THE PITCHFORK OF DESTINY

Also by Jack Heckel

The Charming Tales
The Pitchfork of Destiny
A Fairy-tale Ending (Comprised of *Happily Never After* and *Once Upon a Rhyme*)

THE PITCHFORK OF DESTINY

Book Two of the Charming Tales

JACK HECKEL

HARPER
VOYAGER
IMPULSE
An Imprint of HarperCollins*Publishers*

This is a work of fiction. Names, characters, places, and incidents are products of the author's imagination or are used fictitiously and are not to be construed as real. Any resemblance to actual events, locales, organizations, or persons, living or dead, is entirely coincidental.

Map by Maxime PLASSE (www.maxsmaps.com)

EPub Edition APRIL 2016 ISBN: 9780062359315
Print Edition ISBN: 9780062359322

10 9 8 7 6 5

For Carleigh and Isaac and Taba and Heather

MAP OF THE KINGDOM

I have lost my South Wind.
The sun says I should hold my
tongue and call for her no more.
I have lost my South Wind.
The heavens urge me; fold my
wings and search for her no more.
I have lost my South Wind.
The stars whisper, "Be at peace
and wish for her no more."
I have lost my South Wind.
Still I shall call and search and
wish for her evermore.

An Ode to Magdela by Volthraxus

PROLOGUE

THE MASTER AND HIS DOG

The dragon flew just above the clouds, his golden eyes fixed on a dark mass in the far distance where the Southern Mountains rose to meet the heavens. It was a beautiful day. Bright white clouds dotted a brilliant blue sky, making a fantastical landscape in the air around him. Volthraxus took no notice. He was preoccupied, driven to distraction by the thought of her.

Magdela.

Today would be the day that he would brave the fairy's curse and win his Magdela, or at least that was what he had been telling himself. He certainly thought he could win her. Hoped he would win her. But he knew that if he was being totally honest with himself, he would have to admit that he had his doubts. Would he be strong enough to break the curse? If he did, would she be angry with him for waiting so long to come free her?

He had been trying to figure how long she'd been gone but couldn't quite work it out. It didn't seem like it had been that long but he'd had an ongoing dispute with that troublesome Sir George, then all those times he had been forced to chase off those hideous dwarves (or were they dwarfs?) and their invisible pet halfling, who kept trying to steal his treasure, and then to top it off that idiot Jason came along looking for golden fleas, or something like that, and put him to sleep for several years.

"Excuses, excuses." He sighed and shook his massive head. He did not think Magdela would be particularly sympathetic.

Putting aside whether he could convince her not to be angry with him, the bigger question was whether she would be interested in him. She had, after all, come to these strange southern lands at least in part because she had wanted to build a legend of her own. And look what Magdela had become: *the* dragon of legend, the Great Wyrm of the South. Would she even remember who he was?

And if she does, will she think I'm worthy of her?

After all, who was he? There were the titles, "the Killing Wind," "the Gray Terror," "the Dragon of the North," but he had never been certain he warranted any of them—well, except perhaps the one about being from the north, that seemed undeniable. Also, he thought "Swine Savager" a rather appropriate moniker, but for some reason it had never caught on.

In the end, his list of "terrors" wasn't that impressive. It had never really been his *thing*, the burning and the pillaging and the eating, at least of people—stringy creatures, and in his opinion not worth the trouble. Actually, most of the acts of carnage that been attributed to him were rather more in the nature of collateral damage.

If he was being completely honest, he would have to admit that the name "Killing Wind" had been given to him for an unintended and ill-timed, but particularly lethal, belch.

Was it his fault if humans, and their villages, were altogether too fragile? You came swooping down to capture a horse or a cow or a nice, juicy pig—mostly the pigs—which the humans kept so thoughtfully and conveniently in easy-to-access pens, and the next thing you know the whole place is in flames, and there are people running about screaming and shooting things at you.

Beastly creatures, humans, and so unreasonable.

He made a point of avoiding them as much as possible, but he really did have a weak spot for their pigs, which meant he avoided them less than was generally good for his, or more typically, their health.

Bacon.

All this thinking of swine was making him rather peckish. He raised a claw to wipe a long drip of flaming drool from his mouth.

Focus.

Yes, he needed to focus, focus on what he was going

to do when he got to Magdela and what he was going to say to her when he saw her. He pondered the point a moment, put on his best smile—revealing as many of his shining, serrated teeth as possible—and said to the passing clouds, "Hail, Magdela! I, Volthraxus the Terrible, the Great Dragon of the North, the Killing Wind, the Gray Terror, have come to free you from the fairy's curse!"

Did that sound lame? It sounded lame. He let out a shuddering sigh of noxious steam. What was the point of being the size of a mountaintop, or having talons that could crush boulders into sand, or scorching flames that could set whole forests ablaze, or a roar that sounded like thunder, if when he finally saw her, he froze?

Pathetic, he scolded himself. *I am the Dragon of the North and she is the Great Wyrm of the South, and we were meant to be together.*

The mountains, dark and purple, had been growing in his vision for some time. Now the billowing clouds that were gathered on their heights parted, and he could see Magdela's tower, dark and gray, like a giant's dagger plunged into the earth. His doubts, renewed in strength, assailed him again.

What if I do freeze? What if there's something in my teeth? Should I have brought her a snack? What if my scales aren't shiny enough? What if my scales are too *shiny? What if I cannot overcome the fairy's power?*

He was slightly embarrassed that the last thought had also been his last concern and not his first, but the Dracomancer he had interrogated before leaving had assured him that all he needed to do was melt this silly little golden key or lock or something.

Strictly speaking, it wasn't right before you left, Volthraxus reminded himself. *It has been some time since you learned how to break the curse.*

When had he spoken to that funny little man? It couldn't have been more than a couple of years since he'd caught the fellow lurking around his lair. Certainly less than ten?

"Time!" Volthraxus grunted. Such a tricky concept, and so human.

Anyway, the point was that whenever it was that they'd spoken, this Dracomancer had been quite confident, in a kind of smug, obnoxious way actually, that while fairy gold might be immune to conventional fire, the infernal fires of a magnificent and ancient dragon like Volthraxus would melt it in an instant. He had to admit that, despite being obnoxious, the enchanter had also been quite skilled at flattery. Of course, he had been warned that the enchantment Magdela was under might compel her to attack him, but he was secretly quite thrilled at the thought of rolling about with her claw to claw, tooth to tooth . . .

He opened his eyes from this marvelous daydream and realized he was about to crash into the tower. He pulled up with a great buffeting of wings, and only by an enormous effort did he manage not to smash into the wall and plummet into the thick rosebushes below. Instead, he landed with a resounding thud face-first on her balcony.

Did she see that? He rolled onto his feet, trying to act as though landing on his nose had been the plan from the beginning.

He paused, eyes darting here and there, and took a deep breath of relief. There was no movement from within.

Perhaps she is asleep?

The thought of waking her and breaking the spell filled him with a sudden thrill. He gathered himself and ran his forked tongue over his teeth to remove any debris and across his eyebrow scales to smooth them into place.

This was it.

All he had to do was to enter her chamber. Suavely. Say his piece. Eloquently. Grab the key from around her neck in his talon. Forcefully. Then melt it into a pool of liquid gold. Flamingly. He made sure to take a moment to visualize each action, each pose, each word. And then he caught movement within the room, and he froze.

A wolf stepped into the main chamber from some hidden alcove. It was a dark, mangy cur, scrawny, with long, bristly black hair, and the moment it saw him, it also froze. It was clear that this was not what either had been expecting. Volthraxus ran through all the scenarios he had considered in his head. Not a one involved a wolf.

Maybe it is a pet?

"Where is your mistress, dog?" boomed Volthraxus. The wolf, hair on end and tail between legs, flattened himself on the ground and its teeth began chattering. Volthraxus stepped forward into the room and in an instant took in the dusty rugs and hangings that lined the floor and walls.

It was clear that Magdela had not been here for some time.

"Answer me!" he roared again. "Where is she?"

For a moment, he thought the wolf might not have the power of speech. All the wolves in the forests of the north did, but he had never been this far south. If it couldn't talk, there was not much point in keeping the beast alive. He tried to decide what to do. He should probably kill it. He couldn't imagine Magdela would keep such a useless creature as a pet, and if the beast hadn't been invited, it was rather cheek of the thing to be roaming about her tower.

Besides, she never struck me as a dog lover. Come to think of it, I can't remember her having a particular fondness for any creature except perhaps based on taste and crunchiness.

On the other hand, he had spent a good deal of time over the past week hunting down flocks of sheep so he could use their wool to buff up his scales and wasn't anxious to get wolf blood on him.

This is a complication.

A whine drew him back to the moment, and he frowned in annoyance. He extended a talon and put its sharp edge against the top of the wolf's skull.

"Either you won't tell me where she is, which would really make me quite angry, or you can't tell me where she is, which is just aggravating. Either way, I think I'm going to kill you and use your carcass to fertilize her roses. At least then you would be serving some useful purpose."

Perhaps realizing speech was the only way he wouldn't end up as plant food, the wolf opened his mouth and started talking as though his life depended on it, which in this case it quite literally did. "I'll tell you anything you want, O Terrible and Magnificent One! I just don't know who we're talking about. If you mean the Princess, she was gone when I got here—swear to the Moon. And, had I known you were still alive, I promise you, O Wicked and Frightful One, I wouldn't have been within a hundred leagues of here. I never meant to invade your tower. Really, I'm not like that, I—"

"Wait." Volthraxus applied a little pressure on the wolf's head, which had the admirable effect of silencing the thing in an instant. "Did you say, '*my* tower'? Do you think *I* am the Great Wyrm of the South?"

"Mmmph," the wolf replied.

"You should enunciate better, I really can't understand a word you're saying."

"MMMMph!"

Volthraxus looked down and saw that he had buried the creature's muzzle into one of the rugs. He raised his talon a fraction. "Sorry about that. What were you trying to say?"

"Uh . . . uh . . ." The wolf panted. "Yes."

"Yes, what? What were we talking about?"

"I was saying that you are obviously the Great

Wyrm of the South, Your Incredibly Talony One, no one could compare."

Volthraxus let out a puff of steamy annoyance, snatched the wolf up in his claw, and lifted it so they were snout to snout. "Are you blind? I am obviously a *male* dragon. Look at these horns. Look at the mottling on my scales. I am a *very male* dragon."

"Got it," said the wolf in a wheeze, as Volthraxus squeezed him. "My apologies. No offense, O Very Male One."

"Stop that, it's embarrassing for both of us. Now, tell me what you are doing here, and be truthful, or I'll roast and eat you out of principle."

"Actually," said the wolf, "I was hoping there might be an extra sleeping princess lying about, or at least a few leftover bones. I haven't eaten in days."

"I really couldn't care less about all that, you insipid little beast," said Volthraxus, and he shook the wolf about for added emphasis. "Tell me this instant: Where is Magdela?"

The wolf blinked in vacant confusion. Volthraxus rolled his eyes. "The other dragon. The Great Wyrm of the South."

"Oh . . . you don't know."

"I don't know what?"

The wolf started to say something, then stopped and tilted his head, considering. "How are you with the whole good news, bad news thing? I mean, are you a kill-the-messenger kind of guy?"

Volthraxus narrowed his eyes at the wolf's questions

and at the sudden creeping sensation that something had gone horribly wrong with his plan. "I will tell you who I am, cur. In my country, they call me the Killing Wind, and if you do not tell me where Magdela is, the dragon the people of this land named the Great Wyrm of the South, I will demonstrate—viscerally—why I *earned* that title. Do you understand me?"

The wolf, eyes wide as saucers, nodded silently. Swallowing hard and wetting his muzzle with his tongue, he said, "I hate to be the one to tell you this, O' Killing Wind, but she's . . . she's dead."

Volthraxus dropped the wolf, barely noticing the high-pitched yelp the beast made as he fell headfirst onto the hard stone floor of the tower.

Dead? Magdela is dead? I came too late.

He had failed. A wave of sorrow and loss rolled through his body, and he suddenly felt the weight of the centuries on his bones. He was old and cold and tired.

He noticed a large worn patch in the rugs covering the floor. He moved across the room and curled himself into the space, his tail sweeping the wolf into the wall behind him with a dull thud. *This must have been where she slept. Is this also where she died?*

He had to know. He had to know how she had passed, what terrible calamity had taken her from him. *Dragons don't just die.*

The wolf would know. He swept his eyes across the room and spotted the creature trying to skulk his way down a dark stairway at the very back of the chamber.

He flicked out just the tip of his tail and, using it like a massive spear, pinned the wolf against the wall.

"How did she die, wolf?"

The wolf tried to wriggle away from the sharp end of the tail, but it followed him like a dancing snake ready to strike. The wolf whimpered and panted in fear. "It was a dragonslayer, or at least that's the story that went through the kingdom. She was hunting in the Southern Valley, near a town called Prosper, and a dragonslayer found her and killed her."

"A dragonslayer?" Volthraxus's voice cracked across the room like a whip. "Only *one*? That isn't possible. She has been known to lay waste to small armies without so much as breaking a claw or scratching a scale. I once personally saw her allow six armored knights to surround her, so she could gut them all without having to stir from her bed. Who is this mythical dragonslayer?"

"Well, it's William Pickett, now King William. He was crowned in recognition of his slaying of the dragon—I mean, your Magdela."

"He was, was he? Made king by the blood of my beloved."

A terrible fire ignited in his breast, something more intense than any flame he had ever breathed. *Vengeance.* The thought echoed in his head. Never before had he wanted to kill more than he did at that moment. He rose, his body bristling with anger, the heat from his rage warming the room like a forge.

"Well, you seem to know what you're about," said the wolf, which drew back toward the stair, limping slightly from all the battering he'd received. "Seems to me you have an audience with the King. He lives miles away to the north at Castle White. If you left here now, you could get there in no time as the crow . . . er, dragon flies."

"Perhaps," said Volthraxus, and he lashed his tail around the wolf, surrounding the creature in its coils. "And yet, the dragonslayer, King William, was able to kill Magdela single-handedly, and, as I've chronicled, she was considered one of the most ruthless fighters of our kind." He stared about the room, and his eyes fixed on a tapestry of a dragon, a rather poor rendering of Magdela carrying off a princess from the high tower of a white castle. "Tell me more about this King William. Pray, does he have a queen?"

The wolf paced within his coiled cage, talking and looking for a way out. "Well . . . well, understand the news does not always reach us in the woods by the quickest route, but I have heard that the King is planning on taking a bride soon though I do not know her name."

Still staring at the tapestry Volthraxus asked, "Do you think she would be at this Castle White, with him? Now?"

Perhaps he had finally grown fatigued at being terrified, or perhaps he heard a change in the tone of the questions, but some of the fear left the wolf's eyes, and a sly grin spread across his muzzle. "I don't know, but," he said smoothly, "I could find out."

"Could you now?" asked Volthraxus, pulling his

eyes away from the tapestry and fixing them on the beast.

The wolf calmly lay down, crossed one paw atop the other, and cleared his throat. "May I suggest a partnership, O Vengeful One? If you want to"—he paused and studied his claws before returning his gaze to Volthraxus—"*avenge* yourself on King William, and I mean *really* avenge yourself, not simply roast and eat him, but to make him suffer, you will need someone who knows the lay of the land, who can help you gather news, and who can help you navigate the kingdom. I can do all that and more."

Volthraxus blanched at the thought of eating a human—disgusting. He hoped the wolf wouldn't notice. "And why would you help me?"

The wolf shrugged his bony shoulders. "Partly, because it feels just. This dragonslayer has taken your love from you and profited most obscenely from his crime. Partly because you have not been the only one harmed by the death of your Magdela. Without her as a constant threat, the huntsmen and the guards and the knights of the realm have turned their attention to lesser villains, like me. We have been hounded and harried from our hunting grounds to the point of starvation. I have not had even the scent of a lost child for months now." His stomach growled at the thought. "And partly because I think the droppings from your table will surpass the spread of my own."

"I see," said Volthraxus dryly. "I think you hit nearer the mark with the last point, wolf."

"I admit it," said the wolf. He stood and, with a sweep of one paw, gestured at his scrawny body and matted hair. "It would be ridiculous for me to deny that I could use the largesse of a rich patron to get me back to form. I only ask for a fair share for my contribution."

Volthraxus nodded. He could understand this wolf. "What is your name, wolf?"

"Beo."

"Very well, Beo, my name is Volthraxus, and between us we have an accord. If you serve me well, you will be rewarded beyond the imaginings of your kind. If you fail me"— his voice dropped ominously low— "then I will mete out on you and your kin such punishment as will make future generations howl in fear."

Beo, shivering now, nodded.

"Excellent," said Volthraxus, uncoiling his tail from around the wolf. "Your first duty is to point me to the place where Magdela died. I feel the need to make an appearance."

"O Menacing One, may I humbly advise less haste," said Beo, as Volthraxus began to turn toward the open balcony. "It takes time to do revenge properly, and if we raise the alarm now, before we are prepared—"

Volthraxus swiveled back and felt his golden eyes kindle into molten flame with his anger. Beo drew back beneath the force of that awful gaze. "I am not a fool, Beo. I will let you scout the castle before I attack, but we go now. I am roused to a rare anger, and my blood boils as it has not in many lifetimes of men. Right now

I would do untold destruction in the cause of my despair, and there is nothing that can stand before me."

He did not add the question that was at the back of his mind. *How long can it sustain me?*

Beo lowered himself to his forepaws in a bow. "I am yours to command, Volthraxus, Avenging One."

"That will do," replied Volthraxus. "Which way is Prosper?"

"Northwest."

Volthraxus snatched the wolf up in his talon again and turned in the direction of the unsuspecting town, spreading his wings to catch the wind. Magdela would be avenged, and William Pickett would suffer for what he had done.

Gwendolyn was in the kitchen garden, carefully weaving a green tendril of wild rose through an arched trellis Montague had built for her and wondering when he would return from the market, when she saw the dragon. At first it was just a black speck against the orange of the evening sky, and she mistook it for a crow, but then it began to descend lower and lower in wide, looping circles. Now there was no mistaking the sharp shape of those wings or the long, sinuous tail that flowed behind it.

Gwendolyn froze.

The dragon drew nearer and nearer, and it became obvious from the ever-narrowing spiral of its descent that it was not coming for Prosper but for the farm. It had something, perhaps an animal, clasped in one of its massive talons.

It is Magdela returned, she thought, and shook her head at her own foolishness. After all, she had seen Magdela's bodiless head lying bloody on Prosper's green. It was the first sight that greeted her on waking from the fairy's spell. A more frightening possibility came to mind. *It is the fairy. She has found a way around Will's proscription and has come for revenge. She will take me away again, and I will be lost forever.*

The memories of her waking nightmare, for so many happy months locked away in a remote corner of her mind, sprang forth anew. The shadows under the trellis seemed to stretch unnaturally toward her. Gwendolyn began to shake uncontrollably, her eyes fixed on her coming doom, a scream trapped in her throat.

But then the dragon did something strange. It stopped about a hundred feet above the ground and hovered there, its silver-gray wings beating against the now-blood-red sky, and she could see that it was looking at the flower-covered mound out in the field where Magdela was buried. Gwendolyn could also see that this dragon had horns issuing in two sinister curves from the top of its head.

This is a male dragon, she thought.

"He is silver like starlight and has a long tail that can flow like water," she mouthed thoughtfully, remembering Magdela's description from so many years ago.

The dragon loosed an earsplitting roar that shook the ground beneath her feet. Then, spitting fire, he rose, and like an arrow loosed from a bowstring, launched himself to the north.

Gwendolyn stood there, unmoving, watching the dragon's flight until the frantic sound of the bells of Prosper brought her mind back from old memories. She felt a stabbing pain and noticed that she had closed her hand around the rose vine and that it had pierced her forefinger. A brilliant drop of crimson arose from the wound. She stared at it a moment, still lost in the past.

She heard the sound of running footsteps, and Montague was beside her. "Gwendolyn, are you okay?" he asked breathlessly. His arms were about her. "I came as soon as I saw it—but you are hurt," he added, cupping her hand in his.

"It is nothing." Her voice sounded distant and hollow.

"Did the beast do anything? Did it try to harm you?" He asked this as though her response would answer for him whether he needed to go after the creature, and she knew he was being earnest and loved him all the more for how ridiculous the sentiment was.

Her back still to him, Gwendolyn shook her head. "No, Montague, he had no interest in me."

"He?"

"Of course, he was her love—Magdela's—or he should have been. He has finally come back for her, but he is too late." Gwendolyn turned herself in Montague's arms and buried her face against his chest, so he would not see the tears in her eyes as she began to cry.

CHAPTER 1

UP IN FLAMES

Once upon a time in the Kingdom of Royaume, a land of fairy tale that had been recent witness to no less than three verifiable happily ever afters, on a hill of green stood a shining castle of white where lived the young bachelor, King William. By all accounts, he was a good king. He was wise but not haughty, generous but not frivolous, and even if he was a bit prone to odd turns of phrase better suited to an alehouse than a throne room, he seemed to earnestly wish the best for his people. Indeed, the only real complaint to be raised against him (and this came solely from the lords and ladies of the realm) was that perhaps he was a bit too fair in his judgments, failing quite often to give his peers their proper due in disputes against the less-landed classes.

His reputation for fairness was only one of the reasons that King William had become a popular subject of toasts in taverns throughout the land; another was his romance with Lady Rapunzel.* Their love affair was the talk of the high and the low, and the recent announcement of their upcoming nuptials had set the kingdom atwitter with anticipation.

Lady Rapunzel had, in the space of less than a year, gone from being a lunatic social outcast to the most admired woman in Royaume. Ladies everywhere had begun to copy her style, and her short hair had become all the rage with the more fashionable set.

All in all, as a new spring approached, most of the people of Royaume could not remember a time of such peace and tranquility. And, if there were rumors in the South of a dragon's being spotted above the skies of Prosper, most people dismissed them as a hoax, just another attempt by the increasingly inventive Prosper town council to increase tourism. So, on a beautiful night in the middle of March, beneath a moonlit sky bejeweled by a thousand twinkling stars, the kingdom slept soundly in the surety that King William, Lord Protector and Dragonslayer, watched over them.

Of course, things might have been different had those soundly sleeping people known that on a mountainside several miles to the west, the Gray Terror, the Killing

* One other less dignified, but infinitely more toastable, point in his favor was his now nearly legendary night of drinking at the Cooked Goose. In Royaume, a good night out with the lads is commonly referred to as pulling a King Willy.

Wind, Volthraxus, the Great Dragon of the North, was watching and plotting and waiting, but mostly waiting.

Volthraxus gazed down from his mountain perch at the castle, which, even with his preternatural eyesight, was at this distance little more than a ghostly spot of reflected moonlight glowing among the foothills below. He sighed. While he had fully intended to attack the castle when he left Magdela's tower, the journey had been too long, and his white-hot rage had faded on the flight. Somewhere between there and here he had come to the conclusion that the wolf had been right. He needed information. What if he attacked while the King and his love were at a hunting lodge or touring the kingdom? He might never live the humiliation down. So, he had stopped and given Beo clear instructions to learn all he could and return.

Now here he sat.

Waiting.

In his younger days, he never would have diverted to this hillside or sent the wolf to spy on his enemy. He would have flown straight to the castle, flaming and raging, torn this upstart king to pieces and burnt his kingdom to the ground. It would have been glorious, but then again battles were terribly messy and painful. He still had scars from the lance and arrow wounds he'd received during the misadventures of his youth, and the idea of getting poked at by dozens of metal-bound lunks held no appeal for him.

I sound like an old Wyrm, he thought. *I'm only seven hundred and still in fair shape.*

At this, he craned his neck around to examine his armored sides and the rippling muscles of his taloned limbs.

Well, obviously I still have it, he reassured himself silently. *I'm just being strategic. The plan is sound, and the beautiful symmetry of its revenge will be far more satisfying on an intellectual and spiritual level than would merely killing a bunch of random people. And, the satisfaction will be all the greater for having taken some time to come to ripeness.*

The thought of stealing the dragonslayer's love away as he had stolen Magdela away did carry a certain amount of retributive justice. Forcing his love's killer to feel the agony of loss and the keen sting of dashed hopes that Volthraxus had been made to suffer also seemed quite appealing. And yet he felt empty.

He had been on these windswept heights for what seemed an eternity now, watching the wolf come and go with nothing new to report, and he was growing impatient. It was a barren piece of rock, and he hated it. No matter what he did, he could never seem to get warm.

As if on cue, a night wind began to whip its way across the face of the mountain, and, bored and cold, Volthraxus retreated back through a copse of dark green fir trees to the cave he had appropriated from a none-too-happy family of bears.

"And who's been eating *my* fish?" he said in a fair

mimic of the question the largest of the bears had asked just before discovering the dragon asleep in his den.

Officious freaks, he thought as he used his long tail to sweep aside the bony remains of his last meal, adding as he curled himself up for sleep, "I should have eaten them to make a point, but the big one really was too muscly, the middle one too fatty, and the little one not worth the effort. Besides, bear is stringy. They are all tooth and claw, and the fur gets stuck in my teeth."

He hadn't had much of an appetite lately anyway. Three days, and all he'd had were a dozen or so cows, the odd sheep or two, five or six deer, two elk, and a very ill-fated flock of geese. There was no hunger in him. He hadn't even touched the deer he had caught earlier that afternoon, and he usually appreciated good venison. All he could think about was Magdela, his poor Magdela, lying cold and alone in that farmer's field. He had hoped that this revenge business would give him some measure of satisfaction, or failing that, at least distract him from her death, but it wasn't working out to be as therapeutically destructive as he had imagined.

I will waste away at this rate.

He tried to work up an appetite by imagining the dragonslayer's lifeless body dangling, mangled and bloody in his claws, while the lamentations of his beloved hung in the air. Nothing. He just could not work up the energy to *do* anything. It was hopeless.

Face it, he thought in a sudden burst of self-loathing, *you just don't have the necessary bestial rage and demoniac ambition to attempt a real massacre anymore. You are old and weak.*

"And possibly sick," he added aloud in an attempt to provide an explanation that was less existential in nature.

He coughed, and a little cloud of noxious gray smoke came out. *Gray smoke, hadn't his mother told him something about that?* He tried to remember the advice she'd given him on smoke color, but it had been several hundred years ago, and all he could recall was, "Black smoke your fire's stoked, White smoke your fire's choked." *Or was it the other way around? And what does gray smoke mean?*

He was in the middle of repeating the expression aloud in different ways to see which sounded more correct when he heard the soft, rhythmic fall of padded feet along the path outside the cave. Beo was back and trying to sneak. Volthraxus smiled. It amused him that the wolf thought he could spy on a dragon. Volthraxus calmed his body and steadied his breathing. He then closed his eyes and waited, watching the mouth of the cave through the thin membrane of his outer eyelids.

A few moments later, the bright red and orange silhouette created by Beo's body heat appeared in the opening. He came on tentatively, darting from shadow to shadow, making his way toward the slain deer. Volthraxus could hear the slimy smack as the wolf licked his drooling muzzle greedily with his long tongue. The dragon recalled that kind of hunger fondly and sighed at the memory. The wolf froze, a hindquarter of deer clenched between his teeth.

"Good evening, Beo," Volthraxus said, eyes still closed. "Hungry?"

The wolf, tail between his legs, backed into a dark corner and spit the hunk of meat to the floor between his feet. Panting nervously, he said, "Very hungry, Your Awful Eminence. I see that the hunting was good today."

Volthraxus opened his eyes and grimaced in disgust. Now able to see the wolf in living color, he was reminded again of the creature's terrible eating habits. The wolf's muzzle and face were covered in a gory mixture of fresh blood and innards, and a string of tendon had caught in his teeth and hung limply out of his mouth.

"Still not hungry, O Avenging One?" the wolf asked, licking enthusiastically at the foul mixture on his face.

"Becoming less so with every moment," Volthraxus said with disdain and some jealously. *God, I remember days of rending that would put this little dog to shame.*

Beo glanced anxiously down at the mangled hunk of meat at his feet. "Do you mind if I . . ."

"Yes, yes, just take it outside. Watching you eat nauseates me."

"Of course, Most Fastidious One," the wolf said with a bow that he completed by grasping the bloody haunch in his mouth.

He began to slink away, but was stopped as Volthraxus whipped his tail out to block the cave opening. Beo sat back on his haunches and again dropped the meat with a wet *thunk*. "Was there something else, Your Unpredictableness?"

"Yes, there is *something* else. Tell me what you have

learned. I grow tired of feeding you and getting nothing of value in return. You have become fat enough that I think you might well be worthy of *my* table if you do not soon provide me with the means of exacting my revenge upon this dragon-slaying king."

"I do have news, O Beneficent One, but sneaking through Castle White is not easy, and I have not eaten for days. I thought if I could have just a bite to refresh myself—"

Volthraxus wrapped his tail around the wolf's body and, coiling it inward, began to tighten his hold. "Tell me what you know. Now!" His voice snapped like a whip.

"As you wish, Your Impatientness."

"And stop with the titles," Volthraxus roared. "Some of those weren't even proper words."

"Again, your wish is my command, Grammatically Correct . . . I mean . . . Volthraxus."

"Good."

Volthraxus unwrapped his tail from around the wolf, and Beo visibly relaxed, lying on the floor, both paws positioned possessively on either side of the haunch of deer. "Do you wish to hear the good news or the bad news first?"

Volthraxus glared at the wolf, who responded by crouching lower to the ground in supplication. "No games, Beo, I wish to hear all the news."

"Yes, I understand. It is just an expression meant to prepare you for bad—"

"I do not have any desire to banter with you,"

Volthraxus managed to put enough anger in his belly so that a trickle of steam escaped his nostrils. "Tell me all you know, or your life is forfeit. My patience is at an end."

Eyes rolling with fear, Beo began to tell his story in a rapid-fire fashion. "The King and his betrothed are both in the castle preparing for the upcoming wedding. However"—and here the wolf paused and gave a meaningful glance—"as I warned, visiting Prosper was not advisable. Tales have been spreading through the realm that a dragon had been seen in the skies over the South Valley."

"It was necessary," Volthraxus said, then asked nonchalantly, "What is the reaction among the people?" Oddly, he realized, he was hoping for the worst—total bedlam.

"Most believe it to be just village hysteria," Beo began, but at an angry snarl from Volthraxus, quickly added, "but a growing number clamor for King William to seek you out and slay you."

"I see," said Volthraxus sourly, not fooled by the wolf's hasty improvisation. "Well, if he did seek me out, it would make things easier."

The sight of me in all my glory didn't cause a kingdom-wide panic? Of course, they were used to Magdela, and she always was more bloodthirsty. Nevertheless, it was annoying. He absentmindedly began to scratch the outline of Castle White in the stone of the cave floor with one of his claws, adding flames here and there for ghastly artistic effect.

Warming to the topic, Beo began to speak at great length about all the preparations the King was making at the castle in case the rumors proved true. "The King sent a *large* contingent of troops south to investigate, *and* he doubled the standing guard on the castle . . ."

That he was being "handled" by a creature no better than a common dog only added insult to Volthraxus's feeling of injury, so he paid little attention as Beo continued to add ever more elaborately to the King's defenses against him.

" . . . and I have heard rumors that he has made a plea for dragon hunters or even someone called the Dracomancer to attend him."

Volthraxus held up a taloned claw. "The Dracomancer?"

"Y—yes."

"I know this Dracomancer. I questioned him about Magdela and the fairy at one point. He is a vain and foolish man. If he is the best advisor the King can manage, then my victory is assured, and if this is all the news you can gather, your use to me may well be at an end."

"There is one more thing . . ."

Volthraxus looked up from his drawing and fixed his attention on the wolf. "Well?"

Beo squirmed. "I . . . I may have discovered where Lady Rapunzel is staying in the castle, but . . ."

Volthraxus was on his feet. "Tell me. I go tonight."

"This is what I was afraid of, Volthraxus." the wolf whined. "Do not be so hasty. With a double guard, there will be dozens of archers on the walls. On a clear, moonlit night like tonight, they will see you coming. We should only attack at the new moon. There is no need to—"

"Need? NEED?" Volthraxus roared, flame licking across his teeth in answer to his rage. "There is every need. The dragonslayer must feel the pain of my loss, and it must be tonight." He did not add that another reason it had to be tonight, or at least soon, was that he could feel his fire ebbing. Soon, the sadness of Magdela's loss would drown the last of his anger, and he would sleep again, and there in the bosom of dream try to escape his sorrow. His revenge could not wait.

"I don't understand the rush," Beo said.

"You do not need to understand," Volthraxus spit. "Your job is to serve me and hope that I continue to spare your life." He pulled the wolf closer with his tail and gestured down at the crude, talon-drawn sketch of Castle White. "Show me where she is."

Beo hesitantly pointed at a large tower in the center of the castle with his paw. "There," he said. "Halfway up on the east side is a large balcony. A trellis of jasmine grows about the window. That is her room."

Volthraxus fixed the point in his mind's eye and, sweeping the wolf aside, made for the cave entrance.

"I think you should reconsider, Vengeful . . . I mean, Volthraxus. This is a needless risk."

Volthraxus paused outside the cave and turned his eyes, twin flames burning with the passion of his hunt, on the wolf. "Look to your food, Beo, and leave this to me. When I return, it shall be with Lady Rapunzel as my prisoner. Then I too shall have a reason to feast."

With that, he tore through the trees to the edge of the mountain cliff and flung himself into the sky.

Beo watched the dragon fly away with a curiously disappointed expression. *Pity,* he thought. *I have never eaten so well.*

Beo, like most wolves, was an eminently practical creature. He could not understand any act that was not rooted in fulfilling either a carnal or digestive need. It baffled him every time a knight, surrounded by fair maidens and fine food, left the comfort of his castle to risk his life jousting other knights or traveling to far-flung bridges to fight smelly trolls. It was an enduring mystery. The wolf stared after the dragon until it was a speck on the horizon, then shrugged his bony shoulders and turned back to his food.

A few miles west and a few thousand feet down, in a wonderful, high room in the Royal Tower of Castle White, Lady Rapunzel, dressed in a lovely nightgown, sat on her bed, trying to make her way through an exceedingly dull book on court etiquette. Normally, she loved to read, but she found this particular topic tedious to begin with, and the author of *Brummell's Guide to the Courtly Arts* had not made it any easier by filling his "authoritative" tome with personal anecdotes that mostly involved extremely detailed descriptions of what everyone was wearing. However, the fact that fashion was so central to Brummell's text did explain why the Royal Librarian had referred to it as "Charming's Handbook."

Yawning, she stuck a finger between the pages of the volume to mark her place—Chapter 3: "The Essential Elements of the Backhanded Compliment"—and closed the book, letting her gaze drift across the room, where it settled on the other reason she was finding it so hard to concentrate tonight. On a mannequin in the corner by her dressing table, in all its white-laced splendor, was her wedding dress. The tailor had delivered it this morning and, as foolish as she knew she was being, just looking at it made her happy. It didn't seem possible that in a little less than a month, she and Will were going to be married. It was too fairy-tale. But, looking at the dress made it real.

It had only been a month past a year since they had returned to Castle White from Liz and Charming's wedding—such a short time—but her old life seemed to be, well, a lifetime ago. She remembered only vaguely the strange madwoman that had made herself a social pariah by attacking Prince Charming in the middle of a Royal Ball. Elle no longer recognized herself in the needy, insecure girl she had been and cringed at the memories of those days. It seemed the kingdom had also forgotten her past. She was on everyone's invitation list, and every day she saw more and more of the women of the court mimicking her down to the way she wore her hair. Initially, of course, she had intended to grow it out, but each time the hairdresser came, she asked for the same style. Besides, Will really did seem to like it short.

Stop that, she lectured herself. *Liz would tell you that the point is not how he likes your hair but how you like your hair.*

Like all of Liz's advice, this admonition was much easier taken than followed. She let her eyes wander from the dress to a mirror set on the wall behind the dressing table. She cocked her head from one side to the other and watched her hair swish and fall across her face. No, this seemed right. Besides, the style had become so associated with her at this point that some part of her felt that to abandon it would be to abandon a part of her own personality.

No! You are NOT your hair. She refused ever again to be known simply for her hair—long or short.

"And, that is why I will become the best queen this kingdom has ever known, which means reading bloody Brummell!"

With that, she threw herself back into her studies. But, a few pages later, her eyes crossed, the book slipped from her hand, and her head began to drop to her breast.

It was in this half-asleep state that Elle heard the castle watchman in the East Tower shout the alarm. Her thoughts had grown so languorous that the echoed cries from guards in towers across the castle and the sudden flare of watch fires being lit outside her window blended naturally into a dream she was having where she and Will were being married in a carnival tent with the lords and ladies of the court all around as spectators. A ringmaster was shouting at them to jump through a hoop of fire. Elle started to argue with the man that it simply wasn't possible for her to do such a thing without catching the skirt of her dress ablaze, when a sound like an avalanche stopped her. She and the ringmaster turned at the source of the noise, which seemed to be coming from outside the tent. The cloth walls began to tremble and ripple, then tear.

Elle came awake with a sudden start beneath a shower of glass and wood and stone. She threw up her hands instinctively and felt dozens of stings as the debris cut into her face and palms. She looked between her fingers in confusion and saw that the glass-paned doors to her balcony had shattered inward, taking part of the stone wall with them, and there, amid the ruins of white trellis and jasmine, was a nightmare.

The dragon, for that is undoubtedly what the beast was, was perched on her balcony, trying to force its bulk through the opening and into her room. It was armored in silver-and-gray plates, and seemed to be all sharp edges and angles. Hundreds of teeth like knife blades jutted from its mouth, and a pair of horns curved sinisterly out of the top of its head, but it was the eyes that were its most striking feature. Set beneath jutting brows, the golden orbs seemed terrible and hard, and flames, deep red dancing flames, burnt where the pupils should have been. It stared at her from across the room and renewed its assault, battering its body several times against the castle. She flinched at each jolting impact, but the walls of the tower did not yield any further, and it was simply too large to fit through the door. It beat its wings in frustration, and a hurricane wind ripped across the room, extinguishing her lamps and plunging everything into a darkness that was relieved only by the ruddy glow of the fire that still burnt in her grate.

Later, Elle would be embarrassed to remember that in that first moment of panic, her thoughts did not initially turn to her own safety or the safety of the castle, but rather to whether her dress had survived, and despite herself, she looked to the corner of the room, where the headless mannequin bride still stood untouched by the dragon's attack. Then the dragon withdrew slightly and leaned down, thrusting its head and long, sinuous neck through the remains of the door.

Elle screamed and scrambled backwards off the bed. She pressed against the wall farthest from the balcony, but she couldn't run any farther away.

The dragon opened its jaws and roared—an earsplitting sound that brought Elle to her knees in sobs of terror. As the hot, sulfurous breath of the dragon surrounded her, Elle closed her eyes, whispered a goodbye to Will, and prepared herself for death.

Nothing happened.

Elle was still alive. She opened her eyes and saw that the dragon had withdrawn to the balcony. It perched there, talons gripping the stone, seemingly relaxed, despite the sound of arrows plinking off its scales. The monster was absently scratching something into the balcony stone. Elle was reminded of a cat playing with its food.

Nonetheless, she took this respite to examine her situation. She was alive—that was certainly a plus. She was mostly uninjured, with nothing but a few cuts, scratches, and bruises—again definitely a good thing. It appeared that the dragon could not actually reach her, which she realized might account for her first two observations, or that she was still observing at all. And then Elle remembered the most important thing of all—the door was on her side of the room and only about twenty feet away. If she could make it there . . .

"Have you worked it out yet?" the dragon asked in a deep voice that was tinged with an oddly archaic but certainly cultured accent.

"Wh—what?" Elle choked, her mind still trying to grasp that she was now talking with a dragon.

"Have you worked out that I cannot reach you and that your escape lies but a few feet away?" He (for she decided that anything with a voice like that must be a he) said with an arch of his plated brow and accompanied by what she could only describe as a wry smile.

"Ummm," Elle intoned noncommittally. She refused to acknowledge that this had been her exact thought because she was not sure whether the admission would lead to her immediate and fiery death. The dragon could probably incinerate her and everything else in the room—including her dress—anytime he wanted.

"I see," the dragon said with a sigh. "You have already reached the next stage of understanding, namely that I could burn you to a cinder if you tried to escape. We seem to be at a bit of an impasse. What are we to do?"

Elle bit back the snarky answer she wanted to give, which was that this was his show, and asking her for a solution was not particularly good form. Instead, she said, "We could call it a draw and go our separate ways?"

The dragon shook its impressive head. "No, I'm sorry, I must leave here with you—preferably alive."

"Why?" she asked, realizing that if she was talking with the dragon, that meant she wasn't being eaten or burnt up by said dragon.

"I don't have enough time to give you a full answer. I am afraid your betrothed and . . ." The dragon cocked its head to one side as though listening " . . . at least a score of his knights are mere moments away from reaching your door."

As if on cue, Elle heard the sound of dozens of feet pounding in the courtyard outside. Hope bloomed. Will would save her. He would lead his knights up the tower to her and drive the dragon away. All she had to do was keep the beast from doing something hasty and nasty for a few minutes more. She glanced at the door and saw that she had latched the bolt the night before—something she had done to keep Will from walking in and seeing her dress before their wedding day.

"Damn," she hissed, then silently added several more colorful curses about stupid wedding traditions.

"Yes, I noticed that the door was bolted myself," the dragon said dryly. "Unusual for a lady of your position, as it makes it difficult for the lady's maid to attend. However, if it makes you feel any better, I don't think that door, as heavy as it is, will keep the King or his men from attempting your rescue. It may delay them for a minute or two, but no more."

Elle was exhausted by terror and confused by the dragon's calm. The combination made her momentarily reckless, and she said, "Since none of this seems to matter to you, it seems a shame to put them through the trouble. Why don't I just unbolt it?"

She had actually taken several steps toward the door and extended her hand to the latch when the dragon, its voice ominously low, said, "I wouldn't."

Elle almost responded, "I know *you* wouldn't," but the threat implicit in the dragon's voice froze the words in her throat. She turned back to the dragon, her fingers hovering just above the door's handle. "Why?"

"Because I am living death. Within me burn the infernal fires, and I will consume any man that enters that door in a hellish fiery doom. And, because we both know that your future husband, the *dragonslayer*, King William, will be the very first man through that door."

That he made these statements as fact lent them greater weight. But even more terrible to Elle was the raw anger in the dragon's voice when he gave Will's title. She knew now that this was not about her. The dragon was here for her fiancé.

In answer to this thought, she heard the sound of

men running along the corridor outside, then a hammering at the door. "Elle!" Will's voice thundered. "Elle, are you alright?"

Her heart skipped at the sound of his voice, but she dared not answer. Her earlier hope at his coming had turned to a deep dread. Shaking, she pulled her hand back away from the latch.

She squared her shoulders and stared back across the room at the dragon. The flickering light of the fire cast the dragon's face in shifting shadows of orange and black, so that it was hard to read his expression, but those flaming eyes—half-lidded now—danced menacingly in silent confirmation that the creature's threat was not idle. If Will came through that door, he would die.

Elle knew what she had to do.

She heard Will just outside the door. He was only a few feet from her. "It's bolted. Back! Stand back, damn you!"

She heard him strike the door with a tremendous blow, but though it shuddered, the door held.

Will's actions steeled her own resolve. "Wh . . . what are your terms, dragon?" she asked, finally finding her voice.

The dragon grinned toothily and nodded. "Practical and to the point, I like that. If you will come with me, I will leave and, for the moment, spare King William his doom."

Elle hesitated. A thousand doubts flooded her mind, but in the end only one question mattered—could she trust the dragon to spare Will? She would willingly sacrifice herself if it meant that Will would be safe.

There was another resounding crash, and the wood of the door trembled but did not yield. She heard Will yell, "Elle! I'm coming!"

Elle swallowed. "You swear that you will not harm him?"

The dragon nodded and placed a taloned claw to its chest. "I promise that if you come with me before he breaches this chamber, he will live to see the dawn. I cannot swear that I will be able to stay my wrath if we come face-to-face this night. I also cannot vouch for him in the coming days. It seems unlikely that he will let your capture go unavenged. If I mark his character correctly, he will hunt me, and only one of us shall survive the meeting if he should find me."

It was as much as she could ask.

"Very well," she said softly. "Let us go."

Another blow came against the door. This time a distinct crack and pop issued from the oaken timbers. Elle knew that time was short, but the knowledge that Will was inches from her and that she was leaving him and that this might be the last time that she was ever this close to him was too much for her courage to bear. She reached back and touched the wood of the door. She waited and felt the door jerk against her hand as, once again, Will's body impacted against it, because she knew without a doubt that he was the one battering against it. This time, the latch flexed and bent inward against the force of his assault.

"Lady?" the dragon said somberly. "If we are to away, it must be now."

Elle nodded silently, and whispered, "Goodbye, Will." She turned and walked away, letting her hand on the door trail behind her.

As she marched across the room toward the dragon, her eyes fell on her wedding dress, and despite herself, she began to cry. Still, she kept moving, knowing that to stop now was to stop forever and sentence Will to death. The tears running down her face stung where the salt met the scratches from the glass. She pulled a lace handkerchief from the sleeve of her dressing gown and wiped her eyes.

She reached the balcony as another blow came from behind her. She did not turn to look, but heard the audible *groan* as the door began to give way. Will shouted, "Elle, I am coming, Elle! If you touch her, dragon—" but the threat was never completed as he prepared for his final assault.

Standing beside the dragon she was more aware than ever of the creature's sheer bulk. Arrows from the castle's archers bristled here and there on the beast's body, lodged between its armored plates and ridges, but they seemed like pins in a cushion—insignificant and laughable. The dragon balanced on one of his hind legs and turned the other over to make a sort of platform.

"If you will be so kind," the dragon said, indicating with his head the upturned claw.

Carefully, she sat in his scaled palm, holding on to

one of the talons for balance like an infant grasping her mother's finger. The dragon carefully closed his claw, encircling and cradling her. Instantly, the heat from the dragon's body warmed her so that she did not even notice the bite of the night air through her thin dressing gown.

"Be ready, Lady," the dragon said earnestly. "If you are afraid of heights, this will not be pleasant, but know that I will keep you safe."

She felt the creature's muscles tense, and, like a stone from a sling, he launched his body into the air. Despite the dragon's warning, Elle shrieked involuntarily as they began to drop from the sky. And then the dragon extended his wings above them and caught the air. Roaring and spurting flame, the dragon flexed his shoulders and began rhythmically beating his wings against the sky. At every stroke, they climbed higher. With a speed that made Elle gasp, the castle fell away beneath them.

In the rush of wind that followed their passage, Elle's handkerchief was torn from her grasp. She turned and watched it flutter back down toward the ruined balcony. For an instant, she saw Will, far below, silhouetted against the red light of the doorway. He was standing at the edge of the balcony, sword in hand, pointing up at the sky, then the dragon banked, and the sight vanished.

She was alone with the dragon in the arms of the night.

Standing on the balcony of Elle's chamber in the Royal Tower of Castle White, Will watched impotently as the dragon disappeared into the night sky. Rage and disbelief warred within him. He heard himself giving orders for the archers to fire and for the huntsmen to be summoned and the soldiers assembled for pursuit, but everything that was him was elsewhere in a roaring place of terrible despair.

Something small and white fluttered to the ground at his feet. It was one of Elle's delicate handkerchiefs, identical to the one she'd given to him all those months before at the crossroads where he had fallen in love with her, but unlike that one, this was stained with her blood.

"No!" he said with a choking sob. Will fell to his knees, his sword clattering to the stones at his feet and his hands clutching for the bit of cloth.

The captain of the guards, Sir Alain, whispered in his ear. "Don't worry, Your Majesty, we already have our fastest horsemen following. The dragon won't stay hidden. We will find her. I swear on my life, we will find her."

Will nodded. Bracing himself against Alain, he rose and picked up his sword. "Tell the men to assemble in the courtyard. We march within the hour."

Alain saluted, and, with a few shouted orders, the men departed. Alone, Will looked about at the ruins of the room, his mind recreating the moments of terror

Elle must have felt. At his feet, carved into the hard stone of the floor, was a message from the dragon.

You deprived me of my love, Dragonslayer. Now, I deprive you of yours. –The Dragon of the North.

The old lie had come back to haunt him. The fault truly was his. His eyes fell on her wedding gown. The dress she hadn't wanted him to see. The dress that now he wasn't sure she would ever wear.

"No, that will not happen," Will said in a voice that sounded brittle even to him. He felt an indescribable pain, which he could only imagine was the shattering of his soul.

Whatever it cost, he swore to himself that he would find the dragon, save Elle, then slay the beast and send its vile spirit screaming to Hell. He didn't care about the kingdom, or his crown, or his life. His life and his rule no longer mattered. They were forfeit. He had failed in his most important charge—to protect his beloved. He would go north and face this dragon, but he knew that he would need help. There was only one man in the entire kingdom who had spent his entire life training to kill a dragon.

"I need Charming."

CHAPTER 2

OLLY, OLLY OXEN FREE

Panic is like fire: It only takes a spark to light it, and it spreads quickly when fed by the right fuel—rumor, fear, and ignorance. In the Kingdom of Royaume, all the conditions were perfect for a panic following the kidnapping of Lady Rapunzel. King William had ridden from the castle in pursuit of the dragon only an hour after the attack. His advisor, Lord Rupert, tried to calm the people, but given his terrible history with dragons, sensible folk ignored him. Less sensible folk made up their own accounts of what happened, and as a result, the event known as the Great Dragon Panic spread like wildfire through the land.

During those early days of the Great Dragon Panic, it seemed that no amount of absurdity was beyond the people's belief. Dragons were seen everywhere, and they all seemed to be bent on ridding Royaume of its young maidens. If the tales traded by the merchants in the village markets were to be believed, the skies above Prosper teemed with whole flocks of dragons, and with every claim of a dragon sighting from Prosper, the town of Two Trees responded with two claims of its own. Several families in both towns actually claimed that their daughters had been kidnapped, even while voices that sounded like the young women in question were heard from behind a pantry door or an upstairs window. Old stories and superstitions about dragons were also revisited, including tales of wizards and fairies and witches who could defeat such creatures. These stories soon began to lead people in search of the author of *The Dragon's Tale*, a man known as the Dracomancer.

However, any references to *The Dragon's Tale* also led to people talking about another man—Prince Charming. Although he had lost his title and vanished from public view since Princess Gwendolyn's usurpation of the throne, the reappearance of dragons had meant a resurrection of his legend. The prophecy that Prince Charming would slay the dragon and free the Princess had ingrained itself so solidly in the minds of the populace that many saw the kidnapping of Rapunzel as a sign that it was still valid. Indeed, many began to say that the first dragon had not been the dragon of prophecy at all and that this was why the Prince had never gone to slay it. After being ignored by nearly everyone in the kingdom for over a year, the people of Royaume were suddenly begging for Prince Charming's return. The only problem was that nobody seemed to know where he might be found.

As for Charming himself, he had retired to a quiet cottage in the woods with his wife—the King's sister, Elizabeth Charming—and life was going well . . . perhaps too well.

Increasingly, a sense of restlessness had crept over Charming. While he had unsurpassed skills as a hunter, the animals in the enchanted forest surrounding the cottage had no fear of humans. In fact, they seemed to have an unnatural attraction to people. They would simply walk up to Charming, nearly begging to become dinner. It took all the challenge out of the hunt and, quite frankly, was a little creepy.

He had suggested at times to his wife that they should return to Castle White so Elizabeth could advise the soon-to-be-queen, Lady Rapunzel, and he could advise King William, but Elizabeth had little desire to go to court and thought that her brother and Elle were doing quite well on their own. Although Charming thought his wife's view of court was tainted by her previous experiences, he couldn't argue with her. All things considered, Charming and Liz had all they needed and more at their little cottage, which perhaps explained the ox.

Edward Michael Charming sat down heavily on a stump at the edge of his newly plowed field and cast a critical eye across his handiwork. He had done everything himself. Well, he and the ox had done everything themselves. Of course, Liz had protested that her little vegetable garden was sufficient for the two of them, but Charming knew that once she saw how he had tamed the very land to his command she would come to appreciate his efforts—and also to appreciate Goliath, the ox, to whom she had not exactly warmed yet.

The buying of the ox had been a real test of their relationship. When he had first pledged to her a field so bountiful it would make other farmers weep with envy, she had told him that she thought it was a bad idea, but that if he was determined to "try his hand at farming," she would make sure he at least had a proper draft horse and plow to prepare the earth. This idea of "plowing" had intrigued Charming, and, not wishing to appear ignorant, he had quickly written to King William, the only other farmer he knew, so that he might explain what exactly was required to "farm." The answer, or rather answers, as Will's response had been quite lengthy and filled with many details that Charming did not follow, gave him to understand that there was more to farming than simply dropping seeds onto the ground.

Who knew?

But the one thing that the letter had confirmed was the need for a plow animal—the bigger the better. Liz, of course, had wanted to get involved, but he had informed her that he was quite capable of handling everything. He was renowned throughout the land as having a fine eye for horseflesh—flanks and withers were no mystery to him. So, he had gone to market and found a merchant who had not only sold him a fine plow but the largest animal to pull it possible—an ox—whom Charming had immediately named Goliath as the creature was magnificently huge.

Charming's luck hadn't ended there, for, after Charming had confessed that he knew little of farming and that perhaps purchasing such a large creature was premature, the merchant had assured him that Goliath was magical and not only had the ability to understand Charming's words, but that he also knew all there was to know about farming. All Charming had to do, so the merchant explained, was to point Goliath at a field, and the beast would plow it himself. Such good fortune had its price, of course, but Charming had gladly given the man a bag of gold for such a renowned beast.

The proof of this claim lay before him, a fully plowed field. Charming studied the rows, which zigged and zagged this way and that and bent in odd loops and curves. It didn't look exactly like the fields he'd ridden past on his jaunts through the kingdom. Those always seemed to have perfectly straight lines of crops, but then he reflected that those farmers hadn't had to contend with so many obstacles. His field was littered with stumps and rocks and all sorts of things that Goliath had needed to plow around.

The point was, there had been much churning of the earth, which from Will's letter Charming understood was necessary for the sowing of the ground, or was it the reaping of the ground? Farm terminology was a bit stupefying. Still, he was beginning to wonder how much Goliath really knew about farming. He had specifically asked the creature whether or not they should remove all those things from their path before starting, but Goliath clearly shook his head no.

Charming regarded Goliath, who stood quietly beside him munching on grass. *Such a noble beast.*

"I'm glad you know what you're doing."

The ox lifted his gaze and stared back at Charming with those big brown eyes, his jaw moving in a slow circular motion as he chewed. *Such intelligent eyes.*

"You do know what you're doing, don't you?"

Goliath shook his head, flapping his ears and sending a cloud of flies that had been buzzing around him scattering to the winds.

"You don't?"

The ox dipped its head in an ambiguous motion that Charming couldn't interpret and ripped more grass from the ground. The flies returned, settling again on the creature's head.

"It is all well and good for you to understand me, but we really need to work on me understanding you. Perhaps if you could moo, or whatever you do, once for yes and twice for no?"

Goliath shook his ears again, and the flies took flight once more.

Charming kicked at a dirt clod and mumbled, "Next time, I should probably ask how much an ox usually costs before buying one."

Goliath snorted.

"Yes, you are quite right. It wouldn't have mattered. You are certainly worth a mere bag of gold."

Goliath's ears twitched, and the animal lifted its head ponderously to glance at the cottage. Charming followed the ox's gaze and saw Liz heading down the hill toward them.

"It is an amazing field, isn't it, Goliath?"

The animal made no response to this except a deep belch.

"I mean, who would have thought that I, Prince Charming, could have plowed a field? Of course, I'm not a prince anymore, so perhaps I should be called Farmer Charming."

The ox stared at him with a look that Charming thought might be incredulity.

"You're right, it just doesn't sound believable. Even with my hands roughed and sweat on my brow"—he wiped his forehead dramatically with a silk handkerchief—"I'm too dashing to pull off being a farmer. I'm not even sure what tights a farmer should wear, or if they even wear tights. Perhaps I should try the Farmer-formerly-known-as-Prince-Charming?"

The ox shook his head and looked away.

Charming was about to suggest to Goliath that matching outfits in greens and browns could work when he noticed Elizabeth was now standing at the other end of the field, hands on her hips, staring across at him.

She must be impressed, he thought. *I don't think she every really believed that Goliath and I could finish the work—and so quickly!*

She began making her way through the maze of crisscrossing furrows Goliath had carved into the ground, and he watched her red hair catch the light as she came closer. His heart pounded with the joy he always felt upon seeing her, but this time it was multiplied by the pride he felt at having accomplished something. He could scarcely believe he had plowed a field.

"Edward! What have you done?"

He smiled and swept his arms across the expanse of broken earth. "Behold! The magnificent, unsurpassed, amazing fields of the Charming's! Am I not now the great and humble farmer I promised you I would become?"

"This is . . ." She searched for a word.

"Stupendous?" he supplied.

"Terrible," she replied darkly. She made a half-shrugging gesture that reminded Charming of her brother, Will. "I mean, I didn't think you could do too much damage, but really, look at these furrows. It looks like they were plowed by a drunk, blind man. What were you thinking?"

"Well, I trusted the arrangement of the rows and things of that sort to Goliath, naturally."

The ox bowed his head modestly and chomped down on more grass.

Liz's eyes flashed. "You trusted the ox? Is that what you said? Wait, where is the other half of the plow?"

Charming felt that, for some reason he didn't quite understand, things weren't going well. "Of course I put my trust in the ox, he is magical after all. And, if anyone is to blame for the broken plow, it's him."

"But, Charming," she said gesturing about at the field. "It is no wonder that the plow broke. You have to clear the land first. I mean, there's a rock over there, and there, and there, and there, and more stumps than—" Liz stopped her lecture suddenly, her face flowing from disgust to disbelief. "Wait, did you say a magical ox?"

Charming nodded. "You see, I was going to clear the field, but Goliath didn't seem interested in pulling out the stumps or in moving the rocks, and he is the expert." Charming dropped his voice, so Goliath would not overhear them, "Between you and me, I think he's a bit lazy."

"But a magical ox?"

"Exactly," he said, smiling. "I did tell you when I brought him home that he was magical. I mean, I wouldn't have spent a whole bag of gold on a regular old ox. I'm not an ass."

His smile was wiped away as Liz's face turned as red as her hair. She pointed her finger at him. He would have rather faced a sword than her angry pointing.

"I . . . I thought you were being witty and wry, not daft. You really spent a whole bag of gold on this ox?"

Charming nodded silently, not sure what to say.

"And, how *exactly* do you work a magical ox?"

"Well, since Goliath is the expert, I simply tell him what to do and he pulls. At one point, he didn't want to turn around, and I had to help him, but by and large, I thought he did an excellent job."

Charming looked down at the ox for support, but the ox just blinked and went on chewing.

Liz fell silent. Her green eyes drilled into him. "So, you gave him instructions?"

Charming swallowed. "Yes, I hitched up the yoke and I gave Goliath instructions. The merchant said that the ox knew everything. I assisted as I could." She said nothing to this, and Charming filled the silence by smoothing his tunic, then stumbling on. "I must say, I felt that I was giving orders at a superior level. I instructed him just as you said. There was a slight manure-break incident, but the two of us resolved it amicably."

"I told you to guide him . . . to . . . to lead him!" she spluttered.

"And that's what I did, fairly eloquently, I might add. I pointed and shouted a great deal of encouragement."

Liz gave an exasperated sigh and turned to march back toward the cottage.

"Elizabeth?" Charming pursued her but made certain not to overtake his wife. "I did my best. I know I'm not the greatest farmer, but I thought we did well for our first time."

She whirled on him, and her pointing finger planted itself in his chest. "You stood in a field and shouted instructions to an ox."

He smiled again, but this time with less certainty. "Yes, that's exactly what I did. I . . . I can't believe it worked."

"It didn't work, Edward!" She clucked her tongue,

her expression full of scorn. "I didn't expect much, but I can't believe how *badly* you messed up such a simple job . . ."

Charming felt his face fall. He suddenly realized what a fool he had been to think that he could ever be a farmer.

She raised her finger to shake it in his face. "And, to imagine that you were duped by some market trickster into spending our gold on a magic ox . . ."

He lowered his eyes to the ground in shame as she pointed out all the flaws in Goliath, his swayback and patchy coat. Of course, the ox wasn't magical. Of course, the field was ruined. Everything was ruined. He sighed deeply as he contemplated the fact that, once again, he was a failure.

Liz fell silent and her hand cupped his chin and she raised his eyes to hers. "I am sorry, Edward. You know I don't really care about the field or the ox or the gold, right? I just want you to be happy, and I never believed that being a farmer would make you happy. But, if it is really what you want to do, then I will support you."

A great sense of weariness came over Charming. What did he want to do, to be? It was a question that he had asked himself for months. He was no longer Prince Charming. He had no duties to speak of. Thanks to the dwarf . . . ves' play, he had a wife who was even wealthier than he was. He had no idea what to do with himself, and it was obvious that farming was not in his future.

"Liz," he said, "I don't know. I trained my whole life

to slay a dragon, and that never came to pass, which is fortunate, since . . . well, never mind. And, when I wasn't preparing for that, I was readying myself to take my father's throne, and that responsibility has fallen to your brother. I guess I'm still trying to find my purpose."

Unexpectedly, she kissed him. It was a fierce, passionate kiss, the sort that stole his breath.

When she pulled away, a smile shone on her face. "That is one of the most humble, self-effacing things that I've ever heard you say."

"Thank you, my love."

"But," she added, "you will never be a farmer, and that ox is not magical."

He looked at Goliath, who looked back at him, then shook his head violently.

"Traitor," Charming mumbled, but he said it with a light voice. He knew she was at least partially right. He would never be a farmer, but he was pretty sure that Goliath was, if not magical, amazing. In any event, he would find something to excel at, perhaps cheese making. There was an old cave nearby where he might age the milk. He would, of course, need the most magnificent cows available and . . .

"Come on. Let's unhook this poor beast," Liz said, linking her hand in his and making him forget becoming the most famous cheesemaker in all the land, much to the loss of the kingdom.

They were in the middle of removing the mangled plow from Goliath when they heard a clatter of hooves on the path to their cottage.

"We weren't expecting anyone, were we?" he asked.

Liz shook her head. Charming picked up a length of broken plow handle from the ground and stepped in front of her.

"Charming!" came a familiar shout, and they watched as King William Pickett, his red hair blazing in the sun, plunged his horse down the hill toward them.

"Will?" said Liz, stepping out from behind Charming.

Will galloped his horse recklessly across the uneven field. Charming and Liz could see that the poor creature had been ridden too hard, its body heaved with the effort of breathing, and its flanks were white with foam. As Will drew near, he pulled hard on the reins and threw himself from the saddle. However, his feet tangled in the stirrups, and he crashed to the muddy ground. Without pausing, Will picked himself up and rushed unsteadily toward Charming. Will looked for all the world like a madman, and Charming knew had it been anyone else, he would have brained them with his makeshift club as a matter of courtesy. Even so, he was sorely tempted.

"Your Majesty?" said Charming, going to a knee briefly before rising as Will stumbled again and fell to his knees breathing hard. It was obvious that he, like his horse, was exhausted.

Liz discarded ceremony and went straight to her brother. Kneeling beside him, she put an arm on his shoulder. "Will? What's happened? Is it about the wedding?"

Will ignored Liz and, reaching up, grabbed Charming by the tunic. "I need you, Charming!"

"My King, I am at your service, you know you have but to ask," said Charming with a gasp as he struggled to keep Will from dragging him down.

"Will! Have you gone mad?" asked Liz. "Let go of my husband and tell us what is wrong!"

Will stared between the two of them, his mouth moving soundlessly, clearly not knowing how to begin.

Liz put her hands over Will's and pried them loose from Charming's lapels. "William Jack Pickett, tell me what is going on!"

Will's voice was suddenly very young. "There is . . . there is . . . a dragon. It has captured Elle. I mean, kidnapped Elle. It took her."

"A dragon?" asked Liz.

"A dragon!" exclaimed Charming.

"Yes, a dragon," said Will. "There's a dragon, and it took Elle."

Will's eyes suddenly became wet, but they were unspent tears of anger, not sorrow. "It thinks I slew the Wyrm of the South." Will swallowed hard and put his head in his hands. Sobs began to wrack his body. "My lie is going to get Elle killed."

Liz and Charming exchanged a silent look over the top of Will's head.

Will's hands lashed up with a sudden violence and grabbed Charming's tunic again. This time he managed to pull Charming down to the ground beside him.

"They say if you need to catch a rat, find a ratcatcher. Do you know what I mean?" Will asked, eyes streaming.

"No," said Charming. "As far as I know, I've never seen a rat in my life. I did catch a glimpse once of a pair of mice, but I think they were on an errand for the Royal Tailor. I mean, why else would they be carrying ribbon and thread?"

But Liz seemed to understand something that Charming had not grasped yet. "Will? I mean, King William? Don't . . ." she said, a hint of hardness in her voice.

"Liz, there's only one man in the entire kingdom who knows how to slay a dragon. I need Charming."

With a rush comprehension, Charming realized what Will was asking. An odd mix of emotions passed through him. His heart was sick for Will and desperately worried for Lady Rapunzel, even if she never missed an opportunity to mention his treatment of her hair, but there was part of him, a real and not insignificant part of him, that was intrigued by the thought that there was a new dragon and thrilled that he was being asked to fight it, and yet questing against a dragon was an uncertain prospect even in the best of circumstances, and if Will's condition was any indication, these were not the best of circumstances. He hesitated. It would mean leaving Liz, but this was what he had been waiting for, a purpose, and he couldn't abandon Will and Elle. He raised himself onto his knees and thrust the plow handle into the air like a sword.

"I, Edward Michael Charming, pledge my . . ." he grimaced at the piece of wood in his hand, "sword and my life to you, my brother-in-law, the King, and this just—"

"NO!" interrupted Liz.

"What do you mean no?" said Will, wiping the tears from his eyes with the back of his hand and leaving a streak of mud behind.

"He's . . . he's a farmer," stuttered Liz.

"You said I'd never be a farmer," Charming pointed out. "Besides, this is about a dragon. This is what I do. This is what I was always meant to do." He paused as his doubts returned, and he continued less certainly. "Of course, that was before I met you, Liz. You are my one true love, and . . ."

"There you have it," Will interrupted. "This is Charming's destiny. You are his true love, and Elle is mine. You would expect Charming to come after you, and I must go after Elle. You do want us to rescue Elle, don't you?"

"Of course Elle must be rescued," Liz said with a cluck of irritation. "But where will you go? What is your plan? Why don't I see an army behind you?"

"Yes, where are your soldiers, Your Majesty?" Charming asked, looking about to see if they might be hiding among the furrows of the field.

"Plan? Go? Soldiers?" Will asked uncertainly.

"Yes," Liz said in a clipped voice that bit each word viciously. "Where is this dragon? What kind of dragon is it? Where will you be taking *my husband* when you go on your *fool's* quest? How will you kill the thing when you find it?"

"He's the Great Dragon of the North, so he must be somewhere in the north," answered Will uncertainly. "As for how to kill him, that's why I'm taking Charming."

Liz raised an eyebrow, as Charming nodded in agreement at this last point.

"So, the plan is for you and Edward to ride off alone? Against a dragon?" asked Liz.

There was a moment of strained silence that was interrupted when Charming asked, "Seriously, where have you hidden your guard?" He turned in circles, glancing this way and that. "And did you say Great Dragon of the North, as in, Volthraxus?"

"I don't know," mumbled Will. "Things were a little confused when we rode out. At some point, we stopped to pick up fresh horses. I think I rode ahead while they were arranging things. And yes, it was the Great Dragon of the North. I don't know anything about a Volthraxus."

"You mean you rode that horse without stopping from Castle White?" asked Liz, pointing at the exhausted stallion.

"Yes." Will nodded glumly. "Everything was taking too long."

"You mean you, the King, rode here alone and unguarded?" Charming asked. "And you actually saw Volthraxus?"

"Um . . . yes and yes?" Will answered.

"Madness!" shouted Charming, then catching himself, he amended, "I mean that wasn't very prudent, Your Majesty."

"Which? Riding without my guard or seeing the dragon?"

"Both!"

"But it's the sort of thing you would do," Will said defensively.

"Well, possibly, but I have never been the King," Charming rebuked, while giving a quick glance at the sky. "Don't you remember our last journey together? The woods are filled with brigands and trolls and things. As for Volthraxus . . ." Charming wasn't able to put into words the dread he was feeling, having heard that name.

"Well, nothing happened. And now we can ride together, and you will keep me safe."

"I suppose so," replied Charming, rubbing his chin in thought. He quietly mouthed the word *Volthraxus* to himself.

"It's perfect," said Will, warming to the argument. "Last time we had no trouble defeating whatever we ran into."

"I guess that's right," Charming agreed, but his brow knitted.

"Listen, Will," said Liz, stepping in quickly before Will made the decision a *fait accompli*. "I love Elle like a sister. However, it is too late for anyone to do anything today. You are exhausted from your ride, and your horse is near death, and Edward has been 'farming' all day. Let's all go inside and eat and get some rest. Edward, can you tend to the King's horse? In the morning, we'll talk about everything and make a plan. Then the three of us will find a way to help Elle."

"But, you are staying here," said Will and Charming together.

"No, I'm not," said Liz. "I'm not sure what fairy tale you two are remembering, but the last time the pair of you went off alone, a troll almost took Edward's head off, and Will nearly died of blood poisoning from drinking at that foul tavern."

Charming and Will flinched as Gnarsh the Troll and the horrid beer of the Cooked Goose blended together in a noxious mixture of memories.* They both sunk into a melancholy at the remembrance, which for Charming also included the disgrace of being disowned by his father, which, no matter the time or distance, still stung.

"But . . ." Will began.

"No, 'buts,'" Liz said sternly. "This time the two of you will not ride away and leave me behind to worry and wait."

Charming opened his mouth to say something, but Liz's emerald eyes met his, and something in her look silenced him. This was not about him, or at least not entirely. This was about Will. It was obvious that the King was not himself, and it was just as obvious that Liz had decided that they needed to delay him as long

---

* Author's note: If you would like a sampling of that noxious mixture pick up a copy of "A Fairy-Tale Ending" where you can read all about the early adventures of Will Pickett and Prince Charming. Also, Charming wanted us to add that in that story, he wears many thrilling styles and colors of hose, a fact which he assures us will help to boost sales.

as possible and give him time to come to his senses, and perhaps for his army to find him.

Ultimately, Liz managed to coax Will back to the cottage and get him to admit that he was both tired and hungry. Admittedly, she was helped by the fact that Will was on the point of collapse and simply didn't have the strength to do much more than gesture wildly and mumble. She prepared supper while Charming tended to the horse and made sure Goliath was well.

As he brushed and fed the animals, his thoughts were on Volthraxus. He knew with a certainty that the best course, and the one least likely to get the King or Liz killed, was for him to take on this quest alone. Perhaps his reputation coupled with sheer audacity would be enough to win the day.

It would give me a chance to make up for past failures: never killing the dragon, never saving the princess, wearing that feathery hat after summer. Why doesn't fighting a dragon sound as attractive as it might once have?

What he didn't want to admit, what he had never admitted to anyone, and what he would certainly not reveal now was that after reading everything ever written about fighting dragons, he had determined without any doubt that no man, no matter how skilled, had any hope of defeating a dragon in single combat. And this was Volthraxus, the Killing Wind. If the legends were true, he was an ancient male dragon of immense power. Charming vaguely recalled something about a weakness that Volthraxus had, but he couldn't remember exactly what it was, and it probably didn't matter. In the stories, every dragon always had a crucial weakness, but in truth, they were rarely useful. You needed two things to slay a dragon, for it to make a mistake and lots of luck, and having an army at your back didn't hurt either. Okay, three things. And, even then, fighting a dragon was almost universally a death sentence, and now Charming had Liz and a happily ever after that he wanted to live.

Nevertheless, it seemed inevitable that he would ride forth to battle the beast, so Charming's thoughts naturally turned to the far more important question of what he would wear. Unfortunately, there his confidence was not what it once was. He was not at all certain what condition his questing clothing was in, and as he made his way back to the cottage, he came to the sudden, horrible realization that even if they had been properly pressed before being packed away, they would definitely be so *last year.*

When he finally joined the siblings, it was over a melancholy meal, during which Will mumbled incoherently about what had transpired at Castle White, and Charming worried over how he was going to brave being seen on an actual quest in out-of-date clothes. Besides being distracted over the age-old question of cape or hood, trying to focus on Will's story was not helped by the fact that, to Charming's mind, Will was a terrible storyteller. His descriptions were lacking and his word choices abysmal. But, as they pieced the tale together, Charming's mood began to rise.

The behavior Volthraxus exhibited, and particularly the note he had left behind, seemed to confirm the stories about him, that he was a creature that understood the proper forms. The dragon would, of course, take every opportunity to kill anyone coming to slay him, but he would probably treat Elle quite well and would certainly not raise a claw against her until he could face Will or Will's appointed hero. Charming tried to explain this as they ate, leaving out the fact that the King's champion would almost certainly die, but Will was in no mood to hear reason. After a time, Charming sunk into his own brooding silence as he thought about what he would need to pack.

The hat will have to be discarded, but my old jacket was definitely fashion forward, he reminded himself. *A few alterations to the cuffs and collars, and I might be able to get away with it.*

By the end of dinner, Will was asleep in his chair. Charming, on the other hand had mentally addressed every issue that he was liable to face except for the insoluble ones like how to prevent a full-grown dragon from boiling one before you have time to parley for the release of its prisoner and the fact that he lacked a valet and would have to buff his own boots for the entire length of the quest. Liz interrupted these troubling thoughts as Will began to snore beside him.

"Edward, help me with him," whispered Liz.

Charming carried Will to the guest bedroom. Liz began unlacing the sleeping King's breeches and vest while Charming held him upright.

"What are you doing? That is the King!" whispered Charming.

"Yes, he is." She sighed. "But, he is also my little brother, and he has exhausted himself with grief, Charming. Don't forget that. He has never had to face what he is facing now, and we have no idea how he is likely to react or what he is likely to attempt."

After they had tucked him in, Liz gently smoothed her brother's hair and sang him a lullaby.

"Poor, Elle," Liz said with a sad shake of her head. "She must be so afraid. In the morning, when we are all fresh, we can come up with a plan. Tonight, we need to get some sleep. Hopefully, Will's guard and his wits will catch up with him tomorrow. Even if they don't, we have to find a way to convince him that rushing after Elle isn't going to save her. I remember the last dragon, Charming. If this new dragon is anything like that one, then no man can face it."

He did not argue, and they rose and left the King to sleep in peace.

They went to bed, and although Liz fell asleep, Charming lay awake thinking about her last words as the moonlight traced strange patterns on the ceiling. She was wrong, of course. Any man could face a dragon. In fact, it was trivially easy. The trick he reflected was in not worrying overmuch about the outcome. He used to be a master at not worrying. He wondered if he still could. He fell asleep with the question still echoing in his mind.

He woke a few hours later to find a large, callused, and meaty hand clamped over his mouth. Charming was slightly alarmed to see a shadowy Will leaning over him.

"Shhh," whispered Will, slowly removing his hand. "Come with me."

Still half-asleep, Charming did as he was instructed, shutting the door quietly behind him so as not to wake Liz.

Will was dressed and had his sword belted to his side. A few candles had been lit in the kitchen, and they threw a wavering light about the room. "Get dressed," said Will, indicating a pile of Charming's work clothing sitting on a chair.

Though the cobwebs were still thick in his mind, Charming knew that whatever was happening was a bad idea, particularly if Will had any intention of sending him out in those clothes. "Wait," he said. "What are we doing?"

"Isn't it obvious? I've saddled both horses. We are leaving," said Will.

"No, Will, we should wait until daylight. If you insist on going, I'll wake Liz. Besides, I would never wear that shirt with those tights."

He half turned to go back to the bedroom.

"No, you won't," ordered Will, placing a hand on the hilt of his sword.

Charming was now awake, and the edge of anger pawed at him. "Will, brother or not, please don't threaten me in my own home. I place a high value on hospitality."

"I'm not *threatening* you, Charming. I'm *telling* you not to wake her," Will said, his voice assuming a measure of command that Charming was unaccustomed to. "This I do not as your brother or friend, but as your King. You will journey with me, and *you* will teach *me* how to kill the dragon."

In that instant, Charming was no longer Edward Charming the man, but Edward Charming the boy, and he faced his father, King Rupert. Years of memories and training flooded through him and warred in his breast against what he knew was right. In the end, his duty to his King and kingdom won. This was not his brother-in-law. It was King William, giving him a Royal Command.

It was only later when Charming was dressing himself in a set of appropriate clothes—he had been unyielding on this point at least—that something else King William had said struck him. He had said that Charming would teach *Will* how to kill the dragon. Suddenly, Charming felt sick as he realized what it was Will was really asking.

As Charming slipped on his last boot, he asked as casually as he could, "Your Majesty, what do you intend my role to be in this quest?"

"You are going to be my squire," Will said brightly.

It was like a slap in the face, and Charming physically recoiled as though Will had struck him. Fortunately, Will did not seem to notice his reaction, and turning about, began picking up his pack. As Charming went through the motions of finishing his preparations, he recalled his own former squire, Tomas. He lapsed into a silence as he reevaluated both his relationship to Will and also his past treatment of Tomas and the many others who had served him.

"Are you ready?" asked Will.

Charming bit his lip and nodded. He was at the door taking one last look at the little cottage when he realized he could not leave Liz without a word. He turned back and grabbed a scrap of paper and a quill from a small writing table near the fireplace.

"What are you doing?" Will asked irritably from the door.

"I am leaving a note for Liz."

"No," Will said, and, crossing the room, seized the quill from him. "I don't want her following us."

"I understand," Charming said, and grabbed at his arm to keep him from taking the quill. "But if I don't leave her a note, I assure you, she will follow us. And when she finds us, she'll be furious. More than that, Will, we are going to face a dragon, and I do not want to leave anything unsaid between us."

Will's expression turned down. Perhaps it was the thought of his angry older sister that made him hesitate, or perhaps it was the memory of all the things he wished that he could have said to Elle before she was taken, but whatever the reason, Will sighed, "Okay, go ahead."

Charming quickly scrawled a note to Liz.

My dearest Liz, your brother, the King, means to face the

dragon and has ordered me away with him. I swear to you that I will do everything in my power to return him home to you. I will always love you. Edward.

He placed it on the mantel behind one of the figurines Liz kept there. Will was in the open door shifting impatiently from foot to foot. "We must go," he said.

"My King, where do we start?"

"North. The beast is the Great Dragon of the North, so that's where we are going. North."

Charming opened his mouth to ask another question, but Will cut him off with a gesture. He stared at Charming, and said sternly, "On this quest, I must insist that you follow my lead, Charming. We must rescue Elle. I will not argue the point."

Charming nodded, but his insides were empty. Charming was not on a quest with Will. Charming was on a quest with King William, who had lost his bride-to-be almost on the eve of their wedding. With a heart full of dread, Charming left the cottage with King William. Using a lantern to light their way, the two men slowly rode away to the north, past the newly churned earth of Charming's field, leaving Elizabeth dreaming on her pillow.

CHAPTER 3

A TEMPEST AND A TEAPOT

In fairy stories, most heroines are demure and proper. They sigh when appropriate, swoon when necessary, and never, ever, are given to complaint—unless, of course, they are forced to sleep on anything but the finest pea-less eiderdown, then all bets are off.

When she woke the morning after Will's arrival, Liz felt nothing like those fairy-tale ladies. She was angry with Will, furious at Charming, her stomach was tied in knots, and as for being demure, that was right out. For at least an hour after waking, she stomped around the house, retching into a bucket and swearing like a sailor. But it would not be fair to judge Liz too harshly for her unfairy-tale-ladylike behavior. She had her fair share of reasons.

Reason one became apparent to her almost as

soon as she opened her eyes. She rolled over to find an empty spot in the bed where Charming usually lay. This was not alarming in itself, but when she turned the other way and found her bedside table also bereft of her customary morning breakfast, she knew that something was wrong. Charming had, from the first morning of their marriage, always made sure that she had a little pot of tea, freshly cut flowers (usually lavender), some bread, and a pot of sweet jam to eat. This morning there was nothing. In an instant, she felt her heart empty with fear and her stomach churn violently. Charming was gone.

There was a part of her that wanted to go back to sleep, and not just because the room seemed to be spinning in a peculiarly sickening way, but because she simply did not want to face the cold loneliness of her empty house. However, she was Elizabeth Charming, and avoiding difficult, maddening, infuriating truths was simply not what she did. So, she rose and did the only thing that she could do. She made herself a pot of tea.

It was over her second cup of chamomile, after she had settled her stomach and confirmed that indeed two horses were missing from the barn, that a second reason for being angry suddenly occurred to her. Charming had lied. He had looked her in the eyes and agreed to help her stop Will from leaving. This realization led to a storm of profanity that turned an entire flock of bluebirds red from blushing and also led to her dashing the entire tea set against the fireplace, one satisfying piece at a time.

It was while waiting for a new pot of tea, literally a new pot as the old one had been smashed to bits, to steep properly that the third and final reason for her anger was revealed. She had been sweeping up the fragments of her tantrum from the hearth when she found Charming's note, standing on the mantelpiece and tucked discreetly behind a little ornament of a cheeky dwarf, or as the dwarves had called them when they gave her a set of these figures, "merchandising." She read Charming's brief letter and gave a cry of frustration and anger. From the tone of his writing, it appeared that Charming knew full well that Will was out of his senses, that his desire to hunt down the dragon was both ill considered and ill conceived, and yet he had still been fool enough to follow her mad little brother. This was the last straw. What was left of her self-control broke.

It was during the resulting invective-laced tirade against her absent sibling and husband that Charming's old squire, Tomas, arrived. She had just snatched up a particularly smug figurine of her dwarf friend/tormentor Grady and was going to hurl it against the wall when she saw the man, scruffy and misshapen as ever, staring at her through the open door of the cottage, with the biggest grin she had ever seen him wear stretched across his face.

"Don't mind me," he said in his characteristic rasp. "I was just taking notes for the next time I need to talk to my local clergy." He chuckled, a deep and throaty laugh, at his own joke.

Liz had never been happier to be laughed at in

her life. She put the statuette of Grady down, rushed across the room, and, throwing her arms around Tomas's neck, began sobbing violently.

"There, there, Lady Charming, no need for all that," he said while thumping her back solidly like he was trying to burp her.

"But . . . but . . ." she said gasping for air, "but Edward has left me."

"I don't believe it," Tomas said in a gentle growl. "He was never that smart, but he couldn't be that much of a fool. I mean look at you . . ." He pulled her away from him and cast his eyes up and down. "You may have put on a couple of pounds, but your figure is still fine. I ask you, what more could a man need?"

The cheekiness of this comment was shocking enough that it gave Liz a chance to gain the upper hand on her emotions. Clucking her tongue in indignation, she pulled a handkerchief from her pocket and wiped the tears from her eyes.

Dignity somewhat restored, she said, "No, you old fool, he and my idiot brother have gone off to track down this dragon."

Tomas glowered at this news. "I was afraid of that. I told Alain as soon as the King gave us the slip that we should've come straight here, but he wanted to follow 'procedure.' Bah!"

"So you didn't meet him . . ." she started to ask, but then stopped and exclaimed with wide-eyed disbelief, "Wait, Alain has a 'procedure' for this? How often do you lose kings anyway?"

Tomas went red in the face and muttered something about "affairs of state" and "complicated," but quickly lapsed into silence under Liz's glare.

They stood a moment without speaking, both frowning, lost in whatever dark thoughts their minds had constructed. Liz recovered first. A sly gleam crept into her eyes. "Well, how rude of me. I can't leave you standing in the door. Come in, come in."

She took his arm and led him to the table in the kitchen, where she had set out her second-best tea set. She moved her thankfully unused vomit bucket aside and grabbed a second cup. "Have a seat. I was just planning how I was going to track down Charming and Will when you arrived."

Tomas looked at her sideways with suspicion. "Oh, is that what you were doing? Well, if the speech I heard is any part of this plan, then I feel sorry for those fellows."

Liz ignored this barb and took a demure sip of tea. "Yes, well, now that you are here, we can decide on our next steps together."

" 'We' and 'our' and 'together,' " he repeated, emphasizing each word. "I am honored to be made part of your war council, Liz, but . . ."

"No buts, Tomas," she interrupted sharply. "I am sick and tired of 'buts.' Besides, there's nothing you can do to stop me from going after them unless you want to stay here in the cottage and sit on me, which, I would remind you, would require you to abandon your own search permanently, because as soon as you leave, I'll follow, even if I have to do it alone and on foot."

"Why . . . why . . . why . . . you're blackmailing me," Tomas spluttered. "This is extortion, plain and simple. You know I couldn't let you go traipsing off into the wilderness all by yourself. Why the whole idea is . . . is . . ."

Tomas seemed unable to come up with words strong enough to express what he thought the idea was, so he worked his mouth noiselessly and glowered at her. Liz took another, slightly less demure but infinitely smugger sip of tea and did her best to ignore his glares.

Something about the set of her face or the way she held her teacup must have convinced Tomas that there was no use arguing the point because he eventually relented. After swearing that all women were mad as snakes and as aggravating as mules, and adding that Liz was the worst of the lot, he asked, "Fine. What's the plan? Not that Charming ever had a plan to kill the first dragon. He would always just say something like, 'My good man, we will away to her dark tower there to claim that measure of glory that is my due.' Or some equally meaningless rubbish!"

Liz was silent for a moment, her teacup frozen midway between saucer and lips. The fact was had Tomas asked his question without comment, she would have had no answer, but this last grouse by the man about his days squiring Charming had given her an idea, a most definite idea. She ran to the sitting room, pulled a large, leather-bound volume down from a shelf, and, sweeping the tea to one side in a great clatter of china and silver, plopped it on the table between them. It was an atlas of Royaume, and she flipped to a well-thumbed page near the back that showed a detailed map of the southern portion of the kingdom.

She stabbed a finger down at a point in the mountains south of a small valley where a town labeled "Prosper" lay, and said, "We go there."

Tomas squinted hard at the map, and his face grew white and serious. "What, you mean to the old Dragon Tower? But that dragon is dead."

"Exactly," she replied, then stood and began bustling about the kitchen, filling cloth bags with odds of this and ends of that.

Tomas stared at the map for a minute and then, scratching at the scruffy stubble on his neck, said, "I don't understand."

Not slowing in her feverish packing, Liz asked, "What do we know for certain about this dragon?"

He picked up a tart from among the spilled contents of the tea and said between bites, "Well, that it really hates Will."

"Perhaps," she said, pausing for a moment, a loaf of bread in one hand, a jar of pickled preserves in the other, and a wistful look on her face. "But we know for certain is that the dragon must have really loved the Wyrm of the South. Where better to act out its final revenge than in the nest of its fallen love?"

Tomas could say nothing to this, and so wisely sat eating a pastry and drinking his tea as Liz made their final preparations.

Despite the urgency both felt to get going, it was not until midafternoon that Tomas and Liz found themselves slipping out of the cottage gate. It was fortunate that Tomas had brought several fresh horses along with him because Charming and Will had taken the best mounts from the barn, and after examining the one Will had ridden in on the previous day, Tomas declared the beast needed at least a week's rest before it would be fit for any journey, much less a journey of the length they were proposing. So they let the poor creature out into a fenced field of spring grass with Charming's ox, set the chickens and the geese free, and headed off.

On their way down the path, they passed Charming's field, and Liz gazed wistfully at the mad crisscross of furrows and wondered why they had aggravated her so much the previous day when now she would not change a single thing about them.

Tomas grunted. "What happened here? Did a twister hit, a flood, maybe a giant?"

She nodded and laughed. "Something like that, Tomas. Yes, you could say that a Goliath struck."

By afternoon, they had reached a small road that would lead them in a few days' time to the village of Quaint. It was early spring, and thus far they had traveled little-used ways dotted by the brilliant green of new growth, and the going was actually quite pleasant, or would have been pleasant had not Liz's nerves kept her, and her stomach, in a state of constant upset. But in

Quaint, where the Southern Road to Prosper made its beginning, there seemed to be an unusual number of travelers, and the bustling streets combined with recent rains had turned the town into a quagmire of mud filled with people and carts all jostling this way and that, trying desperately to make their way somewhere else.

"Tomas!" Liz shouted over the sea of noise around them. "See if you can find us a room."

He tipped his cap, dismounted, and maneuvered his way around a pair of families arguing over the contents of their upset handcarts and toward a two-story building with a high, steep-pitched roof that had a colorful sign over the door showing a cross-eyed badger juggling beer bottles. Liz took the horses into a nearby opening between two buildings and watched the people pass by. After a few moments, she frowned. There was something frenzied about the way they were moving, and the carts she was seeing were not loaded with goods but with whole households: furniture, clothes, animals, children, and all. With a sudden chill, she realized that this was not just high traffic from a market day or a festival weekend; these people were on the run. They were fleeing the dragon.

Tomas returned a few minutes later, stalking his way through the crowds and across the mud-filled streets with a sour expression on his face.

"I take it there are no rooms?" she asked, still studying the people with a frown.

"Oh, there are rooms" he said with a grimace. "If you don't mind selling your soul for one. I'm ashamed to tell you what the landlord of the Drunken Badger wants for a single room for you and a spot in the stalls for me. If his prices are any sign of what things cost around here, it's no wonder everyone is running."

"It doesn't matter," she said flipping him a purse of coins. "Go and get us *two* rooms."

"But, Your Ladyship!" he said in protest.

"No arguing, Tomas," she said sternly. "I'm tired and sick from camping out on the road, and you are no longer a squire. I will not have you sleep with the horses while I stay warm in a bed."

Reluctantly, Tomas agreed, mostly because he was also not really keen on sleeping in a tent again if he could help it, but also because an inn promised ale, and in his mind, any promise of ale is a promise that should be kept.

They paid dearly for what appeared to be two closets that had been hastily converted into rooms for them. As for information, their fellow guests had plenty of rumors and gossip to share. According to the people they spoke with, who had ALL apparently witnessed at least one dragon attack personally, the beast had been seen raiding farms from Prosper in the south and the village of Modest in the west to the town of Quiet in the north. What was more, the creature seemed to have a bottomless appetite and a particular fondness for fair maidens. In fact, if all the stories she heard were true, Liz was not sure that a fair maiden existed anywhere in Royaume that remained unmolested by the dragon. She was beginning to feel a little left out.

Later that night, they both squeezed into Liz's room to see if they had learned anything useful.

"Totally useless," Tomas groused as he leaned against the wall at the foot of her bed. "I don't think a single one of them has ever seen a dragon or would even know a dragon if it came up and bit them on the ass. One of them had the nerve to tell me that the creature was half lion, half snake, and quarter raven. I'm no scholar, but that doesn't even add up. If you ask me, they have no idea what they're running from or where they're running to. Half of them seem to think the dragon is in the north and are running south, half seem to think the dragon is in the south and are running north, and the other half are running west or east, depending on which way the wind is blowing that day."

"I know," Liz said, pointing down at her map of Royaume, which she had marked with dozens of neat little *X*s, all of which represented a "confirmed" dragon sighting. "I can't say for sure if the dragon is even in Royaume anymore, much less where it might be or be heading." She sighed, and tucking her legs under her, leaned back against the headboard of the bed. "Did you learn anything that might lead you to believe that *we* are headed the wrong way?"

Tomas thought carefully for a moment and shook his head. "No. Your logic still makes the most sense. But . . ." he began, then seemed to think better of whatever it was he was going to say, and instead said, "No, I say we go on to Prosper like we planned."

Liz studied him over the edge of her map. "Out with it, Tomas."

"It's nothing, Your Ladyship," he said, twisting his hands nervously.

"Tomas . . ." she said, letting the warning note of her voice do the work.

He let out a deep breath. "Well, I heard a couple of people talking about a Dracomancer down south in Two Trees who's been telling everyone that he knows how to kill the beasty. If he's the fellow I think he is, he certainly had a reputation for knowin' about dragons."

Liz glanced back at her map and chewed her lips in thought. "It would add a day's worth of riding to get to Two Trees. Do you think it's worth it? What could he do for us? Are we sure he's a real sorcerer?"

Tomas studied the ground at his feet intently for a moment, then raised just his eyes and fixed them onto hers. "Well, I don't know anything about magic or sorcerers or the like, Your Ladyship, and I don't know if this will be a count for or against him, but he is the one that gave the original prophecy to King Rupert that his son, your Charming, was going to rid the kingdom of the last dragon."

"Right," Liz said stiffly after a minute of bitter silence, "we will stop in Two Trees. I've always wanted to have a word with that man."

CHAPTER 4

NORTH BY SOUTHEAST

The Kingdom of Royaume is known for many things, including the number of public houses with disturbing names, such as the Boiled Badger, the Dead Drunk, the Pernicious Porcupine, Something in My Mustache, and the Cooked Goose.* It also holds the distinction of being particularly well endowed in abandoned manor

* In a marketing effort that had some questioning his sanity, the owner of the Cooked Goose had, at this time, officially changed the name of his inn to the Infamous Cooked Goose. No records are available to confirm or deny whether the new name was successful in bringing in any more customers, but as only a few years later the inn was demolished by the local council to make way for a pigsty, a move everyone agrees to have been a major improvement for the district, this author assumes that it did not work out. The more charitable among my readers dispute this inference and have even suggested that the owner might have had the inn demolished out of concern for the public health. All the author can say is that if you believe that, you really don't know the owner of the Cooked Goose.

houses and darkened woods. However, without question, Royaume is best known for having the single most confusing road system ever devised.

This confusion arises principally because Royaume has an inordinately large number of roads for a kingdom of its size, but paradoxically, also an embarrassingly small number of road signs. The fact is if one goes off the beaten track in Royaume, one is likely in short order to find another beaten track, which to all appearances rightly resembles the first beaten track. Many believe that lost towns and hamlets lie undiscovered in the interior of Royaume, hidden not by wilderness, but a maze of roads winding this way and that. And some say that the disproportionately large number of little hooded girls that go missing in the woods of Royaume each year is the direct result of the lack of any meaningful way of telling where you're going unless you've already been there.** That and the wolves that like to eat them, of course.

** Historians say that some good has come of the dense and indecipherable nature of Royaume's roads. One, possibly apocryphal, tale that is a favorite in many of the disturbingly named pubs mentioned in this chapter recounts how in the reign of King Durward the Uncurious, Royaume was actually invaded by a nearby kingdom. The army that was led into Royaume was enormous and would have easily crushed King Durward's own army, the King never having had much interest in either raising an army or figuring out what to do with the bit of one he had. However, on their way to attack Castle White, the invading army got lost in the Northern Forest and spent the next several years trying to find its way back out. It is said that many of the towns in the north of Royaume were actually founded by members of the invading force who got tired of trying to find their way back home and simply settled down.

While Will and Charming never admitted out loud to each other that they were lost, it could be stated as fact that a week after leaving his sister's home, Will was pacing along the side of one of Royaume's many unmarked roads, having no idea where he was. What was more, and this he was more than a little embarrassed about, Will had no idea how they'd gotten wherever it was they were either.

He had, admittedly, been distracted over the last week worrying about Elle and the dragon and trying to absorb the bizarre bits and pieces of dragon-slaying lore Charming kept throwing out, but the fact was, after giving Charming the order to head north, Will had simply stopped paying attention to the hows, whys and wheres. What was driving the King of Royaume to distraction was that Charming, though he had ostensibly been leading them, also seemed lost.

Will had been watching Charming ponder a merging of paths for at least a quarter of an hour when he finally boiled over. "Charming, do you have any idea where we are going?"

"None whatsoever, Your Majesty."

"Do you have any idea where we are?"

"None, Your Majesty," Charming said, gazing up and down the dirt path they found themselves on. "I suppose that tree looks a bit familiar, but I don't know if that's a good sign or a bad one."

Will's head began to hammer, and he put a hand against his temple. "Well, which way goes north? We'll take that one."

"Neither, Your Majesty," Charming said.

"How is that possible?"

"Well, if my sense of direction has not failed me," Charming replied in a tone that seemed to dismiss the idea as an absurdity, "then that one"—he pointed right—"is going mostly west and south, while that one"—he pointed left—"is going mostly south and east."

"Fine," Will barked. "Pick the one that is going more north."

"Right," Charming said, and began moving his finger between the two trails while mouthing, "eeny, meeny, miny, moe." Finally, his hand settled on the way to the right. "That one, Your Majesty."

Will grunted in disgust and spurred his horse into a canter along the right-hand path.

The week had been filled with these twists and turns and forks in roads, sometimes left and sometimes right. Will was increasingly frustrated by the fact that, despite the enormous distances they were covering, they did not seem to be getting anywhere, much less anywhere north. Sometimes, they had gone east to go north. Sometimes, they had gone west to go north. And, at more than a few points, they had gone south in the hopes that the particular road they had chosen would eventually turn north.

They traveled down this new road into a sinking sun until it dipped below the horizon. It was only after full night had fallen that Will let them stop. In short order, Charming had snared a pair of rabbits and was cooking them over a crackling fire. Because of Charming's bizarre fixation on trivialities like styles of cuffs and collars or the number of buttons on his lapel, this having been the subject of a two-hour lecture the previous day, it was easy for Will to forget that Charming had been trained to be a master campaigner. He'd studied under the greatest woodsmen and hunters of the time. Which suddenly made Will even more frustrated that the man couldn't seem to figure out something as simple as which way was north.

The more Will thought about this, the more irritated he became. The way Charming was lounging against that log was irritating. The way he was buffing a shine into his leather boots was irritating. The way he was now studying the sleeves of his coat to see if they had been dirtied by the day's ride was exceedingly irritating.

"Why can't you find a road north?" Will asked sharply, his voice disturbing the peace of the night.

"What?" Charming asked vaguely. "Road?"

"Yes," Will said, sitting up straight. "Are you purposefully trying to prevent me from going after the dragon?"

"What are you talking about, Will . . . I mean, Your Majesty?" Charming peered across the fire at him. "Have you been drinking? If you have, you know you ought to have shared. In the haste of our departure, I left my flask behind."

"No, I haven't been drinking." In a sudden eruption of anger, he spit, "If you're this great hero, why can't you find a bloody road north?"

Charming's face clouded briefly with anger, but the expression passed, and a nonchalant smile lifted the corners of his mouth. "I think you are laboring under a few misconceptions about heroes, Your Majesty. First"—he held up his thumb—"I didn't learn wood craft to find a creature like Volthraxus, I learned it to hunt game. As for my dragon, the Great Wyrm of the South, I knew exactly where she lived. Everyone knew where she lived. She dwelt in Dragon Tower, so there was no need to track her."

"Second," he said, adding his forefinger to his thumb, "as I think I explained to you in great detail last time we rode out together on a quest, if you are going to be a hero, you must look like a hero. I think you understand about buttons after yesterday, but perhaps I never explained properly the importance of looking impressive. You may think you're alone out here, Will, but you never know when you might meet the public or some traveling minstrel or bard. Unfortunately, looking impressive while riding takes a great deal of concentration. You must always lift your gaze to the far horizon. So, while it is true that I have ridden over nearly every hill and dale in Royaume, I never actually looked at where I was, only where I was going."

Will was nearly speechless, as was often the case after Charming "explained" something to him. "Didn't . . . didn't you get lost?"

"Never." Charming said emphatically. "Getting lost is simply not heroic. No, I always had Tomas with me. He handled mundane matters like directions."

A thought occurred to Will. "Charming, when we rode out together to fight the troll, you were always in the lead."

"Of course," Charming said as he happily ironed the points of his collar between two smooth rocks he'd been heating by the side of the fire. "A hero must always be in front."

"If you were in front, how could Tomas be picking the direction you were going?" Will asked in earnest confusion.

"He would lead from behind," Charming said, as though this was the most obvious thing in the world.

"Lead from behind?"

"Yes, it's one of the essential skills of being a squire," he said as he frowned at a speck of dirt on the breast of his shirt. "A good squire must be able to give direction without appearing to give direction." He appeared satisfied with the outcome of his inspection because he gave Will a big smile. "But, you know all this. You've been doing it since we left the cottage. You're actually quite good at it—very subtle."

A rush of dread went through Will as the sudden realization struck him that they had been traveling at random for nearly a week.

"Oh, God, no!" Will said with a strangled yell, rising to his feet, unable to contain the sense of failure and futility that washed over him. "I've wasted a whole week."

"What?" Charming asked. "Seriously, have you been drinking?"

"I HAVE NOT BEEN DRINKING, YOU HALF-WITTED MORON!" Will shouted. "THIS IS ALL YOUR FAULT! YOU ARE MY SQUIRE! YOU ARE SUPPOSED TO GUIDE ME!"

Charming raised an eyebrow at him. "Your Majesty, I have as little idea about how to be a squire as you have about how to be a dragon hunter."

A cloud of blind rage descended on Will, and he launched himself at Charming with arms outstretched. Tangled in his clothes as he was, Charming had no chance to react. Luckily or unluckily, depending on your perspective, Will's foot caught in a depression. He tumbled to the ground, and his head struck the side of the log Charming had been leaning against. Will heard a roar of light and noise, and before he could figure out how light could roar, everything went black.

Charming spent the night by Will's side, applying cold cloths to the bump on his head and bandages to the fingers where Will had chewed them down to the quick. He wondered at the change that had come over his friend. Charming had long marveled at how Will seemed to rise to any occasion. With Gnarsh, with the fairy, with Gwendolyn, with the bandits in the woods, even with the Wyrm of the South, Will had seemed immune to the sort of panic that would have overwhelmed most people. Until now, he had seemed incapable of being overawed, and it had made him a great king, far better than Charming thought he himself would have been. But, Will now more closely resembled the type of man Charming had been when they met: emotional and brittle.

Elle's loss had broken something in Will. It was understandable, but Charming needed Will to see that trying to become "Prince Charming" and fighting this dragon was not the solution, it was just a way to die. Liz would have been the best person to help her brother. He had considered suggesting that they return to the cottage, but even if he could have convinced Will to acquiesce, an uncertain proposition at best, his friend was so reckless with despair right now that he was a danger to everyone around him. Charming would not risk Liz, not even to save his King. On balance, wandering aimlessly along Royaume's roads for a while might be for the best.

Wandering also gave Charming time to consider what they should do about Volthraxus. In the past, he would have been in Will's camp: ride forth, swords flashing and pennants flying and his white charger charging . . .

Charming shook his head, and the glorious vision faded. "That is the sort of thinking that got us into this mess in the first place," he chastised himself.

He placed a cold cloth over Will's forehead. The "old" Charming would have had no doubt that they could outwit and slay even a dragon as mighty as Volthraxus, but the "new" Charming suspected that the "old" Charming felt this way because the "old" Charming had never thought about the consequences of any of his actions. Now all Charming could think about were the logistics of fighting such a monster. Ostensibly, they were going to face one of the most powerful Wyrms alive, but they had no armor, no shields, no men-at-arms to support them or archers to distract Volthraxus while they made their charge. And that was assuming that they could lure him to the ground in the first place. Trapping Volthraxus in a lair where he couldn't fly would be ideal, but where was he sleeping? The list of problems seemed endless. He wondered if these were the sort of details his squire Tomas used to fret about.

"That would explain why he was so grumpy all the time," Charming muttered. "But is it also why he was so fat and bald?"

Charming ran a worried hand through his thick brown hair. He was still pondering the question and his waistline when the soft blue light of dawn began to seep into the land around them. Charming cooked a very light breakfast and waited for Will to wake up.

Finally, Will murmured, "I didn't kill the dragon. I'm not a dragonslayer. I don't even know how to kill a dragon! Take my crown. Just give me back Elle."

Charming leaned close, and said softly, "Your Majesty, it is okay. I am here."

On reflection, Charming wasn't sure whether Will would see him being there as reassuring, particularly given how the previous night had ended.

Will shook his head and blinked open his eyes. "Charming?"

"I'm afraid so, Your Majesty."

"Where are we, and what time is it?" Will asked with a groan, and levered himself to a sitting position.

"Well, Your Majesty," Charming said, biting his lower lip. "It is about six in the morning, I think on a Tuesday, if that helps. As for where we are, we seem to have misplaced ourselves."

Charming watched carefully for another explosion, but it didn't come. Instead, Will just sat there, stupidly looking at the dancing flames of the fire.

"Would you like some breakfast, Your Majesty?"

Will gave a shake of his head.

"How about some water, Your Majesty?"

Will nodded, and Charming handed him a water-skin he'd filled earlier in a nearby stream.

The cold water seemed to revive Will. "I'm sorry about last night."

"No apology necessary, Your Majesty. No harm done. Well, to me anyway," Charming said wryly, trying to raise Will's spirits.

Will glared at him.

"Don't mock me, Charming" said Will coldly. "I am still your King, and we are on a serious quest. Instead of trying to play the fool, why don't you work at being my squire and get us ready to move out of here."

They stared at each other, but Charming could see the doubt and guilt creep into his friend's eyes. It was a familiar, haunted look, and Charming felt that it was the precise look the Beast had seen in his own eyes when they first met. Will was lost, and it would be up to Charming to lead him back home. But first, Will was going to need to be knocked off his pedestal, and Charming knew he needed to do it before he was tempted to knock the King on his backside.

Charming nodded, and rising to his feet, made a deep and elegant bow of supplication. "As you wish, Your Majesty."

Will looked away and said nothing. Charming crossed to the fire and made Will a plate of food. He knelt in front of the other man, and, holding the plate above his head, said, "Your Majesty, your Royal Breakfast."

"Stop that!" Will said with a shout, rising to his feet to loom over Charming.

"I am merely trying to serve," Charming said innocently. "Am I not pleasing, Your Majesty?"

"No!" Will said still shouting. "Elle has been taken by a dragon, and you're playing games and making jokes and getting us lost! You never take anything seriously. You never . . . You . . ."

Will spread his arms wide and yelled incoherently, and he kept yelling as loudly as he could until he finally ran out of breath. He was swaying on his feet, and a vein on his temple pulsated violently.

"Your Majesty?" Charming said, putting the plate to the side and rising to give him a steadying arm.

"I . . . I need to save Elle," Will gasped, leaning against Charming.

"I know we do."

Will shook his head. "You don't understand. *I* need

to save her, and *I* need you to be a squire, not a hero. *I* lost her. *I* failed to protect her. *I* need to find her. *I* need to prove to her and to myself that *I* can keep her safe."

"First, Your Majesty, may I call you Will?" Charming asked, moving closer so his face was close to his panting friend's. "It will make what I am about to say a lot easier for me to say, and hopefully for you to hear."

"Yes. Fine. Call me Will."

"Thanks, Will," Charming said, and helped Will pull himself back upright.

He stood there a moment, realizing again how enormous Will was and thinking how much better it would be if he could take a step or two back in case this conversation became more physical.

"Well?" Will said impatiently.

Right, here goes, Charming thought, then said quickly, "No offense, Will, but you're being an ass."

"What did you say, Charming?" Will said with a hiss, knocking Charming's arm away.

"You are being an ass, Will, and you can take that from someone who has been one for most of his life," Charming said, certain that he was very close to being punched in the face.

"Why?" Will fumed. "Because I want to save Lady Rapunzel, my wife-to-be, the love of my life, the wheat in my field?"

"No," Charming replied flatly, "because you seem to think that I don't," and he added in disbelief, "Did you really say 'wheat in my field'?"

Smacking his forehead with the palm of his hand,

Will cried, "You ask me that, then question how I can think you aren't taking this seriously. How in the world can you be so dense and infuriating at the same time?"

"I suppose that's part of my charm," Charming said with a raised eyebrow, trying to break the tension.

Will flushed scarlet with anger. Charming held up his hands in a gesture of peace. "I know you think I'm taking things too lightly, but it is only because you have enough rage in you for the both of us. Do you honestly believe that I don't know what you're feeling? Have you already forgotten what I was like when we first met? Do you really think the only way to save Lady Rapunzel is to become *that* guy?"

He gestured helplessly, trying to put into words what it was he was feeling back when he tried to kill Will in the throne room of Castle White, and when he tried to battle a troll single-handedly, and when he tried to betray Will to bandits. "When you came, you took my whole world away. I was so intent on hating you and on trying to prove my greatness that I was blind to everything else. In my blindness, I moved from disaster to disaster, and you will suffer the same if you don't find a way to stop feeling and instead start thinking."

Charming took a deep breath and gathered his courage. This next thing would be hard to admit.

"I . . . I . . ." he hesitated, then plunged on, "I always thought my squire Tomas was trying to undermine and humiliate me when he made jokes at my expense or groused at my excesses, but I see now that the brutal little hobgoblin"—Charming couldn't help describing him this way—"was trying—unsuccessfully for the most part—to keep me from being an idiot." He sighed. "I suppose you could say I am trying to be your squire."

Charming was emotionally spent. To compare himself to his former squire was one of the hardest things he'd ever done.

"And that's all I want from you," Will said as he chewed once more on the side of his hand. "I am probably making mistakes right now—" He stopped, then started again. "No, I know I am making mistakes right now. Elle is lost, and I can't think of anything else. Every time I sleep, all I dream of are the things that might be happening to her. Every time we stop, all I can think of is that I should still be going. I just want to find her. I need to find her. Edward, help me find her!"

Will began pacing up and down, chewing on his fingers and mumbling. Charming shook his head. He knew that he had gone as far as he dared. Will was in no state to deal with the larger issues, so they would just have to start with the small ones first.

Charming sat down on a log and gestured for Will to join him. Will ignored the gesture and kept pacing. Charming shrugged and, moving his head back and forth to keep Will in his sight, said, "Fine. Let's start with why we are traveling this direction. You keep insisting that we go north by the most direct route, but, in case you hadn't noticed, it's rather easy to get lost in this kingdom. We should stick with the main thoroughfares. They may wind here and there, but they will get us where we need to go reliably even if the distance is a bit longer."

"Nonsense," Will mumbled from around his thumb. "If we try to use the larger roads, you know I would be recognized, and Tomas and Alain would catch up with us, which would mean an escort of soldiers, which would mean a caravan of supply wagons, which would mean delay. Besides, I always took back roads from the farm to Prosper, and I never had any trouble."

Charming gritted his teeth in irritation. Alain and Tomas and a troop of soldiers were exactly what they needed. Also, that Will would compare going at most a league from his farm into town to the hundreds of leagues they would need to travel to the Northern Mountains was exactly the sort of thing Prince Charming would have done.

After several deep breaths, Charming decided to try a different tack. If Will intended to act like Prince Charming, then he needed to see how it was done.

"So, you mean to go after Volthraxus, the Great Dragon of the North, without soldiers or archers to support you? You, alone against a hundred-foot-long fire-breathing monster. Exactly what I would have done." Charming smiled his most obnoxious smile. "I'm curious what you are planning, though. You know, I am a bit of a student of dragon-slaying tactics. Maybe I could give you a couple of pointers. Although, maybe not. A real dragonslayer would never take advice from his squire."

Will looked over at him with alarm painted clearly on his pale face. "What are you talking about? You know I have no idea how to kill a dragon. That's why you're here. You need to tell me how to kill the dragon."

"You mean slay a dragon," Charming said seriously. "It's important to have the verb right. You don't kill dragons, Will."

"Why?" Will barked. "Why do our clothes have to be right and the words we use have to be right and our posture on the back of a horse has to be right? What does it matter? Maybe I'm not doing it right. Maybe I haven't spent my entire life training to fight a dragon, but I can't see that any of it matters. We keep going north until we find the monster. We fight it. We kill it. We rescue Elle. Simple. Stop trying to complicate it."

"I'm not trying to complicate things. I'm . . ." *I'm trying to work up the courage to admit what I have never admitted to anyone.*

"You're what?"

Charming didn't answer immediately but instead stood and began to saddle his horse.

"You're what?" Will asked his irritation rising again in his voice.

"What must you think of me?" Charming asked in an apparent non sequitur.

"What?"

"If slaying a dragon is simple, then what must you think of me? I had years to slay my dragon and knew exactly where it was. Didn't you wonder why I never tried?"

Will shrugged. "No, I just thought you were . . . well . . . you know . . ."

"Busy? Going to get around to it after I finished my dalliances with the ladies of the realm? Forging a master plan?" Charming asked as he tightened the straps on his saddle. "No, Will, I wasn't doing any of that. Perhaps I was trying to decide what armor to wear, it was a subject that could occupy my thoughts for days at a time, but that's not important. What is important is that I spent years studying dragons. I was determined to learn everything I could about them. I had tutors to help me, and a library stocked with every book of dragon lore imaginable. Do you know what I learned?"

"No. That's why you're here," Will said with an impatient grunt.

Charming took a deep breath and, leaning his head against the side of his horse, said, "What I learned is that it isn't possible."

"What are you saying?" Will asked in a voice several octaves higher than normal.

Charming turned back to Will. "What I'm trying to say is this . . ." He stopped, searching for the right words. "Will, imagine for a moment that a creature with scales harder than iron flies at you and breathes flame hotter than a forge down upon you. What do you do?"

Will bit his hand, then hastily pulled it out of his mouth. "I raise my shield and use it to hold off the fire."

"No, Will." Charming shook his head sadly. "You

roast alive in your armor. That's what you do. If a dragon has his wits about him, you die."

"But you said that hunting and killing dragons was 'what you do.'"

"I never said anything about killing dragons, Will," Charming said pointedly. "That's what I need you to understand. Killing dragons happens very rarely and only when the dragon makes a mistake. The best way to get a dragon to make a mistake is to make it fear you. In order for that to happen, you have to make the creature believe the impossible—that you can actually kill it. That you are so certain that you can win that you are more concerned with your dress and appearance than with real strategy or tactics. But, Will, this is Volthraxus. He's a legend. He's old and he's smart and he knows what humans are capable of. He won't be impressed by a feather cap or even a well-turned set of calves. I'm saying that if we make our quest to kill Volthraxus, then short of divine intervention, we die, and Elle is never freed."

Will was staring at him, white-faced with shock. Charming took a deep breath before continuing in a quiet voice. "However, maybe, if we appeal to his sense of honor and decorum, and are very lucky, we might make a sufficient impression on Volthraxus that he will agree to exchange one or both of our lives for Elle's. I will help you do that even if it means leaving Liz a widow for the sake of your bride, but I will not help you immolate yourself for no purpose trying to kill Volthraxus."

With that, Charming mounted and started off down the trail.

Charming set a slow pace. Even so, it took some time for Will to catch up. They rode in silence until Will cleared his throat. "Charming," he began, then stopped. "Edward, I'm sorry about the way I've been behaving. I never gave a thought for the sacrifice I was asking you and Liz to make. You . . . you don't have to come with me. I release you from your pledge."

Charming reined his horse to a stop. "I care too much for you as Liz's brother and my friend to abandon you on this quest. I only need you to understand what we are riding into." Charming shifted in his saddle, and added, "And it would help me if you would stop referring to me as your squire. I would hate to think that you might be calling me a gnarled hobgoblin behind my back."

"Agreed!" Will said, and extended his hand. They shook, and Will added, "Thank you, Edward. I mean . . . for everything . . . for . . ."

"Please, don't mention it, Your Majesty."

The two men turned and spurred their horses onward again.

After a time, Charming asked, "Now that we know what we are riding toward, can we talk about why we are going north?"

"We are hunting the Great Dragon of the North, Charming! Where else would it go?" Will said, as though this logic was so compelling as to forestall any further debate on the issue.

"Will," Charming said, trying to keep the irritation from his tone. "Just because he's called the Dragon of the North doesn't mean Volthraxus went north. Few people know this, but the Wyrm of the South was originally from the north."

Will shrugged. "This is all we have, Charming. Where else would you have us go?"

"I would have us go back to the castle to await word from your Royal Huntsmen," Charming said sharply. "I would have men-at-arms about us so that we don't have to set up and take down camp every night, and so a group of bandits or a passing troll doesn't end our quest prematurely. I would have a proper valet so I don't have to press my coats on rocks. I would . . ."

"I get the point," Will said with a growl. "But the answer is still no. If I go on a quest as King, then everything I do, every decision I make will involve the whole kingdom. Your father and Tomas and Alain and every courtier will want me to consider their opinions in every step I take. I will not turn this quest into a bloody carnival."

Will raised his arm and pointed dramatically to the horizon off to their right. "We go north!"

"Will, that's south," Charming said dryly, pointing at the afternoon sun, which was behind them.

Will put his arm down, raised his other, and pointed in the opposite direction.

It was at this point that the trail they'd been riding on for the better part of the day simply stopped. They were surrounded by trees and bushes.

Charming grunted in disgust and began to turn his horse around, saying, "The last turning I saw was around noon. I suppose we will have to backtrack.

"No."

"Well, what would you suggest we do?" Charming asked, turning back around.

"We skip the road and go north until we find a new road," Will said, pointing at the dense forest.

"That's a terrible idea," Charming said.

"I know, but you are the one who's been trying to convince me to change my approach," Will said with a flicker of a smile.

Charming wondered if any man in the kingdom had ever been so pigheaded and stubborn. As he contemplated that question, he felt certain that someone had.

The next few hours were spent hacking their way through the dense brush. The day had faded to evening when they finally emerged onto a new road. They were covered with scratches and cuts from pushing through the thick branches of the woods, and Charming knew after only the most cursory of inspections that his clothes were ruined. They looked like vagabonds. Charming resigned himself to the fact that unless they fixed their appearance, not only would they not receive assistance along the way, but it was likely that they would not even be allowed into respectable establishments. They had lost one of the few advantages they had started with: noble names and noble bearings. They were common travelers now.

No, he thought grimly. *We are worse than common travelers. We will be seen as either brigands or beggars. If only I could make him believe that sometimes, just sometimes, clothes do make the man.*

"Charming!" Will shouted from somewhere ahead. "A road, and it goes north! While we still have the sun, onward!"

Charming emerged onto the road to see Will riding south. "Other north, Your Majesty."

Will reined his horse in and, without comment, turned about and headed the opposite direction. Charming followed, muttering darkly about mad kings and the fools that followed them, a topic he found was rich with poetic possibilities. It had been a long time since he had used couplet.

He was trying to decide which was more euphonious, *insane* and *fame* or *inflamed* and *brain* when Will interrupted his train of thought. "What are you mumbling about, Charming?"

"Nothing, Your Majesty. I was just trying to determine how to put our journey into verse."

Will's response was utterly unprintable.

Will's idea of "having the sun" was extremely liberal as they continued to ride long after the sun had set. Suddenly, Charming had the strongest feeling that the road was going to make a bend ahead and go between two large oaks, and it did. A little later, Charming knew that the road would take a sharp dip, and it did that also. Either he had developed the Sight—a distinct possibility as he had always considered himself peculiarly sensitive—or he had recently been along this section of road, which, given the distance they'd traveled, seemed improbable.

Finally, the eerie and continuous sense of déjà vu became overwhelming, and he felt he had to say something. "Will."

"If this is about stopping, poetry, or fashion, I am not in the mood," Will barked back over his shoulder.

Charming glared at Will's back, and said with barely contained disdain, "I thought you should know that I think I have been in this forest before."

Will drew his horse to a stop so that Charming could catch up. "Do you actually know where we are?"

Before he could reply, he heard someone coming fast along the path, then a voice yelled, "Run!"

Charming swiftly drew his blade and rode in front of Will.

Three terrified men came into sight running down the road. They wore ill-fitting dark green and brown clothes that had enormous rips and tears in them. All of them were badly injured and sported blackened eyes and bloody gashes along their faces and bodies.

"You can tell from their clothes that they are desperate men, Your Majesty," Charming said, as the men continued to approach. "Let me handle them."

Will waved his consent. "Just don't let this delay us any longer than necessary, Charming. We will soon lose the light."

"What light?" Charming asked under his breath, looking up at the stars that filled the now-night sky.

Will made a show of ignoring him.

Charming moved slightly forward and into the middle of the road to block the fleeing men's path. As they came nearer he boomed in his most authoritative voice, "Halt!"

Charming raised his hand and positioned his blade so that somehow, the edge caught the light of the moon as it filtered through the trees, causing the steel to gleam. The men froze on the path.

"Oh, Lor' bless us, it's robbers," one of the men said, and held up his arms in surrender.

The others followed his example, and one said, "I told you that going it alone as outlaws was too dangerous. We should have stayed with the Heinous Hooligans."

"Don't you mean the Boisterous Brigands?" the third countered.

"I don't know," shrugged the second. "I could never remember what the Violet Varlet wanted to call us!"

"Don't you mean the Green Phantom?" the first asked.

"No," the third said confidently, then, as though reciting something he had memorized, continued, "If you recall he gave up the title Green Phantom because it didn't have the proper all-it-er-ative im-pri-matur." He pronounced these last two words as though they might be dangerous if said incorrectly.

"The proper what?" asked the other two.

"I don't know, that's what the Scarlet Scoundrel said last time he was on about the subject, 'all-it-er-ative im-pri-matur.'"

"Alliterative imprimatur," Charming interjected to startled glances from the men, who had clearly forgotten he was there. "That would be a first-consonant rhyming scheme that would serve to give the name additional gravitas, like the Daring Duke or the Dread Dragon. I have never been one to subscribe to such cheap poetic flourishes, but there are those that find them useful."

"Oh," said the men.

Will moved his horse forward. "Can we get on with this, Charming? We are wasting time."

Charming cleared his throat and pointed his sword at the men. "Why have you accosted the King? Answer or forfeit your lives to his just doom."

The men dropped their hands and squinted their eyes in the feeble light. One of them, Will wasn't sure which, said, "That's never the King then. Look at his clothes."

Another of the men said, "Yeah, what do you take us for, fools? No respectable king would be caught dead in that."

Charming dropped his sword to his side and sighed piteously. "I warned you this would happen, Your Majesty. And, how can I argue. They are both proper and correct, no king would be caught dead in that outfit."

"Never mind all that," Will said to Charming, then growled. "I am your King, and if you do not move aside, I will order my man to cut you down where you stand!"

The men scattered to the edge of the road, and Will began to spur his horse forward.

"Wait!" Charming said sharply enough that Will hesitated. "What were you men running from? What attacked you? What is ahead on this road?"

"A witch!" said one.

"A demon!" countered the other.

"A werewolf!" replied the third.

"A monster!" all three shouted together, with one of them adding, "Of an undetermined nature."

Charming sighed and turned to Will to tell him that he thought they were lying, but there was a mad eagerness in Will's face.

"Could the monster have been a dragon?" Will asked

"That's it!" they all cried in ready agreement. "It was definitely a dragon!"

Will rose in his stirrups and pulled his sword from his scabbard. "Where is this dragon? Tell me now!"

"Back at the house!" said the first, pointing behind them.

"It's just off the road!" said the second, following the man's gesture with one of his own.

"In a clearing in the woods!" said the third, repeating the first two men's gestures just in case there was any confusion as to direction.

"We were trying to rob . . ." the first started to say, but a sharp elbow in the ribs cut his confession short.

Will didn't notice the slip, but spurred his horse past the men, screaming, "Give me Elle, you monster!"

Charming paused for a moment trying to decide what to do with the men. They were clearly criminals, but it was just as clear that Will could not be trusted not to get himself killed. He shrugged. "You have my leave to continue running for your lives, but if I ever catch you around here again . . ."

"You won't!" the men shouted.

"Good," Charming said sheathing his sword. "Now, if you'll excuse me, I'm afraid I have to save the King."

The men scattered, and Charming urged his own horse after Will. By galloping hard, he managed to reach the clearing in time to see Will, sword drawn, marching resolutely toward a moonlit cottage nestled quaintly in the trees, an orange glow flickering warmly from behind curtained windows. The sight of the clearing and the cottage froze Charming. This was not just any cottage or any clearing, but one utterly familiar to Charming. It was utterly familiar because it was the one he and Liz lived in. He was home.

Several thoughts struck him at once and with enough violence to send his head momentarily spinning. First, that they had just spent a week traveling in a big circle, which meant both that he had a terrible sense of direction and was not clairvoyant. Second, that King William was about to batter down the door of his home to kill a dragon that could not possibly be inside. Third, that if those brigands on the road had been telling the truth, then someone or something dangerous was in his house. And lastly, that if Liz was in there, then she was in there with someone or something dangerous.

Charming sprang from his horse before this last

thought had even had time to fully form. Somewhere between the saddle and the ground, he drew his sword, then sprinted to catch up to Will. He watched as Will reared back his foot to kick open the door.

"Will, stop" he cried.

It was too late. The door broke inward under Will's assault, and the man disappeared into the cottage, a guttural cry of challenge on his lips. A terrible, inhuman noise issue from within, followed by the sound of a mighty struggle as furniture crashed, crockery shattered, metal rang, and bodies fell. Will's scream of rage was transformed into a bellow of pain. Perhaps there was a monster. Charming put on a burst of speed and launched himself through the door.

What he saw by the flickering light of the fire would have been enough to cause even the most inveterate of drunks to swear off booze. The room was in chaos. Furniture and odds and ends were strewn about. In the middle of the destruction lay Will. He was breathing, snoring actually, and seemed uninjured with the exception of some scratches and bruises to his face and forehead. Over him stood a swayback donkey with a long gray beard, a thick-bodied black-and-brown dog with a squashed face, a rather chubby orange cat with white stripes down its sides and white circles around its eyes, and a scrawny, red-feathered rooster with an inordinately long, skinny neck. The rooster was actually standing atop Will's chest.

This scene would have been extraordinary in and of itself, and for the ordinary man might have frozen him into inaction, but Charming was trained for the extraordinary, and so the presence of the animals and Will's state of unconsciousness actually didn't bother him in the least. What did bother him, what froze his blood in his veins, was that Liz was nowhere to be seen.

Charming's paralysis lasted long enough for the animals to turn their gazes on him, and for the donkey to say in a drawling bray, "Not another burglar. Man! This neighborhood is going downhill. Let's get him, guys!"

The animals moved toward him as one. The donkey lowered his head and charged, the dog leapt over a broken cabinet, teeth snapping, the cat launched itself from the back of a chair toward Charming's chest, with its claws outstretched, and the rooster took flight in a flurry of wings and talons.

There are many things you can say about Edward Charming. He is vain, conceited, and often an ass, but it is also true that he is accounted the best swordsman of his generation, and some say of all time. On this day, at this moment, his skill was augmented by a towering rage, and the results were terrifying.

Charming took two long strides across the room, meeting the animals' charge with his own. Then, in one fluid movement, he dodged out of the way of the charging donkey so that it barreled past him to slam into a bookshelf, kicked the dog squarely in the ribs and pinned it to the floor with his foot, pivoted his body so that the flat of his sword knocked the leaping cat back, sending it flying across the room to smash into the far wall, while at the same moment he plucked the rooster out of the air by the neck with his off hand. By this time the donkey had recovered and was turning to charge again, but Charming had reversed the grip on his sword and lunged so that the tip of his sword came to rest against the donkey's throat.

Everything froze, then the donkey, whose rolling eyes were fixed on the blade touching his neck, asked, "Can we help you, man?"

"Yes, you can," Charming said with icy calm. "You can answer a question for me."

"Okay," said the donkey, "but could you ease up on Rooster there, he's turning blue, man."

"I'll consider it," Charming said coldly, "depending on how you answer my question."

"What happens if I don't give you the right answer?" the donkey asked.

Charming said nothing but instead shifted his weight forward so that the sword tip now dug into the skin on the donkey's throat, and the dog under his foot gave a yelp of pain.

"I swear we don't have anything against you or your friend," the donkey pleaded. "We were just afraid he was a robber like the last cats that came in here. Dig?"

Charming did not respond but tightened his grip on the rooster so that the bird squawked in pain.

"Okay, man," the donkey brayed in alarm. "Ask your question. I'll try to answer."

"Normally," said Charming, and his hard eyes bore into the donkey's, "I would care about my friend, and normally I would be asking why you are in my house, but this isn't normally. My question, and answer very, very carefully, donkey, is . . . where is my wife?"

CHAPTER 5

DINNER FOR TWO

When reading fairy tales, it is never a good idea to think too much about the realities of a damsel's distress. Sleeping Beauty sleeps, but it is a mystical sleep, and so she can wake fresh as a daisy kissing her prince after one hundred years without brushing her teeth. Cinderella sweeps, but despite all the time she spends on her hands and knees scrubbing dishes and cleaning out hearths and how callused and bruised those same hands and knees must have been, all she really needs is a new dress and a pair of pretty shoes to make her a princess. And, should we even discuss what state Ms. Riding Hood and her grandmother would have been in after having been extracted from the guts of a wolf via a woodman's axe?

Rapunzel actually had a bit of experience with the

pain and inconvenience of being a fairy-tale damsel. The stories she could tell about how much time and effort it took to maintain her hair were, well, hair-raising. But the trials she'd had detangling her hair and preventing split ends were as nothing compared to the sheer discomfort of being abducted by a dragon and its wolf henchman, or henchwolf, and flown up to a barren cave in the mountains at the end of winter in nothing but a nightgown.

At first, Elle was far too nervous to complain. When your jailers are a distraught dragon and its deranged and constantly hungry pet wolf, being the squeaky wheel might get you eaten. However, in the end, she decided that she would not survive long if she did not complain, and so complain she did.

She complained about the cold, and the dragon used its flaming breath to heat the rocks of the cave until they fairly glowed with heat. She complained about her state of undress and about sleeping on the rock-hard ground, and so the dragon and the wolf raided several noblemen's estates and brought back wardrobes full of dresses (this took some time as neither the wolf nor the dragon had any concept of sizing, cut, or color). They also brought back a beautiful canopied bed that she swore she'd seen in the Duchess of South Southingham's boudoir. She complained about the food, what there was of it was all raw meat, and so the wolf was sent to fetch all the pots and pans and dishes and implements necessary for a proper meal. He was also later sent to fetch some spices when Elle complained of the blandness of the fare, and some lovely spring vegetables to serve as an accompaniment. The wolf balked briefly when, later still, the dragon, on its own initiative, suggested that for Elle to really appreciate the fresh game properly, she would need a nice wine, but when the dragon reminded the wolf, quite forcefully, that its continued existence depended entirely on the dragon's good humor, it grudgingly agreed.

So on this particular night, Elle was seated at a lovely polished dining table (slightly marred from where one of the dragon's claws had grazed it as the creature was liberating it from Lady Greenleaf's castle) beneath the glow of two silver candelabra (both slightly askew from being clutched in the wolf's teeth as he carried them back from one of his most recent raids) eating a delicious meal of roast venison with smoked eggplant on china (mostly unchipped), which from the gold-plated crest looked to have come from Lord Easterly's formerly famous collection. She lifted a crystal goblet and took a sip of a wonderful Chardonnay the dragon had recommended, and sighed contentedly.

Volthraxus lay on the floor on the other side of the table, his massive head resting on his crossed forelimbs and his red-gold eyes half- lidded but fixed intently on her as she ate. "Didn't I tell you that the '56 *Chateau de Chateau* would be a perfect complement?"

She nodded and wiped her mouth delicately on a linen napkin the dragon had insisted she must have, his exact words to the wolf being something like, "We are not barbarians, Beo. You would not set a table for your guest without a clean tablecloth (which the wolf had also been forced to obtain), and you certainly would not ask a lady to wipe her mouth on the back of her sleeve."

From the corner behind her, there was a whine as Beo begged to be allowed to eat. The wolf had been on the run for the past week, gathering all the "necessities," as the dragon called the finery they'd looted, and the way he was drooling and panting and the way his ribs pinched together made Elle wonder if he'd eaten at all in that time. The dragon gave the wolf a sharp look, and for a moment his eyes seemed actually to be aflame. The whining stopped, and the dragon returned to his contemplation of her, his eyes gentling and the gold flecks slowly returning like fine particles rising to the top of a stream of molten lava.

Elle pointedly ignored this exchange and took another bite, and, after another sip of wine, said, "The meal is delicious, Volthraxus. You have quite a lot of skill with roast deer. I usually find the meat either dry or underdone, and often quite gamey, but here there is a wonderful browning on the outside while the inside remains marvelously tender. How do you do it?"

The dragon's eyes rolled with pleasure at the compliment, and he replied in his deep, rumbling voice, "Years of practice, my Lady. I would happily give you the recipe, but unfortunately it requires roasting the meat at a temperature that can only be obtained using the infernal fires of my kind. However, I must say that I think this venison is second-rate."

"You are being too modest," Elle replied instantly.

Beo snorted at this, but Volthraxus either did not hear or chose to ignore the wolf. Instead, he smiled contentedly, and said, "No, I feel my roasted venison is only barely passable. My real specialty is pork. I am renowned throughout the dragon world as the preeminent expert on swine-flesh, and I have been fortunate enough to locate a large herd of pigs that I shall soon be visiting."

Elle had felt a bit of remorse at the wolf's and dragon's raids against her friends and relations in the court, but they had deep cellars to hide in and could afford the loss of a few bits of china and furniture if it meant keeping the two beasts from real mischief. She knew from having talked to Will that a dragon attack on a farm could mean devastation to the farmer. This was partly why she kept asking the dragon for wild game: deer, geese, elk, fish, and so on.

She decided to try once more to forestall the proposed raid. "But surely," she said gesturing over at the enormous spit of roasted deer he had just prepared, "we have more than enough food for several days."

The dragon glanced quickly at the side of meat and gestured at it with a dismissive flick of one of his claws. "I could not possibly ask you to eat leftovers, Lady Rapunzel. My table is not so ungracious."

"But I hate to see such waste," she urged. "It would make me feel a poor guest."

"Don't worry yourself, Lady Rapunzel," he rumbled soothingly, "If it bothers you so much, I will give the scraps to the dog."

There was a deep growl from behind her, and Volthraxus opened one eye wide and fixed it on the wolf. "Do you have something to add to our discussion, Beo?"

The dragon's eye was blazing, but this time Beo did not back down. "Yes, I do. I have a bone to pick with you, or more precisely a *lack* of bones," he said, or Elle thought that was what he said, for whereas the dragon had a very sophisticated accent, far more cultured and refined than most courtiers she'd met, the wolf's human speech was punctuated by odd yips, barks, and growls.

"Do you? Do the 'scraps' from my table then turn out to be insufficient for mighty Beo?" the dragon asked condescendingly.

"Not the scraps themselves, but in *how* you have ordered your table, *yes*," he said, biting each word short in his anger.

The dragon closed his eyes, and said contradictorily, "I am listening. Go on."

The wolf moved to the side of the table between Elle and Volthraxus. "Why does this human get a place at your table as honored guest? She is your prisoner. Remember, it is her betrothed that slew your beloved. Why should she not be made to suffer in his stead while you await his arrival?"

Volthraxus opened his eyes, but just an inch, so that they were transformed into menacing red slits. "You have a nasty habit of reminding me of painful things, Beo. It is a trait that you should work on remedying lest one day I grow weary of your company. As for Lady Rapunzel, I remember well how her King William wronged me, but she is not King William, and I enjoy her conversation. How I choose to pass my time is my business, not yours. If you cannot behave with better grace, then you may absent yourself from our dinners."

"We are meant to be partners . . ." Beo grumbled with something approaching a growl, and began to pace back and forth reminding Volthraxus about their bargain and about all the terrible things Will had done. The dragon in return rumbled deeply about what the wolf was doing, or more precisely *not* doing, to bring him the revenge they had agreed was the sole goal of their partnership.

Throughout this exchange, Elle was careful to betray no emotion, but inwardly she smiled. She had realized quite quickly after her capture that the dragon did not really like the wolf, and the wolf did not really like the dragon. They were each using the other, but there was little trust and certainly no mutual respect. She did not know how yet, but somewhere in their natural enmity she hoped was the possibility of escape.

The wolf had just finished his appeal to the dragon, and Elle decided it was time to test the dragon's hostility to the creature and, by comparison, his incomprehensible sympathy toward her.

She assumed a look of anxious concern, and said, "Volthraxus, if my behavior has been offensive to you, or if being in my presence causes you pain, I understand." Here she paused and added a womanly quaver to her voice. "I also know what it is to lose someone you love, though for me I hope that there is still some small chance that we will be together again. I . . . I will go." She put her napkin to the side of her plate and rose as if to leave.

The dragon's eyes flew open in alarm at this prospect. "My dear Lady Rapunzel, I am sorry that Beo and I have been airing our personal business in front of you. It was ill done." At this, he shot the wolf such a menacing glare that the creature dropped to the ground and backed away from the table and out of the cave on his belly. Volthraxus turned back to her, his eyes molten gold. "I can only say that your company has made the last few days bearable. I am keenly aware that my own actions toward you could not have been more unwelcome and that you would be right to despise me, and yet you have treated me with a kindness that I would not have thought possible from one of your race. I thank you for that and for the wit of your conversation."

He ended his speech with a slight bow of his head, and she sat again with a demure smile.

"Thank you, Volthraxus," she said. "I was worried that you might have been growing tired of me."

The dragon did not answer but smiled indulgently and asked if she needed more of anything. She declined politely and took another bite. Elle knew that the time had come to broach the topic of his plan for revenge against Will, but she did not know what the best approach would be. She picked up her wineglass and took another sip. Somehow, she had to get the dragon to understand that killing Will would not bring him any satisfaction and less still would it bring back Magdela—heaven help the kingdom.

After pondering the topic silently for a few minutes while she ate, Elle decided that she would just have to try and hope for the best. So, laying her fork aside, she said, "Volthraxus, I wish to speak to you about something."

The dragon had appeared to be half-asleep, but Elle knew by now that the creature was always alert even when apparently in deep slumber, so it came as no surprise when he opened his eyes, and said, "Yes, Lady Rapunzel, is there something else you require?"

Rapunzel blushed a little at this because she'd never been more demanding than she had made herself over the last week, and she heard in the dragon's tone an undercurrent of reproach at her selfishness. "No," she said. "I am sorry if my requests have been bothersome."

"They have not," the dragon said dryly. "I know that you have been trying to keep Beo and me from rampaging through the countryside by sending us on these silly quests, but I do not resent that little subterfuge."

"You knew?" Rapunzel exclaimed.

He chuckled deeply. "Of course I knew. Do you think I am some upstart fresh out of the egg that can be turned by a kind word and a pretty face? I also know that you have been ever so subtly trying to turn me against the wolf, and that now believing that I am more sympathetic toward you, you will attempt to convince me to give up my campaign against King William."

"But why? Why go along with it?" she asked, a growing emptiness replacing the calm confidence she'd had mere moments before.

The dragon shifted his body and recrossed his front talons under his head. The entire movement had the effect of a kind of shrug. "Because your plans, up to this point, have served my purposes also. Take the raids on the nobles for one." He began absentmindedly scratching a complex pattern on the cavern floor with one of his talons. "It is easy for a king to ignore a dragon that attacks farms. King Rupert and Prince Charming ignored Magdela for the better part of thirty years. Ahhh . . ." he exhaled and a puff of smoke came out, "but have that same dragon attack nobles, and the entire court will rise up and demand that the King act. I do not want to be here thirty years. I do not want to be here even three months. I want King William to come at me at once, and so I raid the nobles and steal their riches. Also," he added with another smoky chuckle, "it annoys Beo, and I like anything that annoys him."

"I don't understand," she said, feeling suddenly very small, very simple, and very stupid. "Is Beo your partner, or is he not?"

The dragon paused before answering, his head cocked to one side as though listening for something. Finally, he said, "Beo is a useful tool, but he is dangerous. He is the blade that would happily turn in your hand. I have enjoyed having you as a foil to remind him how disposable he is to me and also to remind me how far I can safely push him."

Elle sat in her chair, her body slumped in defeat. She had been naïve and silly to imagine that her simple machinations would be enough to sway the dragon's heart. He had been playing with her the whole time, and now there was nothing she could say that he would not second-guess as self-serving. Tears pooled in her eyes at her failure, and she said miserably, "I realize now what a fool I've been. Please, if I have made you angry, remember that it was me and not Will who tried to deceive you."

Volthraxus stopped his doodling. "Given your situation, you would have been a fool not to try. I know only too well how you must hate me. The fact that you have been able to maintain your composure and this persona for so long is a testament to your character. I spoke truly earlier when I said that I enjoy your company and that your conversation has made the last week bearable. I only wish that we had met under better circumstances and that you were not quite so human."

She nodded thoughtfully at her plate, then came to the sudden conclusion that she would have to use a more direct approach. Elle sat up straight in her chair. "Volthraxus, I intend to convince you to abandon your plan to kill Will. I hope that by getting to know me, you will see that I mean you no harm, and I have every intention of proving to you that killing Will won't bring you the peace you seek."

Volthraxus nodded, then rose so that he loomed above her and the table. "Now we have the truth. Although I think it is a waste of time and will make our conversations increasingly tedious, I will not try to dissuade you from your course, Lady Rapunzel. You will defend your love using the weapons available to you, just as I will avenge my love using those weapons available to me. In the end, we will see whose resolve fails first. Now, if you will excuse me, there is pork on the menu for tomorrow, and for once in weeks, I am hungry."

He began to move very carefully past her toward the mouth of the cave. Just as he was passing out into the forest, the dragon looked back at her. "You will do what you must do Lady Rapunzel, but if I could give you advice from one that has loved and lost to another, do not put your faith in hope. She is the cruelest of mistresses."

With that, he flew off into the night, leaving her alone.

CHAPTER 6

WHEN PIGS FLY

Liz and Tomas made their way down the Southern Road toward Prosper for more than a week. Refugees, confusion, and panic choked the towns and inns, but nowhere could they find any sign or word of Charming and Will. She had been certain that, with the extra horses and more level heads on their shoulders, they would overtake the two men before they made it to Prosper, but the chronic nausea that had gripped her that first day in the cottage continued to plague her, and it was slowing them down. Liz was beginning to wonder if it wouldn't be a better idea for her to send Tomas off on his own, but thus far she had been unwilling to abandon the search.

Something else that was growing as they got farther south was the legend of the Dracomancer. The mysterious man's name, or at least his title, seemed to be on every traveler's lips, and with each passing mile, the stories grew more and more fanciful. The Dracomancer had killed a dozen dragons in his time, perhaps two dozen. No, the Dracomancer kept dragons as pets and could call them from the sky like songbirds. And the craziest, that the Dracomancer had a magical talisman that allowed him to summon dragon spirits. By the time they reached the road that would take them to Two Trees, they found themselves in a long caravan of pilgrims all trying to reach the legendary man.

In this part of Royaume, the Eastern and Southern Mountains crowded close together, and while the Southern Road followed the valley that ran between them, the way to Two Trees climbed steeply up, cutting back and forth across the mountains through a deep forest of fir and pine. Tomas and Liz settled into their saddles for the long, slow ascent.

"Tell me more about the Dracomancer," Liz said, as the path narrowed, and the trees closed in over their heads.

"Well, what do you want to know?" he asked, taking a drink from a leather skin that Liz suspected held something other than water. "He was an apprentice to a court magician, but he only made a name for himself later when he made the prophecy. After that, he got pretty famous, wrote that book *The Dragon's Tale*, and for many years was traveling about as a sort of seer for hire to the gentry."

"I thought Hans Perrault Grimm wrote *The Dragon's Tale*?"

"Pen name," Tomas said with a loud belch. "Did pretty well with it too as I understand."

Liz was silent for a minute or two as she grappled with the fact that her favorite book was written by a man who called himself a "dracomancer." After a while, she asked, "So, what happened to him after the dragon died? How did his reputation survive after his prophecy proved false?"

Tomas snorted. "It didn't. After that dragon died in your field, he was run out of Castle White. Two Trees probably gave him sanctuary because he had been so good for business for so long. In the heyday of the Great Wyrm, Two Trees got most of its money out of the King's coffers."

She frowned at this. "I know Two Trees was attacked now and then, but no more than Prosper, and probably less."

Tomas took another swig from his skin. "All I know is that the town elders were constantly at the castle requesting funds to rebuild the town from the latest dragon attack. The other courtiers used to call them the beggars court. Not nice, but true."

Liz returned to the question that had been bothering her this whole time. "Do you think the Dracomancer will actually know something about how to fight dragons?"

Tomas shrugged. "I don't know. King Rupert brought

him in to tutor your husband, but Charming didn't like him much. I can tell you that back in the day, he had a really good look, and in my experience, that counts for a lot in these sorts of things."

"Look? Look?" she repeated, her voice raising several octaves. "Are you telling me we're going all the way to Two Trees because he *looked* like a sorcerer?"

Tomas glanced about nervously and gestured for her to lower her voice. "I'm not saying that's the only reason, I'm just saying he had the air of magic about him. And, if I were you, I wouldn't voice your doubts too loudly because I think a lot of our fellow travelers *really* believe, if you know what I mean."

He glanced meaningfully at several of the carts and riders surrounding them. Liz saw that a number of the wagons, if not a large majority, had crude drawings of dragons in various poses and of varying levels of ferocity sketched, painted, or carved into their sides.

"Is one of those his symbol?" Liz whispered.

"All of them are, I think," Tomas said with a nod. They rode on in silence. Liz spent her time wondering exactly who or what they would find at the end of this winding road and whether she would regret the decision to seek him out.

It was late afternoon when they caught their first glimpse of Two Trees. The road crested through a high pass in the foothills of the mountains, and the town lay in a wooded vale below, tightly surrounded by the steep, folded land. As they began their dizzying descent into the valley, fields and farmsteads perched on little terraced clearings began to appear among the trees. Many of them had visible scorch marks though the pattern seemed random.

"Probably still rebuilding from the last time the Great Wyrm of the South attacked over a year ago," observed Tomas.

The closer they got to town, the thicker the mingled smell of woody smoke and animal grew. Also growing thicker were the crowds. About a mile from the wall of the village, cart and wagon traffic stopped altogether. There were tents on the sides of the road and in the farmers' fields. The last half mile, Liz and Tomas walked, leading the horses carefully through the throngs of carts and horses, men and children, beggars and thieves.

The going was slow, and not just because of the traffic, but also because, as in Quaint, the people coming to Two Trees seemed to have packed their whole lives with them. On one side of the road, a family was tucking their children into a curtained canopy bed that they had arranged beneath the sheltering arms of a tree. Opposite them, a farmer was herding his livestock, cows and sheep and chickens, into a corral formed of odd bits and pieces of furniture—a set of chairs, a chest of drawers, a wardrobe turned on its side. A whole clan of pig farmers had set up a sty in what might have at one time been a churchyard. The church itself had obviously been destroyed by the previous dragon and never rebuilt though there was a large donation box still present to accept "Alms to ease the burdens of Dragon Attack." The array of people and animals and things was dizzying, and so was the smell. The stench from the hogs in particular, and their snorting screams, set Liz's already frayed nerves on edge and her still delicate stomach turning.

They had to stop several times to let Liz rest and recover, and she could see from Tomas's face that he was worried about her. She did feel a little weaker than normal, but she was determined to keep going as long as she could. What she was worried about was the chaos that was spreading through the kingdom. If Will was not returned to the castle soon, the whole place might erupt, and she was not sure if his rule would survive, or who would come to take his place if he fell.

By the time they passed the wooden gates of Two Trees proper, the sun had set. The light of evening painted everything in a deep red while the darker shadows of night pooled beneath the trees and in the gaps between the buildings. The combination of light and shadow lent a carnival-like atmosphere to the streets, which, even here, were lined with tents and carts and people and homemade banners flying their version of the Dracomancer's symbol. And over everything hung the heavily mingled smells of cooking fires, unwashed people, and animal manure.

Despite the chaos, finding the Dracomancer was easy. The first man they asked pointed them straight to a low-slung tavern near the center of town. Its signboard, which appeared to have at one time sported a crow dancing a jig, had been crudely modified so that the crow now resembled a sort of beaked dragon surrounded by a circle of red flames. A mass of people crowded about the front of the building, but blocking the door were two burly-looking men with battered, rusty pikes.

Liz and Tomas tied up their horses and made their way toward the tavern. As they reached the edge of the crowd, one of the guards announced, "The sun has set! The Dracomancer will not be taking petitions until the morning!"

People began shouting back at the guards, entreating them to let them in. They also began to argue with each other over the relative urgency of their needs. One man pushed another. A punch was thrown that missed, and another was thrown that did not. It looked like a riot was mere moments from breaking out.

Tomas asked Liz frankly, "Do you really want to get in there and talk to him?"

"Yes."

"You're absolutely sure?"

She looked at the crowd, which in the few seconds of their exchange had grown even more restive, then nodded. "Yes, but it's impossible. We could be here days trying to see him." Just then, a woman screamed, and two men began wrestling in the mud of the street. Liz took a moment to frown. "And that's assuming we don't get killed in the process."

Tomas laughed harshly. "Lady Charming, you don't know me very well."

He grabbed her hand and dragged her through the

crowd, using his compact muscular body to bowl people out of the way. As the going got thicker, he bellowed above the general bedlam. "Her Ladyship, Lady Charming, sister of the Lord Protector and Dragonslayer King William, wishes an audience with the Dracomancer!"

He repeated this twice before a silence fell, which was quickly replaced by a hushed murmur that spread out in ripples through the crowd. People near Tomas and Liz began to back away, forming a path up to the steps of the tavern. Liz raised her head and threw back her shoulders in what she thought might be taken for a Royal Air. Shedding Tomas's hand, she strode with dignity through the avenue of people and up to the guards, who both stood unmoving as she approached.

"Guardsmen," she said, and made a sweeping motion with her hands.

The guards held their ground. One even managed an awkward sort of bow, and said, "I am sorry, Your Ladyship, but His Eminence the Dracomancer is not taking any additional visitors this evening."

Tomas bristled at this and stepped forward, clearly intending to open a way through them by force, when a voice, deep and melodious, rang out from within. "Let the Lady pass."

The guards jerked to attention and stood aside, and Liz and Tomas walked through a swinging half door into the smoky gloom of the tavern. Behind them, the murmurs of the crowd instantly grew to a cacophonous roar as the news spread that Lady Charming was consulting with the Dracomancer.

Liz bent low, and whispered to Tomas, "I'm not sure that was the wisest course. We may never make it out of this village if this interview doesn't go well."

Tomas whispered back, "Your point seems a bit academic now."*

Liz blushed at Tomas's response, but as the interior of the tavern was only lit by a couple of utterly inadequate oil lamps and a log fire that was in the process of dying to embers, Tomas never had the pleasure of seeing her reaction.

Despite the door guards' injunction against visitors, there were a fair number of people still milling about, clustered in groups here and there. Liz peered around the hazy room to see if she could spot the Dracomancer, hoping that someone would clearly stand out as having the "look" of a sorcerer about him.

From a smoky recess at the back of the tavern near the fire, a single flame sparked, throwing into momentary relief a man with deep-set eyes, a sharply sloping nose, and a long gray beard. Perhaps it was his voluminous robes or some trick of light and shadow created by the dancing flames of the fire, but he seemed to be too large for the room, like a giant crouched in a cave.

He sat by himself, two men, just silhouettes in the dimness, standing on either side. On a table in front of

* Editor's note: It is generally agreed that the word Tomas used in this exchange was not academic. In fact, friends of the Royal Squire could not be certain that Tomas even knew the word academic. By all accounts, the actual word he used was far more colorful, far more evocative, but, unfortunately, far less printable.

him were the remains of his supper and a half dozen or so mugs, all but one empty. The sorcerer took a few deep puffs on a bone-white pipe shaped like a dragon's head, the glowing tobacco ember in its bowl illuminating his face beneath the deep cowl of his hood in flashes of orange and yellow. With each inhale, a small ring of smoke issued from the side of his mouth and floated up toward the deeper darkness that lay among the rafters. He regarded her silently as he smoked, his dark eyes luminous in the flickering light of the pipe.

Liz moved forward hesitantly, feeling the weight of attention as everyone watched her. She stood in front of him for a moment at a total loss as to how to begin, her hands clasped one in the other to keep from shaking. She had been so sure that when she finally met the Dracomancer, he would turn out to be just an ordinary man, like the street magicians who passed through Prosper now and then, but now, face-to-face with him, Liz found that she was not sure how to behave. She had never dealt with a sorcerer before, much less a sorcerer as grave and dignified as this one. Liz turned to Tomas for support, but somewhere between the door and the table, the squire had slipped away.

Liz cursed quietly to herself, then opened her mouth to speak, but before the words could come, the Dracomancer spoke. "Lady Charming, welcome. Please, sit." He gestured to a low chair across from him.

She shook her head, indicating that she would rather stand, but then decided that was rude and stuttered out, "No . . . no thank you. I don't want to disturb your supper. I . . . I just wanted to see if I . . . I could ask you some questions about the . . . the dr . . . dragon?"

The Dracomancer threw his hands wide, his pipe spilling smoke into an arc in the air above the table. "Come. Talk with me, Lady Charming. Burden me with your troubles. That is why I'm here."

His voice was deep and sonorous, almost mesmerizing, and he spoke as though each of his words was filled with a deep and equal significance.

She stepped a bit closer and coughed from the thick tobacco smoke around the man. "Well, you see, Your . . . I mean . . ." Liz stopped and gathered herself, finally scolding her nerves, if not into submission, at least into a brief retreat. "How do I address a sorcerer?"

The tavern had been mostly silent since she'd entered, but now a murmur of shock and outrage filled the room. He held up a long, pale finger. "I am a Dracomancer, in fact, The Dracomancer, not a mere sorcerer or wizard."

"The Dracomancer?" she asked, having a hard time keeping her tone measured. Up until this moment, she had been maintaining the earnest hope that the title Dracomancer was some kind of ill-advised joke. It seemed too ridiculous.

"Yes, the Dracomancer," he said with a significant flare of his eyes. "Through long study and dark sacrifice, I have harnessed the magical spirits of the dragons to my bidding." To punctuate this statement, he placed his pipe on the table and traced a complicated series of symbols in the smoky air.

Liz didn't really know how to respond to this without giggling, which she knew would not go over well, so instead she asked, "So, should I call you Dracomancer?"

He laughed, a rich and hearty sound, and his laughter was echoed by his watching followers. "You may, if you wish."

"Dracomancer, I need to know how to defeat the dragon."

The room fell absolutely silent. Liz thought that she saw, just for a moment, the Dracomancer's gravitas break, and he appeared to nearly swallow the long stem of his pipe. He recovered himself by taking a few deep puffs and rebuilding the clouds of smoke around his head. When he finally spoke, his voice rang like a tolling bell. "To defeat the dragon, one must put aside all fear. Fear"—he paused dramatically—"is the ambrosia of the beast, consuming the soul even as surely as the dragon's flame consumes the body."

Liz silently digested this obvious bit of advice, hoping that he would say more, but when he did not, she decided she would have to press him. "Yes, Dracomancer, I understand that fear would be . . . problematic, but do you have any *practical* tips, perhaps a weakness that we might be able to exploit?"

This time he was ready and, after a pregnant pause in which many smoke rings were blown, he said significantly, "The ancient sage, Lochnar Zagroot, teaches us that the Wyrm bathes in flame beneath the earth."

"Is that a bad thing for them?" she asked in real confusion. "I mean, the bathing in flame? Do they do it every night? Do you know where the baths are? Are you suggesting that we attack the dragon while it's bathing?"

The Dracomancer's eyes widened at her questions, and when he responded, his voice had lost a bit of its timbre and much of his earlier cadence. "In . . . in the mad poet Mudthug's *Black Tome*, he writes, 'A wet Dragon never flies at night.' "

"What?"

The Dracomancer had recovered his earlier calm and leaned back comfortably in his chair. He took a deep puff on his pipe before responding quite solemnly, "A wet Dragon . . ." he paused significantly, his eyes wide with intensity, "never flies at night."

Liz rubbed her temples, which were beginning to throb violently, and snapped in frustration, "What the bloody hell is that supposed to mean?"

"The wisdom is perhaps too deep for a layman, or even a laywoman."

"No," Liz snapped, and literally snapped as she punctuated her denial with a snap of her fingers. "I don't mean I don't understand it, I mean that's nothing but gibberish!"

A collective gasp erupted, and the Dracomancer rocked back so violently that his chair slipped out from under him, and he clattered to the floor in a flutter of robes and a cloud of blue-gray pipe smoke. The two shadowy figures that had been standing to the sides of the Dracomancer quickly helped him up. The man wobbled a little as he tried to get his feet back under him in a way that made Liz think that he must be wearing very-high-soled boots if not actual stilts. The Dracomancer grasped the table to steady himself, exposing pale, rail-thin arms that suggested much of his looming bulk was made up by the incredibly large cloak he was wearing. He leaned forward so that his face came out of the smoky shadows, his eyes ablaze with indignation.

"How dare you call my words gibberish?" he shrieked in a voice that had grown surprisingly squeaky. "Your ignorance of dragons is astounding! Have you never read the *Ars Dragonica*, or the collected works of Shuuman the Meddler, or Balgethar the Drunkard, or . . . or . . . um . . . well, anyone?"

It might have been a devastating rebuke if the Dracomancer's beard, which was now revealed to be at least partially a fake, had not taken this opportunity to slip down his face, exposing a weak chin and a mouth of yellowed teeth.

Liz was too angry to take any notice of the angry murmurs around her. She felt a tug at her sleeve and saw a very nervous Tomas, who had appeared out of nowhere, desperately gesturing toward the door. She shook him off and instead stepped closer to the Dracomancer, so that only the table separated them and pointed her own finger at him.

"I call it gibberish because it is gibberish. 'A wet Dragon never flies at night'? 'Bathing in flames in the earth'? 'Ambrosia of the beast'? I defy you to tell me what any of it means. Personally, I don't think you know the first thing about dragons. Your prophecy about Lord Charming was proved false, and now you sit here spouting nonsense and drinking free ale. You are a charlatan, plain and simple."

Shouts of indignation mixed with a few rumbles of tentative agreement, mostly about the amount of ale he consumed, spread through the tavern. The Dracomancer, perhaps sensing that the crowd was turning on him, gazed about anxiously and threw his arms out broadly. "Enough!" he roared, and resumed his overly emphasized speech pattern. "Having offended the dragon spirits I serve, you, Lady Charming, have sealed your own doom. The ancient flames that stir within my blood boil at your blasphemy! The spirits, they rage within me! I can no longer control them!"

Suddenly, he convulsed, his eyes closing and his arms opening wide so that his chest was thrown painfully forward. "I warn thee, flee while you can, the Dragon Spirit Comes . . . the Dragon Spirit Comes."

After this pronouncement, Liz saw his eyes flicker briefly back to her. She frowned at him, put her hands on her hips, and began tapping her foot on the ground in irritation.

His eyes closed again, then opening wide, they rolled back so that only the whites could be seen. He began shaking, his mouth working spasmodically back and forth. Then a hideous throaty babble began to spew from his lips, along with a great volume of spittle. *"Dwarlivish canthon fraxus thrilbit quantrotont lishish, Lishish, LISHISH!"*

He was shouting and shaking so violently that many in the crowd began to draw back, likely in fear that such a dramatic display of madness might turn out to be contagious. Liz, however, stood her ground stoically, watching his performance with open disdain. She started to say, "When you are quite done," but at that moment, the Dracomancer's body seemed to collapse in on itself. His arms and head rolled forward violently, and his legs bent under him so that he dropped to the ground, and nothing could be seen behind the table where the Dracomancer had formerly stood except a large bundle of deep purple robes.

Almost on cue, but a bit prematurely, one of the tall, shadowy shapes that stood in the darkness behind the table moaned, "Woe to us. The Dracomancer, who was our only hope, is now gone, consumed by the dread forces he once kept at bay."

A stunned silence greeted this latest development, and someone by the bar shouted, "'E's dead?"

The other shadowy figure said, perhaps in reply, though it seemed too prepared for Liz's ear, "Who can say if he may die, when his spirit can with the dragons fly."

A deep and deeply slurred voice behind an enormous tankard of ale said, "Lor' bless us all, 'e musta' been taken by da' dragon spirits!"

A particularly warty woman stomped toward Liz with an accusing finger, and shrieked, "It's ta witch what done it to 'im. I saw 'er a castin' a curse at 'im wit' her evil eye!"

"That's absurd," Liz said stiffly, a little stunned at the Dracomancer's sudden collapse.

She knew that leaving—and leaving now—was the prudent thing to do, but she could not believe what had happened and continued to stare at the pool of gathered cloak where the Dracomancer had been.

"I don't understand," she replied softly and mostly to herself. "He was a fraud. He had to be a fraud."

She was about to turn away and follow Tomas when the Dracomancer's cloak rippled and pulsated like an animal had been trapped beneath it and was trying to escape.

There was a collective gasp as something crawled from among the folds of the cloth accompanied by a cloud of smoke. The shape, still only a silhouette in the dim light beneath the table, rose, serpent-like, higher and higher, until it emerged into the oily orange light of the lanterns. Its head, for that was all they could see, was slightly larger than a man's hand, virulent red and covered here and there with mottled patches of black and blue. Wide, unblinking eyes stared, doll-like, from beneath glittering metallic brows, and short, bristly green scales ran along the back of its skull, where two twisted brown horns sprouted from the sides of its forehead. An elongated snout jutted out of the middle of the face. Another puff of smoke surrounded it.

"Preserve us," one of the men behind Liz shouted, "it's the Dragon Spirit come to life!"

At least two women fainted dead away, and several men ran screaming for the exit. Even Liz and Tomas took a few tentative steps back. The head took no notice of the commotion it was causing but began to move sinuously back and forth atop a skinny, oddly fuzzy red neck, now and again bathing in puffs of smoke that rose from the floor beneath it. It opened a wide mouth filled with crooked white teeth and a limply forked tongue. It hissed, and a sibilant voice issued from its general vicinity.

"I am the ssspirit of the dragon. From dark forcesss beyond mortal ken have I sssprung, and by dark powersss beyond human endurance or imagination hasss the Dracomancccer sssubdued me to hisss will. Who quessstionsss him, quessstionsss me."

The voice was clearly that of the Dracomancer, only higher in pitch and slurred. Liz ducked her head and, as she expected, saw the dark shadowy form of the Dracomancer crouched beneath the table, pipe in his mouth and arm extended upward above the edge of the table. The illusion having been broken, Liz now recognized that the spirit of the dragon was a puppet. A puppet, it appeared, constructed of a pair of threadbare men's hose, bits and pieces of fabric, some beads and bobbles, and a couple of twigs. It was an effort the dwarves would have mocked mercilessly as amateurish. Liz started to laugh, but stifled it when she saw that, all around her, men and women, were prostrating themselves on the ground.

"Ssso," the dragon puppet said, fixing its staring eyes on Liz, "thisss is the unbeliever." Another puff of smoke rose up, this time accompanied by a cough from beneath the table.

Dozens of people around her all agreed, in various ways and varying degrees of profanity, that Liz was indeed the unbeliever.

"How ssshall we punisssh her?" hissed the Dracomancer somewhat breathily between puffs on his pipe that threw more smoke into the air. Liz snuck a peek and watched as the Dracomancer twisted his arm about so that the puppet's head moved around as though calling for suggestions.

Even more people voiced their opinions, in remarkably colorful terms, as to what should be done with her.

"Excccellent sssugessstionsss all," the snake snickered sibilantly, "but I think the Dracomancccer himsself ssshould pronounccce her doom. Ssshall I raissse him back from the deep placesss where now he liesss in ressst?"

Voices from all around begged the puppet to do this.

"Very well," the puppet said, and started to say something else, but speaking in such a high pitch must have been taxing the Dracomancer's voice because he had to break off his speech and clear his throat before continuing. He took the moment to make the dragon spirit glare menacingly at Liz, but since there was no way for him to control the puppet's eyes, he did this by pointing the puppet's head at Liz and shaking it. It would have been comical had not everyone else in the tavern, including Tomas, been taking it so seriously.

The Dracomancer, his throat somewhat recovered, continued in a slightly lower pitch that was, Liz thought, more sustainable. "But I warn you, the Dracomancccer can travel through worldsss asss the common man might travel the road to Two Treesss. If you anger him again, he may flee thisss world onccce and for all and leave you all to the doom of the Wyrm."

The people begged for his mercy, and the dragon spirit looked about in a pleased, almost smug manner, if you can judge smugness by the way his cloth snout wrinkled.

After a moment of preening, the puppet shouted, "Sssilenccce!"

Not a sound was to be heard, then a guttural scream began issuing from under the table, and the puppet dragon shook and danced at the end of its arm neck. The paroxysms of the puppet were so violent that one of the twig horns came flying off, though Liz doubted anyone but she noticed.

Then the Dracomancer stood up.

It was neatly done. One moment, only the dragon puppet was visible, then, with an upward swirl of his cape, the Dracomancer was standing in all his mysterious glory. The crowd roared in exultation, and the Dracomancer took a bow. He allowed the cheers to wash over him for a few minutes, the same smug, self-satisfied expression on his face as he had mimicked on the face of the puppet earlier. Then he held up one hand for silence.

"Thank you my friends, my followers, my Dracolytes."

Another cheer greeted this.

He again held up one hand to quiet the crowd, and that was when Liz noticed that his other hand remained conspicuously tucked among the folds of his cloak.

"I have returned—"

"Show us your other hand!" Liz shouted.

The Dracomancer blanched and tried to continue. "I have returned from the dark regionsss where—"

"Show us what's under your cloak!" Liz shouted again. Tomas grabbed at her sleeve again, but she shook him off. She felt sick that this fraud might be causing trouble for Will. She felt angry that Charming was out hunting a dragon while this idiot sat in a tavern and claimed to have all the answers. She had to expose him, for Will, for Charming, for the kingdom.

The Dracomancer puffed himself up and glared down at her from beneath his bristly gray brows. "You, Lady Charming, are in no posssition—" He hesitated a moment as he realized he was still speaking in the puppet's voice. He cleared his throat and adopted his deep, significant cadence again, "I mean, you are in no position to question me. You are condemned by the spirit of the dragon itself."

Liz thinned her lips and frowned at him. "You mean the dragon spirit that's hidden in your cloak?"

"That is absurd," the Dracomancer said with a nervous lick of his lips.

She turned her back on the Dracomancer and addressed the crowd. "I'll tell you what's absurd. What's absurd is that an entire tavern of otherwise sensible people have been taken in by a trickster. He is no sorcerer and certainly no prophet, and his 'dragon spirit' is a bloody hand puppet. And you all should know better." She ended by shaking a finger about the room in general approbation.

Although there was mostly angry denial at her speech, there were also a handful of people who looked genuinely ashamed. They cast their heads down and shuffled their feet in embarrassment.

From behind her, the Dracomancer tried to rally his followers. "Do not listen to her," he grunted. "She is . . . she is," he huffed breathily, "trying to deceive you from the . . . from the"—he gasped again—"from the truth of the dragon spirit's words—"

There was something odd about the way the man kept huffing and grunting as he spoke. Liz turned about and saw that both his hands were now hidden in the folds of his cloak as he struggled to pull the hose puppet from his hand. She was about to point this out and also to question how it was he knew what the "dragon spirit" had said if he had been banished to some other realm, when a howl of rushing wind shook the tavern, sending the shutters and the doors clattering on their hinges and tearing great chunks of thatch off the roof.

Just as suddenly, the wind was gone, leaving people flattened on the floor from its passing fury. As Liz,

Tomas, and many others began to pick themselves up, a flash of reddish-orange light lit the night sky through the gaping holes in the ceiling. This was followed by a blast of heat and a sulfurous smell. An echoing, ear-piercing roar rolled down upon them from above, louder than thunder, and Liz's blood froze.

She grasped at Tomas, standing beside her, and said, almost like a prayer, "Bless us all, Tomas, it's the dragon, the Great Dragon of the North."

The Dracomancer, his eyes ablaze with intensity, reached across the table toward her. "Did you say the Great Dragon of the North? Are you absolutely sure?"

Liz backed away from him, nodding. A strange, hungry look came over the Dracomancer's face, and he murmured, "There's a chance. It actually might work."

She was staring at the Dracomancer, trying to figure out why the dragon's name held such significance for him, when Tomas grabbed her and began physically forcing her toward the back door. "We've got to get out of here," Tomas said in a voice that made the hair rise on the back of her neck, not because it was panicked, but because it was eerily calm.

There was another deafening roar and another blast of heat and light from the street in front of the tavern, then more and more people began scrambling wildly away from the dragon and toward the back door. Despite the maelstrom of people and chaos around her, Liz was protected by Tomas's guiding hand and his powerful fists, elbows, and ironclad boots. He did not so much carve as bull his way through the crowd.

As they went out the back, Liz caught a glimpse of the Dracomancer pushing toward the front of the tavern. His robe and hood had been thrown back exposing his skinny pale body, his high, stilted shoes, and, of course, the dragon puppet on his right hand. He should have looked ridiculous, but he did not. There was no panic in his face, no thought of flight, only a look of mad determination. Then he was lost in a sea of bodies.

The town was still under attack when they made it outside. Tomas led Liz up a rise at the back of the building and stopped next to a well. A din of noise—a mixture of screams and shouts—followed them as the pilgrims below transformed into a terrified mob.

"Stay here, Lady Charming. If it comes for you, use the well for protection. I'll try and get the horses."

She grabbed his arm with a strength she didn't know she had. "No. Don't leave me here."

From their position, Liz could see the devastation caused by the dragon. Much of the sprawling village of tents and wagons around Two Trees had been swept aside by the flight of the beast, and here and there, blazes had sprung up in the debris. Most horrifying were the people. Everywhere she looked, there were people. Like ants from a kicked mound, the former townsfolk and pilgrims scattered. Some were running back down the road away from the village with nothing, while others still swarmed around the devastated tent city, trying to salvage what they could.

Above it all flew the dragon, a black stain in the

sky. The creature was attacking an area near the edge of town. Over and over it dove down below the walls and houses, then rose again with one or more writhing things in its talons. It was too horrible. Liz knew that she could not remain in safety while countless men, women, and children were devoured by the beast. She would have to go down there to do what she could, even if it was futile, even if all she accomplished was to care for the wounded or comfort the dying.

"We have to go down and help those poor people, Tomas," she said.

For once, Tomas didn't argue. He touched his cap, and said, "Very well, Your Ladyship."

Liz continued to study the dragon as they made their way back down the hill. He was larger than the Great Wyrm of the South, and he had horns. His scales flashed silver when the torchlight struck them. As he beat his wings, tents fell over and collapsed. She saw a fire erupt, but it was near a mass of panicked people, not even close to the dragon. And the things he was gathering, they didn't have clothes. They weren't people, they were . . .

Pigs.

"It's pigs. The dragon's eating pigs," she said.

"What?" Tomas said.

"It's concentrating its attack on the churchyard where that sty was. I don't think it's going after people."

"What about the tents and the fires?" he asked, pointing to the devastation of the village and rapidly spreading fires.

She watched the dragon swoop down once more. Tents flew in the air as its wings buffeted to slow its descent. When it flew high again, another pig squirmed in its talons.

"The wind from his flight is enough to send the tents flying," she pointed out. "And as for the fires, I suspect most of those are from people knocking over their cooking in their panic." Even as she spoke, a new fire erupted on a distant hill, far away from where the dragon was attacking.

"You may be right, milady. It's a bloody madhouse down there, and if the dragon had started the fires, they'd be more concentrated. See how they're scattered about?"

She did see this. She looked across the valley and saw that hundreds of people were, just like her, watching the drama unfold below almost like the town had become a stage and the hills about the town the seats of some vast amphitheater.

"So, the dragon hasn't attacked anybody," she said now, staring at the beast with a thoughtful expression as the creature continued to dive up and down like the hook at the end of a fisherman's rod.

"Nobody," he agreed, and added after a pause, "Although, that may be about to change if that crazy Dracomancer has anything to do about it."

"What do you mean?" she asked.

"Look," he said pointing. "The damned fool is marching right toward the dragon, waving his stick and that silly puppet." He punctuated his disgust of the man by snorting emphatically. "It's time for us to go. In my opinion, Two Trees is no place to be and will be even less inviting once the dragon leaves, and all those people start trying to sort out whose stuff is what."

Liz nodded absentmindedly, but she was busy studying the Dracomancer. He was standing in the square in front of the ruined church, gesticulating wildly up into the air with his staff. Almost directly above him loomed the dragon, which was still glutting itself on the pigs—swooping and rising, swooping and rising.

"He seems to be trying to fight it," she said

Tomas squinted, then scratched at his head and chuckled. "What a lunatic. He's damned lucky that dragon seems to prefer the taste of pork to man, or the kingdom would have one less sorcerer about now." He turned to Liz, and said, "I'm sorry I brought you here, Your Ladyship. You were right. The man's a fraud, and worse still, a harebrained, one-sock-short-of-a-pair, candle's-burning-but-there's-nobody-home madman. All we can hope is that this little display will make all these people sit up and take notice, and we'll have no more of these fools following him about and causing mischief."

Liz watched as the little man continued his dance with the dragon. In its frenzied feasting, she doubted it even saw the little man amid the general chaos below. He was such a small, insignificant figure compared to the massive winged creature, but where the contrast in their size and the utter futility of the

Dracomancer's efforts might have made the man appear comical, they did not. If anything, it made him seem larger than life.

Again and again, the dragon seemed to swoop toward him although Liz could see that the real target was the pigsty, and again and again, the Dracomancer gestured wildly with his staff at the swooping dragon. After a few more minutes of this apparent struggle, the monster rose one last time into the air, two squealing pigs clutched in his talons, and, without a backward glance at the town or the sorcerer, flew off to the north.

As the dragon disappeared into the mists high above, there was a roar from the surrounding hillside. Liz watched as all of the people, those who had believed and those who had not, came streaming down into the town toward the square in front of the church where the solitary figure of the Dracomancer lay slumped to the ground, exhausted from his battle.

From behind her, Tomas called out, "We should really go, Your Ladyship."

She nodded. "Yes, Tomas," she said. "It's past time for us to be gone."

"Perhaps it is," came a harsh voice, and a group of six black-robed followers of the Dracomancer surrounded them. "But you aren't going anywhere, Lady Elizabeth. We are holding you and your man for heresy and treason against the Dracomancer."

Tomas moved between Liz and the lead figure. "They aren't nothing but farmers, Lady Elizabeth,"

Tomas said over his shoulder in a voice loud enough for the men to hear. "Let me deal with them." His hand went to the hilt of his sword.

They did look like farmers, and each carried a tool instead of a real weapon. One had a club made of a piece of a fence post, one had a hatchet, another had a scythe, but Liz' gaze rested on a young man with a pitchfork in his hands. His eyes were wide with fear, but there was a grim determination on his face. He reminded her of Will.

Perhaps Tomas could cut his way through them. They were untrained and might flee once one or two had been struck down, but they were not soldiers, they were simple people driven by fear, and she would not bring about their deaths if she could prevent it.

"No, Tomas," she said calmly. "We will go with them."

"What?" he said incredulously, and, turning, lowered his voice to a whisper. "Trust me, Your Ladyship, I wasn't fooling when I said this is not a place you will want to be now that the dragon's gone."

"That is a risk we are going to have to take, Tomas."

They were led in front of the tavern, where they saw a mob of cheering people carrying the Dracomancer on their shoulders toward them. A chill went up her spine as she looked out over that multitude of faces, all lifted up in a kind of frenzied rapture. She didn't give voice to the fear, but it struck her that, though she was worried for Elle, perhaps this man and the mob of fanatics he had drawn to him was more of a threat than any dragon.

Liz suddenly felt a wave of nausea. She leaned over to retch and found herself falling. Tomas was beside her, and she heard him say, "The Lady is unwell," and she fainted.

CHAPTER 7

MY, WHAT BIG TEETH YOU HAVE

In fairy tales, danger is almost always foretold, and when misfortune strikes, it comes from the direction you expect. If you're a princess and get engaged to a frog, then you can't be surprised when he hops up to your door one day looking to get married. If you're a pair of starving children wandering through the woods and come upon a delicious house made of all sorts of yummy things, should you really be shocked when you discover that the mad crone who lives inside it likes to eat children? And when you're a little girl with golden locks wandering through the woods and come upon a cute little cabin with three bowls of porridge and three wooden chairs and three comfy beds, and you decide to take advantage of this uninvited hospitality, you should hardly be taken aback when the owners return and are a trifle miffed.

However, Elle was completely unaware that the cave that served as her prison previously had been the home of a family of bears. If she had known, she would have slept far less soundly, despite the presence of a lovely, four-poster bed. She would have been even more nervous had she known that the pile of furs and odds and ends of splintered wood that the dragon used as his bed represented the entirety of the previous inhabitants' earthly possessions. And she would have been positively terrified to know that the bears were only one ridgeline away, spending their considerable free time pondering their revenge and whether they would ever be able to get the dragon smell out of their cave.

Beo the wolf, on the other hand, was keenly aware of all these facts. Being a practical wolf, he was growing tired of the endless tasks he was being required to perform to please Elle. He was losing any benefit that he had gained from the dragon. In fact, he was working far harder than hunting had required, and his ribs were beginning to show again. His growing emaciation led him to one conclusion: Elle must die. When she did, the dragon would give up his quest and let Beo free from his contract. The tricky part was that Beo couldn't be implicated in Elle's death, or he would surely be roasted, eaten, or both.

He had initially tried to be subtle. He reasoned that if she committed suicide to save her love (which seemed the sort of ridiculous thing humans did), the dragon couldn't possibly blame him. First, he left a rope next to her bed, then some deadly hemlock tea, and, finally, a sharp knife, hoping that she would take the hint. However, the woman clung to hope, believing that she would be rescued or that her Will (Beo was so tired of hearing her whisper that name) would find a way to save her. It was very disappointing.

Something more "proactive" would clearly have to be done. He had been pondering for a couple of days now on how he could effect her death without actually risking his own hide. That was when he struck on the idea of using the bears.

After Volthraxus had flown off on his latest hunt, and Elle had fallen asleep in her comfy bed, Beo slunk out of the cave. Making use of his superb nose and their awful smell, he easily tracked down the three mightily grumpy bears, two males and a female, huddled together in a shallow, uncomfortable depression on the side of a hill.

Beo studied them from behind a large fir tree as he considered how he was going to convince them to kill Elle. They shouldn't have any trouble with the physical part of the job he thought. Each of them looked like a furry boulder with claws and teeth, one large, one exceedingly large, and one absurdly large. Any one of them could easily make a meal of the woman, or more accurately a light repast, but Beo had to be sure that they would not add a side of wolf to the feast. Wolves and bears did not always get along as they often competed for the same prey, notably children—hopefully juicy girls—who had lost themselves in the woods.

After watching for a time, during which the three bears did little more than snore heavily, shuffle about uncomfortably, and scratch themselves with their knifelike claws, Beo came to a few conclusions. First, the bears were really really big. Second, they would be unhappy at being woken up. He recalled that they had been a bit groggy when the dragon evicted them. Beo believed that the dragon had turned them out of their cave before the bears had, strictly speaking, finished hibernating. The last thing he realized was that while he knew these bears were more intelligent than your average bears—and certainly more verbal—they were still bears and not known for their wits. If he were not properly direct in explaining the plan, the entire scheme would likely fly over their heads.

Right, so I'll be direct, he thought. He stepped out from behind his tree and cleared his throat rather loudly.

"Hmmm."

The smallest of the large bears rolled over and snorted. Otherwise, there was no reaction.

"Hmmm." He cleared his throat again a bit louder and added even louder still, "My dear bears!"

This time, the absurdly large one (as opposed to the large and exceedingly large ones) sat up with a jolt and opened his eyes, but only for a second. Then, his body fell forward, and, chin on ground, he began to snore again.

Beo took a few more cautious steps forward until he was sitting directly in front of the absurdly large bear's nose but out of claw reach. Putting a paw to his muzzle, he veritably shouted, "My dear bears, I have a proposition!"

Three roars echoed through the night. He had awoken the bears. All three jumped to their feet, teeth bared and claws extended, growling growls with varying depths of ferocity. They were all staring hard at him.

The largest of them said very deeply, "Wass all this then?"

The second largest said only slightly less deeply, "Yea' wass the idea?"

The third said a little less deeply still, "Waking us up like that?"

Without waiting for an answer they then asked in varying degrees of pitch and wording, "Who are you anyway?"

The wolf had anticipated this question and so had a ready answer, but he shifted slightly back so that he could immediately spring away. "I am the dragon's wolf?" he said as though it were a question.

His anticipation of violence was prescient as the biggest bear took an absurdly large-sized swipe at him, the slightly less big bear took an exceedingly large-sized bite at him, and the still even less large bear attempted to put him into a simply large-sized, but still undeniably fatal, bear hug. Beo leapt backwards and danced away from his attackers.

"Let's not be too hasty. You haven't heard my proposition yet."

"Why should we listen to you? You and dat beasty frew us right outta our hawse!" roared the absurdly large bear in an absurdly large voice.

"Yea, and now we've gotta live here in a hole!" roared the exceedingly large bear in an exceedingly large voice.

"And the least ya could do ta make it up is ta let us eat ya!" roared the simply large bear in a still-quite-deafening voice.

"Well, if I did that, then I couldn't tell you about the proposition," the wolf replied. He wondered if he hadn't been terribly naïve to think that he could reason with bears.

"We don't give a fig about no propy—propysotioun," the largest bear said, trying to circle around behind the wolf in a large-sized circle.

"'E's right. Why should we care about your propulozytion?" asked the larger bear trying to circle around behind the wolf in a middle-sized circle.

"This propo—what's it, can you eat it?" asked the large bear as he tried to circle around behind the wolf in a little-sized circle but tripped over his own feet and sprawled onto his backside instead.

The other large bears were interested enough in the answer to the littlest of the large bear's question that they hesitated in their attacks. Beo saw an opening, and he raced past them and jumped up onto a boulder. "Yes, of course you can eat it, my friends."

"Right, less hear da propy—propy—the deal," said the absurdly large bear, sitting down on his absurdly large backside.

"Yeah, we're listenin'," said the exceedingly large bear, sitting down on her exceedingly large backside.

"But, if we don' like wha' we 'ear, we're gonna eat you instead," said the simply large bear, finally getting back up off of his simply large backside.

"Sounds more than reasonable," the wolf drawled as he sat down on the boulder and spread his front paws wide in a gesture of acceptance. "Let me start by saying that I never wanted to drive you out of your comfy cave in the first place. The dragon was quite unreasonable on the point, and as you have no doubt observed, the dragon can be quite violently persuasive when he wants to be."

"Yeah," all three bears replied at once, and each pawed at an appropriately sized patch of singed fur somewhere on their bodies.

"Well, I'm going to tell you *why* the dragon is here and what you can do to make him go away—permanently."

"We're listenin', Yeah, we're listenin" the absurdly large bear said, running his absurdly large tongue over his absurdly large snout.

"All ears," the exceedingly large bear said as she scratched at an itch on her back with a claw that would only be considered middling by comparison to a battle-axe.

"And teeth," the simply large bear said, eyeing him

largely like he was trying to decide which bit of the wolf he would like to eat first.

"There can be no doubt of that," the wolf said, backing further away from the littlest of the large bears, who, he had decided, was either the most pathological or the hungriest of the bears. *Although,* he thought, *with bears the two may be the same.*

Despite his continued misgivings about whether he could trust the bears, the wolf was feeling more confident than ever. He had managed to avoid being killed outright, and he had convinced them to listen. All he had to do now was sell them on the plan, and selling things was what the wolf did best. He drew himself up on his hind legs and began to spin his yarn.

"There can be no doubt that you have been wronged," the wolf said to general grumbles and growls of profane agreement, the level of profanity seeming to correspond inversely to the size of the bear. "What you all do not know is that the cause is not the dragon himself but the dragon's guest."

"'E's brought a pest into our cave?" asked the absurdly large bear with a large amount of shock.

"It's a bloody outrage!" said the exceedingly large bear with a moderate amount of shock.

"Bedbugs, I knew it," grumbled the simply large bear with no shock at all. "Dragons are filthy beasts."

The wolf slapped a paw to his forehead in frustration. "Not pest, you damned—I mean," he amended hastily, "dear bears. He has a *guest*, with a 'G.'"

The bears all looked at him with varying amounts

of confusion, from puzzled to baffled to utterly clueless.

Be patient and be direct! Beo counseled himself silently. He took a deep breath and said, "I mean, there is someone else in your cave with him, and she is the reason he is living there."

"Right," said the absurdly large bear with little comprehension.

"Someone else," said the exceedingly large bear with only moderately more comprehension.

"Bloody hell," the simply large bear said with so much comprehension that he invented his own facts. "Wif two dragons in dere, we'll never get our cave back."

"Ahhh," purred the wolf, "but there is the delicious irony. His guest isn't a dragon at all, but is a helpless, and, might I add, delectable, young woman." He emphasized the delectability of Elle by running his long tongue suggestively back and forth over his whiskers.

"What, a girl?" the absurdly large bear asked with a large rumble of his stomach.

"A lass, you say?" the exceedingly large bear asked with a medium smack of her lips.

"Yummy, a delectablized girl and a delishikous imony!" The simply large bear shouted with a little twinkle in his eye that was distinctly disturbing.

"Ummm, more or less," the wolf said. "So, now you see my proposition. You go and eat the girl, then the dragon will have no reason to stay in your cave. Simple."

"Yeah, simple!" said the absurdly large bear with a great deal of enthusiasm.

"But, what do we do about the delicioumus irony?" asked the exceedingly large bear, still moderately confused.

"Forget the imony, what do we do about the dragon?" asked the simply large bear with more than a little skepticism.

Beo assumed an innocent pose, which is inherently difficult for a wolf, and replied, "Oh, didn't I mention, the dragon is gone. There is no one currently guarding the lady in question. Just a short stroll over the ridge, and she is yours."

The largest one looked at the wolf for a long second, and asked, "But wha' if da dragon comes back while we're at it?"

Beo was not concerned in the slightest that Volthraxus might return. It would take the bears no time at all to deal with the girl. Still, he made a point of looking up at the moon as though considering. "He will be gone for hours still, more than enough time to dine as long as you don't linger."

The middle large one looked at the wolf for a medium second, and asked, "Wha' if da dragon don't leave after we et' her?"

Beo was surprised at such a perceptive question. He understood why the bears cared, but the answer didn't really matter to him. He would be rid of Elle. "That I can all but guarantee," he lied. "The dragon will be gone before morning, and if he is not you are no worse off and considerably better fed."

The little large one looked at the wolf for less than a second, and asked, "Wha' stops you from tellin' the dragon it was us an' settin' him ta eatin' us?"

This, in the wolf's opinion, should have been the bears' only question. Indeed, fear of the dragon's wrath was the reason Beo wouldn't devour the woman himself. He intended to play dead as long as necessary and hope that the bears would give Volthraxus enough victims if he wanted to seek retribution for the loss of his pretty little plaything. "I am supposed to be guarding the girl. If he will be angry with anyone, it will be with me. Do you think I am going to wait around and risk his wrath?"

The bears pondered this point ponderously as bears will do. Beo, however, was beginning to feel anxious. He would never have admitted it to the bears, but he had no idea how long Volthraxus would be gone, and if the bears were going to make an attack, he didn't want to be anywhere nearby. He decided to bring the debate to a close.

"My dear bears, while we argue and debate, the moon passes overhead." He swept a paw eloquently up to point at the shining orb. "The dragon will return. Will you take this opportunity to fatten your bellies and reclaim your home?" He pointed a paw dramatically back in the direction of the cave. "Or will you remain here in this miserable condition?"

Watching the reaction of the bears, it was not clear to Beo whether the idea of getting their cave back, or being happily stuffed, or not wanting to return to the cold little hole they'd been sleeping in made the decision for them, but whatever it was, the three seemed to come to a mutual, unspoken agreement. The absurdly large bear ambled off toward the cave with his large strides, the exceedingly large bear ambled off in the direction of the cave with her medium strides, and the simply large bear ambled off in the direction of the cave with his little strides.

As they crested the ridge, the little large bear called out, "I call dibs on da delicimous imony."

Beo shook his head muttering, "Irony . . . irony."

He loped off southward, where rumor had it that a lot of people were on the move, running from the dragon. Beo knew that where people were on the road, there would be children, wandering and willful children, that an enterprising wolf might be able to make a meal of. He licked his lips, only regretting that he wouldn't get to hear Elle scream.

As he ran south, the bears returned to their cave. They found their home much changed. Gone were their stores of honey and berries and lovely, crunchy fish bones, and instead there stood a long, polished, wood dining table set with fine china, sparkling crystal, and gleaming silver. The largest bear sniffed at the remains of Elle's meal and, with a swipe of his paw, scooped an entire flower-patterned plate into his mouth and crunched it between his teeth.

Between bites of splintered china, he said in a deep, gruff voice, "Someone's been eatin' in my cave, and it's scrumptimous though a bit sharp."

The middle-large bear was poking around at the pile of furs that had previously been their beds and the dragon had confiscated as his own. She scrunched up her middle-sized nose in distaste. "Someone's been sittin' on my seat, and now it reeks of dragon."

The littlest large bear had gone straight to the large four-poster bed where Elle lay in a slumber of exhaustion. He peered under the covers and grinned a greedy little grin. "Someone's brought us a proper bed, an she's been good 'nough to stick about as a snack."

The other bears shuffled over at this, the largest still slowly grinding at a crystal goblet and the middle one still rubbing at her nose to get the smell out. Elle awoke with the three bears staring down at her with greed and hunger in their large-, middle- and small-sized eyes. Naturally, she screamed.

"It's jus' like da wolf promised," said the absurdly large bear with a smile that showed off his absurdly large teeth.

"Right down ta da delectablized squeal o' fear," said the exceedingly large bear with a grin that displayed her enormously large teeth.

"But, I don't see no delicimous imony," the simply large bear said, pawing through the covers and peering under the bed with a frown that mostly hid his large-by-any-other-measure teeth.

Elle pulled the covers up to her chin and, hoping that bears were like people at least insofar as not generally being impolite enough to eat things that were talking to them, she said the first thing that came to her mind. "My! What a great number of teeth you all have. How do you keep them so white?"

"Wha'?" asked the largest bear with a large-sized crinkle of confusion stretched across his brow.

"Our teef?" asked the slightly less large bear with a confused tilt of her slightly less enormously sized head.

"Oh, we eats lots of fishes and crunch da bones. Best way to keep your teef clean," said the still slightly less large bear, and he took the opportunity to open his little, only by comparison, mouth wide so she could admire all of his teeth—front and back.

Elle swallowed hard as she stared down the throat of the massive creature. "F . . . f . . . fish you say?"

"No," the absurdly large bear said in a largely pedantic tone, "he said fishes."

"Yea, you know fishes," the exceedingly large bear said with a wiggle of her huge paw in a moderately fishlike manner.

"Da fings what have scales," the simply large bear said with little regard for syntax or grammar.

"Oh, fish," Elle said with a nod.

"Right, an' now we're gonna use dem to eat you up," the largest bear said, and he put out his great large-sized claws to grasp Elle's arms.

"Yea'," agreed the middle-large bear, and put out her middle-large-sized claws to grasp Elle's legs.

"An we've gotta get goin' afore the dragon comes back," said the little-large bear, grabbing one of her feet with his little-large-sized, but still quite lethal claws.

"My what lovely large claws you all have, how do you keep them so sharp?" Elle gasped, backing as far up against the carven headboard of the bed as she could.

"Wha' now?" asked the absurdly large bear, staring perplexedly at his large-sized claws. Elle was beginning to believe that the largest of the bears was pretty much in a permanent state of confusion.

"Interestin' you should ask," said the exceedingly large bear, looking proudly down at her own exceedingly large-sized claws. "I use river rocks meself. Best fing in da world to sharpen up your claws and make 'em shine."

"Nope," said the simply large bear. "If you wants 'em really sharp, you gotta use flint. It gives 'em da best edge." He demonstrated by slicing away half the bedspread with a single motion.

The question of which rocks you should use to properly sharpen claws engaged the bears for quite some time, during which they each took turns demonstrating the sharpness of their claws by hacking away bits of the four-poster bed, the dining-room table, the chairs, the china, the linen tablecloth, and so on.

Finally, the largest bear cut a stalagmite in half with a massive sweep of one arm, and roared largely and loudly, "ENUFF! WE ARE WASTIN' TIME!"

"Das right," said the middle-large bear, smacking her middle-large-sized chops. "We come ta eat ya, and we gotta get on wi' it."

"Yup, we gotta eat and run," said the little-large bear and licked his little-large-sized tongue in anticipation of the feast to come.

Elle tried to come up with something else to say, but suddenly their claws were on her, and the heat of their breath was in her face. As she closed her eyes, there came two high-pitched squeals followed by dull, fleshy thunks. Elle opened her eyes and saw the bodies of two bloody and broken pigs lying in the mouth of the cave. A vast shadow filled the opening, and a deep resonant voice said, "Leave her alone."

The bears froze where they were, their eyes wide with fear.

"My, what big eyes you have," Elle said wryly. "I think you might want to change your plan of eat and run to run before you're eaten."

The three bears looked at her with puzzled expressions, trying to figure out her meaning.

The dragon roared behind them, "What the lady meant to say is, 'GET OUT'!"

All three turned and fled past the dragon to the woods beyond. There was a bright flash of light and heat and howls of pain from the bears as the dragon exacted his measure of punishment.

Volthraxus turned back to her. "Are you unharmed, Lady Rapunzel?"

"Y . . . yes," she said, letting out a deep breath she

hadn't known she was holding. "I am happier to see you than I have ever been in my life."

The dragon smiled ironically. "That is nice to hear, Lady Rapunzel, but I don't know that it counts for much as I don't think you have ever been happy to see me."

"You have a point," she said, trying to smile, but the realization of what had almost happened struck her, and she began to shake with fear.

In an instant, Volthraxus was beside her, holding a crystal snifter of brandy ever so delicately in one enormous, taloned claw. "Drink this, Lady Rapunzel, and put your hands on my side. The warmth will help."

She took the drink and leaned herself against the dragon's body, and in a few minutes, she was able to stop trembling.

"I . . . I'm sorry, it was just . . ." She did not complete the thought.

"You have nothing to be sorry for, Lady Rapunzel," the dragon said gently. "It is I who should apologize. Beo was to stand guard over you while I was gone, else I would never have left you. Speaking of which, where is my erstwhile partner? He and I shall have words."

Elle was about to say that she did not know when something the bears had said struck her. "I . . . I think he led them here." She shivered at the thought. "One of the bears said that 'it was just like the wolf promised.'"

She felt a deep rumble of anger pass through the dragon's body.

"I see." Wisps of black smoke came from his mouth. "I have been betrayed."

He was quiet for a time, and Elle looked up at his eyes and saw that they were glowing a deep red, like a blacksmith's forge. "What are you thinking, Volthraxus?"

"I am thinking that I do not like this cave any longer. I am thinking that it is not secure enough. I dare not leave you alone again, and yet I will need to hunt and gather other necessities." He glared at the shredded bed and the mangled table.

"I don't need those things, Volthraxus," Elle said, feeling oddly guilty. "I can bear far more hardship than I have let you know."

His eyes lost their red anger and grew molten and gentle. "I know that, little princess, but I rather enjoy spoiling you." He grew silent after saying this, as if he were considering his statement. His head tilted in thought, and his smile twisted into something less pleasant, more self-mocking. He rose suddenly and strode toward the cave entrance.

"Volthraxus—" she began to say, but he cut her off.

"There is a second reason, of course. While this cave is no longer safe, it is paradoxically also too remote. It suited Beo's purpose well, which I now see was to delay my meeting with your King as long as possible. Now, I wish to force the issue. I must go somewhere that word of my presence will be sure to find him, somewhere that will be marked by all, somewhere . . ." His voice dropped low, almost to a whisper, and Elle thought she heard him say, "Somewhere of legend."

CHAPTER 8

CHAOS IN FOUR-PART HARMONY

In fairy tales, events unfold in ways that always seem to draw the story to a neat and satisfying conclusion. Some people see in this neat arrangement nothing more than random chance, while others find in it evidence of fate at work. Is it her destiny or whim that leads Beauty to ask her father to bring her a rose from his travels when it turns out that plucking a rose from his arbor just happens to be the one transgression of his hospitality that the Beast cannot abide? Is it simply bad luck or her doom that Sleeping Beauty finds the one surviving spinning wheel in her father's kingdom on the day of her cursed sixteenth birthday? And what of the poor wolf of the woods? Is it chance or some unseen hand that guides that woodchopper to grandma's house at the very moment the wolf has just finished the best meal of his life?

Will would often consider whether chance or fate guided him in the days that followed his battle with the animals. Was it written that he would wake from his donkey-kick-induced slumber just in time to hear someone or something with a thick accent and a voice like gravel say, "I'm telling you Charming, brother, the King has lost it."

Was it just bad luck that Charming replied, "I swear to you, he's not normally like this. He's really a levelheaded fellow, but he's not been himself since Lady Rapunzel was abducted."

Will opened his eyes. Morning light streamed through a paned window on his left to illuminate the spare bedroom of Liz and Charming's cottage. Not liking the reality that greeted him, he closed his eyes again, hoping against all reason that he was dreaming and would wake up. He reopened his eyes. Nothing had changed. It was true. He was back in Liz and Charming's home.

His first thought was that Charming had betrayed his oath and abandoned their quest, but this seemed to go against everything he knew about the man. Still, Will could think of no other explanation for being where he was. He almost jumped out of bed to confront Charming right then and there, but lately he had been wrong about so many things. Will decided before accusing Charming, he would see if he could piece together the events that had led them back. That this would require some eavesdropping did not bother him in the least. Everything he did was for Elle. Slowly, he pulled back the covers, and, making every effort to remain stealthy, he crept to the door in his stocking feet and peered into the room beyond.

Charming sat in an armchair by the fire. Arrayed in a half circle about the chair were the four animals that had attacked him or that he had attacked. The whole thing was a little unclear in Will's memory. What was clear was how ferocious they had seemed at the time, and yet now they appeared embarrassingly docile and ordinary. There was a rather chubby orange-and-white-striped cat curled in Charming's lap, a stout, black-and-brown bulldog sitting on a footstool to his right, a very scraggly red rooster perched on the mantelpiece among the dwarf miniatures to his left, and directly across from him, splayed across the couch, was the graying donkey that had landed the knockout blow to Will's chest.

The five were passing around a stubby pipe from which an aromatic smoke was issuing. Charming took a deep draw and handed it to the cat, which cradled it in both paws and also took a puff, before giving it to the dog. They must have been at this for some time because the air around them was obscured in a thick haze.

Exhaling smoke, Charming said in a very mellow voice, "I'm not saying he doesn't have his reasons, but somehow I've got to get the old Will back. Liz's note"—he waved about a piece of paper he'd been holding against his breast—"changes everything. She says she's going south toward Dragon Tower. That makes a lot more sense than the King's plan. I swear, if he says, 'We're going north' one more time . . ."

Will narrowed his eyes in suspicion. It was nearly a confession.

"You shouldn't have to put up with it, Edward, darling," the cat purred, stroking itself against his chest.

"Yeah, you should go solo, man," brayed the donkey.

"You're an artist," barked the dog. "The way you handled us last night was like . . . it was like . . ."

"Like poetry, man," the donkey suggested.

"Yeah, like manly poetry," the cat echoed, stroking her head against Charming's chest.

"Painful Poetry!" the rooster crowed hoarsely rubbing at his long neck.

"Really," the dog said in that same rough, gravelly voice Will had heard before. "My ribs still hurt, brother. Talk about out of control. You were like out of this world."

"Hey, there's a song in there," said the donkey. "On three. One . . . two . . . three . . ."

Will held his hands to his ears, expecting the worst, but the rooster crowed and the dog howled, the cat yowled and the donkey brayed, "Painful poooetry, Out of controool, Painful poooetry, Out of this Wooorld," in perfect four-part harmony.

Will watched Charming's face light up as they sang to him. "That was beautiful," he said with a tear in his eye. "I always did think of my sword skills as worthy of verse, but I could never find the right words. I had thought that maybe there were none. I wonder what you could do with some of my couplets." In the shadow of the door, Will rolled his eyes. It was like throwing a lit oil lamp on a dry hay bale.

"So, you are musicians?" Charming asked, as the pipe moved from the dog to the donkey.

"Yeah, man," said the donkey, raising his ears as he inhaled deeply. "We're the Bremen-four! We used to open for The Seven Players, but they said our sound didn't fit in with their new quasi-existentialist exploration of the intersection between fairies and oversized pumpkins."

"They sold out," said the dog gruffly. "I remember when they wrote real plays about real subjects, now it's all princesses and princes and paupers and glass slippers."

"Sold Out!" cried the rooster from the mantel.

Will watched Charming's face flush as he realized, at about the same time as Will did, that they were talking about Liz's story. He could see Charming trying to think of a way to change the subject. "But, you all must still be on good terms with them," he prompted. "You are here."

"Oh, sure we're still good friends, brother," the dog barked briskly. "They're just sellouts. They would tell you that themselves if they were here, or at least Grady would."*

"Yeah, don't get us wrong, man," the donkey said, taking another deep puff on the pipe. "We would love to sell out. I, for one don't want to go back to carrying sacks of wheat and flour for the man, man."

"Absolutely," the dog said, scratching himself behind the ear with his back paw. "Best thing that could happen to us, brother. I just don't have the build to herd sheep."

"And I hate the taste of mice." The cat shuddered.

"Sell Out!" the rooster crowed, flapping his wings.

"Be honest with me, darling, Edward," the cat said, licking one of her paws and smoothing back an ear. "Have you heard of us?"

"I'm afraid not," Charming said, then Will watched him realize the implicit insult, and quickly add, "But, I've been out in this cottage for the past year or so, and this area isn't a hotbed for music."

"It's not your fault, man," the donkey said with a resigned sort of sigh that blew out his white beard like

* Editor's Note: Solicitors representing The Seven Players™ have asked us to insert the following advisory notice or risk being subject to swift and crippling legal action.
ADVISORY NOTICE: The views expressed by the Bremen-four concerning The Seven Players™ and whether Ash and Cinders™ is in fact an existentialist exploration of anything are only the uneducated opinions of the Bremen-four, and do not represent the opinions or views of any member of The Seven Players™, particularly Grady Dwarf™, who would not bother with the existentialist school if you held a knife to his throat, and he'll teach anyone who claims otherwise a lesson they won't soon forget.

a sail. "We don't get good press, man, so we don't get good gigs, man. The critics just don't know how to handle a band like the Bremen-four, man."

"Yeah," the dog gruffed. "Where do we fit into the mainstream music scene, brother? What's our genre?"

"Folk!" cried the rooster, who Will was beginning to believe was unable to say more than one or two words at a time.

"Yes, darling," the cat purred up to the rooster. "The question is, what type of folk group are we?"

"That's what I was trying to say, sister," the dog barked, his long tongue lashing out to lick across his snout. "Critics have said we are folk baroque, folk pop, folk revival, indie folk . . ."

"Chamber folk, avant folk . . ." continued the cat with an irritated flick of her tail.

"Proto Anti-folk!" cried out the rooster.

"Yeah, man, it's like how can we grow a fan base, man, when the fans don't know what we stand for, man," the donkey said, taking yet another deep draw from the pipe, which he seemed loath to pass on.

"It doesn't help us," the dog said gruffly to the donkey, "that every time we talk to a critic, you tell him that we don't believe in labels, brother."

"Critics!" crowed the rooster.

"And pass the pipe," the dog growled at the donkey.

The donkey guiltily passed the pipe up to the rooster, who snatched it up in a talon and began puffing violently on it.

Charming waited till the pipe was in his hand,

then said authoritatively, "But, I think the question of your genre is elementary." He puffed a few times and pointed the stem of the pipe around the circle at the animals. "It is clear to me that you are a proto-farm folk group with elements of barnyard-madrigal and neo-Orwellian primitivism."

Will rolled his eyes at this new absurdity, but the animals all seemed enthralled.

"That's us, brother!" the dog barked, wagging his tail enthusiastically.

"Us!" screamed the rooster.

"It's nothing," Charming said with a casual wave of his hand. "Fitting a group to a specific genre is rather mechanical. Genre is nothing more than a stylistic specification that intrinsically relates to classification. You merely compare an artist to what they share with or in how they differ from other similarly situated artists. In your case, your music obviously takes elements from the Pied Piper of Hamlin, who is a perfect example of proto-folk, but you add in an inherent animalia quality, similar to what the Little Pigs were doing in their primitivism phase."

Will hadn't understood a word of this, but it was clear that whatever it was Charming had said had truly impressed the four animals.

"How do you know so much about music, man?" the donkey asked, his mouth hanging open in disbelief.

"Understanding the essence of critique is essential to being a dragonslayer," Charming replied as he passed the pipe back to the dog.

"You're a critic, man!" the donkey brayed in alarm.

"CRITIC!" crowed the rooster.

"No, I just understand critique," Charming said, then asked, "What's your beef with critics anyway?"

"I don't know, man," the donkey said, stroking his gray beard with an upraised hoof. "Music runs on good vibes, man. Critical negativity dampens creativity, man."

"I see that, but critics are essential," Charming urged him. "Look at me. I have had plenty of critics over the years, he is too handsome, too witty, his voice is too pure, his poetry too poetic, his calf is too well turned—"

"I don't see anything wrong with your calves," the cat on his lap purred softly. "I've never seen anyone who looks better in hose."

Charming winked at the cat. "It took years to perfect the look. I have some fascinating anecdotes about my early struggles with tights and hose that I could tell you—"

Will realized that Charming might spend the rest of the night and the next day on this topic, and the musicians seemed perfectly willing to indulge him. Unable to contain himself, he groaned.

Charming looked back at the door Will was hiding behind. "Did you all hear that? I think King William might be starting to come around. Maybe I should check on him."

Will held his breath as all five craned around to stare at the door.

"I guess it was nothing," Charming said after a time. "I have to figure out what to do next."

"Yeah, man. What are you going to do about the King, man?" asked the donkey.

Will leaned closer to the door.

Charming sighed and waved off the pipe as it came around to him again. "I don't know. I've pledged to follow him, and that is what I have to do, but I feel guilty. We have no plan other than 'go north,' and he won't listen to me."

"I wanted to ask you a question about that, brother," the dog huffed. "If you went north from here, how did you wind back up here?"

Here it comes, thought Will. *Here comes his admission of guilt.*

"I don't have any idea." Charming shrugged. "We traveled on whatever path we could find. Each morning we would start out going north, but the road would turn or end, and we would have to go east for a bit to go north, then west for a bit to go north, then sometimes south to go north. In end, we made a circle. I was shocked to find out I was back home. If we had stuck to the large byways, I think we could have made it to the Northern Waste by now, but . . ."

Will stopped listening. His heart felt empty. This was his fault. The entire delay had been because he was too stubborn to take Charming's advice. He had endangered Elle again.

Well, he thought. *We will have to start over. This time we will take the main roads, and we will make our way to the Northern Waste. We will ride day and night if necessary. No stops.*

Having decided on his course, Will began to open the door to command Charming that they would start at once, but then by fate or chance, Charming said, "I know I have to follow him, but Liz is out there all alone with no one to protect her. I have a duty to my King, but what about my duty to my wife?"

"And Liz is actually the King's sister, brother?" the dog asked.

Charming nodded, staring at the paper in his hands.

"Woof," the dog said grimly. "Sorry about the comment earlier about her play, brother. It isn't her fault, just . . . just the Players didn't do it justice."

"Don't worry about it. Liz hates the play. She . . ." Charming's voice caught. "She thinks the pumpkins are ridiculous."

"Don't you think the King will care enough about his sister to let you go after her, man?" the donkey asked.

"It sounds like he does not think about anyone but himself," the cat hissed in disgust. "Typical King."

"No," said Charming. "He is thinking of Elle. We cannot hold that against him. He has the best of intentions."

"If you say so, brother," said the dog. "But in my experience, the man only thinks about the man."

Will sat back against the wall, the judgment of the group ringing in his ears. They were right. He had been selfish. His own negligence had cost him his beloved, and now, through his own arrogance, he had endangered Liz.

As Will pondered what to do, Charming asked, "Is it really that bad out there?"

"Bad, man?" brayed the donkey. "The whole place looks like the end of a music festival. People going this way and that, strung out and crazy."

"Crazy!" crowed the rooster.

"Put it this way, man. We are broke and need gigs and are hiding in a cottage in the middle of nowhere, man," said the donkey, taking a long drag at the pipe. "There is no way we are going back out on the road with that dragon out there."

"Besides," barked the dog. "There's that crazy Dracomancer and his Dracolytes to worry about, brother. They've taken over the whole southern part of the kingdom."

"Dracomancer!" the rooster gave a strangled cry.

"You shouldn't go either," the cat purred, rubbing the side of her body back and forth across his chest. "Norm has been telling us all about you, darling, about your poetry and your dreams."

"Norm says you have an artist's soul, brother," the dog said enthusiastically.

"Wait!" Charming said, putting up a hand. "Who's Norm?"

This was a question that was also puzzling Will.

"OX!" screamed the rooster.

"My ox? You mean Goliath?" Charming asked in stunned disbelief.

"Yeah, although he's not sure about that nickname, man," the donkey said.

"He says it may feed into the stereotype that oxen are just big and dumb, brother," the dog growled.

"Sizeist!" the rooster called.

"He's actually very delicate, like me, dear Edward." The cat sighed.

"Although he's got a great baritone, man," the donkey said, gesturing about with the pipe. "We may ask him to join the group."

"You've been talking to Goliath . . . I mean, Norm, my ox?" Charming said, and gestured for the donkey to hand him the pipe. In the other room, Will desperately wished that he could do the same.

"Yeah, and he's been telling us how cool you've been, man," the gray-headed donkey said, nodding.

"About how you were the first person to really let him express himself through his soil sculpture, brother," continued the dog.

"You are too sensitive to be roaming about trying to kill dragons, Darling," the cat said as she licked a paw and ran it over her fur. "Stay here with us, and we can make beautiful music together."

"No!" Charming suddenly stood, dumping the cat in a disgruntled heap on the floor, and began pacing back and forth. "As tempting as it sounds, and as much as I want to get to know Norm, Liz is going right into the heart of this Dracomancer's territory. I must do something! Somehow, I must convince the King to let me go."

In that moment, Will realized Charming had to go south, and he had to go north. Their partnership was at an end.

"Good travels," he whispered.

He gathered his things quietly and slipped out the window while in the other room, he heard Charming announce, "I'll give him another hour till dawn, then I'll wake him and see if I can't explain everything. Perhaps I can talk some sense into him." Charming sighed. "In the meantime, I'm hungry as a dog . . . no offense."

"None taken, brother," the dog said in his gravelly voice. "I'm hungry like the wolf myself."

"Hey," the donkey brayed loudly, as Will slipped out the window. "There's a song in that . . ."

Outside, Will saddled his horse and led it quietly out of the clearing to the path before mounting. He began riding at a measured pace in the direction he *knew* would take him to the main north–south road. There would be no more shortcuts, and he would not abuse his mount. He still felt guilty about his treatment of the horse he had first ridden after Elle had been taken. He might have killed it.

The road turned and twisted through the woods. When the sun reached its height, Will came to a partially collapsed bridge that had formerly spanned a rushing stream. A narrow plank had been placed across the two standing ends of the bridge. It was just wide enough for his horse, but he would have to dismount and lead it across.

Will stepped onto the plank.

"Aha!"

With an impressive leap, a man came out of the trees from the other bank to land on the opposite side of the ruined bridge in front of the plank. He held a wooden stave in his hands and wore a feathered cap.

"Oh no," said Will flatly. "It's the Scarlet Scoundrel. Or rather, the Green Phantom."

"Aha! My reputation precedes me."

"No," said Will. "We've met. I rescued King Rupert from your clutches about a year ago. Don't you remember?"

"King William, is that you?" the Scoundrel asked skeptically. He leaned against his staff. "You look terrible. What has happened to your clothes, and your face, and my God, your hands? Have you been in a battle with trolls or bears or perhaps something even more dark and sinister that has yet to be given a name? As you know, I have a particular skill with names."

"No, Phantom, I've encountered nothing." Will said, clenching his jaw in anger. "Just get out of my way. I'm not in the mood."

The bandit bowed. "My apologies, Your Majesty, but I can't let you pass. First, you are the King, and as such, you are my sworn enemy. Second, as you have proved, I have a reputation now to think of, and letting my sworn enemy cross the bridge I have claimed as my own without challenge would ruin me. Also," he said in a lower voice, "I've decided to steer away from the Green Phantom name. I have a new theory about alliterative—"

"Alliterative imprimatur," Will said in disgust. "Yes, I've heard it."

"You've heard," the Scoundrel said with surprise, then brightened. "My fame must be growing faster than even I suspected. This makes the current debate over my name all the more important to resolve. I would like your view, Your Majesty."

"I don't care."

The Scoundrel either didn't hear or ignored him. "I'm debating between the Scarlet Scoundrel and the Violet Varlet, although, I have also thought about the Verdant Vigilante, but I'm not sure it's right for my own particular . . ."

"Idiom?" offered Will.

"Idiom!" the Scarlet Scoundrel shouted.

"Can we hurry this up?" Will asked.

The Scoundrel looked at him crossly. "You have changed, Your Majesty. Last time we met, you were far more courteous and a great deal more fun. I believe the crown must be ageing you. Be wary of that. Kings never look as good when they leave the palace as when they enter it. However, enough banter; if you wish to rush straight to your own humiliation, let's have at it."

The Scoundrel extended his staff in a challenge but did not yet step on the plank.

"You have a staff, and I don't," complained Will.

"True," replied the Scoundrel. He whistled. A hand

reached down from an overhanging branch near Will, holding a staff. A quiet voice from above said, "Here you go, Your Majesty."

Will dropped the reins of his horse, grabbed the staff, and stormed onto the plank toward the Scarlet Scoundrel. The Scoundrel took one disappointed look at him, and said, "You don't seem like the quick-witted young man I remember."

Swinging his staff wildly, Will shouted, "I'm not a stupid peasant anymore. I'm the King now!"

"Yes, you are a king now," the Scoundrel said sadly. "Pity."

With that, he kicked the edge of the plank off his side of the bridge. The next thing Will knew, he was falling, then he hit the water. The stream was freezing cold, and Will realized he couldn't breathe. A heartbeat later, he felt something tug at the back of his tunic and his head burst to the surface. The Scarlet Scoundrel was holding Will up with his staff. He swung him over to the bank.

"Now, if you will be so good as to drop your sword, my men will liberate you of any valuables. Please understand, Your Majesty, this isn't personal. It's just business."

Will coughed and spluttered. He could hear men in the trees laughing at him. He lay on the bank of the stream, cold and miserable and feeling completely and utterly defeated.

He heard a commotion in the trees. "We've got a problem," a hidden voice said.

"What is it?" asked the Scoundrel. "Someone deal with it, we've got the King here. Show some respect. After all, this is a Royal Robbery. Oh, I like that one."

"It's a lone rider, and he's coming fast," came another hidden voice.

"He looks really impressive," said yet another voice.

"Wait. Does it seem like he's staring at the far horizon?" asked the Scoundrel.

"Yes, that's it," called another in a worried tone.

"My God, we've got to get out of here," said the Scoundrel.

There was a clatter of hooves on the road.

"Ahem, too late," came Charming's voice from atop the bridge. "Hello, Daniel."

"Don't call me Daniel, Edward," the outlaw hissed. "You know I'm the Scarlet Scoundrel. And why are you here anyway?"

"Oh, didn't you know," Charming said in his most obnoxiously superior voice. "I'm the King's personal squire."

"A squire? You?" The Scoundrel laughed. "Squire Charming?"

"The one and only," Charming said, and Will looked up to see him tap his heels against his horse's flanks, and the horse gathered itself and leapt the gap in the bridge.

Charming stared down at the Scoundrel. "Now, the way I see it, Daniel, we can do this the easy way, and you can drop the staff and run, or I'll take it from you and dunk you in the water in front of all your Hardy Hooligans."

"Now, listen, Charming. I can't just back down. And *ixnay* on the *Anielday*, I'm the Scarlet Scoundrel, and these are my Heinous Highwaymen."

There was a murmuring in the trees and the sounds of several arguments.

"Well," admitted the Scoundrel. "Some of our names are still under discussion."

"Personally, I like Heinous Highwaymen," said Charming, confidently. "Are you going to back down, or do I beat you with your own stick?"

The Scarlet Scoundrel began to back up, holding his staff defensively in front of him as Charming advanced on his horse. "Be reasonable, Charming."

"No! No! No! This isn't right!" shouted Will.

Both Charming and the Scarlet Scoundrel paused. Charming cleared his throat. "Your Majesty, it's perfectly fine. The Scoundrel knows I can thrash him. I've done it a dozen times although he's got me when it comes to archery."

"And swinging on ropes."

"True, that has never really been part of my milieu," nodded Charming. "Don't worry, Your Majesty. This thrashing will take no time, then we will be back on our way north."

Will sat up and put his head in his hands. "It's impossible. I can't do this."

The Scoundrel put his staff against the railing of the bridge and, approaching closer to Charming, whispered, "Edward, this seems like a bad time."

"I know. Let me handle this."

"Please tell me that he's not crying. I couldn't stand it if I brought the man to tears."

Charming nodded. "Maybe you should help him up out of the mud there. Oh, Heinous Highwaymen," Charming called out. "Can you come down out of the trees? I think we need to regroup."

Men began climbing down from the branches.

"Wait, I give the orders," shouted the Scoundrel.

The men paused.

"Okay, do what Charming said."

The bandits resumed climbing down the trees.

Will didn't care about the Scoundrel or Charming. All he cared about was Elle, and he realized that he had no idea what he could do or where he could go to help her. Charming was right. There was no reason to go north. Even if, by some miracle, they found the dragon, Will had no idea what to do, and from their conversation on the road, he knew that Charming didn't really know either. They had wasted a week riding around the kingdom. He had failed as a man to protect the woman he loved. He had failed as the King to keep his subjects safe. The last great thing he had done was to place Princess Gwendolyn in judgment over the fairy.

Then it came to him.

He shook his head and laughed, as the Scarlet Scoundrel threw him a rope. He was still laughing when the Heinous Highwaymen helped him onto the bridge.

"I know what to do."

Charming came over to him. "Will?"

"I know what to do."

"Go north?" Charming asked with resigned voice.

"We aren't going north," Will said with a bemused laugh.

"What are you talking about?"

"Who knows how a Dragon thinks? Who understands Dragons? Who has talked more to Dragons than anyone else?" Will headed over to his horse.

The Scarlet Scoundrel and Charming shared confused glances and shrugged.

"I'm telling you what Liz figured out a week ago," said Will. "We need to go south! We need to head to the one place that I can always find—home. We have to go back to Prosper."

"Why?" asked Charming.

"Because that's where we will find the one person who can help us—Princess Gwendolyn Mostfair!"

And with that, Will mounted up and started riding south.

CHAPTER 9

THE MAGICAL MYSTICAL TOUR

In fairy tales, no two prisoners have the same story, either as to their treatment or the reasons for their imprisonment. Beauty is held prisoner because the Beast wants her to love him, and she is treated like a princess. Hansel and Gretel are held prisoner because the witch, after so many sweets, craves something savory, and they are treated like livestock.

Unlike most other fairy-tale damsels, Liz was being held prisoner because she *wanted* to be held prisoner. She and Tomas had plenty of opportunities to escape. The Dracomancer's trusted confidants, whom he called the Dracoviziers, weren't the best watchmen, and they didn't seem to think she could or would go very far. For her part, Liz needed time to get over whatever illness was afflicting her. She also felt it was important to stay close to the Dracomancer in the hopes that she might be able to reason with him or at least gain an understanding of the bizarre sway the man held over his followers, and how she, or more preferably Will, might break it.

But if Liz's motives were clear, at least to herself, the Dracomancer's reasons for keeping her with him were a mystery. She made, or at least took every effort to make his life a misery. If she wasn't interrogating him, she was ribbing him about the absurd and amateurish nature of his "act," as she called it. Her aggressive combination of sarcasm and curiosity clearly nettled the Dracomancer, and Liz reflected that had she been the Dracomancer, she would have exiled herself, or put herself in stocks, or done something, anything to get rid of herself, and yet the more she criticized and questioned him, the closer he drew her to his side. By the end of her second day with the Dracolytes, Liz wasn't allowed out of the Dracomancer's sight. It was a mystery.

In fact, everything the Dracomancer did was a mystery to her. The first few days Liz spent in the Dracomancer's company were at his bedside in the back room of his tavern headquarters, where he was recuperating from his "battle" with the dragon. There the Dracomancer received a constant stream of select followers—selectness being determined exclusively by the person's generosity to the Dracomancer and his cause. She saw instantly that he was swindling them, and she, or at least her title, was being used to lend him extra credibility. Then news arrived that the dragon had been spotted flying to the dark tower south of Prosper, and the Dracomancer made the announcement that the time had come for him to rid the kingdom of this new terror.

To say that Liz was surprised would be like saying that there are a few trees in a forest, or that trolls have a slight odor about them, or that the ale at the Cooked Goose has an interesting flavor. More accurately, she was utterly gobsmacked. Liz had never had a high opinion of the Dracomancer, and her time in Two Trees had only reinforced her belief that the man was nothing more than a charlatan and a crook. She had come to the conclusion that the Dracomancer's sole aim was to milk his followers for every free meal and tankard of ale and copper he could manage, and that one day he would slip away into the night before the tar could get heated and the feathers plucked. Indeed, she had become increasingly convinced that even his reputation as a scholar of dragons was an exaggeration if not an outright fabrication.

So great was her cynicism about the Dracomancer that she was initially convinced that the announcement of his departure must be part of some larger con, or perhaps its culmination. *This is the moment,* she thought, *where he convinces Jack to sell his cow for three magic beans, or the emperor to walk naked in the streets.*

But the next morning, the Dracomancer donned his black cloak, took up his carved black staff, and mounted his black mare, and with Liz and Tomas on his left and a few of his closest Dracolyte supporters on his right, he rode up the street toward the town square.

Liz had only ever seen so many people in one place once in her entire life, and that was at Gwendolyn and Will's almost wedding at Castle White. While she and the Dracomancer had been cloistered in his rooms at the back of the tavern, outside, the town had continued to swell as new followers flowed into Two Trees, lured by tales of the sorcerer's brilliant defeat of the dragon. The hundreds had grown to thousands. It looked to Liz as though someone had draped all of Two Trees in a patchwork quilt of humanity. They were seated on the ground and crouched in the trees. They had clambered atop wagons and horses. They rose in ranks up the sides of the hills and sat perched like birds atop the roofs of the buildings.

It was a gray day, full of dark, heavy clouds that spoke of rain to come. As the group reached the edge of the square, the Dracomancer made a signal for them to halt. A strong breeze whipped and swirled across the dirt market square, kicking up clouds of dust. The Dracomancer waited a heartbeat or two, then rode out to the center of the open space. Dressed all in black, with his long, twisted staff, and his face hidden within the folds of the deeply cowled hood, he looked arcane and otherworldly, an effect that was only heightened by the strong winds, which pulled and tugged at his horse's mane and tail, and at the cloth of his robes, so that he was a flowing, undulating silhouette of black.

"I was led here to this place to await a sign," he

began with no preamble. "That sign has come. The dragon has returned to Dragon Tower, there to fulfill the draconic cycle long prophesied." He raised his staff in dramatic emphasis. "Now it is *my* time to take leave of this place and fulfill my role. To face the dragon. To fight the dragon. To slay the dragon. I go with no regrets and with no fear. I go only with happiness that I may serve you, my friends and people, and that we may rid the Kingdom of Royaume once and for all of this scourge. Know that whatever the outcome, my friends, I shall remain with you all in my spirit."

Liz did not know what she expected. Perhaps that he would get a rousing cheer or a plaintive protest for him to remain, but the crowd remained eerily quiet throughout his speech. They made no response of any kind. They did not shuffle impatiently. There was not a cough or a sneeze. Instead, as the Dracomancer turned his horse back onto the road out of Two Trees, the host of his black-clad followers, without any debate or question, simply fell into step behind him. She turned about and saw that at least a hundred men and women were on the march.

Liz felt again that quiver of doubt that she had felt watching the Dracomancer face down the dragon on her first night in Two Trees. She leaned over to Tomas, and asked, "What do you think of the Dracomancer now?"

Tomas looked at her grimly. He had been made to work during his captivity, clearing away the burnt remains of tents, caravans, and wagons left behind in the wake of the dragon's attack. He was dirty and haggard. "I still think he's a madman, Your Ladyship, but his is the most dangerous kind of madness . . . madness with potential."

"Perhaps," she said with a frown as she studied the retreating figure. "Or, perhaps he is not as mad as he would like us to believe. I think I see in these machinations a distinct plan. A plan with a crown at the end."

On a good horse with fair weather, it was only a day's ride from Two Trees down the mountains and across the River Running to the South Valley and Prosper. The Dracomancer had a good horse, but many of his followers didn't even have shoes. The going was slow, taking them two full days to reach the river basin.

As they descended from the hills, they devoured everything in their path. Fields were stripped bare of crops and livestock. Whole houses, barns and miles of fencerow were torn down to burn in their campfires. And every man, woman, and child they met was conscripted into servants for the Dracomancer's army. Pleas for mercy were only met by the wrath of the Dracolyte mob.

Around noon on the third day of their journey, they came out of the woods. The sun was playing peekaboo with the few wispy white clouds that remained, casting huge flying shadows down across the gold-and-green fields. The road turned sharply to the west and struck off through the grassy hills toward the River Running, which sparkled and flashed in the distance.

The Dracomancer reined in his horse to take in the sight. His attendant Dracoviziers protectively flanked him. It almost seemed to Liz as if the Dracomancer was trying to pose, and for a brief moment, her thoughts turned to Charming. She wasn't worried about him as such, but she did hope that he was keeping Will safe. Some part of her felt guilty that she did not worry about Charming more. Some part of her knew that the aura of invincibility that surrounded him was just that, an aura, an illusion. Still, she was glad that those parts were, for now, being quiet because she also knew in her heart that once she did start worrying about him and fearing for him, she might never be able to stop.

"Where is Lady Elizabeth?" the Dracomancer asked. The Dracoviziers silently parted to indicate where she had been riding, immediately behind them. The Dracomancer eyed them all suspiciously.

"Oh, go away, all of you!" he barked, sharply waving his hands at the Dracoviziers as though shooing flies. The Dracoviziers turned their horses and shuffled slowly back toward the following masses.

The Dracomancer beamed a crooked smile at Liz. He gestured for her to come forward. "Lady Elizabeth, let us ride together for a bit."

She sighed wearily, but she spurred her horse to move up beside his. The prospect of riding the rest of the day in his company was not a welcome one. It was not so much that the Dracomancer was a cruel captor or that she felt her life was in danger. Indeed, if asked, she would have had to admit that she was being treated rather well. He had actually been very solicitous about her health after her fainting spell. Regardless, she simply could not stand to be around the man.

Why did he bother her so much? She did not believe that he actually commanded magical powers or was possessed by the spirits of dead dragons. Tomas had said that the Dracomancer possessed the "unsettlin' weirdness of the true wackaloon," but she didn't think that was it either. What she really felt when she was in his presence was used. He had a preternatural ability to manipulate people into doing what he wanted, and it made her feel dirty when he turned his attention on her.

The Dracomancer fixed her with his gaze. His eyes were such a deep brown that they were almost black, and illuminated by the midday sun, they gleamed like polished onyx. "Is it nice to be back?" he asked.

"Where? In Prosper?"

"Yes, Lady Elizabeth," he said with a knowing smirk. "That is exactly what I mean. Have you been back to Prosper since leaving for the castle?"

"No." She wondered what exactly he was getting at.

"Haven't you been curious about your old farm?" he asked with an exaggerated indifference. "Haven't you wanted to see the resting place of the Great Wyrm of the South?

A warning tingle raced across her scalp. "First, the farm is not my home any longer, and Edward and I have been busy building a life of our own. Second, I never want to see a dragon again or even the resting place of a dragon."

"That's right, your farm, your brother—"

"King William" she corrected.

He waved her interruption aside with the back of his hand. "Yes, yes, your brother, *King William*, he gave it to Gwendolyn Mostfair, didn't he?"

The warning tingle became a dull roar of alarm as her thoughts raced. *How could I have forgotten Gwendolyn? Is that why he was so eager to go to Prosper? What does he mean to do with her?* Afraid to say anything for fear that it would reveal her internal distress, she stiffly nodded.

"What interesting stories she must have," he said, far too casually.

Liz made no response.

"I *know* King William keeps the dragon's golden key as a scepter when sitting judgment at court," the Dracomancer said in a jarring shift of topic, "but what did he do with the other artifacts from the dragon? Like the pitchfork—the Pitchfork of Destiny, the weapon that slew the creature? Did he keep it?"

"The pitchfork was destroyed, I think," Liz answered absentmindedly. She couldn't actually remember what happened to the pitchfork, and her mind was distracted by thoughts of Gwendolyn. The princess had spent a lifetime in the company of the last dragon; did she know something about this dragon also?

They rode in silence for a time. She could see the line of old willow trees that marked the banks of the

River Running less than a league ahead. The bridge would be in sight soon, and with any luck, they would be in Prosper by early evening. Behind her, the Dracolytes chanted a marching song. They had borrowed an old nursery tune, but some inventive member of the group had changed the words, and now floating over the road on the breeze came:

"Ding dong the King is gone,
The dragon stole his Lady Fair,
It flew her off
To who knows where?
DING DONG!
Ding dong the King is gone,
He abandoned us
Gave up his trust.
And where he is, we do not care.
DING DONG!"

A throaty roar that made Liz want to flinch, punctuated each "ding" and each "dong." She glanced over at the Dracomancer. A half-twisted smile spread across his face at the words "we don't care." He was enjoying his rise, but more than that, he reveled in the fact that his rise was coming at the expense of Will. She wondered what injury Will had done to him. Was it merely that Will's rise had come at his own expense?

"Ding dong the King is gone,
We all went down on bended knee
To swear to the King our fealty
Now the dragon rules and we feel like fools.
DING DONG!"

They had made it to the edge of the River Running. Ahead lay the bridge that would lead them over the river and into the district of Prosper. Liz decided that she had to press the Dracomancer. She had to know what his intentions were with Will, with the dragon, and with Gwendolyn.

Straightening herself in her saddle, she said steadily, "What's your game?"

"My game?" he asked innocently. "Whatever could you mean, Lady Elizabeth?"

"You know exactly what I mean," she snapped, and pulled her horse to a halt, forcing him to follow suit. "You don't speak to dragon spirits, you have a hand puppet. You didn't drive the dragon out of Two Trees, it left because it had eaten an entire herd of pigs and desired no more. I'm not sure how you knew you wouldn't be attacked that day, but somehow you knew. You don't have the skill or power to fight the dragon, and I believe you have no intention of doing so. So, I repeat my question, what is your game?"

The Dracomancer stiffened as though struck but otherwise betrayed no outward emotion. The half smile remained frozen on his face, but it was a rigid thing, lacking any warmth or humanity. He fixed his eyes, now jet-black in the shadows beneath the willow trees, on her, and said very softly and calmly, "You know all that, do you, Lady Elizabeth?"

Staring into those eyes, so lacking in compassion or emotion, Liz was suddenly unsure how to answer. Still, as firmly as she could she replied, "Yes. I know that you value your own skin too highly to risk it facing the dragon in real combat. My question stands. If you don't intend to kill the dragon, why have you brought your followers with you? Do you really want so many to bear witness to your inevitable defeat? Are you that mad?"

The question hung in the air between them like a poisonous snake.

Gnarsh the Troll lurked gloomily in the shadows beneath his new bridge, staring through the cracks in the wooden spars at the figures on horseback standing so tantalizing close. In the old days, he would have leapt right out and eaten them and their horses for good measure. But still he sat, hesitating, as foul, black spittle dripped from his maw and mixed with the murky water of the river.

It wasn't right. Not at all.

He looked down at his daggerlike talons and reflected on the fact that he had been at this bridge for almost a month and had yet to actually attack a traveler. This time he could not blame the bridge. It was a good bridge, elegantly decayed and with an excellent caliber of mud beneath it, but what made it really special was its location. Gnarsh knew that location was everything in picking a bridge to lurk under, and this one was perfect. It was on the main north–south road and was the only bridge for miles. When he'd found it, he had known that this would be the start of a new chapter in his life. And then the new dragon had arrived, and he had lost his courage. So he lurked under his bridge and ate fish. Fish! He, Gnarsh, had become a fish eater!

It wasn't right. Not at all.

He hated dragons almost as much as he hated goats. One mad goat had shattered his dream—taken away his chance to become legend. He had been so close to eating Prince Charming! Now each time he heard hooves of any sort, he would cringe and cover his black-and-green-scaled head and cower. He didn't want to risk leaping upon the bridge, expecting to find a horse, and have to face a goat instead. He knew he needed to get over his fears. But still, he would wake up hearing their bleats in his nightmares.

It wasn't right. Not at all.

He pressed one of his googly eyes to a knothole and stared up at the people. They didn't look like goatherds. He raised his ooze-dripping nose and sniffed. They didn't smell like goatherds. They smelled like humans, crunchy, juicy humans. The more he stared and the more he sniffed, the hungrier he became. He ran his black tongue over his razor-sharp teeth. His stomach gave a grumble, and he looked at the mud bank littered with fish skeletons. In a moment, some of the old fire returned. He had lurked too long. Was he just a troll, or was he a troll under a bridge? He had to eat these two. Anything less wouldn't be right.

Giving himself no more time to dither, Gnarsh swung himself up on the bridge and let loose a terrible roar. "I am the dread troll, Gnarsh! And I will eat you both up!"

There was a woman who gave a satisfying cry of terror and jerked her horse back away from him, but the old man who rode beside her, holding a staff just stared at Gnarsh, seemingly unafraid.

"Dracomancer," the woman shouted. "Run!"

Gnarsh gnashed his razor-sharp teeth and clashed his daggerlike talons, but still the old man did not move. Instead, he turned his horse and addressed the woman. "You want an answer to your question, Lady Elizabeth?"

"No," she said, still trying to control her own nervously prancing mount. "I just want us not to get eaten."

"But you won't, Lady Elizabeth," he said calmly, "because although you are quite right that I don't have the power to fight dragons or even trolls, and that I have no intention of fighting either, you fail to understand that I did not bring my followers with me to bear witness to my deeds. I brought them to *be* an army."

At that moment, the ground began to shake, and a mass of humans, more humans than Gnarsh had ever seen, topped the little rise behind the man and began rushing toward the bridge. The old man in the black cloak held up his staff, and they stopped.

He rose in his stirrups and pointed the staff at Gnarsh. "Friends, Dracolytes, this creature wishes to stop us from reaching Prosper and fulfilling our destiny. Teach him what happens to those that stand in the way of the Dragon Spirit."

There was an inhuman roar of deranged anger from the mob, then they surged forward and around the man in the cloak like a living wave. Gnarsh swung about with his boulder-sized arms and his daggerlike talons. Dozens fell before him, and the bridge grew slick with the blood of the dying and the dead, but the living showed no fear of Gnarsh, or of the random bits and pieces of their comrades that were strewn about. In a moment, he was swarmed and grasped from all sides. He tried to fight back, but there were too many of them, and before he realized what was happening, they had started pulling him apart.

Gnarsh felt one arm, then the other pop free from his shoulders. He heard his legs snap and break. They hefted his head high, and tossed it off the bridge, where it landed with a splash in the river.

It wasn't right. Not at all.

"This is not right," Liz shouted as she watched the mayhem on the bridge with horror. "Make them stop," she pleaded with the Dracomancer. "Can't you see that people are dying? Your people are dying!"

"Yes," the Dracomancer said in a slow, low drawl, not taking his eyes from the melee. "They are, aren't they? Sacrificing themselves in my name."

"Don't you care?"

"Of course I care," he said.

"How can you let this happen?" she asked, her voice breaking.

He had a strange, twisted smile on his face. "You misjudge me, Lady Elizabeth," he said in a hissing whisper meant only for her. "I don't care that they are dying, but I do care a great deal that they are willing to die for me. When we left Two Trees, I had some doubts about their devotion. This demonstration puts my mind at rest. Their unquestioning zeal will make sending them after the dragon that much easier. Don't you think?"

The Dracomancer watched, quite placidly, as his army disposed of the last bits of the troll. When they were finished, he held up his staff, and the Dracolytes who were not dead or maimed all turned to salute him, each in their own unique fashion.

Over the groans of the wounded and dying, he exclaimed, "Today, my Dracolytes, thanks to the power of the Dragon Spirit, we have achieved a great victory. This dark and gruesome beast was clearly in league with the dragon, and had been sent here to prevent our reaching the dragon's lair. Let this day be a testament to those who still doubt. There is nothing that can stand between our destiny and us. The dragon will fall!"

The Dracolytes roared in exultation and the Dracomancer leaned over to Liz. "Forgive me, Lady Elizabeth, but I think we will have to continue our fascinating conversation at another time." Then the Dracomancer rode across the bridge and led the mob down into Prosper. As they marched, they picked up the song they had been singing before.

"If you ask why we sing
And why it is that bells should ring
If you need our one true answer
It's because we follow . . . the Dracomancer!
DRACOMANCER, DRACOMANCER!
He commands the spirits and the mystic flame.
He shall make the dragon writhe in pain
All must acknowledge the world's new master.
Put your faith in the Dracomancer!
DRACOMANCER, DRACOMANCER!"

Liz sat motionless on her horse, an island trapped in a tide of the Dracomancer's followers. Finally, Tomas reached her. To the grizzled old squire, she looked lost. He went to her.

"What's the matter, Your Ladyship?" he asked in as kind a tone as the gruffness of his voice would allow.

She was silent a moment, then shook her head sadly. "I'm sorry I got us into this mess. I've been a fool, Tomas."

"Come on, now, don't say that."

"But, it's true, Tomas. I didn't see. I didn't understand what he meant to do."

"What does he mean to do?" he asked, the gruffness returning as he readied himself for the worse.

"He . . . he means to send all those people to their deaths," she sobbed. "He's going to march them up the mountains to Dragon Tower to attack the dragon. So many will die, and for what? The dragon will kill them all. It is pointless."

"It's madness, that's what it is, Your Ladyship.

They won't do it," Tomas said hopefully. "He can't make them, and they won't do it. No one will listen to him."

"But he can, and they will," she said, looking up at him with tears running down her cheeks. "That's what I didn't understand. I thought he was a charlatan, but he does have power, only it isn't over dragons, it's over people. He has them so convinced he is a prophet that they would follow him off a cliff if he told them it was their destiny."

"Then they must be barking also."

"Maybe," she said with a resigned shrug. "Who knows? But even if they are, we can't let this happen."

"But how can we stop it? As long as the dragon is there, the Dracomancer seems determined to try something."

Liz stared at Tomas, her head cocked at an angle as though listening to something very far away. "I don't know that we can stop it, but maybe I know someone who can."

One of the Dracoviziers rode over and gestured for them to move on. Liz and Tomas rejoined the marching horde. While her time with the Dracomancer had been illuminating, it no longer suited her purposes. She needed to escape.

Liz leaned down so that she was close to Tomas's ear and whispered, "How good are you at distractions?"

Tomas cracked his knuckles and bent his mouth into an evil grin. "Fair, Your Ladyship."

Carried downstream by the current of the River Running, Gnarsh's head bobbed along with the other remains of his body. Gnarsh would have sighed had he still had lungs. Instead, he satisfied himself with rolling his googly eyes in despair. It would take him weeks to regenerate.

It wasn't right. Not at all.

And it was at that moment that Gnarsh vowed to abandon lurking and bridges altogether and return to retirement in the mountains, where he could live in peace—where all he would have to worry about were the goats.

CHAPTER 10

DRACOMOCRACY IN ACTION

When Will Pickett first made up his mind to seek out Gwendolyn Mostfair, there had been no doubt in his mind. Being that rarest of person, someone who has spoken with a dragon and not ended the conversation inside the dragon's belly, the former Princess would know far more about dragons than anyone else in the land, and Will knew in his heart that Gwendolyn would help him if she could. She wouldn't suffer any woman to be imprisoned by a dragon. With her as his goal, the stubborn determination that he had wasted on his attempt to head north was now completely redirected to getting back to his old farm.

As the days passed, however, he had time to reflect on his decision. It wasn't that the prospect of talking to Gwendolyn frightened him, but she had used her magic to enslave him and nearly forced him to marry her. It wasn't that he worried about the reception he might get from her, but who was to say how she felt now that she'd spent months as a common farmer on, to put it mildly, the humble Pickett homestead in Prosper? Will recalled quite vividly how delicate she was and how particular she was about her comforts. What if her thankfulness for his mercy had turned to thoughts of revenge? What if she'd turned back to sorcery?

Will felt that he should talk about his doubts, but the only person he had to share his concerns with was Charming, and Charming was now taking his role as dragonslayer instructor very seriously. Will knew that this was exactly what he'd been asking for, but the timing, order and subject of these lessons was, peculiar, to say the least. One moment, Charming would be talking in intimate detail about dragon anatomy and the best points to strike for maximum effectiveness, and the next he would be discussing, with equal seriousness, the relative effects different hat styles had on one's profile. Charming was currently, and had for the past hour, been talking about one of his favorite topics, the state of their clothing and his appearance.

"Will, I wish you hadn't run off from the cottage like that. It makes the second time you haven't given me the proper chance to pack extra clothes, and now we are beginning to see the consequences. I don't think dirt is a look that I can pull off. I mean, if I were going to be a farmer, I suppose I'd have to find a way, perhaps by being more of an advisory-farmer than a laboring-farmer. Oh, and I think it would be better for us not to use our real names unless absolutely necessary. Our reputations would suffer terribly. I also wanted to talk to you about your eyebrows. A well-shaped eyebrow must be at the very top of your . . ."

Will stopped listening, something he was getting better and better at. Even if he did broach the topic of Gwendolyn, he couldn't envision Charming giving him the sort of levelheaded advice he was looking for. Besides, what could they do? Whether Gwendolyn hated him or not, they still needed to at least try to speak to her. And, if she wouldn't help, he still felt confident that every moment they came closer to Prosper was a moment closer to Elle.

At his mind's mention of her name, his thoughts wandered onto the topic of Elle and lingered there as they rode. At some point, Will realized that it was almost evening. Long shadows covered the road. He looked about. They were riding in a deeper part of the wood. Ruins could be seen partially hidden among the trees. There was a crumbling stone wall, covered in vines, and through the broken stones, the last few rays of the setting sun fell on gravestones. He thought of Elle, about how long she had been gone, about what he might do if the unthinkable happened. His throat tightened. His eyes burned, and he started blinking.

"Getting tired, I see," said Charming. "Understandable. I have been cramming a lot of dragon-slaying wisdom into you, and it must be exhausting. I know it has been for me." He put a hand to his jaw and flexed it. "Let's stop and set up camp."

Charming dismounted and began tying his horse to a tree directly opposite the cemetery. In the next moments, Charming was setting up camp. Will was distracted and useless. He kept looking at the graves and thinking of Elle.

"Charming? Do you ever worry about dying?" Will regretted the question as soon as he asked it.

A fire crackled to life, and Charming fed larger and larger sticks and branches onto the growing flames as he answered. "Yes, of course. Rather goes with the trade, you know." He sat on a log and extended his booted feet to the fire. "It used to be a bit of a hobby of mine, actually. I've always been pretty sure I'd do it well. I have imagined dozens of different dramatic and poignant deaths. In one, I expire, wounded and bleeding, after victoriously battling dozens of enemies to save the kingdom. In another, I sacrifice myself to stop an evil enchanter from stealing all the children of the land away using a magical flute or something like that. I'll admit it's a bit of a rough draft. Though lately, I've been thinking that, perhaps, if I'm lucky—"

Charming stopped and looked thoughtful.

"What?"

Charming said wistfully, "Maybe I'll pass quietly in bed as a wrinkled old man with Liz stroking my forehead and my children all about me."

"You have changed, Charming."

"I know," said Charming. "I've gone terribly soft."

"No, it's a good thing," Will assured him. "I guess I thought your advice on dying well would be . . . I don't know, more dramatic."

Charming laughed. "No, no, Will. It's a common misapprehension for the layman, but the truth is that one of the great boons of being a dragonslayer is that you are guaranteed a good death. You might be boiled alive by dragon fire or lashed to pieces by its tail. You might be bitten in twain between the dragon's jaws or ripped asunder by its claws. Regardless, it will be dramatic."

Will paled at this list of violent ends, but Charming continued airily, "No, the only danger for the dragonslayer is of their death not being properly chronicled by the minstrels. That is why I have already deposited several volumes of suitable couplets, ballads, elegies, laments, odes, threnodies, and, of course, a multivolume epic that may be used on my death. My only regret is that I won't get to hear the verses put to song."

Charming frowned, then shrugged the thought off. "Oh, well, I suppose there is nothing to be done about that now. If we survive this, maybe I'll work with the Bremen-Four and Norm to set them to music." He looked up at Will with a quick smile. "I'm getting a little hungry. How about you?"

Will shook his head. He couldn't imagine eating right now. The discussion of death and dying had been a mistake, and he felt jumpy.

"No? Well, if you don't mind, I think I'll look around for some game," Charming said, rising and grabbing a bow and a quiver of arrows from his pack. "You should rest. You are looking a little pale."

Will nodded and watched Charming stalk off into the night. Almost immediately, a cold mist began rising out of the ground and creeping about the trunks of the trees and the stones in the graveyard. The horses picketed at the edge of the firelight whinnied nervously. Fear born of a hundred scary bedtime stories crept inside Will's head. He began to shiver in earnest and also to become intensely aware of all the little nighttime noises around him, the crackling of leaves, the rubbing of branches, a bird crying in the night, furtive, shuffling footsteps.

Probably Charming, he told himself.

As he listened, the footsteps grew more distinct. Whoever or whatever it was was coming his direction.

Must be Charming, he reassured his nerves.

But, Charming always walked with a bold, determined stride. Whatever this was had a shuffle in its step. It was not the clomp, clomp of Charming, but more of a clomp, clomp, drag, clomp, clomp, drag.

Perhaps he is dragging game behind him.

Will stared into the misty night, turning his head this way and that, trying to locate the source of the sound. At first, he could see nothing, but as the ominous "clomp, clomp, drag" grew closer, he saw the silhouette of something approaching through the mist. It was a shuffling misshapen form, ragged and hunched. Will fumbled in his pack for his sword, got to his feet, and stood with his back to the fire, watching the figure approach.

Will heard a strangled coughing sound and the shuffling "clomp, clomp, drag" began to come faster. The figure was much closer and making low, groaning noises. Will wiped the sweat from his palms and gripped his sword even tighter.

A rasping strangled sound came from it. The figure stopped and hacked for a moment. There was a terrible wet noise, and Charming said, "There you are. Much better, I'm sure. When we get to the fire, I can make you some tea."

"Oh, thank you, dearie," came the voice of an old woman.

Will exhaled as Charming came into the circle of light carrying a heavy bag in one hand and supporting an ancient-looking woman with his other. She was wrapped in a deeply hooded cloak and was so bent that her body was almost doubled over.

Charming carefully lowered the woman to sit on a stone near the fire, then dropped the bag with a thump onto the ground beside her. The top of the bag opened, and a handful of apples so red and beautiful that they were almost irresistible rolled out.

"Apples!" proclaimed Charming. "They look wonderful. May I?"

"Of course, dearie," cackled the old woman. She drew back her hood, and long white hair spilled out. "I'm sorry I interrupted your hunt, young man, I was just heading home, and the time got the best of me. Thank you ever so much for inviting me to share your fire."

"It's nothing," Charming said, "My brother . . ." he winked elaborately at Will, "*Van* Winkle and I . . ." he winked again, "*Rip* Winkle, are always ready to assist our fellow traveler."

Will's thoughts whirled about. He didn't mind Charming's making up names for them, although Rip and Van Winkle sounded ridiculous, but the apples bothered him. It was the wrong season, and they were too perfect. He remembered tales about witches and poison apples. If she was a witch, what better way than to kill naïve and unsuspecting travelers like Charming than with something as seemingly harmless as an apple?

"Wait," said Will.

Charming held the apple in front of his open mouth. He paused. "What is it, *Van*? If you want one, there are plenty, *Van*. I'm sure the good woman won't mind, *Van*."

"Not at all, not at all," she said with another cackle and, reaching into the bag with her bony white hand, she plucked a particularly juicy-looking one and handed it over to Will.

"No, that's not it, *Rip*. I was just wondering, whether they would be ripe this time of year?"

"Why not, *Van*?" asked Charming. "They look delicious."

"Oh, they are, *Rip*." The old woman smiled a crooked smile. "My pretties are so beautiful, but that dragon's ruined everything. No one guards the roads. No one goes to market. So I haul them there, and no one will buy, so I have to haul them all the way home again."

The woman *was* all alone. What woman of her age traveled at night and by herself? It seemed suspicious. Will grabbed Charming's arm to stop him taking a bite.

"What is it, *Van*? Do you need something? This isn't about going north again, is it?" Charming asked lightly but with a hint of irritation in his voice.

"Nothing like that, *Rip*," Will said with a forced laugh. "I was just going to ask our guest *where* she was heading, and whether she *normally* traveled *alone* at *night*."

Will tried to hint to Charming with his eyes that there was something amiss. Unfortunately, Charming thought Will was trying to tell him that he had some dirt on his doublet and began dusting himself off.

Under his breath, Charming said, "Thank you, Will. Well spotted."

Before he could stop him, Charming took a large bite of his apple. "Delicious, good woman. You must have a wonderful orchard."

The old woman cackled hideously and smiled her crooked smile, and said, "Thank you, young man. So polite."

Charming devoured the entire apple. Will held his breath, waiting for him to collapse or start acting strange, but nothing happened. The old woman and Charming chattered about apples and orchards, and Charming told a mad story about shooting an apple off the head of a childhood friend for a dare, and Will wondered if it was Daniel he was talking about, and if the mental scars from being a friend of Charming's growing up might explain his transformation later in life to the Scarlet Scoundrel. Will began to feel like a fool. His nerves had transformed a harmless old lady into a witch. He relaxed and took a bite of his own apple. It really was delicious.

After a time, the old lady pulled a jug out from one of her many bags, and asked, "Are you boys thirsty? I have some cider here." She took a drink.

Charming's eyes lit up. "I would love some cider. My brother here made me leave home without packing a flask. I've been drinking water for weeks now." He made a grimace as though this was a hardship beyond enduring and took a long drink.

"This is marvelous!" he said, and handed it to Will. "Try some, Your . . . *Van*."

The old woman was humming some song to herself in a creaking voice and did not seem to notice the slip.

Will took the jug and studied it suspiciously. It smelled like nothing more than cider, and the old woman had taken a drink also. He put it to his lips and took a sip. It was remarkable, clean, crisp, and sweet, with just a hint of a bite at the end. He took a longer drink and passed it back to the woman. She took a little sip and passed it back to Charming, who drank deeply.

Soon, the woman had enough. Will found that he and Charming were passing the jug back and forth and having a wonderful time. They told the old woman stories about their adventures, Gnarsh the troll, the Scoundrel, the Seven Players, the Bremen-four, and even going north. In no time, they were roaring with laughter.

"And then . . . and then, Will, here," slurred Charming, "he's sitting in the mud under the bridge remember, and . . ." he laughed and slapped his leg, "and the Scoundrel says, 'It's nothing personal, Your Majesty. It's . . . it's just business.'"

They both laughed, and the woman cackled, then Charming started snoring. Will looked down at the jug in his hands. He raised it to his lips, but only a drop came out. They'd drunk the whole thing. He tried to apologize to the old woman, but his tongue wasn't working properly, and he ended up just mumbling at her.

He looked about, smacking his lips. Sometime in the night, the fire had died low. Across the glowing embers, he saw the old woman sitting on her stone perch, staring at him with a greedy look. His eyes blurred, and he began to nod. He had a feeling he shouldn't fall asleep, but try as he might, the drink was pulling him under.

"Sleep well, Your Majesty," she said, and smiled her crooked smile.

Will wondered briefly how she knew he was the King, as they had been using fake names, but then sleep overtook him, and he began to snore.

Will woke with a blazing headache and the instant knowledge that they were in trouble. He was lying on hard planks, and the world seemed to be moving underneath him, rocking and pitching and jolting. He blinked his eyes open, and bright sunlight stabbed at him, causing intense pain to race about in his skull. He groaned.

There was a cackle of delight from somewhere ahead of him, and he heard the old woman say, "Boys, I think the King is awake. Keep an eye on him."

"Yes, Mother," two deep, drawling voices to his left and his right, said.

Will sat up and, squinting through the pain, looked around. Their campsite was gone. He and Charming, who was still snoring softly beside him, were lying in the back of a wagon. They'd been stripped to their underclothes and chains ran from around their ankles to large iron rings set into the wagon's planks. Perched high on the driver's seat sat the old woman, reins in her hands. Beside her were stacked bags of apples and a dozen or so jugs of cider, and all of Will and Charming's clothes and possessions.

Will groaned again at the memory of how much he'd drunk last night, and his stomach rolled queasily.

"Not feeling too good, Mr. Van Winkle? Or is it King William?" the old woman asked, and, turning about, fixed him with her crooked smile.

Two deep laughs from either side of him drew his attention to two enormous-looking men, probably a few years younger than he and Charming, who were riding alongside the wagon on Will's and Charming's horses.

He responded with a groan and closed his eyes again as though slipping back into sleep. Once his three jailers had lost interest in him, Will quietly tested his bonds and decided there was no hope of breaking free. The chain itself was well made, and whoever had attached them to the wagon had known what they were about. He looked around, trying to get his bearings, but all he could see was that they were traveling along a road under a partial canopy of trees. The sun kept flickering through the leaves. He got a sense that they were in the hills, but beyond that, they might have been anywhere.

"I demand to know where you are taking us," he said, trying to put as much kingliness into his voice as he could given that he was in his underwear.

"Oh?" the old woman said, turning again to look at him. "Did you hear that boys? His Majesty demands to know." They all laughed. "Demand all you want, but we're no longer your subjects. We answer to a higher power now."

She turned back to look at the road.

Will rubbed his temples. "Would you please, good lady, tell me where you are taking us?"

She shrugged and, not bothering to look at him this time, said, "No reason not to tell you, I suppose. We're taking you to Two Trees. Soon, you will be the guest of the Dracomancer. I'm sure he'll give you a proper Royal Reception." They laughed again.

"The Dracomancer?" Will asked confused. "Are you one of these . . . Dracolytes I've been hearing about?"

They began to laugh again. "No, my dear," the old woman said between cackles. "We aren't in the Dracomancer's army."

"If you don't believe in the Dracomancer, then why have you captured us?" Will asked angrily.

"Who said anything about believing or not believing," the old woman said, and fixed him with a knowing eye. "Castle White is a long way from here. In these parts, the Dracomancer is the power. If you want to get along, and we always want to get along, then you work for the Dracomancer, one way or the other. We may not want to go fight dragons for the man, but we do our bit."

"Yeah," said the man on his right. "We don't go in for the idea of throwing ourselves into a dragon's belly for the Dracomancer. Right, Ma?"

"That's right, my lovely boy," the woman said sweetly. "Dracolytes are true believers, and I say let them have their fun. It's no business of mine."

"So, if you aren't Dracolytes, what are you?" Will asked. "And what is your business with us?"

"So many questions," the old woman sighed. "I think I liked you better when you were sleeping." She cackled. "What was that funny saying your friend, Prince Charming, used last night?" She thought for a second. "Oh, yes, it's nothing personal, it's just business. We are recruiters. We go out and bring in 'willing' subjects and give them a chance to swear their allegiance to the Dracomancer."

"But I am the King," Will said angrily. "You know I won't bow down to this man."

She shrugged. "I still get my fee, but more's the pity for you if you refuse. More's the pity. But cheer up, dearie, we are almost there."

The canopy of trees fell away, and they entered an area of fields from which, perhaps a league or so away, they could see the town wall.

Will had never been to Two Trees though he'd heard enough about the place over the years. It had a notorious reputation as being Magdela's favorite target. The scars from those attacks could still be seen around him. The homes surrounding the town and the walls of the town itself had clearly suffered heavily. Every building, it seemed, had some damaged, burnt, and scorched sections of wood, partially collapsed walls, caved-in roofs. He found it odd that people were still living in these wrecks, but smoke curled from chimneys, children played in front yards, women hung laundry from lines. He studied the town more carefully.

Unlike most kings and nobles, Will had a practical eye, and though at first glance the houses and walls of the town appeared to be ruins, the appearance didn't bear up under closer inspection. It was true that blackened ruins of charred buildings stood all around, but these appeared to be facades. Behind them, or in some cases within them, stood newer structures that were perfectly intact. He began to believe that Two Trees' reputation for disaster was perhaps the result of civic planning.

This was only reinforced when signs began appearing at regular intervals, which read, "Suffered another Dragon attack. Have pity. Please donate. Gold preferred—Copper not accepted." Since becoming King, he'd been puzzling over the records coming from Two Trees. At one point, he calculated that the number of people reportedly killed by dragon attack in Two Trees was only slightly less than the number of all the people living in the entire rest of the kingdom combined, but he'd thought at the time that it must be an error in recordkeeping, a misplaced decimal point. Now he wasn't so sure.

Much as Prosper has made an industry of Magdela, they have made an industry of disaster. He sighed. "I never did understand how the people of Two Trees survived, or why, given the number of dragon attacks they've experienced over the years, they didn't abandon the place."

He decided if he ever got out of this and made it back to Castle White, he would have to revisit how much of the Royal Treasury was going to help with repairs to Two Trees every year.

As he was contemplating the problem, Charming groaned next to him, then in a sudden burst of movement, rose to his knees, which was as far as the slack in his chains would allow, and shouted, "Have at you, villain! I'll tear you apart!"

The wagon jolted to a stop, knocking Charming back to the floor. The men laughed deeply, and the woman cackled wickedly.

"Now both my pretties are awake, and just in time," she said.

The wagon had come to a stop at the wall to the

town. A great wooden gate stood closed in front of them. Emblazoned upon it was a picture of a dragon crossed out with a red "x," along with a picture of a crown, also crossed out in the same way. Up on the wooden gatehouse, a sentry held a bow with an arrow notched.

"Who goes there?" shouted the archer. "Who seeks permission to enter Two Trees?"

"New recruits for the Dracomancer," shouted the women in her crooked voice.

Charming smacked his lips, blinked his eyes, and looked blearily about. "What's going on, Will? Where are we? Where are my clothes? Why are we chained to a wagon? Why is that woman telling that man that we are volunteering to be Dracolytes?"

"We are being handed over to the Dracolytes as recruits, Two Trees, in the front of the wagon, and because she's a BLOODY MERCENARY WITH NO MORALS."

"Oh," Charming said with dawning comprehension. "One last question. Why have my silk underclothes been exchanged for these lady's things?"

The woman cackled in delight, and, cracking the reins across the back of the horses, they rolled through the gate into Two Trees.

In short order, Charming and Will found themselves locked in a muddy stockade formed of long poles set deep into the earth with about a dozen other men also in their underclothes, and at least one who had no underclothes at all. A handful of men in black robes were standing atop a wooden platform that rose above the stockade fence. They were picking through piles of clothing and boots and weapons that must have belonged to the men in the stockade. Will recognized his doublet and Charming's sword among the things.

Will had quickly decided that their best option for surviving this was to blend in, get recruited, then escape quickly. Unfortunately for Will, as Charming's faculties returned, his indignation at their situation grew more and more voluble.

"This is intolerable, Will," Charming said loudly. "I have made it a point to never put anything other than silk next to my skin, and now look at me. I suppose this is cotton, but it is so ill made and coarse that it might as well be burlap."

"Charming, be quiet," Will said. "We have bigger problems."

"Bigger problems? Bigger problems?" he shouted, then his voice lowered to a vicious hiss. "What about the chafing, Will? The Chafing!"

"Quiet down there!" one of the men in black robes said. He was wearing a tall cap with what looked like beady eyes and a long, forked tongue of red fabric sewn onto it. "Right you lot, line up and prepare to take your oath of loyalty and obedience to the Dracomancer."

They started to shuffle about aimlessly and formed a sort of ragged line through the middle of the stockade; only Charming stood off to one side. He kept arranging and rearranging the underclothes he was wearing and muttering darkly about numbness and pinching.

"You!" the dragon-capped Dracolyte shouted from atop the platform, pointing at Charming. "Get into line."

Charming looked up defiantly and shouted back, "I refuse to take any such oath, and he is the Ruler of Royaume, King William." Much to Will's dismay, he stuck out a hand and pointed at Will.

"Hah! Good try, but the recruiter put your names down as Rip and Van Winkle," the man shouted back, and wagged his head about so that the red-fabric tongue swung back and forth. "Furthermore, we do not recognize the King."

"Well, I don't recognize you either," Charming said, giving him a rude gesture. "In fact, I've never seen any of you in my life." Under his breath, he whispered to Will, "It's no wonder they don't recognize you, Will. Look at what you're wearing. I warned you over and over about the importance of being properly dressed, but you wouldn't listen. Now look where poor fashion judgment has landed us."

Will slapped a hand to his forehead. The man with the dragon cap said, "No, no, that's not what I meant. I don't mean we don't recognize that he is the King . . ."

Another black-cloaked man stepped forward, and said, "I saw the King once, and he doesn't look anything like him. The King is a giant, almost seven feet tall . . ."

"And he weighs twenty stone," added yet another.

"I saw him bench-press an ox once," a naked, cross-eyed man next to Will said.

"Wow!" Charming said in a low voice. "I have to say, I'm impressed, Will. Your public-relations staff is doing a great job. You've built quite a reputation."

"But, I didn't—" Will started to say.

"Quiet!" screamed the lead Dracolyte so violently that his dragon cap flopped off. He bent to retrieve it and, with great dignity, placed it back atop his head. "This is all entirely beside the point! We don't care if you are or aren't the King, we don't recognize the King's *authority*."

"Why don't you recognize the authority of the King?" demanded Will.

"Haven't you heard? The King abandoned us, so we've abandoned him," the Dracolyte said, and he visibly relaxed as though he was entering familiar conversational territory. "The Dracomancer has established a new kind of authority. We're a dracomocracy, and all of you"—he spread his arms wide—"are now part of it."

"What's a dracomocracy?" Will asked. "How does it work?"

"Simple," the man said with a smile. "We all have a say in everything that goes on now unless the Dracomancer tells us otherwise."

"How is that different from what you had except that you replaced me with the Dracomancer?" Will asked fiercely.

"Because we have a dracomocracy!" the Dracolyte said enthusiastically.

Charming had been deep in thought, now his head shot up, and he shouted, "Wait! Everyone has a say? Not just nobility? You don't rely on good breeding?"

"Nope," the Dracolyte said with another jubilant wag of his hat. "The Dracomancer teaches us to rely only on ourselves, or the Dracomancer, of course, or a council of his select Dracoviziers, or the Dracoassembly for internal matters and issues involving swine, unless there is a split between the Dracovizier Council and the Dracoassembly, in which case the Dracomancer or his Dragon Spirit may decide the matter without further consult to either body, or unless the court of Supreme Dracojudges, of which the Dracomancer is the Chief Justice, determines that a ruling by the Dracovizier Council or the Dracoassembly violates the Dragon Spirit Code, which was laid down in a series of documents that includes the Declaration of Draco Independence, the Articles of the Draco Confederation, and the Magna Draco"— he took a deep breath—"to decide the course of our destinies!"

There was a confused and halfhearted cheer from the men in the stockade.

"I am the King!" shouted Will. "This is rebellion."

"And unnatural besides!" Charming added. "You're telling me that everyone gets the *same* say, regardless of their status?"

The Dracolyte nodded.

"Title?"

He nodded again.

"Poetic talent or general eloquence?"

He nodded yet again.

"Fashion sense, how he sits on a horse, how well turned his calf is?"

The Dracolyte nodded and nodded until the tongue on his dragon hat was swinging wildly about like a pendulum.

Charming put his arm around the naked man. "You are telling me that this man"—the cross-eyed man tried to look at him, but his eyes wouldn't cooperate—"would have the same say as me?"

The Dracolyte spread his arms to the gathered men. "All men are equal in the Dracomancer's eyes, except the Dracomancer, of course, who is exalted above all others."

All the Dracolytes shouted, almost in unison, "HAIL THE DRACOMANCER!"

"Madness!" Charming hissed, wiping the hand he'd been touching the naked man with off on Will's underclothes. "This isn't a dracomocracy, it's a dracomockery. We've got to put a stop to this. If peasants start making decisions . . ."

Will glared at him. "Until recently, *I* was a peasant, Charming."

Charming cleared his throat. "Of course, I didn't mean you, Will, you are both King *and my* brother-in-law. I mean . . ."

"Never mind," Will whispered. "I agree we have to put a stop to this, and I think I have a plan."

"Is it violent and dangerous, and will it allow me to thrash those pompous Dracolytes?"

"No."

"Oh well," Charming said. "It may work anyway. What do I do?"

"For now, be quiet and let *me* do the talking," Will said emphatically.

"Not the best start to a plan I've ever heard . . ."

Will hushed him. The Dracolytes were calling men forward to be sworn into the service of the Dracomancer. The first man was holding his left hand on top of his head as though smoothing down his hair.

"Repeat after me," the Dracolyte was saying. "I, state your name, do solemnly and on pain of my soul being ripped from this mortal coil by the Spirits of the Dragons of Nether, do . . ."

"STOP!" Will shouted, stepping in front of the man.

The man behind him repeated the partial oath adding at the end, "STOP!"

The Dracolyte looked at him with disgust. "Now, I'm going to have to start all over. What do you want this time?"

"I demand a judgment by the Dracomancer," Will cried.

There was a shocked hush at this, but the head Dracolyte smirked down at him. "Too bad! The Dracomancer and all his Dracoviziers are gone."

"Where?" Will asked, honestly interested in the answer.

"None of your business," said the Dracolyte, but the

fellow on his left said, "He's gone down to Prosper to fight the dragon, of course."

The head Dracolyte fixed an angry gaze at his companion.

"What? Everyone knows that."

Will pursed his lips for a moment in thought, then his mouth turned up with a cunning smile. "Very well, then I want to take a vote on whether or not to release the prisoners," Will demanded.

"But you're a prisoner."

"So?"

"You have no right to call a vote," the Dracolyte said, shaking his hat emphatically.

"But you just said that, by the Dracomancer's own decree, 'everyone gets a say in the course of their own destiny,'" Will pointed out, and turned to the other prisoners. "Were you lying to these good people, or do you question the commandments of the Dracomancer himself?"

There was a ripple of murmured protest both from the prisoners and from the other Dracolytes.

The capped Dracolyte licked his lips nervously. "That isn't the way it works. You have to be a Dracolyte before you can vote. None of you are Dracolytes yet."

Will clasped Charming by the shoulder. "You told my friend here that everyone had the same say, no matter what . . ."

"Which is sheer madness—" Charming started to say, but Will covered Charming's mouth with his hand to silence him.

Will cleared his throat. "Do you deny your own words? Do you take us for fools?" He wrapped his other arm around the naked man, whose crossed eyes were either staring at Will or at a goat tied up on the other side of the square.

"Prisoners don't get a vote, and that's final!" the Dracolyte said in exasperation.

Will turned about to take in the prisoners. "Is this a dracomocracy or is it a dractatorship?"

The head Dracolyte looked lost for how to respond. He readjusted his hat a few times and flipped through the list in his hands.

"Down with the Dractator!" Will shouted, raising a fist to the sky.

"Yeah," said one of the other Dracolytes. "What gives you the right to tell me what I can or can't vote on?"

"We want a vote! We want a vote!" Will started chanting.

Soon, everyone was chanting along with him, prisoners and guards alike.

"Fine!" shouted the head Dracolyte, who had begun sweating profusely, and whose dragon cap had slipped partially over his eyes. "You can have your vote."

"All in favor of keeping the prisoners as prisoners," the Dracolyte said in a monotone.

Five of the six Dracolytes on the platform raised their hands. The head Dracolyte stared hard at the sixth, and he slowly joined them.

"All in favor of releasing the prisoners?" Will

shouted. All the prisoners except the naked man raised their hands. Will stared at the naked man, who either returned his stare or was intently watching a washer-woman carrying a bucket of water from the well.

"I don't believe in voting," the man said. "It never really changes anything anyway."

Will groaned in disgust, but then said triumphantly, "It doesn't matter. Releasing the prisoners carries the day twelve to six! Huzzah for dracomocracy!"

"Huzzah!" cried the prisoners.

"Release them," the head Dracolyte said, taking off his cap and throwing his list to the ground.

After getting dressed in their old clothes, all except Charming's underclothes, which the woman had taken with her when she left, Charming and Will reclaimed their horses and led them back out of the town gate. From atop the wall, the head Dracolyte guard with the bizarre dragon cap shouted down, "You're fools to leave the protection of the Dracomancer. It's a harsh world, and only the strong will survive. All of our values are gone. Soon, people will be looting homes for food. We won't all make it. It's safer in a community than trying to make it alone on the road."

Will stopped and turned to the Dracolytes lining the wall. "I've traveled nearly the length and breadth of Royaume . . ."

"Except for the north," Charming said under his breath.

Will glared at him, then, turning his gaze back to the Dracolytes assembled on the wall, he continued.

"It isn't that bad out there. Royaume is still the same kingdom it was. Its people are still a good people. For the love of light, it's only been a week or so."

The Dracolyte was silent a moment, then blurted, "Of . . . of course you'd say that, you're the King."

Will threw up his hands in disgust. "Let's get out of this place, Charming. It looks like I not only have a dragon to slay but a kingdom to save as well. It's time to get to Prosper and have it out with this Dracomancer once and for all."

"I'm with you," Charming said grimly. "I mean, the idea of *everyone's* getting a say." He shivered. "Dracomockery! It sounds like the dracopocalypse."

Behind them, the man shouted from the top of the wall, "Those who are prepared will survive. Those who are not will be devoured like pigs. So says the Dracomancer!"

They made no response but, spurring their horses to a gallop, made their way out of the hills toward the River Running and the bridge to Prosper.

CHAPTER 11

SHADOWS OF THE PAST

The Pickett farm, as it was still known by the townsfolk of Prosper, lay a few miles outside the village down a country lane on a gently sloping piece of land between the River Running and the edge of the Dark Wood. It was a beautiful spot, but it was also widely known to be cursed. In the Pickett barn, Lord Pickett had begun his doomed attempt to breed golden-egg-laying geese. In the Pickett field, the dread Wyrm of the South had died, and her body was buried. And, in the Pickett home the outcast witch, Gwendolyn Mostfair, lived with her fiancé and former amphibian, Montague, or Monty to his friends. It wasn't that people weren't thrilled that such a famous couple lived right in their midst, and it wasn't that Gwendolyn didn't draw a crowd, mostly admiring men, every time she went into market; rather, it was that people were happier having them living "out there" and not "right here."

One person who was particularly pleased that Gwendolyn lived just outside of Prosper, in fact one person who had marched an entire army south to Prosper at least partially so he could see Gwendolyn, was the Dracomancer. He had been a young man of twenty when Gwendolyn Mostfair had stolen his heart. From the moment he saw her, he had been lost, and almost everything he'd done from then to now was directly or indirectly aimed at making himself worthy of her. Now was his time. He was the Dracomancer, more powerful than a king, more beloved and respected than Prince Charming had ever been, and more dreadful even than the dragon. She would love him. It was his destiny.

He had been repeating this mantra to himself for about a couple of weeks now, ever since he learned that the new dragon was none other than Volthraxus. He knew all about Volthraxus. He had even spoken to Volthraxus many years ago when he'd been in the north. He knew that if he played his cards right, he could get the beast to leave without risking a hair of his own head. Then he could claim the mantle that should have been his years ago: "hero and savior."

"And, if things go as I plan, I'll also be King," he said to himself as he rode into the muddy yard of the Pickett farm, scattering chickens.

"I am sorry, what was that, Dracomancer?" one of his Dracoviziers asked.

"Nothing, nothing," he said as he dismounted. "Wait here and make sure we are not interrupted."

They all saluted, one by pounding his fist across his chest, one by slapping his palm facedown across his forehead, and the last by making a strange, fluttering motion, almost like a bird, with his outstretched hands. The Dracomancer grimaced and reminded himself AGAIN that he needed to deal with the whole salute issue.

"If they would just settle on one," he grumbled as he stalked to the little green door of the farmhouse. He adjusted the hood of his cloak, ran a hand through his thin, graying hair and a finger across his thick, bushy eyebrows. He knocked, and seeing the budding roses in the trellises surrounding him, he plucked one, pricking his finger in the process.

He was still cursing and sucking on his thumb when Gwendolyn opened the door.

"Gwendolyn," he said in hushed awe.

"Who . . . Delbert?" Her face went white. "I . . . I mean, DRACOMANCER!"

"It is a pleasure to see you, Gwendolyn." He thrust the rose toward her with a shaking hand.

She ignored the rose. "What . . . what are you doing here?" And then, seeming to remember who he was, shouted, "DRACOMANCER!"

"Please, Gwendolyn, there is no need for titles between us."

"R . . . right, Delbert. I'm just, I'm just surprised to see you . . . HERE."

"May I come in?" He once again thrust the thorny rose at her.

"In?" She carefully took the rose from him. "YOU WANT TO COME IN?" she repeated in a passion of disbelief.

"Yes, dear Gwendolyn, I have much I want to discuss with you, and my time may be rather limited."

He tried to affect a tragic air, but it might not have been entirely effective, as she asked, "Are you ill? Do you have a stomachache? Do you need the privy?"

"No, no, but it would be better not to discuss it here in the open," he said, trying his mysterious mystic face.

There was a noise from within the house, like a door's closing.

"Are you alone?" he asked, trying to peer around her, but she had taken a stance directly in the doorway so that he couldn't see past her.

"I am quite alone. It . . . it must be the cat."

"What about your . . . fiancé?" he asked, unable to keep the disdain from his voice.

"Oh, him?" she said, and sounded surprised that she even had a fiancé, which the Dracomancer took as a very good sign. "He is, um, in town?"

She twirled the rose between her fingers. He shuffled his feet at the doorstep and coughed. Neither one seemed to know what to say.

"So, can I come in?" he asked again.

"Oh, yes, sorry," she said, and added in that loud voice she seemed to adopt now and then, "COME IN, DRACOMANCER."

She led him through the door into a long hallway of cracked plaster painted in a pleasant, if weather-beaten, yellow. Doors opened at irregular intervals on the left and right, and a twisting, somewhat lopsided, wooden stair led to a second floor. Gwendolyn ushered him through the first door they came to, and he found himself in a worn little sitting room that had walls the color of faded roses. Tea for two had been set between two ancient and threadbare love seats, which sat before a grate in which a cheerful fire crackled and popped.

The Dracomancer stared down at the tea service, and said, "I thought you were alone."

"OH!" she said in surprise, a little color coming into her cheeks, "I am. I . . . I mean I thought Monty . . . er . . . Montague might be home by now, but he seems to be running late."

He found the mention of her fiancé's name irritating, and so grunted, "How very inconsiderate of him."

"He is very busy running the farm," she said, and gestured to a seat. "Please sit down, and . . . and I'll pour you some tea."

He looked dubiously at the worn settee and settled himself on the edge of the seat. As she served the tea, the firelight caressed her body, turning the golden locks of her hair into living flame and bathing her profile in a dancing radiance. He traced the light as it flickered along the nape of her neck and down the elegant curve of her arms to her delicate hands, which were shaking as she poured the tea from a much-abused tin pot into a mismatched set of old china cups.

"Would you like sugar and cream?" she asked.

"Yes, four spoons of each."

She opened the little sugar jar and peered inside. "I'm sorry. I have only a couple of spoons of sugar left."

"Fine," he said. "I'll take whatever you have."

She sighed and tipped the contents of the sugar bowl into his cup and added four spoons of a thick cream.

"I make the cream myself," she said proudly. "It turns out it isn't that hard. It only takes a bit of effort."

Something about this comment irked him. His memory of her was of a refined, courtly princess, and while she still had some of the grace that had made her such a famous and desirable courtesan, living on this farm had clearly taken its toll. Her cheeks were no longer as pale as china but were sun-kissed, and here and there a freckle showed. Her hands, while still delicately boned, were rough around the edges, and she had been forced to trim her nails quite short. As for her dress, in her youth, Gwendolyn would not have allowed even one of her servants to wear something so plain. It made him angry to see her humbled so, and it made him feel even more certain that she would swoon when he offered to save her from this hell. Now was his chance.

In a sudden movement, he grasped her hand. The clay pitcher she'd been using to pour the cream slipped and tumbled to the plank floor with a clatter.

"Oh!" she cried, and moved to pick it up.

He held her firmly in his grasp. "Leave it."

"But the cream," she said, as the thick white liquid continued to spill out onto the floor.

"It doesn't matter, Gwendolyn. None of this matters." He gestured with disgust at the little room and the broken-down furniture and the ragged tea set.

"It matters to me, Delbert," she said, and, prying her hand from his, picked up the pitcher and placed it very deliberately back on the tray. She sat back in her chair and crossed her arms.

Reminding her of her low condition was clearly upsetting her. It was harsh, but he had to make her understand that her beauty and desirability were being squandered here.

He adopted a lecturing tone. "Of course it matters, but it matters only because you have been brought low by that wretch of a king, William, and his equally devious sister. They have stolen your title and convinced you that *this* is what you deserve. Don't you see? They have debased you and humiliated you, but that is over now. I have come to place you, once and for all, where you belong, on the throne as queen."

"What are you talking about, Delbert?" she said. "King William has already announced that he will take Lady Rapunzel as his wife and queen."

"But you forget about the dragon, Gwendolyn."

"The dragon changes nothing for me," Gwendolyn replied, perhaps with a hint of bitterness.

"You're wrong, Gwendolyn. The dragon changes everything."

She shook her head. "No, Delbert, even if the dragon kills Lady Rapunzel, I am the last woman in the kingdom that King William would marry."

"You assume that William Pickett will still be king," he said with the confidence of a gambler who had just thrown his trump card.

"What do you mean?" she said angrily. "Do you mean that the dragon might kill King William? Even if that were to happen, either Rupert or Edward Charming will take the throne, and the chances of my becoming queen go from fleeting to nonexistent."

"Pah!" the Dracomancer said with disgust. "The Picketts and the Charmings, they are the past. I am talking about the future." He stood and struck a dramatic pose in front of the fire. "I am talking about you becoming the Dracoking's bride and queen."

"You?" she said, and on her face was a look of utter confusion.

"Don't you see, with the coming of the dragon, and the King's flight from Castle White, the people have no one to turn to but me. I have become the true power in Royaume. With my Dracolyte army, I can march from here and take Castle White in a matter of days, and that is just what I intend to do."

Her face was an emotionless mask. He knew that she must be overwhelmed by what she knew was coming and fearful to show her true feelings. The Dracomancer decided that one more flourish of gallantry would tip her, forever, into his arms.

He came to her side and dropped to one knee. He extended one hand to his breast and swept the other wide. "Come with me, Princess Gwendolyn, and I will make you the woman . . . the queen that you were always meant to be. Come with me, and I will give you the life that you deserve."

Her eyes were wide. She was pale with stunned shock, then as he watched, her face underwent a transformation, and her teeth drew back into something like a snarl. He rose and retreated.

"You . . . you . . . you dare!" she spit, barely able to form the words. "You, who are the author of EVERYTHING that happened to my sister, to me, to this kingdom . . . How could you think that you could come here and expect me to . . . to . . ." She lost her ability to speak but stood and advanced threateningly toward him.

He fell back and found himself pinned against the settee. "I did it all for you. I am offering you everything that you wanted. I only wanted to give you what you deserved."

She raised back her palm to strike him, and he held up his hands to ward off the coming blow, but it never fell. Instead, she threw her arms around her body, and turning her back on him, she began rocking herself to and fro in front of the fire.

"I know you did, Delbert," she said, in a voice hoarse with emotion. "But I did not know what I was asking for."

The Dracomancer licked his lips nervously and cast his eyes about the room as though looking for an escape. How could he have known that she would maintain such an unreasoning grudge for so long?

"I never knew what would happen. If I had—"

She spun and pointed a shaking finger at him. "You knew what the fairy was like, and still you led me to her!" she spit, the anger momentarily giving her voice the force it had lost. "You gave me the spells. You taught me the words to speak. I was an innocent. You knew, and still you . . ." Suddenly, her eyes were filled with tears. "How could you let me do it? I was so young . . . just a girl."

He stood silently, letting the question hang unanswered in the air. *I was such an insipid, pathetic little fool playing with magic,* he excoriated himself silently

Gwendolyn said softly, "You said that you loved me."

And the memories of those days returned to him like a slap. He saw himself at the balls and the fetes, where she and her sister had been the center of the world, and he had been left to skulk about the edges of the crowd like a shadow. She had been so beautiful, and he had been a second-rate sorcerer's apprentice. He would have told her anything, given her anything for a moment's attention. A wave of shame passed through him as he remembered the fawning, grasping, spotty young man he had been, and at how she had dangled him on the end of her little finger.

Anger flared through him. *How dare she judge me! I am the Dracomancer, and she is nothing now. She should be kissing my feet and begging me to return. I will not grovel to a fallen woman. I will not abase myself to a farmer's wife.*

Shielded by his armor of self-righteous anger, he drew himself up, and the cold smirk returned to his face. "Just a girl? Just a girl?" he mocked in a singsong voice. "What a conveniently selective memory you have. Don't you remember who you were and who I was? You were Princess Gwendolyn Mostfair, and I was nothing to you, and yet you dare talk to ME of LOVE?"

He laughed aloud at this.

"You never even *thought* of me," he hissed viciously. "I was just some peon, and you used me, just like you tried to use the fairy. The difference was that in the fairy you met someone even more cruel and unfeeling than yourself. You may believe that I am to blame for your fall, but it was your own stupidity that let the fairy trap you. You may have convinced yourself that you were an innocent, but the wishes that cursed your sister to death came from your own poisonous heart."

He straightened his black robes and stomped toward the door, treading the cream into the floor as he went. At the hall, he turned back and looked down his crooked nose at her, and the bile from long-remembered slights and long-smoldering resentments spilled out.

"I see that you are incapable and undeserving of my attentions. You are where you should be, scrabbling in the dirt like the peasant hag that you are. Enjoy what remains of your life, Gwendolyn Mostfair. I wish you all the misery that you deserve."

An echo of his former longing rose in his breast, but he suppressed it ruthlessly, threw open the door, and stalked away into the night, slamming the cottage door behind him so hard that it rattled the teacups in their chipped saucers.

As soon as he was gone, Gwendolyn fell to her knees sobbing, as a mix of emotions overwhelmed her. There was a rush of feet, and Monty and Elizabeth Pickett were beside her. Monty dropped to the ground and threw his arms about her, pulling her to him.

"Are you alright, my darling?" Monty asked.

Liz watched as Gwen nodded between sobs.

Monty's jaw clenched and unclenched with anger as he held Gwendolyn close. "I shouldn't have let the swine speak to you like that. I should give him the thrashing he deserves."

His face was so tense and his eyes so dark with anger that Liz thought he would have done just that had Gwendolyn not held on to him so that he could not rise.

"Stop, Monty," she said firmly, and pulled away from him enough so that she could lock her eyes on his. "I will be fine, but I need you to be calm because I am not. Do you understand?"

"Yes, darling," he said softly. "I am sorry. It was harder than I knew to listen to those vile things."

They stared into each other's eyes for several moments, and the look that passed between them was so personal and private that Liz felt it would be the worst sort of violation to remain. Coming here had been a mistake. Quietly, she began to withdraw.

Gwendolyn stopped her with an outstretched hand. "Lady Elizabeth, please don't leave. We need to talk."

Gathering herself, she stood and went to a divan

to sit. Liz crossed the room and took the settee opposite her. Gwendolyn clutched Monty's hand in hers. Liz could see the white marks that her nails were leaving on the back of his hand, but Monty said nothing, nor made any move to pull away. He was entirely fixated on her, his face lined with deepest concern.

They remained frozen in this tableau until finally Liz could stand the silence no longer. "You have done a marvelous job fixing up the place. I love the rose trellises."

"What?" Gwendolyn said as if she had just woken.

More brightly, Monty said, "That ill-tempered man interrupted your tea, ladies. Let me freshen it."

He gathered the remnants of the tea and left.

The two women sat staring at their hands and saying nothing for a time. Finally, Liz took a deep breath. "Thank you for hiding me, Lady Mostfair. I have only just escaped from the Dracomancer, and when I heard you call out that he was at the door, I thought I was done for. I can't tell you how much I owe you and Monsieur Montague for taking me in."

"Lady Elizabeth, please call me Gwen. I have been trying to leave my old titles where they belong, in the past. As for taking you in, this is still your family's estate. Monty and I owe you and King William everything. We have a home, food, and an occupation because of your generosity."

"Thank you, Gwen, and please return the favor by calling me Liz. I find it difficult to wear a title in this place. And, thank you for your welcome, but this is your home now. My brother and I agreed, and I am glad it is being put to good use. And what you did today goes far beyond any thanks you owe us. If the Dracomancer were to return or find me here, my presence would put you and Monsieur Montague in terrible danger."

"It's Monty to you, Lady Elizabeth, and you are welcome any time, Dracomancer or no Dracomancer," Monty said from the door, a tea tray laden with steaming pots and new cups and jars of jam and fresh scones in his hands.

"And, don't worry about us, Liz," Gwen said as she arranged the cups in front of her. "Delbert was quite honest when he wished me every misery I deserved, but he won't harm me." She gestured around the little room with a weathered teacup. "I am quite certain that he believes that leaving me here is the greatest punishment he could possibly mete out. I am content that he believes that."

Gwen and Liz engaged in the wonderfully familiar ritual of pouring and spooning and stirring until they were both settled with a scone and a cup of tea. Monty withdrew again with a smile, and said from the door, "I will be across the way if you need anything."

"He is wonderfully attentive," Liz said, taking a large bite of her scone. "I wish that Edward could learn to be as thoughtful."

"Yes, *I* am very lucky," Gwen said with a smile that did not reach her eyes.

Liz wasn't sure but felt that there was something in the other woman's answer—something bitter. Liz thought she understood and nodded her assent as she took another bite of her scone. "I am sorry if my being here has brought the past back to haunt you."

Gwen laughed, and this time, the bitterness was obvious. "After everything I did to your brother, to Prince Charming, to Rupert, but especially to you, I wouldn't have thought that you would ever be sorry for anything that's happened to me. I could have killed you and nearly killed your love. I'm not sure that if our positions had been reversed, I would have allowed you any kindness at all."

They were the very thoughts and feelings Liz felt herself struggling with. She wanted to hate Gwen, but seeing her now and sharing tea with her, she was finding it hard to do. Not knowing how to respond, she took another bite of the scone to fill the silence and was surprised to realize she had finished it. Suddenly, she was famished. She picked up another one and spread cream and butter and jam on it.

They sat in silence for a time, Liz eating and Gwendolyn staring at nothing, then one of the candles sputtered, causing shadows to move around the room. Gwen's eyes went wide, and she pulled her knees up to her chest.

Liz could see that Gwen was struggling. The Dracomancer and she herself had reawakened memories in the woman that would have been better left buried. Though Liz had no love for her, she would not wish Gwen's suffering on anyone. She needed to bring this visit to a close, so they could both go back to forgetting the past.

"Gwen," she said, putting her now-empty teacup and crumb-filled plate back down on the tray. "Soon, the Dracomancer will discover I'm missing. My companion, Tomas, will be captured, and I have made him promise that he will not play the hero, but will tell the Dracomancer everything he knows. I don't know if he will keep that promise, but I must assume that the Dracomancer will know that I have gone, and perhaps he will guess where I have gone."

"I don't have a horse, if that's what you want. We have a mule and two milk cows, but they won't get you very far."

Liz smiled at the woman's joke. It was a shame that they'd had such a troubled past because she thought she might be able to be friends with this version of Gwen. She cleared her throat. "I don't need a horse, but thanks. I need information."

"What sort of information?" Gwen said, raising her head but very carefully averting her gaze from a little patch of shadow that clung to the far edge of the room.

"Lady Rapunzel has been captured by this new dragon and has been brought to the same tower where you were held prisoner. We think the dragon has come to revenge himself on Will for having slain, or at least having claimed to have slain, the Wyrm of the South. Now, the Dracomancer has raised an army that is sweeping across the countryside. I need to know what we, and I guess I mean myself, Charming, and Will, assuming I ever see them again, can do to kill the dragon, and anything you can tell me about the

Dracomancer and his powers that might allow us to beat back his growing influence."

Gwen frowned, then said, "You know I'm not a real witch? I have no power. The dragon—Magdela—taught me a couple of tricks to control fairies because she really, really hated that fairy. Other than that, I know very little."

"Please, Gwen, anything might help." Liz clasped her hands in a sort of supplication.

Gwen pursed her lips in thought. "Let's start with the Dracomancer. To start with, stop calling him the bloody Dracomancer. His name is Delbert. When I was eighteen, he was the court sorcerer's second apprentice. He has no more power, and probably a great deal less, than his mentor had, and that old man was a terrible bungler known mostly for his ability to make coins appear out of the oddest places. This might have been great fun at parties and balls but rather impractical."

Gwen leaned forward and picked up her scone with her long, delicate fingers. "Delbert's greatest single act as a sorcerer was in teaching me to summon a fairy. We all know the result of that. I ended up killing my sister and destroying any chance of happiness for myself or King Rupert, oh, and I also managed to bring a rampaging dragon down on the kingdom and get myself imprisoned for several decades."

She elegantly bit off a corner of the pastry and put the remains back on the plate in front of her.

"So he has no real power?" Liz asked, eyeing Gwendolyn's half-eaten scone hungrily.

"Depends on what you mean by real power," Gwen replied. "He can't do real magic, but he has always been a crafty court operative. I held him in the same regard as I might a trained weasel. However, he was still the one that I went to when I wanted to win Rupert's heart"—she sighed—"and his ambition has only grown. After my kidnapping, he wrote the prophecy that guided the kingdom for most of your life. If it weren't for Will's pitchfork, he'd probably still have his own tower in Castle White. And right now, he has a rather large and loyal army."

"Yes, an army at his back and a hand puppet in his cloak," Liz snorted. "The man is ridiculous."

A suddenly serious Gwendolyn fixed her eyes on Liz's. "It would be dangerous to underestimate him, Liz. He may not be able to cast spells, and he is certainly foolish, but he is ruthless. There is a reason a *second* apprentice and not the *first* inherited the title of court sorcerer. Besides, I wouldn't be surprised if he's a little unbalanced at this point. For all those years that his prophecy held, he was on top of the world, then from one day to the next, he was a pariah. If you think I have had it tough with my exile, try being the magician that misread the tea leaves on the most important and well-publicized prophecy in the history of the kingdom."

She looked about as though someone might be listening and, dropping her voice, leaned in, which Liz reflected was probably a force of habit from her days in the court. "I heard he was reduced to tavern shows and children's birthday parties."

"Alright, so he's dangerous, foolish, and mad. What would you advise we do?" Liz asked.

"Kill the dragon."

Liz rolled her eyes in exasperation. "Okay, yes, but—"

"No buts, Liz," she said, and her blue eyes became hard as ice. "The 'Dracomancer' derives his power from the fear of the dragon. As long as the dragon remains, more and more people will flock to him, but remove the dragon, and there is only Delbert. People will follow the Dracomancer. No one will follow Delbert. However, if Delbert kills the dragon, then he will always be the Dracomancer, and you will never defeat him."

"So, how can we get rid of the dragon?" Liz said in exasperation, and putting propriety aside, picked up the remains of Gwendolyn's scone. "There must be something that could help us fight the beast. Did the old dragon—?"

Gwen cut her off, then, speaking in a sudden heated flurry of words, said, "It is true that Magdela told me lots of things. I wasn't truly awake, more like half-asleep, but whenever I managed to stir, she talked to me. I believe she was incredibly bored. She told me when Rupert remarried. She announced the death of my parents and the birth of Prince Charming. She talked a lot about births and deaths as the years passed by, and she absolutely reveled in telling me of Delbert's prophecy and in how dashing and handsome Charming was becoming. Gossiping to me gave her something to do. I don't think she meant to be cruel, but the effect was the same."

Gwen rested her head on her knees and let out a long, ragged breath.

"I . . . I'm sorry, Gwen," Liz said, losing her appetite at the sudden awareness of how much it must be costing the woman to talk about her past.

"It's okay. I know the dragon that your brother and Edward have gone to fight. Apart from her diatribes against the fairy and her discussions of human affairs, Volthraxus was Magdela's favorite topic."

"What did she say about him?"

"Magdela told me that she left the North because she felt she had fallen into *his* shadow and wanted to prove herself worthy of his attention. She thought that he had never come to court her because he found her unworthy to be his mate. She said that she might spend a lifetime burning villages and devouring towns and still never match the casual destruction he could cause. He is living death, Liz. I'm sorry."

"Is there no weapon? No spell? Nothing?" Liz begged.

"No—" Gwen started to say, but just then a log popped in the grate, sending a shower of sparks exploding against the screen. Gwen turned her head sharply at the sound and her eyes seemed to widen in surprise as she stared at the glowing coals.

"You've thought of something," Liz said, a new hope suddenly blooming in her empty breast.

"Possibly . . ." she whispered, but would say no

more. "Whatever happened to the pitchfork? You know, the one that Magdela impaled herself on? What happened to it?"

"The Dracomancer, I mean, Delbert, asked me the same thing. I can't remember, but why does it matter?" Liz asked.

"Because it's been bathed in the blood of a dragon, Liz," she said half rising in her seat, the volume of her voice rising with her. "I remember, in the early years, Magdela chuckling about the knights and soldiers the king would send to fight her and how it was all so futile. Humans don't have the strength to pierce a dragon's scales with ordinary steel. How, for a man to kill a dragon, he needed a weapon bathed in the blood of a dragon but there weren't any. That was the irony. How could a weapon be bathed in the blood of a dragon if it couldn't pierce the hide of the dragon in the first place? I doubt she ever thought about the possibility of a dragon stabbing itself with one. She landed on it with her full force. Her might was strong enough to force it through her scales."

She snapped her fingers at Liz. "Try to remember, Liz, what happened to the pitchfork? Did it survive?"

"Yes. I remember sticking it in the wagon when Will went up to the tower to get you, but I don't remember seeing it again." She covered her mouth with her hand as her heart sunk. "Oh no! He left it in the tower. I asked him about it, and he told me that he couldn't carry you and the pitchfork, so he left it."

Gwen fell back into her chair. "The only weapon in

the world capable of killing the dragon is sitting in the only place in the world we can't go."

Liz sat silently. To her surprise, Gwen came and sat next to her and grasped her hand gently. They said nothing for a time, then Liz whispered, "They won't stop, Will and Charming. Even if I tell them it's impossible, neither will turn aside. Will would never abandon Elle to the dragon, and Edward would never abandon Will to face the dragon alone. I . . . I will lose them both."

Though she fought them, the tears came anyway, and she found herself being embraced by Gwendolyn. "I'm sorry, Liz. This is the unfairness of being a woman. Men are allowed to march to their doom and fight against it till the end, but we are expected to yield, to sit and accept the inevitable quietly. The only comfort we are permitted is our sorrow."

Something in what she said struck a spark of anger in Liz's breast, and that spark kindled a flame that burst into a conflagration. She pulled herself out of Gwendolyn's comforting arms and stood. "That might be what we are told to do, but that is not our destiny. You proved that. I can and I will do something."

Liz stood and walked out into the hallway, Gwen following just behind. Liz opened the door and looked outside. "Gwen, thank you again for your kindness. I know that it came with a cost."

Monty came out and, nodding his goodbye, wrapped his arms around Gwen and led her back into the sitting room. Liz closed the door and stepped out into the moonlit night. She looked back toward where Prosper lay and wondered if Tomas was safe. The guilt at leaving him behind hung heavy on her heart, but she knew that to try and save him would mean dooming everyone she loved. For a moment she froze, unable to take the first step on what would likely be her last adventure.

"What was it Will said to me," she asked herself. "'Long goodbyes make for long journeys.'"

After leading her horse out of the barn where she'd hidden it, she mounted and rode toward the dark horizon to the south, where the woods and the high, cruel mountains waited.

CHAPTER 12

A BARGAIN WITH THE DEVIL

The Dracomancer was lost in dark thoughts as he rode back to Prosper flanked by his Dracovizier honor guard. Everything he had said to Gwendolyn was justified. She was not the princess she had once been but had fallen and been brought low by her own hand. Yet he still felt hollow inside. He had not wanted to hurt her. He had come to give her a chance to regain the life she had before, to reclaim her standing and position in good society, but she had rejected him. She had made him say those things.

"Why does she have to be so beastly stubborn?" he hissed between clenched teeth. "She should be taught a lesson for her insolence."

"Do you require something, Dread Dracomancer?" the Dracovizier on his right asked.

With a start, he remembered the men around him. "Yes!" he shouted. "The witch, Gwendolyn, must be arrested. She . . . she is too dangerous to remain free. She spent years with Magdela, the Great Wyrm of the South. Indisputably, she is under draconic enchantment and, therefore, guilty of draconic conspiracy. Go back and take her into custody. Her fiancé as well since he's allowed this to happen under their roof."

"At once, Dread Dracomancer." The Dracovizier placed a palm on his forehead and bowed.

"What was that? What are you doing?" the Dracomancer asked.

"That is the dracosalute, Dread Dracomancer," the man said significantly.

"No, it isn't," the Dracovizier on his left said sternly. "The dracosalute is a hand across the body like this." He demonstrated by slapping his arm across his chest with a thump.

"That isn't it either," said a Dracovizier behind them. He rode forward and demonstrated a gesture that required him to drop his reins and flap his hands like a bird.

"What kind of salute is that?" asked the first man. "It looks ridiculous."

"It is not. It is meant to represent a dragon in flight."

They began to argue, and the Dracomancer felt his head throb.

"ALL OF YOU, BE QUIET!" he shouted, and the men fell immediately into silence, each giving him an exaggerated version of their particular salute. The

Dracomancer looked up and issued a silent oath to the skies. He never knew having followers would be so irritating.

"I wish to be alone," the Dracomancer said. "Go back and arrest Gwendolyn. Once that is done, ride ahead and prepare the army for a march. We leave for Dragon Tower in the morning."

I will show Gwendolyn what I am capable of, he thought. *When she sees my army on the march . . .*

"But, we cannot leave you unguarded, Dread Dracomancer," one of the Dracoviziers protested, interrupting his train of thought. "What if—"

"What?" the Dracomancer asked irritably. "I am the Dracomancer. Do you believe me incapable of defending myself from peasants and farmers? Leave me now, all of you, or you shall feel the wrath of the Dragon Spirit."

The men gave their disparate salutes and, spurring their horses, galloped away back toward the farm.

The Dracomancer let out a sigh of relief and turned his thoughts to composing a speech to deliver to his followers. It had to be grand and eloquent, something that would spur them to new heights of frenzied devotion and convince them that being snapped up, squashed, or incinerated by a dragon was exactly what their lives had been leading up to this whole time.

Suddenly, a shadow with yellow eyes jumped onto the road. His horse reared back and nearly unseated him. "Damn!" cried the Dracomancer, and fought with the reins until he had calmed the beast.

The wolf, for that was what it was, paced back and forth across the road, its eyes never leaving the Dracomancer or his horse. The Dracomancer cursed himself for sending his guard away. Here he was, on a deserted road, with a ferocious wolf stalking him. In an attempt to project authority, he waved his staff at the beast, and cried out, "Begone, you cur!"

"That's no way to talk to a friend and admirer," the wolf said, eyes still fixed on the Dracomancer.

"Friend?" the Dracomancer said. "Is it friendly to ambush someone?"

"I am sorry about that," the wolf said, his long, wet tongue extending as he panted. "I had not expected to have a chance to talk to you so soon, but when you sent your guards away, I knew I had to act quickly. I hope you were not too frightened."

"I wasn't frightened," the Dracomancer lied. "But you did startle my horse."

"Again, Dread Dracomancer, my apologies."

"You know who I am?"

"Of course I do." The wolf smiled, and his white teeth gleamed in the moonlight. "I have come a long way to find you."

"Why is that?" the Dracomancer asked, wondering if having such a renowned name might not be a hazard in some cases.

"My name is Beo, and I wish to pledge my services to you, Powerful and Horrible Dracomancer," the wolf said, and, rising to his haunches, placed a paw to his breast, and bowed his head.

The Dracomancer rolled his eyes and stared at the scrawny wolf in front of him. "You wish to serve me, Beo?" he asked scornfully.

"Yes, Great and Terrible Dracomancer."

"And what service can a common wolf be to the Dracomancer?"

"Since you have proclaimed yourself as enemy to the Dragon, I thought someone that had previously been in service to Volthraxus, the Killing Wind, the Gray Terror, the Great Dragon of the North, might be of use," the wolf answered, and, turning to go, said, "Perhaps I was wrong."

"Do not be so hasty, Beo," the Dracomancer said, intrigued by the possibilities. "I would need to have proof of your service to him. Anyone can claim to have knowledge of the dragon. What can you tell me that I do not already know?"

Beo considered. "Did you know that Volthraxus has come to avenge the loss of his love, Magdela?"

"Yes, anyone who has read Gurble Pettiswang's *Tooth and Tail, Tail and Tooth* would know of the connection between the Dragon of the North and the Wyrm of the South," the Dracomancer said dismissively, and began to spur his horse forward.

"Do you know that Volthraxus has a weakness for swine?" Beo asked quickly.

The Dracomancer laughed and rode past the wolf. "You would have to be a fool, or have read nothing of the *Ars Dragonica* not to know of Volthraxus's penchant for pork."

"I . . . I . . . can tell you his weakness," Beo pleaded, stalking alongside the Dracomancer's trotting horse. "Where his scales have gaps, what weapons to use . . ."

"Go back to the woods, wolf, and leave dragons to experts," the Dracomancer said with a wave of his hand. "There is only one weapon in all the world that could have killed Volthraxus, and I know for a fact that the pitchfork that slew Magdela, William Pickett's pitchfork, has been destroyed."

The Dracomancer had gone on another few yards when the wolf's voice, now calm and confident, called after him, "And what if I told you that I know where King William's pitchfork is?"

The Dracomancer reined his horse to a stop but did not turn around. "That's impossible," he said, but his mind was racing with the possibilities. Liz did not actually say that it was destroyed. She had only not disputed his assumption. If it was true . . .

"Not impossible, Your Worshipful Dracomancer. I've seen the pitchfork with my own eyes."

The Dracomancer turned his horse about. "Where?"

Beo shook his head and grinned his toothy grin. "It doesn't work like that. You agree to take me on as your ally, to protect me from the dragon, then I will tell you where it is."

The man and the wolf stared at each other across the gap of road. Finally, the Dracomancer came to a decision. "If you bring me the Pitchfork of Destiny, Beo, then I shall seat you at my right side, and you shall become exalted throughout the land."

"It will be done," said the wolf, and once again he rose onto his haunches, put his paw to his chest, and bowed his head.

The Dracomancer watched the wolf slip into the trees beside the road. If he could get his hands on the Pitchfork of Destiny, it would change everything. He would delay the march long enough to give the wolf a chance to retrieve the thing. It would take several days at the least, but it would be well worth it.

Besides, even if the wolf was lying or couldn't get the pitchfork, he had gained something from their meeting. The salute the wolf had made had actually been quite elegant. The Dracomancer decided on his return to Prosper that he would make it standard throughout his army.

CHAPTER 13

A BRUSH WITH DESTINY

Typically, the pages of a fairy-tale story can only comfortably hold one fairy-tale princess. In their stories, neither Cinderella nor Beauty nor Briar Rose have a real rival for beauty, grace, and wit. Perhaps Snow White's stepmother, for a time, competes with the young princess for title of fairest of the realm, but from the moment the mirror speaks, it is clear that the Queen's reign will soon give way. The fact that Lady Rapunzel's own fairy-tale story was shared with Gwendolyn Mostfair had never set well with Elle, but, even by her own admission, their stories had become intertwined almost to the point of being tangled.

Will's untimely rescue of Gwendolyn, or at least the untimely nature of Prince Charming's learning of the rescue, had resulted in Charming's rapid flight from Rapunzel's tower and the resultant loss of half her hair. The loss of her hair had driven her mad with anger, which had led to her assaulting the Prince at the Royal Ball and her subsequently, and quite deservedly, she had to admit, becoming a social outcast. Gwendolyn's poor treatment of Elizabeth Pickett had led Elle to try to protect Lady Pickett, which bonded the two women in friendship, which ultimately led to her romance with Liz's brother, Will. It was also Gwendolyn who had put Will on the throne, which meant that one day, if Elle lived to be queen, she had to acknowledge that her fairy-tale ending would never have happened had it not been for Princess Gwendolyn Mostfair.

But that didn't mean she had to like the woman, or like the fact that Volthraxus was now suggesting that she sleep in the same bed where Gwendolyn had slept during her imprisonment. The same bed where Will had given, or tried to give, Gwendolyn, true love's kiss.

"I assure you it's an excellent bed," said Volthraxus from behind her.

"How would you know?" asked Elle with a pout of her lips.

"I guess I don't really, but it does look nice," he said brightly. "Look, it even has a little pillow." He leaned his massive snout through the door and sniffed at the bedding. "It also has a lovely scent about it, like faded roses."

"But it's that woman's scent," Elle protested with a stomp of her foot.

"Who, Gwendolyn's?" he asked, and inhaled again. "Lovely."

"Lovely," she mimicked, then added in a sulky voice, "everything *she* did was always lovely. She is a better dancer, wears gowns better, and even laughs better."

"You are jealous of her?" Volthraxus asked in surprise.

"A little," she admitted quietly.

"But she has been banished from court, and you will become queen. What in her could possibly inspire such envy in you?"

Elle shrugged and voiced aloud the worry that had been nagging at her for months now, really ever since Will proposed. "I worry that I won't be the queen she could have been. She was everything a princess is supposed to be . . ."

"She was also mad," Volthraxus said seriously. "Gwendolyn Mostfair spent two of your lifetimes lying in this stone cell, alive and aware but unable to move or speak. Don't forget that, Lady Rapunzel, and do not envy her life."

She knew she was being childish, but she hated the idea of being kept in the same tower as Gwendolyn, to forge yet another link between them. She looked around the room. It was empty save for the bed and a battered pitchfork leaning against a wall in the corner by the door. She went over to the bed. Volthraxus was right. It was very nice. A year had passed, and there was no sign of age or decay in the bedding, not even a hint of dust. She wondered if some of the fairy's magic might still linger among the stones of the tower.

A shiver of fear ran along Elle's spine. *What if Gwendolyn's fate becomes mine? What if I go to sleep on this bed and can't wake up? What if Will never comes?*

Elle felt her face drain of blood, and she turned around to face the dragon, putting the bed at her back. She felt her heart pounding and her head swimming.

"What?" he asked, clearly alarmed at her appearance. "You have nothing to fear here, Lady Rapunzel. The thorns that surround this tower keep all but my kind from gaining entrance, and if anything does try to molest you in the night, they will find me waiting. You can sleep easy."

"I . . . I want to go home, Volthraxus," she said, and tears began to fill her eyes. "I want to go home to Will. Let's stop this charade. You don't want to hurt me. You know that Will didn't intend to kill the Great Wyrm of the South."

"Her name was Magdela." Volthraxus bared his daggerlike, teeth and a rumbling, burning growl resonated beneath his words.

Elle took a half step back. "Yes, Magdela. I'm sorry." She clasped her hands together and, her voice pleaded. "But it was an accident."

"An accident maybe, but what about after? Did or did he not take full advantage of her death to build up his own reputation?" Volthraxus thumped his tail in irritation, and the tower shook. "I tire of this same argument! When we meet," he said, and now his voice was ominously low, "I will give him the chance to prove whether he is a dragonslayer or not."

He turned away from her to stare out at the evening sky.

Elle shuddered at the anger and pain she heard in Volthraxus. He was frightening when he was like this. At last, she said, "Killing Will won't heal your heart. It would only destroy mine."

Volthraxus didn't respond.

"What would Magdela have wanted?" she asked.

"I don't know," he admitted, and the pain and regret in his voice was so strong that it was hard for Elle not to feel for him despite everything.

She turned and stared back down at the bed. It did look warm, and the main room, with its open balcony, was so cold at night. She sat down on the edge of the bed and felt the soft covers and silken pillow. Elle sighed. It was foolish to deny that it would be far more comfortable than another night on the floor next to Volthraxus. She lay down on her side, gazing back out the archway into the main chamber, where Volthraxus sat watching the sunset over the mountains beyond.

That must have been what Magdela did every night, she thought.

Elle suddenly had a need to know more about the dragon that had been such a figure of terror all her life and whose shadow now threatened all of her dreams.

"Come and talk to me while I go to sleep," she said to the dragon's back.

He snorted in anger.

"Don't be like that," she said, sitting back up. "We both have reason for thinking the other unreasonable and pigheaded, but that does not mean we need be discourteous to each other."

"I don't feel like talking," he said irritably.

"If you don't come and tell me stories, then I will keep talking all the night, and you won't get a wink of sleep, and we shall both be out of sorts tomorrow," she threatened.

"Fine," he said with a grumble, and, turning, snaked his long neck along the floor until his head rested just outside the door to her room. "What do you want to talk about, little princess?"

She lay back down, staring into his gray face. A question hung on her tongue for a moment, and her mouth went dry as she waited to ask, wondering if it would be pushing too far.

His lamp-like golden eyes shone on her. "What?"

She decided to come at the topic indirectly, and said, "I was wondering how you met her."

"Why?"

"Don't be like that," she said, shaking a scolding finger at him. "Just answer the question."

His tongue flickered out in annoyance, but, finally, he said, "The first time I remember seeing Magdela was up north many, many years ago." He closed his eyes in the memory. "She was in flight, and we soared and tumbled around each other for a long time. She was such a beauty. At once, I knew that I must have her."

"Did you tell her?" Elle asked softly.

His eyes opened again. "I couldn't speak. She was too beautiful and terrible. I . . . I flew away."

Elle giggled. "So, even big, bad dragons get nervous around girls. Imagine!"

Volthraxus made a rasping sound, which she realized was a sort of draconic cough. "It wasn't quite like that. Things are different with dragons. There are standards of behavior to uphold. You wouldn't understand."

"Oh wouldn't I," she replied with an arched eyebrow. Raising herself on her elbow, she asked, "When you finally managed to work up the nerve to speak with her, what did you say?"

He shrugged. "Most of the time she wouldn't let me catch her. When she did, I never seemed to know exactly what to say. I tried the standard lines. I would tell her of my exploits and my titles. You know, armies killed, villages flattened, swine eaten, that sort of thing, but she didn't seem that impressed. One day, I went looking for her, and she was gone. I heard that she had flown south, and later that she had been enchanted by the fairy and forced to guard Princess Gwendolyn."

"Why didn't you fly after her at once?"

He shuffled uncomfortably. "Dragons can be very proud, and dragon females terribly so, especially those of Magdela's more youthful age. I was afraid that if I broke her free, she would resent it. Eventually, I ran out of things to distract myself with and got tired of waiting for her to break free herself. When I came south this time, it was to rescue her. But I was too late," he concluded with a long, vaporous exhale.

Elle knew they were getting near the heart of the matter now. She took a deep breath. "So you never did get to know who she was, not really."

A rumble of warning came from his throat, and she felt his hot breath rush into the room. "What are you saying?"

Elle sat up so that she could look directly into his eyes. She was beginning to regret finding out so much about Volthraxus. She didn't want to hurt him, but her only hope of saving Will was to make him understand the truth.

"What?" he grumped, as she continued to stare at him.

"What was Magdela's favorite food?"

"Something crunchy, I don't know." He snorted. "Why does it matter?"

She took a deep breath and threaded her fingers together nervously. Making her voice as gentle as she could, she said, "I'm saying, Volthraxus, that you never truly loved Magdela any more than I loved one of my many girlhood crushes like Prince Charming. You were in love with the idea of Magdela, but you never knew her. I'm saying that I'm not sure why you are doing this. Maybe you feel guilty. Maybe you are mad at yourself, but whatever the reason, it isn't because you were in love with her."

His eyes flashed from gold to a flaming red. "How do you know?"

She reached a shaking hand out to touch his scaled

snout. "I know because I know what true love feels like, and it is something that can only grow by knowing someone."

He pulled his head away from her touch. She saw in his body a tension of suppressed anger, and the heat emanating from him was almost unbearable. If he was ever going to kill her, this would be the time.

"I'm sorry," she said, and closed her eyes.

She tensed for an explosion, but in the next instant, there was a tremendous rush of wind. When she opened her eyes, Volthraxus was gone. She went out to the balcony, and saw him between the faint afterglow of sunset and the gentle kiss of the moon as the light reflected off his scales.

The thought rushed through her that now was a chance to escape, but looking over the edge of the balcony, she could see the massive wall of thorns that Volthraxus had mentioned. It completely surrounded the tower's base and covered the door. If she tried to push her way through that, she'd be torn to pieces.

A wind blew in over the mountain, hinting at a cold night ahead, and even colder without the Dragon's heat to warm the tower. She shivered and retreated back to the little room. Lying down on the bed, Elle thought back over her conversation with Volthraxus, picking over each word and gesture in the hopes that she might gain some insight into how the conundrum of Will and the dragon might be resolved without one of them dying. Soon, despite all the thoughts racing about her head, her eyes drifted closed, and she slept.

Elle woke and felt instinctively that something was wrong. The feel of the air in the tower was different. Slowly, she opened her eyes and looked through the open door to the outer room. It was still night, and the main chamber was dark and empty.

Volthraxus had not yet returned.

Apart from knowing that he was gone, Elle could see little else in the dim light of the stars and the moon. She realized that she had become accustomed to the dragon's warm glow being her light at night.

Elle waited for a few minutes and had nearly convinced herself that her wakefulness was nothing more than nerves, when a gray shadow passed across the opening of her doorway. It looked about the size and shape of a wolf.

The hair rose on the back of her neck, and goose bumps ran over her arms. Her heart pounded in her chest. She knew without a doubt that it was Beo. She also knew that if the wolf found her here, he would kill her.

Slowly, deliberately, and quietly as a shadow, she slipped off the bed and crouched behind the stone platform that supported it. Here she would be hidden from the door, but if Beo investigated the alcove, he would be sure to find her.

Straining her ears, she listened for any sign of activity from the outer room, but there was only silence and the sound of her own breathing.

Elle started to relax, thinking perhaps that Beo had

either found what he was looking for or had not found what he had expected and moved on, when she heard the soft flap of padded feet at the door to her room. The sharp sound of metal ringing on stone and the soft thunk as of something heavy being dropped on the carpeted floor of the main chamber followed, then the wolf began to sniff the air. Elle tensed in her hiding place, not even daring to breathe.

"Lady Rapunzel?" came Beo's harsh, clipped voice. "Are you there, little piggy?"

Elle barely managed to suppress the scream that tried to escape her throat.

The wolf took a few tentative steps into the room. "Come out, come out, little piggy," he called in a mocking, singsong voice.

Elle knew that it was darker here, even dark for the wolf's night eyes. Perhaps he was only guessing that she would be here. He would have examined the other parts of the tower, and there were few other places she could be.

She heard his footsteps just on the other side of the bed now. He was sniffing at the bedding. He knew her smell from the time in the cave. He would smell her.

Elle's nerves nearly broke, but at the same moment that she would have sprinted for the door, Beo spit. "Bah! This isn't her scent. Where has that bloody dragon hidden her?"

In his frustration, he shredded the covers and the pillow and sent them flinging about the room. "No matter. I have what I came for, and soon enough, the

Dracomancer will kill Mighty Volthraxus, and there will be no one left to protect the foolish girl." He padded back to the door, chuckling cruelly. "To think that the key to his destruction was sitting under his nose this whole time. The Great and Powerful Volthraxus is not nearly as clever as he believes he is."

There was the sound of something being dragged along the ground, then receding down the stairs to the lower level. For several minutes more, Elle dared not move. Only when she thought she heard movement in the rosebushes outside did she get up. Quietly, she made her way back to the balcony in a crouch. She peered over the edge of the balustrade and, in the light cast by the moon, saw Beo, with something long and glinting of metal clutched in his mouth, making for the trail down the side of the mountain. Although Elle knew the danger was gone, she still did not feel comfortable in the open. She crept back into the alcove to hide behind Princess Gwendolyn's bed.

When Volthraxus returned a few hours later, he found her shivering from a combination of cold and fear.

The dragon's red-gold eyes took in Elle and the tattered bedding. "What has happened here, Lady Rapunzel?"

"It . . . it was Beo."

There was a rumble of anger from him, but it wasn't directed at her. "Come here, little princess. I will warm you up."

She rose, shaking, and walked to him. He gathered her gently into a claw and carried her to a mound of carpets he had made in the center of the chamber for his own bed. Using the barest bits of his breath, Volthraxus ignited a wall sconce. Elle had never felt happier to see the light of a flame. She leaned against his warm body and sighed.

"Th . . . Thank you," she said, as the shakes slowly subsided.

"You have no reason to thank me," Volthraxus said. "Once again, through my negligence, I have put you in great danger. I should not have left you alone, but I thought the thorns would keep you safe. I forgot that Beo and his kind are part snake when it comes to sneaking into places. Tomorrow, I shall block the entrance. He will not get in again."

"Where were you?"

Volthraxus looked embarrassed. "Arguing with you made me hungry. I found a few pigs down on the outskirts of Prosper."

Now that he mentioned, she noticed an overwhelming smell of bacon. "Is that what you were doing? Eating?" she asked indignantly.

"Yes," he said, then added at her glare, "I was also watching what is transpiring in Prosper. There is an army. They speak of the Dracomancer, and there's talk of something they call the Pitchfork of Destiny. It is supposedly the weapon used to kill Magdela."

She gasped. Now she knew what Beo had been carrying. It had been a pitchfork; she could see the glint of the metal tines at the end of the long, wooden haft in her mind's eye. She got up and ran to the alcove. It was gone.

"That is why he came," she said. "It was the pitchfork. I saw him carry it off. I didn't know what it was at first, but that must be it. He has the Pitchfork of Destiny."

"You are overwrought and imaging things, Lady Rapunzel," he said in a soothing tone. "Whatever might have been taken, it wasn't the Pitchfork of Destiny. Frankly, I have serious doubts about whether such a thing even exists. Besides, who would leave an item of such value, a weapon, pitchfork or not, that actually slew a dragon forgotten?"

Volthraxus curled up, much like a cat Elle thought, and his massive body filled the tapestry room. Nothing was going to get past him. She returned to his side and lay against his warm belly. His final question repeated itself in her mind. She finally whispered the answer. "Will Pickett."

CHAPTER 14

UNEASY LIES THE HEAD

If one happens to find oneself a king someday, it would be advisable not to model one's rule after the kings of fairy tale. The kings of fairy tale seem for the most part to be ineffective, lazy, stupid, or just plain evil. We can all laugh at the emperor king who is convinced to walk naked through his kingdom by a pair of hucksters selling invisible cloth, but others are not so amusing. Take Snow White's kingly father. He is apparently perfectly willing to let his new queen plot the murder of his daughter, or at least raises no hand to stop it. And what of the poor weaver girl who is married to the king of the realm based on her purported ability to spin gold from straw? Far from being the devoted spouse a girl might hope for, the king threatens to kill her if she cannot produce bolts of golden cloth for him, and in the end she is forced to promise their firstborn child to the lonely manikin, Rumpelstiltskin, to give her betrothed what he wants.

As he rode toward Prosper, Will Pickett, King of Royaume, knew that he had not been a particularly good king lately. He had failed in his duty to the people of his land. He had let his selfish need to rescue Elle overwhelm all other considerations, and the evidence of his failure was to be seen all around. It was there in the burnt farms and ruined fields that marked the passage of the Dracomancer's army. These people had been depending on him to protect them, and he had failed them just as he had failed Elle. If he wished for one thing, it was to be given the chance to set things to right, to make Elle safe and his people whole. Fortunately, he now knew where he was going. He felt the calm confidence of the man who knows where the end of his journey lay.

Prosper.

It was in Prosper that he would find his sister, Liz, who could give him the practical guidance that he had always relied on. It was in Prosper that he could talk to Gwendolyn, the one person in Royaume who might have an insight on how to defeat the dragon. Perhaps most of all, it was in Prosper that he would come face-to-face with this Dracomancer. This is not to say that he was confident that he would be able to best the dragon and save Elle, or bring the Dracomancer and his Dracolytes to heel, but he at least knew where the ending chapter of this particular tale would be written. Whether alive or dead, king or prisoner, one way or another his fairy tale would end in the place it had started a year earlier.

Ahead, the roofs of the village became visible. It was as if the fairy-tale story of Will's life had run backwards. He knew that all that had been done could be undone and that he had no one to blame but himself, and a part of him wondered if he would not be better off. He would never shirk his responsibility, nor would he willingly subject Elle to the hard life of a farmer's wife, but the smell of the earth and the animals, and the light of the sun in the South Valley felt like a comfortable pair of boots. He was coming back home, back to the familiar, and some of the tension he'd been holding for so long eased in him.

Unfortunately for Will, the calm only lasted until the road turned, and the whole of Prosper came into view. The quaint village he had known and grown up in had been transformed by the Dracomancer's army. Throngs of people and tents lined the road that led into town, and in the distance, he could see a crowd gathering around a wooden stage that had been erected on the green in the central square. Will had never imagined that the Dracomancer could gather so many people to him. He felt his shoulders tighten and his head begin to throb.

Without knowing it, Will had stopped in the middle of the road, too stunned to move. Charming rode on for a bit, then, realizing that Will was not with him, he turned and came back. He moved his horse close in, and said, "I would guess the stage is for the Dracomancer, Will. We need to get closer so we can be on hand to challenge the man when he appears."

Will nodded dumbly. How had so many lost faith in him so quickly?

Charming turned his horse to ride on, and when Will still did not move, he came back again. "Is there a problem, Will?"

"All the people . . ." Will said stupidly. Had he been that bad a king?

Charming's brow wrinkled in puzzlement for a second, and a sudden, knowing gleam came into his eyes. "You're right, Will, there are far too many people to take the horses. We can leave them here and continue on foot."

Charming led the horses to the side of the road and tied them to a fence. Will dismounted in a haze. He wondered if even the people of Prosper had joined the Dracomancer, then remembered how he had basically accused the entire town of being no better than thieves when he left, and came to the conclusion that probably most of them were quite enthusiastic Dracolytes. With a start, he realized the danger that his presence here represented. Even if the average citizen of Royaume had never seen him, anyone from Prosper would recognize him in an instant. All it would take was one of his disgruntled former neighbors to spot him, and they would be captured before they ever had a chance to get to the Dracomancer.

He drew his cloak over his head and whispered to

Charming, "I think we should try not to draw any attention to ourselves. Too many people here in Prosper could recognize me."

Charming glanced down at his clothes and, frowning, also drew his own hood over his head. "Excellent suggestion, Your Majesty. I can't imagine the embarrassment if anyone saw us looking like this. I mean, the Royal Tailor would throw a fit. He might even refuse to work with me again."

"This isn't about the clothes, Charming. It's about finding the Dracomancer without getting caught."

Charming nodded knowingly to Will. "It's fine. I understand that you wish to spare me the harsh truth, but I'm quite aware that my appearance is tragic. The chafing is a constant reminder of my humiliation. As for being recognized, I would not concern yourself. No one sees a king when he's in commoner's clothes."

Will's eyes darted about the crowd, looking for faces he knew. "The problem is that the people of Prosper remember me when I was a commoner."

Charming cocked his head to one side as though considering this for the first time. "How inconvenient it is that you were once poor," he said with a remarkable lack of self-reflection.

Will wisely said nothing and instead focused on maneuvering them through the growing crowds. As they got closer to the central square, the press of people around them became overwhelming. They were jostled and pushed, and the tide of humanity caught them in its motion and seemed almost to carry them toward the stage ahead. Onstage, four men lit four different braziers positioned at the corners of the platform. Flames roared to life, rising high into the evening air. There was a roar of cheering. Someone at the very front of the crowd began shouting "Dracomancer," and others joined in. As more people added their voices, the shouts changed from random cheers into a steady chant. A robed man with a long white beard and clutching a gnarled staff of blackened wood climbed up onto the stage. In an instant, the chant was transformed again into a frenzy of cheers, this time even louder.

The Dracomancer stood, smiling, basking in the adoration of the crowd, then swept up his hands. Immediately, a silence fell.

"What the hell is he doing up there?" Charming shouted in the sudden quiet.

The man beside Charming pushed him, and said, "Shut up, and show some respect."

Charming started to say something, and Will put an arm around his shoulder and pulled him in tight. He whispered, "Are you mad? You are going to get us killed."

"But, Will," he said in a hushed voice matching Will's own. "I know, the Dracomancer. He was my tutor in dragon lore. He's a decent academic when it comes to dragons, although his theory about Agorak the Black, the ancient sleeping dragon, is poppycock and well, we both know about the prophecy. What I never liked about him was that when he didn't know an answer, he always made up some drivel like, 'A wet dragon never flies at night.' Anyway, my point is he doesn't have any mystical powers. Why would anyone follow him?"

Before Will could utter a response, the Dracomancer spoke.

"People of Royaume, once again, we are plagued by the most terrible of monsters, a dragon. But King William"—there were derisive whistles from the crowd at the mention of Will's name—"King William, the man who promised to protect us, has gone into hiding. He has shown us his true colors." Someone yelled "yellow" and the Dracomancer smiled. "The King will not save us."

There was a roar of agreement from the crowd.

"You should speak up," Charming muttered.

"Not yet," said Will. "We need to hear him out."

"But will we be dismayed?" the Dracomancer continued his speech. "Will we to turn our backs on the people of this land as our King has?"

The crowd roared a lusty, "Nay!"

Beside him, Charming was quivering with outrage on his behalf, but Will kept a firm grip on his shoulder as a reminder of the need for patience.

"No! We choose to stand and fight the menace. We will not stand by idle while this new monster savages our brother and sisters. I call on all of you"—he pointed his staff out over the crowd—"my Dracolytes, to answer the call of the Dragon Spirit! The salvation of Royaume will depend on our actions in the coming days. On the deeds of each and every one of you assembled here will the fate of this land and its people depend. I can lead, but I need you, my army of believers, to answer my call. Will you do that? Will you pledge your hearts, minds, and bodies to serving the Dragon Spirit through me, his humble servant?"

A roar of assent echoed through the crowd.

Will had to admit that the Dracomancer was a compelling figure, and he began to wonder if he would be able to turn the tide of passion the man had stirred in the people.

"Our course ahead will not be easy. All around us the agents of the dragon will conspire and plot against us. Some will be obvious to our eyes, as was the monster we faced and vanquished on our hard road to Prosper. But some will be subtle. This day, my Dracoviziers tracked down and imprisoned the witch formerly known as Princess Gwendolyn Mostfair for the crime of draconic conspiracy."

There was a hiss of anger from the crowd and even calls that to "burn the witch."

Will's heart sunk. He couldn't consult Gwendolyn if she was under guard of the Dracomancer. His plan, which had seemed so hopeful before, appeared to be crumbling before him. It was beginning to sink in that he might very easily lose everything.

The Dracomancer spread his arms. "No, my friends, we do not slay the nonbelievers, but treat them with compassion. The minds of these apostates have been twisted by the dragon. It is our charge and duty to try to guide them back to the light of the Dragon Spirit. As I myself have been doing for Lady Elizabeth Charming, who has been my guest and patient for some time now."

Charming's head snapped toward the stage, and his eyes blazed. Will felt a cold fear in his heart. *The Dracomancer has Liz?*

"Although I had made great progress in reforming Lady Charming, as we have moved closer to the dragon, its pull on her mind has become too great for her will to resist. For her own safety, I have had to send her away!" The Dracomancer's body wilted, and he sadly shook his head. "Perhaps I failed her . . ."

"No! No!" came shouts from the assembled masses. "It was her! She's a fool like her brother! The Picketts are all mad!"

The Dracomancer pulled himself back upright. His face set with determination. "This should be a reminder to us all that the power of the dragon is great. Its evil lurks everywhere, and any doubt in our cause or in the power and wisdom of the Dragon Spirit may give that evil a foothold on our souls." He raised his arms high in the air. "Gird your belief. Arm yourself in the surety of knowledge that only through the Dragon Spirit shall we be delivered!"

Cheers erupted from the crowd. Will felt anger boil up inside him, not at the Dracomancer, but at the jeers directed at Liz. He was reminded again of how she, how they, had been treated by the people of Prosper when they had lived here.

He was about to speak, when Charming gave voice

to his thoughts. "How dare they speak of the Lady Elizabeth in such a fashion?" He pulled away from Will's arm and began forcing his way forward through the crowd, a hand on the hilt of his sword.

Will's own anger turned to fear as he realized that, unless he stopped him, Charming would likely call out the Dracomancer and maybe the entire mob in order to defend Liz's honor. Now was not the time to let their passions rule. There was too much at stake. He grabbed Charming's sword arm.

"Please, not now, Charming," whispered Will. "We must first find Liz. Perhaps he will tell us something of where she is."

Charming nodded and steadied himself, dropping his hand from his sword. "I will agree to a delay, but mark my words, Your Majesty, he will face my wrath, and, when the time comes, let no man stand between me and my retribution."

Will swallowed at the anger he saw boiling in Charming's eyes. Part of him actually pitied the Dracomancer—a very, very small part of him.

The Dracomancer spoke again. "We turn to the task at hand. The Great Dragon of the North now lairs in the Dragon's Tower. The nightmare has returned! A time of suffering and fear is at hand if we do not act. I leave it to you, my brother and sisters, my Dracolytes, who would you have come to your aid? Who would you have come to save you?"

Someone, who to Will's ear sounded a bit like his former girlfriend, Gretel, screamed, "You, Dracomancer!"

Chants of "Dracomancer, Dracomancer" filled Prosper. The Dracomancer held his hand up to his ear, and the volume increased. He pointed to one side of the stage, then the other, with the chants increasing with his attention.

After several minutes of sustained chanting, the Dracomancer raised his hands again for silence, and the crowd settled. He placed a hand to his heart and bowed his head. "I humbly accept the duty that you have thrust upon me. I pledge the power and knowledge of the Dracomancer to the cause. I pledge my life for you, the people of Royaume! And I bring you hope. For through my studies and communications with the Dragon Spirit, I have recovered the one weapon in all the land that can be used to slay the Dread Dragon! Dracoviziers, attend me!"

The Dracomancer clapped his hands. Two men in dark robes appeared, carrying between them something long and heavy, covered by a black wrap. The crowd murmured to each other, and the Dracomancer let the tension build.

"There are those," he began quietly, "who have questioned my commitment to facing the dragon." There were many protests from the crowd at the suggestion, but the Dracomancer held up his hands for quiet. "Who have said that I didn't immediately go to face the dragon because I lacked the courage and fortitude." More denials erupted at this, and, again, the Dracomancer had to silence the crowd. "There are some who have even said that I am no better than that human peacock, the former Prince Charming." Outraged shouts erupted at this notion. The Dracomancer smiled patiently and waited till they'd settled. "The reason I have delayed my meeting with the dragon is that I know the truth of how to defeat the dragon. Only one weapon in the all the world has the power to slay a dragon like the one we face now. A weapon forged in the very heart-flames of a dragon. I give you . . ." he paused dramatically, "the Pitchfork of Destiny!"

The Dracomancer attempted to remove the covering in a dramatic flourish, but the cloth got caught on the tines of the pitchfork, and it would not come. The Dracoviziers stepped in and began tugging and pulling. Audible grunts and curses could be heard from the group as they fumbled with the draping.

As they waited, Charming leaned over to Will, and whispered, "You didn't tell me that your pitchfork was forged in the heart-flames of a dragon. If you had, I wouldn't have thought that you were so much of a fraud when we first met. I mean, that's actually pretty amazing."

"It wasn't," Will said irritably. "It just sort of melted after the dragon impaled itself."

"Oh. Fair enough," Charming said, disappointed. "Some advice for you, though, Will. It sounds more impressive if you go with the story the Dracomancer is telling. Use that one for posterity."

Will almost replied, "To hell with posterity," but just at that moment the Dracoviziers managed to pull the cloth away with a great tearing noise.

Panting from the effort, the Dracomancer said in triumph. "I give you the Pitchfork of Destiny!"

A gasp spread through the crowd as the Dracomancer held a pitchfork high in the air. Everyone fell to their knees with the exception of Will, who was too shocked to move, and Charming, who Will noted was shaking his head in disgust.

Will stared at the pitchfork, and without thinking, stepped closer to the stage. The first thing that he noticed was that the haft wasn't blackened and burned, and that his name wasn't visible where he had whittled it on that summer afternoon in the field so many years ago. The tines were also much sharper than he could ever recall their being, and not a point was bent. The metal practically gleamed in the firelight.

The Dracomancer gestured widely with his free hand toward the kneeling crowd. "Tomorrow, I march to Dragon Tower to face the dragon and end his reign of terror. Who among you will join me in my righteous quest? Rise if you will march with me to Dragon Tower to rid our land once and for all of our enemy. Rise if you stand with the Dracomancer!"

As one, the crowd jumped to its feet and roared their assent. The Dracomancer let the people cheer, and when they had calmed, said, "Not all of us will make it back. Many may fall, but our quest is righteous, and we shall prevail. With the Dragon Spirit on our side, and the Pitchfork of Destiny in our hands, nothing can stand before us!"

The crowd erupted once more, and chants of "Dracomancer" began echoing again through the streets of Prosper. Onstage, the Dracomancer urged them to higher states of frenzy by stalking back and forth across the stage, waving and thrusting the pitchfork into the air.

Will's face grew pale. He had thought the Dracomancer would take only trained troops up to face the Dragon, but the maniac meant to take anyone who would follow, men and women, possibly even children, whether they could hold a weapon or no. How many would die? Would anyone survive?

"Charming," he said firmly, pulling his hood away from his face, "It is time we made our appearance. Clear a path."

"With pleasure, Your Majesty."

Charming lowered his hood and, projecting his voice as only he could, shouted, "Make way for Lord Protector of the Realm, His Majesty, King William! Make way! Make way!"

The crowd fell quiet and turned to stare at Charming and Will, but no one moved.

"I said," Charming shouted again, "Make way for His Majesty, King William, or face his swift and sure judgment!"

For emphasis, Charming drew his blade, and the light from the fires around the stage caught on the edge of his sword so that it gleamed as though aflame. A circle of space grew around them. Will squared his shoulders and marched toward the stage with Charming at his side, the crowd parting like wheat before him.

The Dracomancer watched them approach with a smirk as he leaned on the pitchfork. When Charming and Will finally climbed atop the stage, the Dracomancer gestured at them, and said in a lazy, sarcastic drawl, "People of Prosper, brothers and sisters, we welcome King William who has finally revealed himself after his long sojourn in parts unknown. Pray, dread King, to what do *we*, your *people*, owe this *great* honor? We so rarely see you outside of Castle White or in places where the need is greatest. Have you run out of amusements in the court or simply grown tired of running?"

He punctuated his speech with many exaggerated facial expressions and rolls of his eyes. The people laughed. Out of the crowd came derisive shouts. "Down with Cowardly King William!" "We don't want the Yellow King!" "Go back to Castle White, we don't need a false dragonslayer!"

One of the Dracoviziers behind the Dracomancer yelled, "Ding Dong the King is gone! We want the Dracomancer!" The crowd suddenly burst into a chorus of "Ding Dong the King is gone."

Someone threw a tomato at Will, and it hit him in the side of the face. He did not flinch but wiped the remains away with his sleeve. An apple followed, but it never reached its intended target as Charming's sword smoothly speared it from the air. He stepped in front of Will, his face white with anger, his eyes flashing a challenge. The song faltered, and the chants stopped.

With deliberate slowness, Charming pulled the

apple from his blade and took a bite. His face grimaced and he spit out the fruit. "Rotten!" he shouted. "Like this town. Like this Dracomancer." He threw the apple back into the crowd. "So, you, people of Prosper, and you . . ." he sneered, "Dracolytes, would choose to follow this . . ." he sneered again, and this time, it was even more pronounced, "Dracomancer? Let me tell you what I know of him." He moved to the side and gestured at the Dracomancer with his sword, letting the tip dance up and down in the air as he spoke. "You call him Dracomancer, but his real name is Delbert Thistlemont, and when I was a child, he would put on puppet shows for the children. That is the man in whom you have chosen to place your faith. An entertainer. A fraud. He pulls your strings, and you dance for him."

Shouts of defiance rang out from the crowd, and behind him, several of the black-robed Dracoviziers stepped forward, their own blades drawn and at the ready.

Charming spun in a circle around the still-unmoving Will, slashing his sword back and forth, the firelight still somehow catching on the edge of his blade so that it shone and danced in the night air. "Let any who call me a liar say it within reach of my sword. Let any who dare insult King William come and face me!"

Several Dracolytes, men with sewn-on dragon patches of various designs on their tunics, robes, and cloaks, all started shouting and pushing their way through the crowd toward Charming. However, while the more distant Dracolytes were pushing forward, the Dracolytes and Dracoviziers on the stage and in the immediate vicinity, those who could see the eagerness in Charming's eyes, all began to back away.

The Dracomancer, his own face flashing with anger, suddenly produced a dragon sock puppet from beneath his robes and began screaming in a high-pitched voice, "He hasss been corrupted by the dragon. Dessstroy Prince, I mean, the Charming who wasss Prince. DESSSTROY HIM! THE DRAGON SSSPIRIT COMMANDSSS IT!"

Tremendous gasps and screams came from the crowd. The mass of people surged forward. Beside him, Charming was laughing and slashing his sword and challenging the world to come at him if they would.

Will stood, aghast, looking out over the jeering crowd. He recognized faces among the people gathered. There was Tuck, the blacksmith's son, and Hans Pickle, the pig farmer. He saw the Old Geezer who told stories for a drink and Merle, the self-declared one true beggar of Prosper. Agnes the shepherdess was standing to one side of the stage waving her large, hooked staff about. Closer up, he could see Gretel holding her arms up to the Dracomancer as though enraptured. And those were only the ones he could identify in the torchlight. How many other faces did he know?

The people of Prosper may never been have good to Liz and him, but they were still his people. It was his selfishness that had brought them all to this place. He had run off, thinking only of Elle and himself, and not of the kingdom. He knew what he must do.

Will grasped Charming by the arm and, pulling him toward him, said in a low voice, "Charming, you cannot fight them."

"Never fear, Your Majesty. There are several moves that only work when fighting armies of men that I have been waiting a chance to try," Charming said in a voice that matched the eagerness of his eyes as he continued to whirl his sword back and forth, letting the steel whistle.

"No, Charming, I mean that I will not let you hurt them."

Charming's face fell. "My King, I can put an end to this."

Will studied the man at his side. Charming would do what he thought was right and continue to believe that somehow he would succeed right up to the point that the mob overwhelmed him, and he would not stop fighting until they had killed him. He might slaughter half of Prosper before they eventually dragged him down, but Will knew that they could not win. Not this fight. Not even with Charming's sword. And Will was certain that he would not want to. How could he live with himself if he allowed such a slaughter? Will knew that he would kneel before the Dracomancer and surrender himself before he allowed that.

"No, Charming. Do what you can to give me time to speak, but harm no one," Will ordered.

"As you command, Your Majesty," Charming said

grimly, and, with a flourish of steel, he took a defensive position at Will's back.

Will straightened to his full height and spread his shoulders. He stepped to the very front of the stage, and, holding up his hands, shouted, "People of Royaume and citizens of Prosper, your King speaks."

This made the crowd only shout louder, trying to drown him out with their chants of "DING DONG" and "DRACOMANCER," but Will was implacable. He felt his face flush, but as to whether it was from anger or resolve, he wasn't sure.

"ENOUGH!" he roared. "I WILL BE HEARD!"

A hush fell across Prosper. The only sound was the crackle of the torches. The sock puppet vanished inside the Dracomancer's cloak.

Will stared about at the gathered people. His eye fell on Gretel's face. Memories of their time together flooded through his mind. He reminded himself that it was her and all the others like her that depended on what he did next. They were, for the most part, good people. They might be fools for believing what they'd been told, but they did not deserve the death that would await them if he did not succeed here. He took a deep breath and began.

"You have been told many things by this man whom you call the Dracomancer. He has told you that only he can defeat the dragon, and he has convinced you that with his power at your side, the dragon cannot stand before you."

"And he's right!' shouted a tall, thin young man

with straw-colored hair at the foot of the stage. Agreement was echoed all around.

Will fixed his eyes on the young man and addressed him directly. "I have seen a dragon. I have run for my life as it fell upon me. I have felt the unearthly heat of its breath and the hurricane wind of its wings. I have prayed in the darkness of the night that when the end came, it would be swift."

A silence had fallen on the people. They stared at him, spellbound. He felt the tears rise in his eyes and raised his gaze to take in the larger crowd. "I have also borne witness to the attack that this new dragon made on Castle White, when he took . . . took my Lady Rapunzel. I can barely describe the power of the creature. How it tore away the side of the castle. How the steel arrows of our archers bounced from his hide like rain from a stone."

"If this man"—he pointed at the Dracomancer—"tells you that he can keep you safe from the dragon, and that you will return unharmed from the Dragon's Tower to your homes and fields, either he lies, or he is mad. Dragons are not monsters to be faced and fought. They are forces of nature, and going to battle with one is like going to battle with a raging storm. You may scream to the wind, but the wind will still blow. You may shake your fist at the heavens, but the lightning will not be denied."

"This, then, is the courage of the King," the Dracomancer said, stepping forward and giving a mock bow to Will. "His judgment is that we should once again submit ourselves to the ravages of the beast. Rather than face the creature, he would have us hide ourselves in our homes and in our cellars like rats and let another dragon ravage our land for generations. Your name is well earned, Yellow King William."

Once again, jeers rained down on Will. He stood looking out at them with a flat, steely expression. In time, the very lack of reaction from Will seemed to sap the energy of the crowd, and they grew quiet.

"This you have also been told," Will said, and he could not keep the anger from his voice. "That I am a coward. This man has told you that you were abandoned by your King, and that I care not for you. It is a monstrous falsehood. I have never rested in my hunt for the dragon. I have never abandoned you. This dragon has ravaged the homes and flocks of my people. This dragon has stolen my beloved. I . . . I hate it."

This last he spit so viciously that he had to pause before he could continue. He happened to glance down and saw that there were tears in Gretel's eyes, and in the eyes of many in the crowd.

Will steadied himself and felt his face turn to stone with his resolve. "All I ask is that you delay your march and give me a chance to go to the Dragon's Tower. Stay here in safety, my people, and let me prove myself again to you. Let me prove that I am worthy of your trust. Let me, once and for all, earn the title dragon-slayer."

The people were silent. A tension filled the air, as though everyone gathered was collectively holding their breath. For the first time, the Dracomancer looked nervous, and he licked his lips and raised his hand. "Your Majesty makes a stirring speech, but how can we trust you with such a mission? Your sister, Lady Elizabeth, has shown herself to be corrupted by the dragon, your beloved is in the dragon's clutches, and, by your own admission, you have no faith that any man can face a dragon attack. Should you falter and be seduced by the dragon, then your people would be under even greater threat."

Had Will not restrained his arm when the Dracomancer mentioned Liz, Charming might have run the man through right there. "I will not let him speak of Liz like that," Charming hissed.

"Patience, Charming," he said, and gave his friend a knowing look. "I am determined." Charming nodded and lowered his sword.

Will looked down at the Dracomancer, who, even in his bulky cloak and tall boots was still shorter than the King. "I understand that you profess to believe in letting the people have a say in the course of their own destinies." He gave the Dracomancer no time to answer but turned back to the crowd. "I am your King. This fight should fall on my shoulders and not anyone else's, and certainly not women and children. If you will send me on this quest, I promise I will fight the monster to my dying breath, and I will not return save with the dragon's defeat. What say you?"

There was a profound silence that stretched until Will was certain he had failed, but then a single voice that could have only been Gretel's said, "Let's give Will . . . the King . . . a chance."

There was a general murmur of agreement from the crowd. The Dracomancer held up his hands for silence and eyed Will with a shrewd expression. "You would undertake this quest alone?"

"Yes," Will said sternly.

The Dracomancer nodded, and said, "Give me a moment to confer with the dragon spirits." He gestured, and the handful of men in robes who had shared the stage came to huddle about him.

Charming came and whispered in Will's ear. "What about me, Your Majesty? Surely I will join you."

Will shook his head. "No, Charming. Not this time."

"But—"

"No," Will said, clasping the man's shoulder in his hand. "You must stay here and find Liz and Tomas. You must make sure no harm comes to them or to Gwendolyn or to any of these people. It is my last wish as your King. Do you understand?"

Charming nodded and, with his own hand, clutched Will's shoulder. "It will be as you command, Your Majesty, my King."

The huddle between the Dracomancer and Dracoviziers broke apart. The Dracomancer stepped to the edge of the stage. With a sweeping gesture, he announced, "William is our true King. Yes, he may have vanished from the land when we needed him most, but he has sought me out, a sure sign of wisdom on his part. His quest may well end in failure, but I put it to you that he deserves the chance to redeem himself for his failures. Do you agree?"

The people roared their assent.

"It is decided," he said, and to forestall any cheering, he raised a finger to the sky. "But, to further prove my loyalty to His Majesty, the King, I also say that we, the people of the Dragon Spirit, should give him our greatest boon. I say that we render unto him the Pitchfork of Destiny, that with it, guided by his mighty arm and our prayers, he might strike down the ravening beast of the sky, the Great Dragon of the North. What say you to this?"

He thrust the pitchfork high, and an even louder roar erupted from the crowd.

"It is decided. Let no one say that we did not send him forth with every chance to slay the dragon. And now, in the eyes of all assembled, I, the Dracomancer, grant thee, King William, the Pitchfork of Destiny! Take this pitchfork with my blessing, and should you prove worthy of it, surely you will come back triumphant. But remember, should your courage waver, should your heart weaken, should your fortitude fail, the Pitchfork of Destiny will deny you and leave you naked against the beast's wrath!"

The Dracomancer thrust the pitchfork into Will's hands. Will leaned in close to the Dracomancer, and even as he wrapped his hand around the pitchfork's handle, he whispered, "This isn't my pitchfork."

"Yes, I know," the Dracomancer whispered back, "but your pitchfork simply doesn't look heroic enough."

"But this one will have no special power against the dragon," Will hissed.

"I know that, and you know that, but they don't know that, King William," the Dracomancer said in a mocking, singsong voice. "Will you still take on this quest, or will you turn away now and prove once and for all your title, Yellow King William?"

A mad malevolence shone in the Dracomancer's eyes. He meant for Will to fail, and Will knew if he failed, that nothing would stand in his way of the Dracomancer's climb to the throne. "Still I will go," replied Will. "But be warned, Dracomancer, should we meet again—"

"We will not," the Dracomancer hissed, then he grasped Will's arm and raised it to the sky. "Rejoice! The Dracomancer has blessed the King!"

Prosper erupted into cheers. Will turned to face the people, his people. They were rapturous, and Will resolved to give them the one thing that he could: hope. He raised the pitchfork in the air.

A white horse was brought into the square, and the crowd parted to let Will make his way over to it. There were a tremendous number of shouts. Once he was in the saddle, Will felt his course, whether due to chance or fate, was set. He was going to ride to the Dragon's Tower, and once he was there, he would confront the dragon. And he would sacrifice himself to save the kingdom. And to save Elle.

As soon as Will was out of sight, the crowd began to disperse. Charming was still standing on the stage, watching the road up into the mountains, wondering how, once again, he had been left behind.

The Dracomancer's voice in his ear shook him from his reverie. "I suppose, Lord Charming, that you would like to find your good wife, Lady Charming?"

"What?" asked Charming, raising an eyebrow. "I thought you said she'd left."

"Well, that is what I told the crowd," the Dracomancer said. "The truth is that many among my followers did not like the way she spoke to me or of her skepticism of the Dragon Spirit."

"I have no doubt," Charming said with a grin at how much irritation Liz's sharp tongue must have caused the Dracomancer.

"I was obliged to keep her out of sight. For her own safety, you understand," the Dracomancer said earnestly. "Let me bring you to her."

Charming sheathed his sword. "Thank you, Delbert, I appreciate it."

He put an arm around Charming's shoulder and led him from the stage. With a gesture, a number of his Dracoviziers fell in behind them.

"It is nothing, Lord Charming," the Dracomancer said with a deprecating shrug and directed their steps toward a low building set against the tavern. "How could I do anything less for my best pupil? It is a shame it has been so long since last we met to discourse on dragon lore."

"Until recently, I had thought the need for such studies on my part to be at an end," Charming said. They had reached a door set low into the wall of a stone building. It almost looked like a root cellar. Charming turned to the Dracomancer. "You have put her in here?"

"It is perhaps not what I might have wished for her," the Dracomancer said apologetically, "but I assure you it is very secure."

Two of the Dracoviziers opened the door, and a rush of cold air, on which came the smell of wet and stone and wine, issued forth. A low light flickered from within. "Liz?" Charming called into the room beyond and made his way down two low steps to the door. "Liz, are you there?"

A deep groan came back to him. He had heard that groan before. "Tomas?" He leaned forward.

From the corner of his eye, he saw a flash of movement from behind, but before he could react, a sharp blow landed on his head, and someone pushed him forward. He stumbled into the room, his head spinning and eyes dancing. The doors slammed closed, and the sound of a bolt's being thrown shut rang out. He staggered and spun. The room began to tip sideways. He saw Tomas sitting against one wall, a long chain about one ankle and dozens of empty wine bottles surrounding him, against a second wall was chained a mangy wolf, which was gnawing on the end of a bone.

The wolf looked up and growled, "Oh, blessed moon, not another one."

"Shut up you flea-bitten mongrel," Tomas slurred, then raised a bottle to his lips, and said, "To your health, Lord Charming. I see you have also become a guest of the Dracomancer. I hope you had as much fun as I had getting the invitation." With this Tomas smiled broadly and poked his tongue through a gap where one of his teeth had been knocked out.

It's unclear whether Charming's mind fully registered Beo's presence because his last conscious thought was, *What's that wretched hobgoblin doing here?* before the world rolled over and went dark.

CHAPTER 15

UP IN FLAMES REDUX

The road that led through the Dark Wood and up into the highlands of the Southern Mountains where Dragon Tower stood was exactly where Will had described. Unfortunately, Liz's trip up the mountains was nowhere near as uneventful as her brother's. To begin with, it was spring, which meant constant rain, which meant roads that were more quagmire than road. Also, while slipping out of town was essential to her not getting stopped either by the Dracomancer or Tomas, she hadn't planned or packed for the trip. When she went through her saddlebags, Liz discovered that she had with her one spare cloak and only the most meager of rations.

Liz would have gladly accepted being cold and wet, but the food was a problem. She was ravenous and felt that even the couple of days she had been without good food had left her weaker than usual. Still, this was not the greatest of her concerns. That honor was reserved for the inhabitants of the Dark Wood. In the year since the death of the dragon, many creatures that had formerly avoided the Black Road out of sheer good sense had begun to return. This is not to say that the road had become so mind-bendingly dangerous that it lived up to its reputation—frankly, there weren't enough monsters and evil witches in all of Royaume to do that—but it was no longer the walk in the dragon-patrolled park that it had formerly been.

Among the Dark Wood's new denizens were a pack of particularly mangy and desperate wolves, who liked the woods because the King's hunters still believed the old tales about dragons, and, despite repeated Royal edicts to the contrary, wouldn't enter the place. Liz began to hear the pack's distant howls on the first night of her trip as she huddled in her sodden cloak beneath a dense stand of pines. On the second night, it became clear that either they were getting closer to her or she was getting closer to them. Her sleep, cold and miserable and fitful as it was, was filled with dark and primitive dreams of tooth and claw. By the third night, the air around her seemed alive with their howls, and she did not sleep at all. In fact, she did not even stop to rest but, feeling safer on the move, pressed on into the night, walking her horse when it became too dark to see the path.

Liz first caught sight of the wolves at dawn the next

morning. The sun had come up and was just beginning to paint everything around her in its soft light when Liz saw a pair of yellow eyes staring at her from between two trees. Despite her desire to turn and look, some instinct told Liz to keep her eyes fixed on the trail ahead. Unfortunately, ignoring the wolves did not stop them from gathering. One pair of eyes became two, then four, then eight. The wolves were careful never to come directly into her sight, but Liz could sense them soundlessly pacing her on either side of the trail; like ghosts, they slipped into and out of view behind the trees. It took every ounce of her willpower not to spur her jittery and extremely eager horse into a gallop. Somehow, she knew that the moment she ran, they would be on her.

How long the wolves stalked her she did not know, it could not have been more than an hour, but she gradually noticed that the forest was thinning. The rising sun had begun to fill in the colors around her, and the ever-present browns and greens of the woods were interposed here and there with slashes and pools of blue as the sky became visible through the branches. The path was climbing above the tree line, and the thought that she would soon be leaving the forest behind filled Liz with hope.

As if they sensed her change in mood, the wolves closed in. A bold black wolf stepped first onto the path behind her, flanked by a gray one, which bared its teeth. Four more emerged from the forest, two on either side, so that she could hear their deep panting as they padded alongside. Liz could feel her horse shaking, and she held fast to the reins to keep it from bolting.

They began to yip and bark to each other, and Liz realized it was speech and that she could understand it in parts.

"I don't like this, Rem," one whined to the other. "Beo said we were to bother nobody till he gave the word. Beo said a whole army would be on the march soon, and there would stragglers aplenty to feast on if we were patient."

"Beo said, Beo said," growled the wolf Liz assumed must be Rem. "I don't see Beo here now, Rom, do you? And what if Beo's army does not come?"

"Yeah," yipped a third, who was weaving in and out of some trees on her left. "Beo promises and promises, but since we helped him sneak into Dragon Tower, he's been in town with the men, feasting at their table, and we haven't had so much as a scrap."

"I am hungry," Rem said with a bark. "And who will miss one woman?"

The other wolves yipped their agreement and began to close in even tighter on either side. If she was going to do something, it would have to be soon.

She studied the path ahead. In a few dozen yards, it narrowed as it passed between a large, rocky outcropping on one side and a fairly steep drop-off on the other. The wolves would have to fall back rather than run alongside her.

Hoping to surprise the wolves, Liz reined back and

slowed her reluctant horse to a walk. The poor creature was not happy, and its nostrils were flaring and eyes rolling with fear. As she had hoped, the wolves also slowed, and the four on her flanks fell back. Liz took a strong grip on the reins, tensed her body, and as she drew even with the outcropping, she let out a sharp cry and drove her heels hard into the flanks of her horse.

Her mount, already anxious to run, sprang forward with a great leap. She felt the wind catch her hair and send it streaming back behind her. The wolves, momentarily surprised, were slow to react, but then, with a collective, bloodcurdling howl, they gave chase. Answering howls echoed from ahead and Liz saw two more wolves blocking the path in front of her. Beyond them, a horizon of blue sky beckoned.

She slapped the reins hard against her horse's side, trying to urge the last measure of speed out of the animal and leaned forward in her saddle. The waiting wolves, teeth bared, lunged. At the last moment Liz rose in her stirrups, and the horse leapt. Liz felt one of her mount's hind legs connect with the body of one of the wolves, and she heard the snap of jaws, but then they were past, and ahead lay a straight stretch of open ground as the trail traced a high, rocky ridge.

A wild and terrible cacophony of howls erupted from behind her. Liz took one quick glance back as they raced along the rising path and saw a dozen wolves, eyes blazing with anger, sprinting behind her. The horse needed no urging now. It laid its ears back and galloped as fast as it could. Liz barely stayed in the saddle.

A desperate race ensued in those high mountains, with Liz only vaguely in control of her plunging mount. On the rare portions of the road that were mostly straight, she would leave the wolves behind, but often the road would twist and turn back on itself like a writhing snake, and the wolves would close. At these times, their howls, echoing off the rock faces of the cliffs, seemed to surround them.

Finally, they rounded a bend, and Liz sighted Dragon Tower. It sat on a high ridge overlooking the trail at the top of a steep, winding footpath. Liz realized that it would be impossible to take her horse up to the tower. She needed to put as much distance between her and the wolves as she could and leave the horse to see to its own safety.

Leaning into the creature's neck, she slapped the reins hard against its blowing sides. The horse must have been exhausted; foam blew from its muzzle, but still, at her urging, it put on a last burst of speed. The howls of the wolves fell back.

As they neared the narrow stair that marked the entrance to the path, she pulled hard on the reins, and her horse slid to a stop. Leaping off, she unbuckled the straps that held the saddle and bridle in place and slapped the horse on the side. With the wolves' howls growing louder behind them, the mount launched itself along the road and, a second later, had rounded a curve and was gone.

Liz sent one brief prayer to the heavens that her horse would escape as she turned her own feet to the winding footpath and began climbing as fast as her legs could manage. Unfortunately, whether it was the mountain air or the general lethargy and lack of energy that had afflicted her lately, Liz found herself slowing and stumbling after only a few twists of the trail.

About halfway up, her head spinning from exertion, Liz's legs almost gave way, but at that moment, the wolves, their tongues hanging from their muzzles, came into view. She held her breath and hoped that they would miss her scent and continue their pursuit of the horse, but it was not to be. They sniffed about at her discarded tackle, then one caught her scent at the stair and let loose a bloodcurdling howl. The wolves all began to climb after her. Ignoring her shaking legs and the burning pain of her body, Liz resumed her own climb.

The narrow, winding path slowed the wolves considerably, but even still, they were much faster than she was. When they had started their desperate race, she had been halfway up the cliff and the wolves two turnings of the trail behind. A third of the way from the top, they were only one twist of the trail behind her. When at last she reached the top of the ridge and drew even with the thorn-encased tower, they made the last turn. Only a few hundred feet separated them from her and about as much distance separated her from the tower door.

Gritting her teeth against the blazing pain in her side, Liz stumbled forward, but when she lifted her eyes to the tower door, all hope left her. Huge boulders stacked in a haphazard mound completely blocked the entry.

"No!" she wailed.

The strength of will that had kept her moving left her body. Her legs collapsed beneath her, pitching her forward onto her hands and knees. A breath later, the wolves had surrounded her. Liz closed her eyes.

"I'm sorry, Elle . . . Will," she gasped, and clutching her ringed hand to her breast, sobbed, "I love you, Edward."

She felt teeth pulling and ripping at the skirt of her dress. She flailed about with her feet and hands, refusing to die without a last struggle, then a blast of heat like a thousand forges passed over her in a wave, taking her breath away. The stench of burning hair filled the air, followed by wild yelps and howls of pain and panic from the wolves.

Liz opened her eyes and saw a vast shadow descending on her from above. It brought back memories of the night at the farm in Prosper.

"Run, Will," she said in a hoarse whisper. "The dragon has come."

She felt herself being lifted into the air and had enough time to remember vaguely that Will was not here and that she was not in Prosper before she passed quite willingly into the arms of unconsciousness.

As she slept, Liz dreamed that she was sitting on the old wagon from the Prosper farm, the reins to their old nag, Grey, in her hands. Will was standing beside the wagon, looking at her sternly.

"How do you plan on sneaking up on the dragon, Liz?" he was asking.

She said nothing, not having a ready answer at hand.

"How are you going to get into the tower?" he asked in follow-up.

Again, she had no answer, but this time bit the side of her thumb nervously.

"Where did you leave the pitchfork? What are you going to do if you get it? How are you going to rescue Elle?"

He asked these questions one after the other, giving her no time to answer, which was just as well because she seemed to have been struck dumb.

"Liz, what if she is already dead?" he asked earnestly.

She replied with her own question. "Why would you ask that?"

"See," Will answered, but in the voice of Elle, "I told you she wasn't dead. Now would you please hand me that bucket of water."

"Fine," came another voice, refined and very deep. "And I didn't say she was dead only that she *should* be dead. There is a very great distinction between the two, as anyone in the fields of dragon slaying or tightrope walking will tell you."

The scene dissolved. Something cool was being held to her forehead. Liz blinked open her eyes, and there was Elle, her golden hair framing her smiling face. Behind her, also peering down, were the flame-colored eyes and enormous gray head of the dragon.

Liz gave a gasp of alarm and tried to scramble backwards away from the monster.

Elle held up her hands in a gesture of peace. "It's okay, Liz, he's a . . . well . . . he's not going to hurt you." She turned back to the dragon, and, putting her hands on her hips, said, "What are you doing hovering over her like that? Are you trying to scare her to death?"

"I was concerned," the dragon said in an injured tone. "I have no confidence at all that you know what you're doing, Lady Rapunzel. It seems to me that all young ladies are taught these days is how to do needlework and look elegant."

"Oh, and you've had so much practice nursing the wounded?" she replied tartly with a shake of her finger. "Your response to every problem seems to be to try crisping it. I thought I told you be careful, and yet the next thing you're doing is breathing flame all over her."

The dragon drew himself up with what Liz could only describe as an affronted expression. "She was perfectly safe, Lady Rapunzel. I have absolute control over my flames."

"Absolute control? Absolute control?" Elle said in a rising voice of disbelief. "Look at the hem of her dress, it's still smoldering."

Liz followed the dragon's eyes down to the bottom

of her gown, which she saw had been scorched in a number of places. The dragon *humphed* at this, blowing out a cloud of noxious vapor from his nostrils in the process.

"I see you have no intention of thanking me for saving your friend, Lady Rapunzel," the dragon said with a flip of his head. "Will you at least do me the pleasure of introducing us?"

Elle look uncertainly back and forth between Liz and the dragon. She sighed. "Volthraxus, this is Lady Elizabeth Charming. Liz, this is Volthraxus, the Dragon of the North."

"I see," Volthraxus said with a hiss. "So, this is the sister of the dragonslayer, King William."

Liz drew herself up into a seated position, her back against a tapestry-covered wall, and said weakly, "I will offer you my thanks, Lord Volthraxus, and then I will ask why you bothered."

"Why I bothered?" the dragon asked with an arch of the ridge of gray plates above one eye.

"Yes," she said, and her voice grew stronger as her wits returned and her anger at the pain, destruction, and chaos the dragon had caused flared to life. "Do you also intend to hold me hostage?"

The dragon nodded. "Knowing who you are, I will certainly consider the possibility, yes."

"I will not be held hostage."

"Oh, will you not?" he said with a smirk and a derisive flick of his forked tongue. "And, if I choose to keep you, what can *you* do to prevent it?"

"Stop it!" Elle said to the dragon sharply. "Why do you insist on being so cruel?"

The dragon shrugged and, turning away, settled himself on a worn spot of carpet near a large, open balcony that looked out on blue sky and snowcapped mountains.

Elle bent down to Liz and handed her a tin cup filled with cool water. "Drink this, Liz. You look exhausted. Are you not feeling well?"

"I did just get chased through the woods by a pack of bloodthirsty wolves, Elle. Oh, and then got 'rescued' by a fire-breathing dragon," Liz said with a grimace, but she took the water and drank some greedily. She was suddenly very, very hungry and wished that Elle had offered her something to eat also.

Elle cast a glance back at the dragon, which appeared to have fallen into a deep sleep. "Are Will and Charming with you?" she asked in a low voice.

Liz shook her head. "I have no idea where they are, Elle."

Elle frowned at this. "You mean they are on their own? All this time, I had hoped that they would have you to keep an eye on them."

"They took off right after your capture," Liz said, and took another deep drink of the water. "Will was . . . distraught."

"What do you mean?" Elle asked, her face lined with worry.

Liz made a sort of half-shrugging gesture with her hands. How could she possibly explain the state Will was in without throwing her friend into despair? "He is young, Elle," she said delicately. "Apart from our parents, and he was too young to really remember them, he has never lost anyone he's loved, and he has never loved anyone as he loves you. He . . ."

"What, Liz," Elle asked desperately, "whatever it is I must know."

"He is mad with despair," she said. Behind them, the dragon shifted in its sleep, and Liz dropped her voice to the barest of whispers. "He will not stop until he finds you."

"And . . . Charming?" Elle asked, tears pooling in the corners of her eyes.

Liz nodded. "He is with him, and you know that he will not abandon Will, wherever that takes him. Unless we can help them, they will both die trying to save you."

"What can we do?" Elle asked, and her voice was a little ragged. "I mean"—she gestured around at the little, tapestry-lined, round room and the sleeping dragon—"we don't have a lot of options."

Liz pulled her friend closer. "I spoke to Gwendolyn, and I think the answer is here. Have you seen a pitchfork somewhere in the tower? Its ends would have been melted and the handle blackened."

Elle's eyes widened. "Yes, but it's gone."

"What do you mean, gone?" Liz asked.

"If it ever existed," came the dragon's deep voice.

They both flinched and turned to see the dragon staring at them, its eyes the merest slits.

Elle raised her chin defiantly. "It isn't polite to eavesdrop."

"And it isn't polite to plot against your host," the dragon said sardonically.

Anger flared anew in Liz, and she said sharply, "However polite your manner may be, you are not our host, Dragon, you are our jailer, and whatever gratitude I owe you for saving my life from the wolves I balance against the fact that you have kidnapped my friend and announced your intention to kill my brother."

"You have made your feelings toward me quite clear, Lady Elizabeth, and I hope to make mine just as clear to you," the dragon said, rising so that his head loomed above them. "As you have no love for me, I have no love for your brother. He was responsible for Magdela's death—"

"I have told you he did not raise a hand against Magdela." Elle came forward, pleading. "It was an accident."

The dragon did not react to Elle's plea but kept staring at Liz, eyes blazing with rage. "So you have said, but even if that is true, he fed off her death like a vulture." He raised a long claw and pointed it at Liz accusingly. "Your brother, King William, dares call himself the 'dragonslayer.' Either he tells the truth, in which case he is guilty of her murder, or he is a liar, in which case he trades on her death to his own gain. In either case, I will exact my measure of vengeance on him."

Liz pulled herself up from the ground. "Yes, he lied. We lied," she said, breathing hard from the effort of standing. "You seem to be the only being within several kingdoms who was not aware of the fact. And you can say that he was responsible for her death, and I suppose in the twisted logic of your mind, that makes sense, but she is the one who was trying to murder us. If she had let us be that night, then we would likely still be farmers, and she might still be alive."

The dragon stared at her, seething malevolence, and she tried to meet his gaze, but her head was swimming again. She leaned back against wall to keep from falling, gulping air.

"Your appeal is denied, Lady Elizabeth," the dragon said, his voice iron.

Her vision blurred, but she could see that he was withdrawing, turning away. She knew that antagonizing the dragon was foolish, but she would not remain a captive to serve as the same kind of mad distraction for Charming that Elle had become for Will. She would rather die now than become the reason for his death. Quietly, mostly because she could not work up the strength for anything louder, she said, "Of course, had you thought to rescue Magdela from her own fairy enslavement, perhaps she would still be alive today. I suppose you did not think enough of her then to come to her aid."

There was the sound of sudden movement, and she tensed herself for the killing blow that she expected to come. But nothing happened. She looked up and saw to her alarm that Elle was standing between her and the dragon's massive claw.

"Move aside, Lady Rapunzel," the dragon said, his harsh voice having lost much of its earlier refinement. "I mean you no harm."

"Don't you see," she said her voice plaintive, "if you harm her, you harm me. If you kill Will, you will kill me. That is what I've been trying to tell you from the beginning. If I have stayed with you, willingly, it's only because I know that the only escape for me would be through death, and that would kill Will, but if you go ahead with your plan to slay William Pickett, then I will follow him into that final darkness. If you continue, there will be nothing but sadness at the end of this story."

Liz held her breath as the dragon stared down at Elle, his deadly, taloned claw still poised to strike, but how the dragon might have answered or the moment resolved she would never discover as just then, there was a shout from outside the tower.

It was Will.

"Hail, Great Dragon of the North. I am King William of Royaume. I ask for proof that the Lady Rapunzel still lives. If she does, I am ready to discuss your demands."

CHAPTER 16

DRAGON TOWER BURNING BRIGHT

The fire in the Dragon's eyes rekindled as he heard Will's challenge. With a rush of movement that sent the tapestries on the walls fluttering, Volthraxus sprang to the edge of the balcony and screamed his hatred.

"HERE I AM, KING WILLIAM, DRAGON-SLAYER!" Volthraxus roared, beating his wings and sending a terrible wind rushing through the room that knocked Elle and Liz back into the wall. Holding each other for support, the two women tried to fight their way to the balcony, but it was useless.

Will's answer floated up from below, "I am ready to meet your challenge, Dragon, but first show me that Lady Rapunzel remains unharmed."

"I will do more than that, King William, Dragonslayer," Volthraxus said, and he reached back with his tail and pulled Liz and Elle toward him in a sweeping motion so that they found themselves at the balustrade looking down at Will, who was standing before the boulder-blocked door of the tower in tattered clothes with a pitchfork in his hand. He had never looked more like a farmer.

His eyes alighted on Elle first, and he called out, "Are you well, Elle?" But then his gaze took in Liz, and they watched as his face visibly paled, and he shouted, "Liz? What are you doing here?"

"We are both fine, Will," Elle shouted back to him.

Liz added, "Now get out of here, you ninny, before you get yourself killed."

"I would not advise taking your sister's advice, King William, Dragonslayer," the dragon called down with a hiss and a spurt of flame.

"I have no intention of running, Dragon," Will said. "Leave the ladies alone and let us be done."

"AS YOU WISH!"

"Wait!" Elle cried, and reached a hand up to the dragon's chest. "Will you take me down with you so that I may at least say goodbye?" she asked in a fragile voice. "Please?"

"Elle!" Liz said in a shocked voice.

"Liz, be quiet," Elle snapped.

Volthraxus looked down at her with his molten eyes. "Normally, I would grant such a request, but I know you too well, little princess. I fear that your desire to say goodbye is a subterfuge for some grand

and noble gesture on your part that might lead to some harm coming to you. You may say your farewells from here, I think."

"You are cruel."

"Perhaps," he replied. "However, I think that it would be more cruel to King William if he died knowing that you had come to harm when he might have prevented it." Volthraxus raised his head to address Will. "What do you say, King William, Dragonslayer, shall I transport Lady Rapunzel down to the field of combat?"

"He's right, Elle, it would be better if you stayed where you were," Will said from the bottom of the tower. "Besides, I've been two weeks on the road, so you probably don't want to get too close right now anyway."

"You do look a mess," she said with a cluck of her tongue.

They stood in silence for a time, their eyes drinking each other in, absorbing every detail.

At last, Will said, "You let your hair grow out."

Elle touched her head self-consciously. "Yes. I'm sorry, I haven't had a chance to get it cut since—"

"No!" he said brightly. "I like it. The way it spills over your shoulders and how the sun catches in it. I want to remember you like this."

Tears sprang into their eyes and ran down their faces as they gazed at each other.

"Elle, I wish . . ." Will started, but then stopped, and said, "The dress is beautiful."

"You peeked!" she said accusingly, and wiped at her eyes with the edge of her dress.

He shrugged. "Sorry."

Will's face became serious, and he said, "You should wear it someday. It may not be with me, but it should be with someone. Elle, promise me that you will wear it!"

"No!" she sobbed, and reached out a hand toward him. "Will! No! There must be a way. Volthraxus! Please!"

"You monster!" Liz was suddenly shouting, shaking her fist up at the dragon's face. "How can you do this to them? How can a thinking being who says that he has felt love do this?"

"Enough!" Volthraxus rumbled angrily and, using his tail to push Liz and Elle to the side, stepped forward to the very edge of the balcony, beat his wings against the air and threw himself off the tower. He glided down in a half circle so that he landed near where the trail emerged onto the tower's ledge.

"As you can see, King William, Dragonslayer," Volthraxus said, spreading his great gray wings out to the sides, "I have fulfilled my portion of the bargain. The ladies are unharmed, and when our combat is at an end, I will free them and not stop or hinder their flight in any manner; nor will I raise a talon against them unless you choose this day to flee from your appointed doom."

Will nodded. "You have done all you promised, Dragon. I will not run."

"Yes, you will, William Pickett," Liz shouted down at him.

She grabbed Elle by the hand and ran back across the tower to the stair. They raced down the stairs and across the debris-filled lower chamber to the blocked doorway. Through the gaps in the rocks, they could see Will, his back to them, facing off against the dragon.

"I love you, Will!" Elle cried out as she banged her fists futilely against the stones.

"I love you, Elle!" Will cried, and, coming to the other side of the rocks, he reached his arm through a slight gap so that their fingertips touched. He peered through the crack into the darkness. "Liz, take care of her, and tell Charming thanks for everything."

"Will, behind you!" Liz shouted.

Volthraxus had closed the distance between them in two steps of lethal grace. He reared himself above Will, his great gray wings flapping and fire issuing from his mouth, and gazed down at him as molten flames danced in his eyes.

Will circled around to the side of dragon, putting some distance between them and where Liz and Elle were standing.

"Now we fight, King William, slayer of Magdela," the dragon said, hissing flame and steam. "I have the fires of the infernal. You have your Pitchfork of Destiny. I fight for the memory of my beloved. You fight for your kingdom and bride. Shall we begin?"

"No," Will said calmly.

He threw the pitchfork to the side and fell to his knees.

Behind him, Liz and Elle were shouting. "Will, No! Don't!" "Run, Will!"

Volthraxus ignored the shouts of the women and, as smoke continued to leak from his snout, took a step back, and rumbled, "What is the meaning of this? Do you refuse my challenge?"

Will looked up to meet Volthraxus's terrible gaze, and said, "I accept your challenge, Dragon, but I am not here to fight. I am here to end this. If only my life will satisfy your need for vengeance, then I give it to you. I give it to you with the understanding that you will leave Royaume, satisfied by the exchange, and that you will no longer terrorize my people or seek further retribution on my family. Do we have an accord?"

"Will! You can't!" Elle screamed with a sob.

Liz shouted, "Move aside, Elle!"

There was a loud crash as something heavy and wooden was thrown or rammed against the boulder barricade.

Volthraxus ignored the screams and shouts and leaned in close to Will, his hot breath scalding Will's face. "Do you think I will be swayed to mercy by this gesture? Do you think I will let you live because you are willing to sacrifice yourself?"

"No." Will said, still staring into the dragon's molten eyes. "I expect you will kill me, but this is no longer about me. You keep calling me dragonslayer, but since my crowning, I have not claimed that title. I do, however, call myself King, and I understand better now than I did before what that means. It means that my life must be lived for the betterment of my people, even those that reject and scorn me. I give my life for theirs, for Elle and Liz and all the others who would be subject to your wrath should I refuse. Now, do we have an accord?"

Will's steady gaze seemed to be making Volthraxus uncomfortable, and the dragon retreated a step and cocked its head as if in thought.

There were more shouts from Elle and Liz, and more sounds of heavy objects being battered against the stone blockade. One of the boulders shifted.

"I don't understand," Volthraxus growled. "Are you so tired of life?"

"I don't expect you to understand, Volthraxus," he said. "However, I am trusting to your word that you will not harm the people of my kingdom, and that you will see that Lady Elizabeth and Lady Rapunzel make it safely back to Prosper."

"You are putting a lot of faith in the word of a monster," Volthraxus said. "Why?"

Will's grim expression finally broke, and he smiled. "Because I had the best teacher of dragon lore in the kingdom. Prince Charming told me all about you, and he told me that Volthraxus was an honorable dragon."

Volthraxus nodded. "Very well. If this is what you wish. I think it is a pity that we did not get a chance to fight." There was real regret in his voice. "I think you would have made a worthy foe."

Liz's and Elle's shouts grew louder. There was the

sound of more rocks falling and tumbling over one another.

Will smiled a little self-mocking smile. "I probably would have disappointed you. I don't even know how to hold a sword properly." His face grew serious again. "You will keep them safe?"

Volthraxus nodded, then opened his mouth. Will saw within a sight that few in the world have ever seen and lived to tell of, the fiery maw of a dragon. He felt the heat build, said a silent goodbye to Elle, Liz, and even Charming, and closed his eyes.

At that moment, something soft that smelled like jasmine struck him in the chest. Elle wrapped her arms around him and buried her face in his neck. In a startled panic, Will twisted around so that his body would shield Elle as much as possible from the dragon's lethal breath. He felt a terrible heat pass just over the top of him.

"Elle!" "Lady Rapunzel!" he and Volthraxus both shouted once the flames had passed.

"What is the meaning of this?" Volthraxus demanded above them. "I could have killed you, Lady Rapunzel."

"Don't blame her," Lady Elizabeth shouted between heaving breaths. "You tried to burn her to death."

"I did nothing of the sort," the dragon said, indignantly pointing a claw at Will. "I was trying to burn him to death, and she leapt in the way. It's only by a miracle that I managed to redirect the fire at the last moment. I think I may have strained something," he said, holding a talon to his throat.

Behind them came a crackling and the smell of smoke. The dragon's flame had caught the rosebushes that grew around the tower's base on fire and, in seconds, the tangled vines were a raging pyre, leaping up the sides of the stone structure.

"Great," the dragon said with disgust. "Now what are we going to do?" He gestured with frustration at the burning tower. "I can't very well put you and Elle back in the tower, can I? But if I leave you out here, you two are going to keep finding ways to get in my way."

"I hate to say that this is your problem," Liz said unsympathetically, "but it is your problem."

"It is all very irritating," Volthraxus said.

Elle and Will were holding each other on the ground. Elle was saying, "How could you think to leave me like that? You must promise never to leave me." Will was saying, "Don't you ever, ever do that again." They paid no attention to Liz and the dragon's exchange or the fire raging a few feet away.

"And, look at them," Volthraxus said with a strange mixture of disgust and wistfulness. "I mean, it lacks a certain dignity to roll about like that kissing and hugging and touching, don't you think?"

"Yes," Liz said this time with a great deal of sympathy. "I have to admit it is an unseemly sight. I'm not sure that a king and his future queen should be behaving in that manner—publicly."

Volthraxus settled himself on the ground and sighed. "This isn't working out to be as violently cathartic as I had hoped."

"Perhaps," Liz suggested, "you might consider scrapping the whole idea of revenge."

In the dragon's eyes, the flicker of anger kindled, flamed, and grew. "I would like to, Lady Elizabeth, I swear that I would, but as much as we pride ourselves on our intelligence, we dragons are essentially creatures of emotion. I can no more ignore this anger that rages in me than I can ignore a hunger in my belly. I must answer vengeance's call. It is my nature."

Liz sat next to him, and they watched the tower burn and tried to ignore the endless litany of sweet-nothings being whispered between Elle and Will. Finally, she looked over to the dragon. "Why do you think your anger picked Will, I mean, King William, as its focus?"

"I suppose," Volthraxus said thoughtfully, "because he is the most blameworthy. It was his pitchfork that slew her, it was his field where she fell, and it is his head that wears the crown as a result."

Liz was quiet for a moment, then said softly, "It isn't much, is it?"

"No," the dragon admitted sadly.

"In fact, you could put as much or more blame on me," she said. Volthraxus looked at her skeptically. "It's true. It was in trying to protect me that Will found himself in that field in the first place. Had he never gone out there to draw her away from the farmhouse, probably Magdela never would have attacked us. Also, I profited as much from her death as he did. It is only because of Magdela that I met my Charming. Without her death, I would be a spinster desired by no one and doomed to a life of drudgery and loneliness. Would you be satisfied to exact your revenge on me?"

A knowing smile stretched across his face, and the fire ebbed in his eyes. "No, Lady Elizabeth. I am sorry for my behavior earlier, but you may be the last person I would choose to harm."

"But I am as guilty—"

"Your guilt or innocence has nothing to do with it."

"What then?"

"You will know soon enough, suffice it to say my personal code of honor prevents me from harming you. Besides," he said with a sigh, "I am beginning to see that if anyone is to blame, it is I. You were right in the tower, Lady Elizabeth. I didn't love her enough. I should have come for her sooner, but I kept making excuses and finding reasons to delay. Are those the actions of an honorable dragon?"

Liz had no idea what an honorable dragon acted like, and so did not answer, but, as she watched Elle run her fingers through Will's hair and sigh, a sudden thought struck her. "I don't think you are any more to blame than Will and I."

The dragon looked at her with a rise of his scaly eyebrow. "I don't think you have a firm grasp of self-preservation, Lady Elizabeth."

"You just told me I'm the last person you would choose to harm, Volthraxus. Forgive me if I'm feeling a little reckless, but if you are going to keep me in fear of my life, you need to work on your intimidation," she said with a waggle of her tongue.

Volthraxus looked a little hurt. "I think I'm very intimidating." Then, looking around at Will and Elle kissing and Liz, who was now resting against one of his taloned claws, he added, "Perhaps not at this particular moment, but you know what I mean."

"Yes, Volthraxus," she said in an encouraging voice. "I am sure you are usually very ferocious."

"So if I am not to blame, and you're not to blame, and Will's not to blame, who can I blame?" he asked, trying to change the subject.

"Magdela," Liz said softly.

There was a rumble of anger from Volthraxus. "Be very careful, Lady Elizabeth. My patience can be stretched too far!"

The anger in the dragon's voice snapped Elle and Will out of their lover's embrace. "What's the matter?" Will said. "I thought the rumbling part was over?"

"Your sister was explaining how Magdela was responsible for her own death," Volthraxus hissed angrily.

"Liz!" Will and Elle both said in surprise.

"She was!" Liz said, and, standing, began pacing in front of the dragon. "Volthraxus, in the brief time I have known you, I have found you to be a refined dragon."

"It's true," Elle said passionately, running a hand through her mussed-up hair and rearranging her clothes. "He doesn't like to eat people. He doesn't even like to attack or kill people. For the most part, he is satisfied with an occasional pig."

"More than occasional," Volthraxus interjected.

"Fine," Elle said, "I was trying not to bring attention to the fact that you have been overeating since you got here and have put on a few pounds."

Liz giggled at this, and the dragon shot her a glance, and said snidely, "I would not be snickering, Lady Charming, if I were you."

"What's that supposed to mean?" she said, and her face reddened.

"Nothing," Volthraxus said. "I want to know why you would malign Magdela's good name."

"Was Magdela good? You might not like to kill and eat people, but she did. She killed and slaughtered the people of Royaume for decades. On the night of her death, she was coming to kill Will and me. How could you, who seems to dislike, or at least disdain violence, want to be with her?"

Volthraxus thought about this for a long time. When at last he spoke, it was to ask her a question. "How can you, a practical, levelheaded woman, want to be with Prince Charming? According to everything I've heard, he is everything you are not. He is vain, self-obsessed, flighty, given over to deep passions about trivial things like fashion, poetry, and how good his calves look in hose. How can you have fallen in love with him?"

"She was your Prince Charming," she whispered.

"Perhaps." He shrugged his shoulders and settled

his head lower onto the ground. "I have no answer for either of us, Lady Elizabeth. Perhaps there is no answer for why we love whom we do. All I know is that I did love her. I loved her the first time I saw her. In that moment, my heart roared to life as it hadn't for centuries. If it gives you any comfort, though, my rage is gone. I am done with revenge. All I feel is cold."

They were all silent. Liz rested her body against his face and embraced him, and they watched the top of the tower catch and burn, flaring brightly as the flames reached the ancient tapestries and rugs, until the entire structure was a giant torch.

At some point, Will rose to his feet. "I hate to bring an end to this, but I'm afraid I must be on my way back to Prosper to try to reclaim my kingdom."

"What do you mean?" asked Elle, putting her hand in his.

"There is a madman down there calling himself the Dracomancer, and he has gathered an army of zealots, and if I don't find a way to convince those people that he is dangerous, they might just go on following him and put him on the throne. I may not be a good king, but I'm pretty sure he would be a disaster."

"Surely, the people will rally to you once Volthraxus is gone," Elle tried to reassure him.

"I'm not so sure," Will said, frowning. "My disappearance was badly done on my part. The people are convinced I abandoned them, and they aren't wrong. I was being selfish. Also, the Dracomancer has a certain charisma. He is promising them safety and power, and it may sound awfully tempting to a lot of people." He took both her hands in his. "I'm sorry, love, but when this is all said and done, I might be out of a job."

"The Dracomancer?" asked Volthraxus.

"What, you know him?" asked Will.

"Certainly," Volthraxus said, and he snickered a little so that little trickles of flame spilled out from between his teeth. "He's actually a bit of a joke among my kind. He goes about 'studying' dragons, annoying them with questions, really, and picking up bits of old scale and what not. I think he claims to command 'dragon spirits,' whatever that means. The only dragon spirit I'm aware of is draconic brandy,* which is quite delicious, but also quite rare. I questioned him once, quite pointedly, as to whether he had any, and he swore he didn't. He might have been lying, but as I was holding him upside down over the edge of a thousand-span drop, I have some confidence he was telling the truth."

The dragon started to rise, shaking himself like a dog and stretching his wings wide.

"Anyway," he said, tasting the wind with his forked tongue, "if that lunatic is around, I really should be going. He is such a bore."

---

* Author's Note: According to Edward Charming and other draconic scholars, the distilling of draconic brandy requires fermenting apples, grapes, and apricots in honey, then boiling it in the infernal fires of the nether, and aging it for at least a century in a barrel made out of the wood from the timbers of sunken ships.

"No, you won't be going anywhere just yet," said Elle, planting herself in front of the dragon and wagging a finger at him. "You owe me."

"Owe you?" he rumbled deeply.

"Yes," she said seriously. "Your abduction of me started this whole mess. It forced Will . . . I mean King William . . . to leave the castle to come look for me. It brought the Dracomancer to power, and it is threatening Royaume. You have to fix it."

The massive dragon stared down at the little woman, who stared back up at him, utterly unconcerned by the difference in their sizes. Finally, his body slumped, and his horns dropped. "What can I do?"

"Deal with the Dracomancer," she said, a dark note in her voice.

"Elle," Will said with concern. "I don't know—"

She cut him off. "King William, you cannot allow this man to run free in our kingdom. His followers must be made to see that he cannot protect them as you can. Once he is gone, they will fall back in line."

Will and Liz looked at the petite woman with new respect. There was steel in her eyes and her tone that would brook no debate.

Volthraxus nodded. "You are right, Lady Rapunzel, I should put things to right. I owe you at least that much."

To Will, he added, "You have found yourself a marvelous queen, King William. I do not have to tell you that I will take it as a very grave issue between us if ever I hear of you mistreating her. Although, from my experience, I think that she will have no trouble defending herself and those things and people she loves."

To Elle he said, "Lady Rapunzel, if only you were a dragon."

She blushed.

He lowered himself to the ground so that they could climb onto his back, and, with Dragon Tower burning behind them, they floated down over the mountains toward Prosper.

CHAPTER 17

FOR WHOM THE BELLS TOLL

We rarely hear about what happens to fairy-tale kingdoms once the happily ever afters are over. How exactly did Sleeping Beauty's kingdom recover after having been frozen in place for a century? Did the three little pigs really get along living under the same roof? There must have been a reason they decided to build three separate houses in the first place, right? With her stepsisters having had their eyes plucked out and their feet mutilated by her stepmother, how awkward were the holidays for Cinderella?

After the death of Magdela, the Great Wyrm of the South, and the ascension of King William to the throne, Prosper had become a major tourist attraction. One of the biggest draws was the weekly ringing of the bells, when the town reenacted the dragon's attack and death, culminating with the raising of the dragon's head, or at least a papier-mâché version of it, on the maypole in the town square. Unfortunately, early reviews of the staged celebration were rather poor.*

In response to the critical panning, a special effort had been made by the town to up the "wow" factor. One of the first things they did, apart from replacing their homemade dragon's head, was to "restore" the bells of Prosper. That this restoration included expanding the church tower and adding a half dozen additional bells that had never before existed did not appear to bother anyone. Still, no one could have anticipated at the time that the bells of Prosper would ring again, or really ring for the first time since nearly all of them were new, to occasion one of the most important events in the kingdom's history.

Had Edward Michael Charming been asked to write a review of his visit to Prosper, it might not have

---

* Author's Note: S. Tagger's review of the Prosper Dragonfest in his book *Staggering Along: A Guide to Royaume* was particularly harsh. An excerpt is provided here. "I arrived in Prosper at about noon and my first reaction was, 'Is this it?' The town has a lovely green, if what you are looking for in a town green is well-tended grass and little else. There is one inn, one tavern and nothing to do but drink warm, overpriced beer and wait till morning when the death of the dragon is reenacted. The reenactment itself is quaint, if you define quaint as cringeworthy. It certainly does not make the journey south worth the trip. Take the bells, bell really, for at least when I visited, only one bell was working. I had heard about the ringing of the bells of Prosper for months, but in reality they are barely audible over the screams of the children that flock to the papier-mâché dragon's head the townspeople drag out to the green for the occasion. As for the fake dragon's head itself, all I can say is, no. Just, no."

been as generous as S. Tagger's. He spent his days in the town manacled to a wall in a wine cellar underneath Prosper's tavern next to his passed-out ex-squire, Tomas, and the Dracomancer's ex-henchwolf, Beo. After spending most of his life having never been manacled to anything, this made the second time in as many days. Needless to say, Charming was beginning to have doubts about the direction his life was taking.

The worst part about his captivity was not necessarily the fact that he was chained up, or the fact that he had been relegated to a wine cellar, the single cell in the constable's hall currently hosting Gwendolyn Mostfair and her fiancé, but that he had to share his makeshift cell with Tomas and Beo. It wasn't that they didn't have their uses. From Tomas, he was able to learn everything that had happened to Liz on their journey, including her trip to visit Gwendolyn, and his implausible brawl with half the Dracolyte army prior to his capture. While from Beo he heard a blow-by-blow account of the dragon's capture of Elle and of their flight to the south. The problem was that neither of them was particularly lucid. Tomas was drunk most of the time, and so his stories were interspersed with periods of unconsciousness and indescribably bad bouts of singing, and as for Beo, he spent every moment he could grousing about the seemingly endless number of ways life had treated him wrong. At this moment, Tomas was snoring in his corner, and so he was being regaled with another of the wolf's litany of woes.

"Whatever happened to a man's word being his

bond?" Beo asked rhetorically, for he never actually appreciated it when Charming replied.

Charming ignored the creature and focused on the chains that held him to the wall. He had been working at them for days now, but all he had to show for it were bruised and bloodied wrists. Nevertheless, he had vowed not to give up until he was reunited with Liz and Will and Elle. He gathered what remained of his strength, and renewed his efforts, pulling and twisting at the manacles.

Beside him, Beo continued his thought. "Twice now I have made a partnership, once with Volthraxus and once with the Dracomancer, and twice I have been left worse off for the exchange. There can be no dispute that I delivered my part of the bargain in each case." The wolf picked up a bone in his paws and gestured with it at Charming and the unconscious Tomas. "Did I or did I not deliver Elle's location to Volthraxus and make her capture possible? And, did I or did I not deliver the Pitchfork of Destiny, the one weapon capable of slaying the dragon, into the hands of the Dracomancer?" Beo stuck the bone in his mouth and chewed on it a bit. Between cracks and crunches, he concluded, "I did. And what do I have to show for it?"

Charming felt a trickle of warm blood running down his right arm. The pain was growing intolerable. He slumped to the ground, breathing hard. "Nothing." He sighed.

"That's right," Beo snarled around the bone. "Nothing! Worse than nothing, for at least I was a free wolf before. Now look at me. Chained like a common dog."

"It seems to me you've gotten no more than you deserve," Charming said coldly. "You are a spy, a thief, and a traitor."

Beo cocked his head to one side in quiet thought, "Fair point, but I still say it isn't right."

All at once, bells began to ring. At first it was one, then two, but soon, from all across Prosper, bells of every tone chimed, rang, and clanged in dreadful earnest. Soon, other noises began to filter through the thick door of their prison, screams and shouts of alarm, people running, the clash of arms.

"Tomas!" Charming called out. "Tomas! Wake up!"

Tomas sat up and blinked blearily. "Wassat?"

"Something's happening," Charming said.

"Knowing my luck, it's probably a festival to roast the wolf," Beo groused.

"About time," Tomas said with a nod, and rolled back onto his side.

Charming had something he needed to say to Tomas. He'd been thinking about it for weeks now, ever since his disastrous turn as squire. Now was as good a time as ever. "Tomas, in case I don't get the chance again," Charming said. "I want you to know that you were a tremendous squire. I . . ." He took a deep breath. "I apologize for being so ungrateful and insulting over the years."

Tomas began to snore again.

Charming was looking about to see if there was anything he could throw at the man to rouse him when the doors to the cellar flew open. Light flooded in as three Dracoviziers clambered down the steps into the cellar, followed by the Dracomancer, whose hands were shaking.

"Quickly! Bring him and the wolf!" the Dracomancer urged, and, turning, he ran back up the stairs.

"What's happening?" Charming asked, still trying to adjust his eyes to the light.

"And does it have anything to do with barbecuing wolf?" Beo asked, his tongue lolling out of his mouth as he nervously panted.

Without a word, the men unlocked the bolts that attached Charming and Beo to the wall but did not remove the manacles that secured the chains to their bodies. Grabbing the ends of the chains they dragged both of them up from the ground and began to march them out of the cellar. The Dracomancer stood at the top of the stairs.

"Where are you taking me?" Charming demanded.

"Us?" Beo added.

The Dracomancer said nothing but headed in the direction of the town square, with the Dracolytes hauling Charming and Beo along in his wake. The town was in chaos. People, some in the black robes of the Dracolytes and some who were clearly just townsfolk, were running here and there. Occasional screams and shouts of terror could be heard. Lending urgency to everything were the bells, which kept ringing and ringing in a steady peal.

The Dracomancer stopped on the edge of the square. Many of the black-robed Dracolytes were gathered there, milling about nervously. In the square's center, there stood a rough timber post. The Dracomancer made a gesture, and one of the guards dragged Beo over to the post and chained him to it. The wolf lifted his head and howled in misery, but the sound was nearly inaudible over the bells.

"Stop the DAMN bells!" shouted the Dracomancer.

Dracolytes scattered in all directions, eager to obey their master. The Dracomancer rubbed his forehead.

As soon as the bells stopped, the Dracomancer had his face in front of Charming's. "We don't have much time. First"—he pointed to a small dark shape in the sky over the mountains—"Volthraxus is coming. This is a problem. It means that he's killed the King, but he's not satisfied. He wants something else. I'm hoping it's him." He stabbed his finger toward the wolf.

"Will is dead?" said Charming. His heart sunk, and a feeling of desolation settled over him. He had failed.

"There is no time for being maudlin or overtly tragic," the Dracomancer said and, grabbing Charming by the shoulders, gave him a shake. "This isn't one of those idiotic epic poems you would make up about yourself as a child." The Dracomancer thrust his pointing finger once more at the wolf. "That is Beo, the Dragon's former wolf servant. I'm sure he's already told you his sad tale of woe. Ignore it. All you need to know is that Beo betrayed Volthraxus. I have taken the liberty of making him easy for Volthraxus to find."

"You bastard!" the wolf snarled. "You promised me protection, Dracomancer. You promised me a place at your table. You're nothing but a liar and a coward. Have you never heard of honor among thieves?"

The Dracomancer turned and stared at the wolf. "No."

"Fair point," the wolf said after a moment's hesitation. "But . . ."

Whatever else the wolf said was lost as the Dracomancer grabbed Charming by the arm and began leading him away to the side of a building where the afternoon sun cast a deep shadow. He pressed himself next to Charming's ear, and whispered, "Lord Edward Michael Charming, the dragon is coming. Do you remember Volthraxus from your studies?"

"I do. I've been trying to remember everything I could since I first heard the name." Charming nodded. "Volthraxus is the largest of his breed and is named for the destructive winds his wings make in passing. He is rumored to have some missing scales on his breast, but what dragon isn't rumored to have some strategically placed missing scales. He has some odd quirks, the principal one being that he doesn't enjoy the taste of human flesh, preferring swine. You also told me that he was highly intelligent, rather absentminded, had a penchant for doodling, and was the least likely of dragons to go on a rampage."

"Um . . . you obviously did some extra reading.

Remind me to come back to you when this is over and take some notes. Don't spread that around."

"If he has kill . . ." Charming's voice caught, "killed King William, why is he coming here? I assume you've cleared the town of all pigs?"

"Of course I have," the Dracomancer said in indignation. "I'm not an idiot. It was the first thing I did on arriving."

"Well then?"

"I don't know why he's coming," the Dracomancer said, and Charming saw his eye twitch nervously. "Perhaps it is nothing more than the wolf that he wants. Dragons can be very peculiar about revenge. However, this behavior is beyond what I predicted. I'm not exactly sure what is about to happen, but I do know this. We have an opportunity today to actually kill a dragon, Charming."

"How?" Charming asked, as his mind raced to find something he might have missed that would make such a feat even remotely possible.

Townsfolk and Dracolytes from the square had begun to cluster around the Dracomancer. They crowded around him and fell to their knees, begging to be saved and pointing to the sky, where the dragon's approaching silhouette grew larger with each passing moment.

"SILENCE!" said the Dracomancer. He gestured to the black-robed men who had retrieved Charming from his cell, and they began to drive the crowd away with their pikes. When they were once more alone, the Dracomancer beckoned to another of these Dracolyte henchmen. "Bring me the weapon at once!"

The man rushed across the square to the tavern, even as more people joined the gathered masses. With the bells silenced, their wailing and sobbing could be heard clearly. The Dracomancer seemed to take no notice of the people's distress but was pacing back and forth and rubbing his hands together. His lips moved as if he were having a conversation, but no words came out. Charming thought he might be debating with himself.

At last, the Dracomancer stopped, and whispered, "You don't think he'd want Gwendolyn Mostfair, do you?"

"No," replied Charming, shaking his head, and knew that if he had answered differently, the Dracomancer would have quite willingly ordered that she be chained to the post alongside the wolf.

"My thoughts as well," said the Dracomancer. "Just remember, if all goes well, you will have avenged your King and probably regained your throne. You and I, Edward, are about to fulfill the prophecy."

"I don't care about that anymore," Charming said grimly.

"Do you care about these people?" the Dracomancer asked, waving his hands about him at the assembled crowd. "If you refuse to fight, they will all die, but if you listen to me and follow my guidance, you can save them all, and become the legend you've always wanted to be."

Before Charming could ask how, the Dracomancer took a few steps forward from the edge of the building so that he could be seen from all corners of the square. He spread his arms wide, and announced, "My Dracolytes! People of Royaume! I must give you the worst possible news! King William . . . is dead."

The Dracomancer let the words settle. For Charming, the thought of his friend dead brought a chill of sadness, but the death of their King seemed to have little impact on the people in the crowd. Their collective gaze was fixated on the sky. Charming looked up and searched for Volthraxus. The dragon was no longer an indistinct shadow on the blue heaven but had taken a very definite and ominous shape. In moments, the monster would be upon them.

"The dragon is upon us!" the Dracomancer said, trying to bring the crowd's attention back to him. These words, though obvious, made more of an impression, as many of the people began to scream in terror and beg the Dracomancer for deliverance. He held up his hands to quiet them. "Have faith and do not fear. By my hand, we have with us none other than Prince Charming, the man I prophesied would slay the Dragon. However, my prophecy was misinterpreted by jealous and wicked people who sought to ruin my good name. Prince Charming was never to meant to slay the Great Wyrm of the South, but rather, he was born to slay the foul beast that descends upon us at this very moment—The Great Dragon of the North!"

At a signal from the Dracomancer, two of the

robed Dracolytes began to unchain Charming. In another moment, he was free. He rubbed his arms and looked around, still uncertain what the Dracomancer intended for him to do. The Dracomancer waved him to his side with the back of his hand.

Charming stepped forward. At the same time, the Dracolyte whom the Dracomancer had sent off returned, carrying a terribly mangled pitchfork. The haft was burnt, and the tines were bent and looked as though they'd been melted. Charming shuddered to think of Will's last moments. If the pitchfork's condition was any sign, it had been a terrible battle.

"How did you get that?" Charming asked suspiciously.

"Yeah," said a woman in the crowd. "And it looks different. It's all beat-up."

"Th . . . th . . . this morning, the Dragon Spirit brought the Pitchfork of Destiny back to me!" the Dracomancer stuttered, and Charming could see beads of sweat on the man's forehead. "The damage you see is the result of King William's battle with the dragon. The King may have failed, but the pitchfork still retains its power, and in the right hands, the hands of a hero, the hands of the one I prophesied would slay the dragon, in the hands of Prince Charming, it will bring victory!"

With that, the Dracomancer extended the pitchfork to Charming. Charming grasped the handle. He knew there was more to the story of how the pitchfork came to be in the Dracomancer's hands than he was telling, but the dragon was here. First, he would save these people and avenge himself on the dragon for Will's death. After that, he would be able to collect on the Dracomancer's many debts.

Beside him, the Dracomancer once again spread his arms and addressed the crowd. "Let the prophecy be fulfilled! Everyone, find shelter where you can, but you will want to bear witness to these events!"

With that, the Dracoviziers, the Dracolytes, and everyone else in the crowd dispersed. Charming was alone with the Dracomancer. The man led him back over to the shadowy wall of the tavern. "Hide here. The shadows combined with the heat of the afternoon should blind the Dragon to your presence. If even half of what the wolf tells me is true, then Volthraxus will attack him first. You will have the element of surprise. Run under the dragon, pierce him in the heart, and he dies. The prophecy will be fulfilled, and you will once more be the hero, and perhaps the king you were always meant to be."

The Dracomancer turned to leave, but Charming caught his arm. "I know that you bear more blame for what happened to King William than you are saying. That you have this"—he hefted the pitchfork and put the sharp tines against the man's chest—"speaks volumes. When this is over, you and I will have words, Delbert."

The Dracomancer grimaced at Charming's use of his name, but rallied and responded with a threat of his own. "Remember, I have Gwendolyn and that squire of yours, Tomas. I also still have an army of Dracolytes at my command. Do we understand each other?"

Charming nodded. "I understand. Do you understand that I will not rest until I see that justice is served?"

Sneering, the Dracomancer pulled his arm free and ran into the tavern, his billowing cloak flapping behind him. Charming waited, watching the dragon grow larger and larger. This wasn't how he had ever expected to meet a dragon. He had always imagined a field of green. He would be atop his noble steed, with his armor glittering in the sun and the pennon on his lance flowing in the breeze. He imagined the charge and the dragon's fire curling about his shield. In his mind, the moment had always been glorious, but here he was, hiding in the shadows like a thief, dressed in peasant rags, a mangled pitchfork in his hand.

It went against everything in his nature.

Having said that, surprisingly, the circumstances fitted his emotions perfectly. He was not filled with the thrill of battle, but rather, his heart was empty. His friend, Will Pickett, was dead, and it seemed likely that Lady Rapunzel was also gone. He had no idea what had become of Liz. All he wanted was the dragon dead so he could mourn his losses, seek his wife, and exact the necessary measure of revenge against the Dracomancer. It was the height of irony that the Dracomancer's plan was the best means to all of those ends.

The low, steady, beating sound of the Dragon's wings striking the air reached him. Charming could feel a wind rise as the beast made its way closer. Volthraxus was on the outskirts of town. Charming braced himself against the wall, but, as he watched, the Great Dragon of the North suddenly dove and disappeared outside Prosper's town wall. Had Charming been seen? Volthraxus was known for his intelligence.

Perhaps it's a ploy.

Charming stayed motionless. It was time to be a hunter. He had immense patience when he needed it. He watched the wolf strain against its chain. The animal was panting and foaming at the mouth.

Beo was a villain, to be sure, but could he really be the reason for Volthraxus coming?

Charming continued to study the desperate wolf and think on the stories the wolf had told, but the longer he considered the subject, the harder he found it to believe that after Volthraxus had avenged Magdela, he would bother to go after a wolf, no matter what the beast's crimes had been. He adjusted his grip on the pitchfork, Will's pitchfork.

I will avenge you, Will.

As he thought this, there was a mighty rush of wind, and the Great Dragon of the North soared above the wall of Prosper and landed in the town square with his front claws on either side of the wolf. Silver-gray scales rippled across powerful limbs, and he made a horrific roar that shook the buildings and set the bells of Prosper to ringing once more.

Charming was in motion before Volthraxus had his claws set. He threw himself forward, dove, and rolled underneath the Dragon, holding the Pitchfork of Destiny in both hands. He came to his feet directly beneath the Dragon's breast. He thrust the pitchfork upward at the Dragon's heart. The armor here was as thick as anywhere else on the dragon. There were no missing scales or convenient weaknesses, still the tines of the pitchfork pierced the Dragon's side just as the Dracomancer had predicted. Three drops of steaming blood flowed from the wounds, but instead of pushing further into the mighty creature's heart, Charming paused.

Volthraxus froze.

"Great Volthraxus," said Charming, anger coloring his voice. "If you move, you will die. Should I hear the scales on your neck rustle, I will pierce you through the heart. You live only because I have three questions upon which your fate hangs. Do you understand?"

The dragon stayed perfectly still. "Yes, I understand. I have one question of my own if you would allow."

"Ask," Charming said, but tensed his arms in case this was some sort of rouse.

"You have me at a disadvantage," Volthraxus said. "Several actually. However, since you know who I am, may I ask who you are?"

"My name is Edward Charming."

The dragon gave a sigh, it sounded almost of regret. "You may ask your questions, Edward Charming."

Charming took a breath to prepare himself for what was to come. "Did you kill King William?"

"I did not."

Charming almost flinched with surprise, but retightening his grip on the haft of the pitchfork asked, "What about Lady Rapunzel?"

"She also lives. I left her along with King William and Lady Charming outside the walls of the town so they would not come to accidental harm should any archers have been present. They were not happy with the arrangement, and I suspect that, though I asked them to stay away, they will be here soon."

Charming had intended his last question to be about Liz, but to hear that not only were Will and Elle alive, but also Liz, brought him an overwhelming sense of relief, and it took a great deal of willpower not to relax.

Now that his principal concerns had been addressed, his last question seemed obvious. "Why are you here?"

"My actions have allowed that fool"—there was a deep, angry rumbling from within Volthraxus although his body was still as stone—"who calls himself the Dracomancer to nearly depose King William and take over this kingdom. Your future queen, Lady Rapunzel, has insisted that I put that to right. As I abducted her, postponed her wedding, and threatened to kill her husband, I felt that it was the least I could do to make my amends."

Charming continued to hold the pitchfork in place, but he knew this standoff could not last indefinitely. If he removed the pitchfork from the dragon's breast, Volthraxus would be free to act. All it would take would be for the dragon to lower his body and Charming would be crushed. The thought also came to him that all it would take would be one thrust, and the dragon would die.

I would be a hero of the land, a true dragonslayer.

Without consciously meaning to, he braced himself for the killing blow. Then another thought struck him.

If I do this, I will be the instrument that fulfills the Dracomancer's prophecy. I will only be doing what he always said I would.

A bitter bile rose up in his throat, and his grip on the pitchfork wavered.

"What are your intentions, Edward Charming?" the dragon asked calmly, perhaps sensing in Charming's silence his internal debate. "I acknowledge that you have every right to kill me, and would not think less of you if you did. I am, however, getting a little cramp in my right leg. So . . ."

"I have no reason to kill you," Charming replied. "You have spared my brother-in-law and King, his bride, and my own beloved wife. I don't believe that we have any quarrel remaining. You may think it would be justified, but killing you at this point, in my opinion, would be terribly bad form. May I propose instead . . . peace between us?"

Volthraxus made a deep, rumbling sound. It took a moment for Charming to realize that it was laughter. "Peace? The great Prince Charming, the man who was prophesied to slay my Magdela, wants peace between us? Why? Why not kill me and fulfill your destiny?"

"My studies of you indicate that you are a dragon

of honor and would therefore hold to any accord we would set. As for that prophecy . . ." Charming sighed. He reflected on his life. Everything in his entire existence had centered around the prophecy. All the adoration, all the training, all of the expectations, everything had been about the prophecy. He was sick of it. "The Dracomancer created that prophecy." The disdain he felt toward the man came out in his voice. "I find him repugnant and would do almost anything to thwart his designs. Will you accept my offer? Will there be peace between us?"

"Peace? Yes, I would have peace. I would rather not kill you," Volthraxus said, and made another chuckling, rumbling sound. "I find you warriors of Royaume difficult to understand, though. I was all set on a glorious and violent revenge, and was certain that you would oblige, but instead I find myself making peace, first with your King and now with the most renowned swordsmen of the age. Strange."

Charming withdrew the Pitchfork of Destiny and walked out from under the dragon. "I apologize for your injury."

With a groan of relief, Volthraxus stretched himself, much as a cat might, and looked down at the pinpricks of red on his breast. "It's nothing," he said. "Just a scratch. Although," he added, eyeing the pitchfork, "that weapon, as inelegant as it appears, certainly lives up to its reputation."

Charming grimaced at the pitchfork. "Sorry about that also. I am a little ashamed to have had to meet you in this manner. The ambush was ill done and, well"—Charming hung his head and gestured to his clothes—"I am a disgrace."

"Please don't beat yourself up about it," the dragon said gently. "We all have bad days."

Charming regarded the enormous silver-gray dragon. Volthraxus had a majesty and refinement about him, and there was something in his subtle bearing, in the way his eyebrows were so well manicured and his scales so shiny, that made Charming feel a kinship to him.

Charming felt another apology was in order. He squared his shoulders, and said grimly, "I feel the need to apologize to you. You should not have had to face me this way. I have been wearing these clothes for a week. There are rips and tears and stains all over them, my boots lack any sort of shine, and please don't get me started on the state of my hair . . ."

"Also," the Dragon said seriously, "and I hate to mention it, but I wouldn't be doing you a service if I didn't also point out that your collar is last season. I think you may need a new tailor."

Charming's face grew pale with shame.

"Forgive me," Volthraxus said. "I shouldn't have said anything, but I find that these days there is a shocking lack of appreciation for the forms and fashion."

"No," Charming said sorrowfully. "You are in the right, but the blame is mine and not my tailor's. He is . . ." Charming's voice broke. "He is a good man."

The dragon started to say something, but from

inside the tavern came the Dracomancer's ragged scream, "Kill the monster!"

Charming planted the Pitchfork of Destiny in the ground and glared at the tavern. "Come and do it yourself."

"Remember, Charming, I have your squire, Tomas and Lady Mostfair," threatened the Dracomancer.

Volthraxus quietly said, "Lord Charming, I know we've just met, but in my seven hundred years, I've never met the man who would spare a dragon, or who had such well-sculpted eyebrows. Would you mind if I responded to this ultimatum?"

Charming shrugged, curious as to what the dragon would do. "Be my guest."

Volthraxus roared, and flames shot into the sky. "Bring us the Dracomancer, or all shall feel my wrath!"

The door to the tavern opened, and black-robed hands shoved the Dracomancer out into the square. The door slammed behind him, and the clear sound of a latch's being thrown echoed across the green. Charming strode over and, grabbing the Dracomancer by the front of his robe, dragged him toward the center of the square and the waiting dragon.

"I . . . I think you should reconsider, Edward," the Dracomancer stammered. "I . . . I am giving you the chance for eternal fame and glory, and you are throwing it away."

Charming threw the Dracomancer to the ground at the dragon's feet, stripping him of his bulky outer cloak as he did. He reached down and ripped the false beard from the Dracomancer's face, then lifted the man up in the air and out of his high-heeled boots, before setting him back down. He stood revealed without his cloak or boots or beard as a thin, short man with a weak chin.

"Stop! I'm the Dracomancer!" His voice sounded squeaky and scared.

He flinched as Charming searched his robe for its hidden pocket. When at last he found it, Charming removed the dragon sock puppet and held it in the air.

"Everyone!" shouted Charming. "Look at this man, this fraud. Here is your true Dracomancer, not a sorcerer, not a great leader, but a con man willing to sacrifice all of you to the dragon's fire to reach his goals."

"You can't do this!" yelled the Dracomancer.

"Yes, he can," shouted King William.

Will, Elle, and Liz walked into Prosper's square. All three looked exhausted and tired, and perhaps a little sooty, but also happy. Liz practically glowed. As much as he wanted to rush over and embrace her, Charming knew that matters had to be settled first. He twisted the Dracomancer's arm behind his back and led him over to Will. Volthraxus, sitting on his haunches like an enormous dog, watched the entire drama unfold with a playful wag of his tail and a look of amusement.

"King William, may I surrender to you the traitor, Delbert Thistlemont, the self-proclaimed Dracomancer," said Charming. With a strong push, the Dracomancer went down to his knees at Will's feet.

Charming threw the sock puppet to the ground next to him.

Will folded his arms and looked sternly at the Dracomancer. "You have betrayed the Kingdom of Royaume and plotted treason against me, and if it were up to me alone, I would declare you guilty of the charges against you, but I have learned something from you, Delbert."

Will picked up the puppet and, striding to the center of the square, turned in a circle, his hands outstretched in a gesture of welcome. "People of Prosper and visitors, I call you to judge with me the guilt of this man." All was in silence, but faces appeared in windows and at doors, peeking out.

"He has lied to you. He told you that he can speak to dragon spirits, but this is revealed to be a sham." Will laughed and, putting his hand in the puppet, waggled it about ridiculously. Somewhere, a child giggled.

"He told you that he has power over dragons. That he can keep you safe from them. You have seen the dragon, he sits here now before you. I ask you to judge for yourself the 'power' this Dracomancer, this Delbert Thistlemont, has over the dragon."

Volthraxus rose and loomed above the Dracomancer. He roared in the man's face and lifted him in the air with the merest tip of his tail.

"Someone do something! Save me!" screamed the Dracomancer.

There was no response. Volthraxus dropped him to

the grass, where the Dracomancer scrabbled away on his hands and knees like a dog.

"The Dracomancer would have had you fight the dragon for him. He led you here, knowing that many if not most of you would die in the attempt. I call him a liar and a coward, and a traitor to the people of Royaume. Do any gathered here speak for him?"

No word was spoken. No chants of support were heard. A moment passed. Finally, someone reacted. A hand reached out of a window and pulled down a Dracomancer banner.

"It looks like your followers have reconsidered your leadership," said Will. He walked to where the Dracomancer had crawled and stood over him. "Dracomancer, I and the People of Royaume declare you guilty of being a traitor to the crown and the citizens of this land. As they have found you guilty, it is my duty to pronounce your doom." Will looked up at Volthraxus. "I can think of no better judgment than to remand you into the care of the dragon."

Volthraxus smiled, baring all of his teeth. "I will gladly take him, King William."

"If I could make a request on behalf of the people of Royaume, it would be that you not kill him but instead take him far from here to a place where he can make no more mischief."

Volthraxus bowed his head. "It shall be as you wish, King William."

Charming stepped away, and the dragon scooped

the convicted man up in his right-front claw. The Dracomancer fainted.

"I would, in turn, humbly request a boon," said Volthraxus. "I would ask the wolf as a pet. He has many debts to repay me."

"The wolf?" asked Will in confusion.

"Your Majesty," said Elle, beaming. "I would consider it a delightful wedding present if you gave that cur to Volthraxus."

"Of course, my love. Volthraxus, the cur is yours."

Beo whimpered.

The dragon immediately snatched up the wolf, snapping the metal chain as he did. "With that," asked Volthraxus, "may I take my leave? I long for the skies and my home in the north."

Will nodded. "You are welcome to take your leave, Volthraxus, but before you do, may I extend the hand of peace from all the people of Royaume? Should your journeys ever lead you back to our lands, you shall be welcome."

The silver-gray dragon nodded, his eyes glowing with wonder. "Once before, King William, you took the title of dragonslayer. Let it be known to all that you have renounced that title, but let me provide you with another. I pronounce you King William, Dragon-friend."

Will's mouth fell open. He placed his hand to his breast and bowed. "I am honored."

Volthraxus lowered his head. "Before I depart,

Your Majesty, may I have a private word with Lord Charming?"

Will gestured for Charming to join him next to Volthraxus. Liz raised an eyebrow of concern, but Charming gave her a kiss on the check for reassurance and walked to where the dragon stood. Will politely backed away.

The dragon leaned his head close to Charming. "Lord Charming, I wish to be the first to offer you congratulations."

Charming looked at him quizzically. "Congratulations? I consider what happened to be our victory, not mine alone."

The dragon shook his head. "Not on your handling of me although that was neatly done. I mean to congratulate you on your choice of wife."

"Liz is a treasure," Charming smiled. "I'm a very lucky man."

Volthraxus whispered. "I would have told her, but now I think it should come from you. You will soon be a father. Children are the greatest of treasures. Cherish them."

Charming felt tears of joy in his eyes. For once he did not try to suppress them. "Thank you, Volthraxus. You have given me the very best gift possible. I am forever in your debt."

Volthraxus smiled, then, flicking out his tongue, the great Dragon tensed and shot into the air in a rush of wind, a wolf struggling impotently in one claw and the Dracomancer dreaming in the other.

CHAPTER 18

HAPPILY EVER AGAIN

And so it was that the Great Dragon Panic ended nearly as quickly as it began. Within a fortnight, no one who claimed to be a Dracolyte could be found in either Prosper or Two Trees or in the surrounding areas. There were a few reports of dracomocracy breaking out in villages here and there, but wherever they were or might have been, the roads to them must have been so convoluted and ill marked that they might as well have been lost. However, it must be noted that merchants and tailors began a booming business in sock puppets of Volthraxus and nary a silver-gray sock could be found in the land that didn't have button eyes sewn into it.

Lady Rapunzel married King William within a week of her return to Castle White. Any doubts that remained about William's reign were drowned in a sea of praise for Queen Rapunzel. Other than the delay caused by Rapunzel's abduction, every aspect of the wedding was flawless, particularly the dress, and though it would be the talk of the realm for decades to come, it may be even better remembered for a live performance from Norm and the Bremen-Four that marked the beginning of their Great Comeback Tour. The only thing that struck anyone in attendance as curious was the sudden disappearance of Lord and Lady Charming before the Wedding Ball.

While the kingdom danced and drank, Edward and Elizabeth Charming sat in the back of a carriage, blissfully happy to not be at the center of attention.

"Will did well tonight, didn't he?" Liz asked with a sigh. "I think he and Elle are going to be so happy, don't you, Edward?" She placed her head on Charming's shoulder and blinked away more tears of happiness. She thought she must have wiped all her makeup off onto handkerchiefs, but she couldn't help herself when she thought about her baby brother and his bride.

"I have no doubt," replied Charming, putting one arm around his wife's shoulder and gently placing another on her belly, hoping that he might feel a kick.

She snuggled closer. "I love you, my Edward Charming."

"And I love you, my Lady Elizabeth."

They both laughed, recalling the afternoon the previous year when they had ridden out from Castle White after their own wedding. "Do you remember what I asked you the last time we left the castle?"

"Of course, I do. You said, 'Edward, what do you think will happen to everyone?' "

"That's right. So, what do you think will happen to everyone?" she asked, with a yawn.

"Let me see. Elle seems destined to be the best queen this land has ever had. Your brother, probably in large part because of Elle, will be well loved by his people and implement all manner of town councils and other reforms." Charming sighed. "And, though it still seems unnatural, I'm sure it will be for the best."

"What about us?" she asked, raising her head to look into his eyes.

"We will away to our cottage, and you will have the first of our many children."

Liz added, "If it's a girl, we will name her Eleanor, and if it is a boy, Edwin."

"I was thinking that we could name them Princess or Prince."

"You're incorrigible," she said with a chuckle, nestling herself against his shoulder once more before yawning.

"Always," he said, and gave her his most incorrigibly Charming chuckle.

Liz said nothing. He looked down and saw that she had fallen asleep. He listened to her soft breathing, and, suddenly, he felt not one, but two kicks from within her belly. Liz stirred slightly and placed her hand over his before relaxing once more. Charming smiled. For the first time in his life, Edward Charming was well and truly content.

EPILOGUE

A FIELD OF TEARS

The most important day of Gwendolyn Mostfair's life came on a Wednesday in March. A year had passed since Volthraxus had descended like a storm on Royaume. The Royal Couple had been married the summer previous, and the Charming twins were born that fall. In Prosper, spring had arrived. The delicate green of new growth covered the valley and surrounding hills.

That morning, Monty had taken one breath of the clean air and one look at the peerless blue sky and pronounced that today was not a day for work. With a kiss on her cheek and a pinch, he had insisted that Gwen put aside her apron and her cleaning and join him for a picnic. An hour later, they were walking hand in hand, he with a basket of food and she with a blanket. They made their way through the knee-high stalks of their corn toward the little hill in the center of their field that the townsfolk called Dragon Mound.

Monty and Gwen had, from the first, agreed that Magdela's resting place should be left untouched by the plow, and it had become one of Gwen's favorite spots. After her chores were done, she liked to sit on the hill and think and make posies from the delicate blue and white wildflowers that dotted its sides. On this day, they lay next to each other on the blanket, watching the clouds chase each other in the wind and talking about everyday things.

They spoke of how the corn was growing, about when they might have enough money saved to fix the barn roof, and about whether they should think of getting a second cow. Then a pleasant lull came to their conversation.

"Are you satisfied here, my Princess?" Monty asked, breaking the silence.

"What are you talking about, Monty?" she laughed. "What a silly question. Of course I am."

He sat up, his face set, and stared into her eyes. "I am being serious."

"So am I," she replied, and also rose, so that they sat facing each other.

"But, we talk of cows and corn and barns," he said gesturing about dismissively with his hand. "Do you not miss the court? Do you not miss the dresses and the balls, the dukes and barons, and speaking of things of significance?"

"Significance?" She laughed aloud. "I cannot think

of a single conversation I ever had at court that had as much significance to me as our talk today of cows and corn and barn." She clutched his hands in hers. "I will not say that there are not times when I wish I had a servant or two to wash the clothes or churn the milk, but I would not go back to court if King William himself came and begged me." He looked away from her, and she placed a hand on his cheek and turned his face back to hers. "But you know all this, Monty. What is it that you are worried about?"

He plucked a stalk of grass and began twirling it between his fingers. She could tell he was nervous, and suddenly she was nervous, and all her doubts intruded themselves on her thoughts. *He has grown tired of being a farmer.* Her heart began to beat faster. *He has grown tired of me.* Her hands began to shake. *He wants to leave, but does not know how to tell me.*

"Are . . . are you not happy?" she asked, her voice quavering and catching.

His eyes widened. "What?"

"I know that there are better places for you than here, and women that would be of far greater help to you than . . . I." She kept her voice calm but could not help its catching at the end.

"You think I mean to leave you?"

She did not answer, but the tears flowed from her eyes. "We never said that this had to be forever, only that we would try. I . . . I must . . ."

She had to go. She could not let him see her cry. She rose to her feet and began to turn. He caught her, and when she looked down, he was on his knees at her feet.

Gwen tried to pull her hand away, but he held her with a desperate strength. "No, my Princess, I will not let you go, not until you answer two questions."

His dark eyes pleaded with her to stay. Fearing to speak, she nodded.

"Do you love me?"

Gwen knew that what he meant was did she love him truly. It was nearly the same question she had asked him when he was still a frog, and they had kissed for the first time. Her heart whispered the answer without hesitation.

"I do," she said.

He reached with a hand to his breast pocket and pulled out a ring of gold. Her breath caught.

"Then will you make me at last happy, Gwendolyn Mostfair, my only love? Will you do me the great honor of being my wife and spending all the days you have in this life with me?"

Her heart soared. How could it be that from one moment to the next one could go from desolation to transcendent happiness?

"I will," she said, and tears of joy ran down her face as he slipped the ring on her finger. "I will," she said again, and he rose and clutched her to him. "I will," she said, as she buried her face in his chest. Gwen thought that perhaps she might never stop saying "I will," but he raised her face to his and silenced her words with a kiss.

He pulled her down onto the blanket next to him and began kissing her in earnest. She returned his embrace, but as the afterglow of the moment began to fade, a thought intruded itself in her mind, and no matter how hard she tried to ignore it, it would not leave her in peace.

"Monty?" she asked at last.

"Yes, my love," he said, still kissing her throat.

"Where did you get the ring?"

The kisses stopped. "I thought you would wonder about this," he said, then asked, "Does it matter?"

"I think so," she said, twirling the gold band around her finger. "You must know it isn't that I don't love it, but it must have cost a lot, and you know I don't need a fancy ring—"

"It cost nothing," he said, peering down at her and moving a lock of hair that had strayed across her face.

"But it is gold."

"Most assuredly."

"How?" she asked. "We don't have the coin for a gold ring."

He sighed and, rolling from atop her, rose to his feet. "I knew you would wonder about that also, my Princess." He buttoned up his vest. "An admirer of yours helped me. In anticipation that you would agree to marry me, and in appreciation for his help, I have invited him to share this day with us. If you do not mind, I think that he should explain."

"An admirer?" she asked. "I don't have any admirers besides you."

"There you are most assuredly wrong, my Princess," he said, and began waving his arms in the air as though signaling to someone.

She stood and looked about, but could see no one. "Who is it?" she asked, straightening her dress and shaking the grass from her clothes and hair.

Monty pointed up in the sky, at a little black speck dancing among the clouds high above.

"The . . . the dragon?" she asked, her heart suddenly beating faster. "Volthraxus?"

"Yes, my love," and, taking her hands in his, he peered into her eyes. "Tell me now if you do not want this, and I will send him away. He will not descend further unless I signal, but he has been very kind and would very much like to speak to you of Magdela."

"When did you meet him?"

"A month ago, he came to me while I was in the far field near the woods," Monty said. "He was hiding among the trees, and we talked for a time. He told me about his lost love, and he asked after you. Shall I send him away?"

"No," she said at once. Perhaps at one time she might have been scared, but now her heart yearned to talk to the dragon. "I also wish to speak with him."

Monty nodded, then gave another wave to the sky. The little dot began to descend in gentle circles toward the ground. Monty kissed her hands and picked up the basket. "I will leave you to speak in private," he said. "Should you need anything, I will be close at hand."

He walked off through the corn to the house. She

looked after him, then raised her eyes and watched the dragon come closer and closer, his silver-gray tail fluttering out behind him like a pennon. The bells of Prosper began ringing in the distance. And then he was above her. He fanned out his great wings and, like a gentle breeze, Volthraxus landed on the opposite side of the hill. Despite her desire to see him, her throat caught at his size and power.

"Lady Gwendolyn," he said with a flourish of his wings and a bow of his head, "it is a pleasure to meet you at last."

"The pleasure is mine, Lord Volthraxus, Great Dragon of the North." Gwen curtsied elegantly in her simple dress. "I would offer you the hospitality of my home, but I fear we have no swine."

He laughed, a gentle rumbling sound. "I fear few do in this land. I was most greedy during my last visit, and I understand it will take several years for the pig population to recover." Volthraxus settled himself on the hill and lowered his head to the ground so that he did not loom above her. "I thank you for agreeing to speak to me, Lady Gwendolyn. I know that you have glad tidings today and that I have interrupted your celebration."

With a blush, Gwen wondered how long the dragon had been watching her "celebration" with Monty. She cleared her throat. "Please, Lord Volthraxus think nothing of it. The great joy of today is that I will have all the time in the world to be with him. Besides"—she glanced at the ring on her hand and smiled—"I understand that you are to thank for some part of my happiness."

"It was nothing," he said with a shrug. "Your betrothed explained to me his desire to make you a gift on the occasion of your engagement, and I agreed to help him reforge an amulet of gold he had in his possession. I offered to bring him one of the jeweled rings from my horde as a token of my esteem, but he assured me that this would hold a deeper meaning."

Gwen gazed at the band with greater appreciation. This was the fairy gold from his amulet recast by dragon fire. For her, it might be a symbol of future happiness, but she knew for Monty it meant that he was finally free from his past. Her eyes grew misty, and she said, "It is perfect, Lord Volthraxus. You cannot know what this means to him . . . to us. Is there something I can do to repay your kindness?"

Volthraxus sighed deeply. "I would not ask, only request, if it would not cause you pain, to talk to me of her, of Magdela. I never got the chance to know her, and it is the void of her life I feel most keenly."

"It would cause me no pain, Lord Volthraxus," she said with a sad smile. She lowered herself onto the grass in front of him and tucked her legs beneath her. The first thing that Gwen said was, "She spoke of you often, and I think of all your features, she admired your flowing tail the best."

Villagers from Prosper who had been alarmed at the Dragon's approach and come to see if there was trouble, stared in amazement at the great gray dragon and the young lady in the pale white dress, sitting on the flowering hill beneath the spring sky, heads bent close together in conversation. They talked for hours of Magdela as the sun passed overhead and began to bend toward the horizon. At last, Volthraxus had asked all the questions he had, and Gwen had told him all she knew and could remember.

"Thank you, Gwendolyn," he said with a sigh that bent the flowers between them. "It has eased my heart to speak of her."

"It has eased mine also," Gwen said, and knew that it was true. For as much as the memories of that chapter of her life could still bring her pain, talking about Magdela with Volthraxus had been like talking about an old friend. For so many years, Magdela had been her world, and she had never had a chance to mourn her.

Volthraxus stared across at the farmhouse. "Your Montague has been very patient, but I have denied him your company long enough, I think. You know that he has been watching from the window this entire time. He is very devoted, Gwendolyn."

Gwen looked over her shoulder at the light burning in the cottage window. "I know, Volthraxus. I am very fortunate. I only hope that I will be worthy of his love. I am not a particularly practical woman to take as a wife."

"I do not think Montague cares," the dragon said with a laugh.

"I do," she said firmly. "I . . ." she stared at the ring

on her finger, but couldn't find the words to voice her fear.

Volthraxus gazed at her gently. In the growing darkness, his eyes glowed slightly. "I think I understand," Volthraxus said. "You worry that you are not worthy of him, that you will be a burden." She nodded. "You think because people have always admired you for your beauty and grace that this is all you have to give." She nodded again. "From what you have told me of her, I begin to see that Magdela feared something much the same, and it kept us apart when we might have been together."

He rose from the ground and stretched. "Do you see the flowers growing on this hillside, Gwendolyn? Have you ever seen their kind before?"

Gwen plucked one and examined it. It was a simple flower with four teardrop petals in pale blue and white surrounding a yellow gold center. She realized she had no name for them. "No," she said puzzled.

"I doubt it not," he said, staring at the stars that were beginning to appear in the sky above. "They are called dragon's tears, and they bloom only where a dragon has died. You could try and plant them in your garden, but they would not thrive. On this hillside, though, they will never falter. Neither frost nor disease nor drought nor pestilence will touch them. They may appear delicate, Lady Gwendolyn, but they endure. I think the same could be said of you."

Gwendolyn smiled at the flower in her hands and,

rising, embraced the dragon around the neck. "Thank you," she said, and gave him a kiss.

Volthraxus rumbled with pleasure. "Go home, Princess," he said. "And let my blessings go with you."

He watched as she skipped down the hill toward the cottage. The door opened, spilling light into the night, and she ran into Monty's waiting arms. When the door had closed, Volthraxus bent to the ground and kissed the earth at his feet. "Sleep in peace, Fair One, My Magdela."

He lifted his nose to the wind, smelling the possibilities on the night air. Unfurling his great wings, Volthraxus leapt into the sky and was gone.

ACKNOWLEDGMENTS

A fair listing of acknowledgments is never possible, because the page count of such a list would begin to rival the novel itself. Having said that, we would like to try and thank everyone who has helped us on our quest to write this, the most challenging of any author's career, the second book. As always, someone will be forgotten in this list, but this won't be the last. We will get it right next time.

To Taba and Heather, there is no Jack Heckel without the two of you.

To all of our beta readers: Taba, Heather, Kayla, Kim, Dorothy and Carleigh. We cannot thank you enough for everything you do to help us become better writers.

To our families, we love you all and appreciate all you have done over the years to make us who we are.

To our fellow Harper Voyager authors, thanks for the continued friendship, community and support.

To W.R. Gingell, for inspiring us with a dedication.

To everyone at Unboxed Technology, especially the QA team and all honorary members for the encouragement and support.

From John to Mom, thank you for taking all the winding roads on every journey, and letting me explore all those mysterious caves we inevitably found at their ends.

From Harry to Dad, thanks for the support every step of the way.

Finally, again a big thanks to Rebecca and Kelly and Jessie and everyone else at Harper Voyager.

ABOUT THE AUTHOR

JACK HECKEL's life is an open book. Actually, it's the book you are in all hope holding right now (and if you are not holding it, he would like to tell you it can be purchased from any of your finest purveyors of the written word). Beyond that, Jack aspires to be either a witty, urbane world traveler who lives on his vintage yacht, *The Clever Double Entendre*, or a geographically illiterate professor of literature who spends his nonwriting time restoring an eighteenth-century lighthouse off a remote part of the Vermont coastline. Whatever you want to believe of him, he is without doubt the author of *A Fairy-Tale Ending*. More than anything, Jack lives for his readers.

www.jackheckel.com